THE COWARD'S TALE

BY THE SAME AUTHOR

Storm Warning
Words from a Glass Bubble

THE COWARD'S TALE

A Novel

VANESSA GEBBIE

BLOOMSBURY
NEW YORK · BERLIN · LONDON · SYDNEY

Published by Bloomsbury USA, New York

All papers used by Bloomsbury USA are natural, recyclable products made from wood grown in well-managed forests. The manufacturing processes conform to the environmental regulations of the country of origin.

This book is a work of fiction. Names, characters, businesses, organizations, places and events are either the product of the author's imagination or are used fictitiously. Any resemblance to actual persons, living or dead, or actual events, is entirely coincidental.

LIBRARY OF CONGRESS CATALOGING-IN-PUBLICATION DATA

Gebbie, Vanessa.
The coward's tale : a novel / Vanessa Gebbie. — 1st U.S. ed.
p. cm.
ISBN-13: 978-1-60819-772-9
ISBN-10: 1-60819-772-7
I. Title.
PR6107.E29C59 2012
823'.92—dc22
2011015509

First U.S. Edition 2012

1 3 5 7 9 10 8 6 4 2

Typeset by Hewer Text UK Ltd, Edinburgh
Printed in the U.S.A. by Quad/Graphics, Fairfield, Pennsylvania

For Robert Diplock, 1962–1969

By the Town Statue,
Outside the Public Library

'MY NAME IS IANTO Jenkins. I am a coward.'

Those words have echoed through this town once before. And today, they will be said again by Ianto Passchendaele Jenkins, small and grey now in his khaki jacket and cap to almost match, the beggar who sleeps in the porch of Ebenezer Chapel on a stone bench, his kit bag for a pillow and a watch with no hands dropped to the flagstones next to his boots.

The words will be said outside the Public Library, to a boy called Laddy Merridew. They will be overheard by the town statue – a collier struck from a single block of granite, a tumble of coal round his boots. Been there for as long as anyone can remember, that statue, standing and dreaming in all weathers, eyes downcast as though he is deep in thought. When it rains, like today, water drips off his hair and off his chin in memory of colliers lost one September day down the pit called Kindly Light, although it was neither. Colliers whose names once lived for evermore until their plaque was unscrewed by the town lads and thrown in the lake up Cyfarthfa.

But before the words are said, the bus comes down the hill to deliver not only the boy but Mrs Harris and Mrs Price with their shopping baskets and their lists. Mrs Eunice Harris, her hair all mauve and well-behaved under a net, steps down from the bus in front of Mrs Sarah Price, for after all her husband is Deputy Manager of the Savings Bank and Mrs Price's is not.

Ianto Passchendaele Jenkins is at the bus stop, not waiting for anything in particular. He is reading the bus times to see if they have changed since yesterday, and they have not, so he raises a finger to his cap in welcome to Mrs Harris, who does not want a welcome from any part of Ianto Jenkins the beggar, thank you very much. The bus starts to move – then it stops. Someone has forgotten to get off.

A boy of ten or thereabouts comes stumbling down the steps of the bus, his socks round his ankles. His hair is very red and very untidy. His fringe is too long and his glasses have slipped right down his nose. There is no one to meet him. He is clutching a small brown suitcase to his chest, this bright-haired boy in a stained school raincoat several sizes too small, its belt tied in a knot as there is no buckle. He was dreaming on the bus with his head against the window, a bad dream full of the bad words that come up at night through the floor-boards when his mam and dad think he's asleep.

The bus pulls away again. The boy tries to push the glasses back up his nose, trips on a shoelace and falls before Ianto Jenkins can catch him. The suitcase bursts open on the pavement, spilling out a wooden drum wrapped in a pair of pyjamas, a few pairs of old pants, a toothbrush and a blue knitted jumper. The boy looks at his hands. They aren't clean. He's skinned the palms, and skinned his knees. He tries to rummage in his raincoat pockets for a handkerchief without hurting his hands any more than they hurt already, but there isn't one. Tears come, all quick and hot and angry.

Mrs Harris and Mrs Price do not know what to do with a boy's tears. They both take a step back with their shopping baskets, and Mrs Harris opens a black umbrella with a snap, mouthing words that look like *clumsy* and *boys* and *mess*.

It is Ianto Passchendaele Jenkins who hands something that might be a handkerchief to the boy and mutters words like *never* and *mind* before gathering the boy's things back into the suitcase, not forgetting to give the drum a pat. The small sound echoes off the library wall.

Ianto Passchendaele Jenkins starts to smile at the sound as he clicks the case shut, and as he straightens up slowly, muttering, 'Oh my old bones,' but when he looks at the boy for the first time, properly, the words fade. The smile dies.

The boy does not see any of this. He sits on the kerb, peers at his knees and dabs at them with the thing that might be a handkerchief, then he takes off his glasses to wipe his face, leaving behind streaks of blood and pavement. Ianto Jenkins, still looking at the boy, shakes his head as if to clear it. He coughs and points to his own nose; the boy half-smiles and rubs at his nose with his sleeve. Mrs Harris and Mrs Price tut, and the boy winces as he pushes the old man's handkerchief into his pocket. 'Sorry. Thank you. I'll get my gran to wash it,' then he stands up and cleans his glasses on the hem of his raincoat. He pulls up his socks, and when he straightens they fall back to his ankles as if they are more comfortable down there. He sighs and shrugs and looks at the clock that says ten past two on the pediment of the Town Hall, next to the library.

He says again, to no one in particular, 'Sorry.' Then he looks back up at the clock, 'Can you tell me the time? I thought the bus got in at half past, and where has lunchtime gone?'

There is a muffled reply from another timepiece, on Ebenezer Chapel down by the cinema, where the bell was once wound with a rag not to wake the minister and no one thought to take the rag away now there are no ministers left. Ianto Passchendaele Jenkins taps at his watch with no hands, 'Sounds like half past something to me.'

Mrs Eunice Harris pulls back the sleeve of her good coat and checks her good watch. 'Indeed yes. Half twelve,' and waves a hand at the Town Hall clock as if it was hers. 'Always ten past two. Someone put a nail in the time years back.'

The boy doesn't answer, just says, almost to himself, 'Said I'd meet Gran in the library at half past. She cleans it some days,' and he bends for his suitcase. But before he can pick it up, Ianto Jenkins is carrying it towards the library, and the boy is limping behind, 'It's all right. I'll take it.'

The beggar waits for the boy, and says something about the boy's hands being all scraped raw, and he doesn't mind carrying it to the library. Because after all, 'Factual' Philips the Deputy Librarian has a kettle and he makes a good cup of coffee.

They pass in front of the statue of the Kindly Light collier with a tumble of coal round his boots, and the boy looks up at Ianto Jenkins, 'Thank you very much.' There is a pause before he says in a small voice, 'My name is Laddy Merridew. I'm a cry-baby. I'm sorry.'

The beggar doesn't stop walking, doesn't look at the boy, doesn't really answer. Except to say, 'And my name is Ianto Jenkins. I am a coward. And that's worse.'

And the two of them, old man and boy, coward and cry-baby, disappear into the Public Library with the suitcase.

* * *

4

Mrs Eunice Harris frowns and nods as if they needed her permission to leave at all, then she turns to Mrs Sarah Price, who is gazing up at the face of the statue, and she does not lower her voice, 'Did you see that? Pants on the pavement?'

And before the good ladies wander down the High Street with their baskets, they stand in the drizzle under a single black umbrella to contemplate the statue.

'I am sure that is the Harris nose. I wake up with that nose every morning.'

'Aww indeed, it may be the Harris nose but it hangs above the Price mouth, will you see? No mistaking the Price mouth.'

Mrs Eunice Harris sucks at her teeth, 'Hanging in the front room that nose is, sure as anything, in a photograph all tinted lovely. And a real ebony frame as well.'

But whichever way they look at him, and whichever of the town's men he is like, the rain wets the statue's head, and drips off his hair and off his chin. Off the Price mouth and the Harris nose, the Edwards eyes with their beetle-brows, always frowning. It pools in the folds of the sleeves and catches in the crook of a bent middle finger just like the finger of Icarus Evans the Woodwork Teacher who broke his own on a lathe. The widow's peak and curls are the spit of the Window Cleaner's, Judah Jones, the ears beneath the curls could be Baker Bowen's from Steep Street, and are those the long fingers of the Bartholomews, Piano Tuners, or the Littles who like their gardening, and is the way he stands just like Tutt Bevan the Undertaker or more like Philip 'Factual' Philips, owner of the Public Library's only kettle?

Who is to say? But all over the town, on the front room walls, high in the half-curtained dark, the town's ancestors watch from their ebony frames, their noses, ears and mouths all mirrors of the statue's.

The beggar Ianto Passchendaele Jenkins comes out of the Public Library smartish, leaving Laddy Merridew to wait for his gran in the Reading Room under a sign that tells the world to be quiet. There is no coffee to be had today for Mrs Cadwalladr the Librarian has appropriated the kettle for a meeting. Ianto Jenkins stops to check the face of his watch with no hands and it looks back at him all blank and hopeful. He taps that face to see if might tell him anything different, but it doesn't, so he turns away towards the bottom of town, pulling his collar up against the chill. As he does the Kindly Light statue seems to nod. Ianto Passchendaele Jenkins nods in return. He waves to Icarus Evans the Woodwork Teacher, pushing his bike and its trailer full of offcuts up the High Street. Then the breeze blows the beggar all the way down to Ebenezer Chapel, its porch and his home, leaving the statue to wait in the rain for something or nothing to happen.

The Woodwork Teacher's Tale

i

BUT SOMETIMES, THE BREEZE doesn't get as far as the High Street. Sometimes it stops to play with the sheep's wool caught on fences on the hill above the town. Sometimes, it gets through broken windows into the farmhouse that once owned the fences, and shivers the cobwebs on the bedroom walls. It toys with the frayed ends of string tying the front door shut and wheedles itself under the barn door to send years-old chaff rattling against the tin walls. It shakes the windows of the caravan next to the barn, where the carpenter Thaddeus Evans, who the lads call Icarus, may not yet have woken, for it is early. Then it gives up playing with his windows, and ruffles the feathers of two chickens crooning at the bricks under the caravan. No wheels, that caravan. Never goes anywhere. Just sits and slumps on its bricks in the yard, watching Icarus Evans coming and going to the school down the hill where he teaches the lads to work with wood.

'Mr Evans, Mam says can I make a new mahogany dining table for her Auntie May up Penydarren?'

'Of course – best learn to use a chisel first, is it?'

* * *

Icarus Evans will shake his head and smile to himself as he pushes his bike back up the hill after school, with its trailer carrying offcuts from Tutt Bevan the Undertaker, too good to waste. The town is graced with those offcuts. A nursing chair for number eight Tredegar Road, passed from house to house when four babies appeared exactly right. Sets of mahogany and pine dominoes on the shelves of the Working Men's Club at the bottom of the hill, and perfectly matched bedside tables for the Deputy Manager of the Savings Bank and his wife, but their bedroom floor is uneven so both glasses for the false teeth go on one table, where they can smile at each other until morning.

Making a boat, Icarus Evans is now, a rowing boat, its ribs sitting bare on a pallet behind the caravan, each rib a different wood, each plank for the sides. Mahogany, birch, hornbeam, ash, and all their cousins. Covered with an old tarpaulin to keep off the rain.

Over beyond the caravan and the boat and the barn is the single stony field left of the farm, for the rest have been swallowed by the Brychan estate on the edge of town, and its noise. There are no sheep in this field now, all sold at market for mutton, but wild ponies sometimes come to graze. And in the furthest corner, under the roots of rowan trees fenced round by wire long rusted, there is a spring. A spring that sends its water into a stream that once ran free down the hillside to join the river in the valley, but now which disappears into a stone culvert by the track. A spring where the boys from the Brychan come at weekends to play and to watch the growing of Icarus's boat.

'There's lovely, Icarus, that boat. Who's it for then?'

Icarus may not reply except to say, 'Mr Evans to you, lads,' and will carry on planing and shaping the boat's ribs as curls of wood tumble across the yard.

And the lads will go laughing to drop pill bottles into the spring. Little brown bottles that once held aspirin or something for stomachs, half-forgotten behind packets of Paxo in kitchen cupboards, with no pills in now, but messages to girls they may never meet: 'Mine's floating, going see? Going to Australia!'

Some are taken. Off to Australia they go, bobbing under the tree roots and into the tunnels under the town for the water to chuckle at their profanities. And others are swallowed, the words never read except by the earth. They are sucked under when the spring stops bubbling like it does now and then and goes still and dark. Like the water is from a pulsing vein and there's a halt in the heartspring.

Then the lads run off back to their streets, leaving just one, the new boy Laddy Merridew, who has not sent messages. He just hung back to watch the rest, sent out to play by his gran when he was happier not playing at all. He picked at the bark of a tree with a dirty fingernail, then perhaps he waited behind to peer into the spring to see what it might tell him. Maybe the water stopped bubbling again, and just looked back at the boy, reflecting not just his questions but the rowan berries over his head.

In the blear of morning, Icarus Evans may sit on the bench in the yard with a mug of hot tea and some bread spread with jam from the bullaces that grow near the spring. And when he has eaten, he may go back into the caravan and return with a small cage made of rowan twigs stripped smooth and green as fingerbones. A cage no bigger than the cupping of his two hands. And he will be talking soft, whispering to the cage while he sits with his bare toes drawing runes in the dust. Then he places the cage on the earth and bends to unlatch the door, winding a thin string round one finger. A string tied light but strong round the leg of a small bird.

Icarus Evans clears his throat, 'Morning, Bird.'

Perhaps the bird will come out and stand with its head on one side to think about how big it is, this new cage. And with one wing dragging, in small runs and starts it will search the dust for food. Maybe a few rowan berries brought for the purpose from the spring. Icarus Evans will keep watch from his bench, letting out the bird's string, scanning the yard for cats, until there is the bark of a dog on the track, 'Come here, Bird,' and he winds the string in slow, then bends to take the bird up in his hand. It comes to him easy, eye bright, and back in the rowan cage it goes as the dog comes snuffing into the yard before running through the field to the spring to find a drink.

Icarus Evans washes in that spring every morning, for it is the only running water left at the farm. He will splash his face, his beard, shaking like the dog shakes, then smoothing his hair down neat for school. He will cover the boat with its tarpaulin, just in case. Before tying up the door of his caravan with string, he will look round inside. At walls covered in pictures of places he has never been, cut out of brochures from the travel shop in the High Street. Paper palaces on paper canals and mountain cities hung with flags that flap their messages to a paper wind.

Off he goes, pushing his bike across the yard to the track over the culvert, where the water is chuckling this morning deep in its own throat. And he will disappear down the track to the road by the Brychan estate on the edge of town, on his way down the hill, to school, a bundle of offcuts in his trailer and his head full of small plans.

To school he goes, then, on his bike, and on the way he may pass Tommo Price in his suit off to be Clerk at the Savings Bank. 'Morning, Icarus.'

Or he may see the lads from the Brychan in the doorway of the dressmaker's trying to light a butt end found on the pavement, 'Morning, Icarus.'

'Mr Evans to you. Put that out, will you?'

Or he may pass Peter Edwards, Collier until they closed Deep Pit a few months back, the last pit to close round here, too – sitting on the steps of the Kindly Light statue outside the library and looking at his hands – but Peter Edwards just nods and says nothing, for there is nothing to say.

And at the school does Icarus go in with the other teachers, to be all serious with black looks and exhortations to the lads not to be lads at all but to be as old as they are themselves? He does not. Round the back he goes, parks the bike in a rack, then takes the bag of offcuts from the trailer and carries it to a hut with a locked door. 'Carpentry' it says. And 'Mr Thaddeus Evans' in case he forgets he has a name other than Icarus. Through the metal window with its cracked panes he can see his workbenches, his shelves, his tools hung all neat on the walls.

In he goes and shuts the door, lifting his face to an air

hanging full with the sweet smell of pine. He may raise his face and shut his eyes, to breathe in the scents while the lads are still half-listening in the Assembly Hall.

Under the workbenches there are pale curls and shavings, as whorled as fingerprints with patterns that ran once under the skin of trees. Icarus may pick up a few and stand there to uncurl the wood, to feel the oils deep in the flesh. To see if the wood splits and snaps in his fingers, or whether it uncurls easy and lissom. Those that do not split he saves, and puts them in a box on his desk.

He checks the time, then looks at the shelves round the walls of his workshop. At the boxes on the shelves, labelled for every year Icarus Evans has been a teacher in this place. Thirty years. Thirty boxes, on shelves that span floor to ceiling.

Icarus Evans watches the lads crossing the playground, new lads to this lesson, all brave now, swinging their bags and play-punching, most. He is wondering, maybe, if there is a real carpenter among them, such as he has never been, for all the bedside tables he has made, all the chairs, dominoes and benches. Not really. Not yet.

He listens to the lads' chatter as they settle,

'I'll make a cart to ride down the hill,'

'Or a box for secrets,'

'A rocking chair for my gran,'

'A set of wooden spoons,'

'A boat like Mr Evans is making up the farm,'

'A rocket, me,'

'A wooden rocket? That's daft . . .'

Then he tells them to gather round, and he takes down one

box from the shelves, one of the thirty. Lifts the lid to show the lads what's inside.

Is it a set of carved spoons? Loving spoons to show how clever the lads were with their hands, those who left a long time back to work with numbers, letters, things that need no clever hands? Is it blocks of different wood? Blood-red mahogany and the pearl of hornbeam or the glow of pine, for the boys to feel the difference? Not at all. The lads peer into the box to see nothing but a pile of wooden feathers, fashioned from shavings gathered from the floor and saved. Some delicate and others solid and ham-fisted.

Icarus looks at the lads, then, all of them: the boys who tried to light the butt end outside the dressmaker's shifting in the middle of the group, another gang from the Brychan who come to drop pill bottles into the spring, right to the red-haired boy in glasses at the back trying not to be seen.

All new this boy Laddy Merridew, his glasses shining, hair cut special by his gran this morning with her dressmaking scissors to keep it out of his eyes, his parting white as chicken meat. Bitten nails. His school trousers mothball-smelling cut-offs from the back of a wardrobe, belonging to a dead grandad. And that same grandad's shirt, its tail hanging out and smelling of more mothballs while another lad inks 'Stinker' into the hem in blue biro. But Laddy Merridew does not notice this as he is listening and watching as Icarus talks.

'Here's the test, lads. To see the watermarks. To find wood that is made to be feathers. There's feathers made by every boy I have ever taught, right by here –' and he taps the side of the box to hear the feathers settle with a whisper.

Icarus waves at the walls of the workshop, at the boxes with their dates, at the thousands of feathers in the boxes. Then he goes quiet. He picks one maybe two feathers from the box on his desk. The best. And he calls the new boy forward, and asks his name.

'Ieuan Merridew, Mr Evans,' but his words are swamped by laughter when another boy answers 'Stinker' as well. 'But they call me Laddy back home.'

Then more shouts of 'Stinker' and 'Mothballs' and 'Ginger' follow him to Icarus's table, but Icarus takes no notice, just smiles at him. He gives the worked curls of wood to the boy called Laddy Merridew and asks, 'Are these feathers, then?'

'Yes, Mr Evans. No, Mr Evans.'

'Do they feel like feathers?'

The boy runs his fingers along the outer edge of the curls. 'No, Mr Evans.'

'Ah. Sad, then. Do they behave like feathers?'

'Sorry, Mr Evans?'

'Will they float on the air like a feather will? Drop them and see, will you?'

Here, Icarus Evans pulls out a chair and the boy climbs up in his old trousers, his shirt-tail hanging out, and the others laughing but jealous for all that. Laddy Merridew waits for a moment for the air to be right, and he holds first one and then the other wooden feather high over his head and lets them go.

There will be a hush then. Despite themselves, the lads are willing the feathers – made by older lads, their heroes – willing them to find the smallest of up-draughts, willing them to fall a little, willing their carpentry teacher to start a smile as one stops – *there*! Like that. *Magic!* For it to pause in the air on that up-draught like a hand has caught it, invisible. Willing it to catch the movement of the air made by the breathing in and out of thirty boys and one man. Willing it to float, gentle and swaying, willing it to side-slip and be caught in the real ink-stained fingers of a boy. *There! Did you see? It floats!*

But do any do this? Have any done this in all the years that Icarus Evans has been teaching the lads at the school? No. None. The wooden feathers all fall straight to the floorboards to meet the sawdust, for they have never stopped being wood, and are simply going home. Not one, not a single one in all those years has ever floated on the air like a real feather, for all the trying.

Just like these two feathers dropped by the new boy Laddy Merridew, who stands on his chair to hear laughter, and the magic is broken, the 'maybe's have vanished and there's a lad just here holding his nose.

Laddy climbs down and Icarus Evans is saying, 'There you are. You have lessons with me for a year. And by the end of the year maybe one of you will have made me a feather that will float?'

The lads all smile at one another and nod, and not one makes plans to carve wooden feathers that float on the air. For such a thing, as everyone already knows, cannot be done.

'But will we make tables, Mr Evans? And chairs?'

Icarus Evans sighs, puts the wooden feathers back in the box and closes it all up again for another day.

When he goes home at the end of the day, leaving the lads' heads full of plans for anything but feathers, does he stop at

The Cat Public House at the corner of Maerdy Street for a drink, or call in at number eleven to see if old Lillian Harris has anything that needs mending? He does not. He will call by Tutt Bevan the Undertaker's, to ask if he has any offcuts today. He will take those strips of mahogany or pine that were not born to be coffins and home he goes to the farm, to make himself a little supper, and after supper to carve yet another feather himself. And then to work on the rowing boat. To make another piece, another rib for the sides.

The Woodwork Teacher's Tale

ii

BACK DOWN THE TOWN the cinema is getting ready for the next showing and Mrs Prinny Ellis has upped the shutter of her ticket office, sending its noise to fall against the door of Ebenezer Chapel and to wake the beggar Ianto Passchendaele Jenkins dozing on his bench in the porch. Mrs Prinny Ellis is sucking a bullseye while she waits, maybe reading a magazine, something to do with the South Seas and palm trees and sailing ships. Ianto Passchendaele Jenkins the beggar comes down the steps, leans against the peeling wall of the cinema and taps the face of his watch with no hands, for it must be nearly time to be begging again and his watch agrees.

Laddy Merridew brings himself down from the school, for his gran may have told him he is not to come back until suppertime, and given him a few coins for the cinema from the jar on the kitchen mantel.

He may be the first in the queue, and the next in the queue will recognise Laddy from the Brychan, and may ask how his first day has gone at the school.

Laddy will say nothing about shirt-tails with 'Stinker'

inked in blue biro, shirt-tails washed in the school lavvies in yellow soap. Instead, he says, 'We must make feathers. Make them float on air.'

'Aaw. That Icarus Evans. Him and his feathers. I remember that, and it's ten years ago now. Fetch him water in a bucket from the tap outside the workshop. They'll float nice.'

The queue will grow, and someone may ask why the teacher wants feathers from wood and what's wrong with the real thing then, and what started this, and when will it finish? And what is the teacher called Icarus doing with all those feathers, making a flying suit? And there is laughter, indeed there is, but if they ask it right, and if the questions come to the ears of Ianto Passchendaele Jenkins, leaning against the wall just there, he will tap his watch again, wheel his arms in the air as if he is drawing the story down from the wind and look up the road towards the school, 'Listen with your ears, I have a story for them, see, about Icarus Evans and his feathers. But stories need fuel they do, and it is a while since I had something to eat.'

Someone will bring him a coffee with two sugars made in the ticket booth by Prinny Ellis, and maybe someone will open a bag of mintoes, or toffees for him to suck. And Ianto Jenkins begins.

'Ah, that Icarus Evans, he always loved wood. Even as a small boy. Loved the feel of the trees, the roughness of bark and the smoothness of the flesh underneath. The smell of wood when he scraped a twig with a nail, gentle. And the colours, so many he couldn't name them. Colours that were just green or brown to most, but to the young Icarus Evans no two woods were the same, ever. No two pieces from the same tree, even.

Icarus Evans's da was the best carpenter in this town. Up Gylfach Cynon, a little house on the hill with a workshop out the back and Icarus's mam taking in mending done on the treadle machine in the middle room, a machine she got from her own mam, and she from hers. Not called Icarus at all back then, of course. Not yet, but called for his grandfather, the collier Thaddeus Evans.

Never met that grandfather he was named for. Not even once – Thaddeus Evans the grandfather died years before Icarus was born, and when his son, Icarus's own da, was just an apprentice carpenter. Thaddeus Evans the grandfather died up Kindly Light pit one September morning a long time back now, put to sleep by the afterdamp. Terrible, that Kindly Light accident. Terrible.'

Here, the beggar will pause and rub his eyes. He takes a slow mouthful of coffee and shakes his head. Then he continues.

'Before Thaddeus Evans the collier died sudden like that, he left his son the carpenter with a question, the answer promised but never given. A secret taken down Kindly Light pit and left down there in the dark, sure as anything. You will see.

But now, the boy Icarus learned to breathe in an air heavy with the scents and sounds from his father's workshop. The green scents of the wood wound themselves about his head, Icarus just a baby in his basket by the sewing machine, as his mother turned collars for men who worked in insurance offices. So the tick tick tick of the machine and the shunt and pulse of the treadle were his sleeping song.

And in his workshop out the back his da made chests for the big houses high on the hillsides out of town. Oh and there were chairs for the chapels, and boxes for lovers to keep their secrets in. Kitchen tables for Tredegar Street and Plymouth Terrace. Careful wedges decorated with robins for the doors of the old houses strung along the river, where the old ladies live.

The boy Icarus learned to crawl among the sawdust and the curls of wood under the plane bench in the workshop, and he learned to love in that very same place. First, he loved the softness and the scents of the sawdust, he loved it for its colours, how they flickered away from the colours of the sawn wood. He grew, and saw how mahogany unreds itself, how beech whitens in its own dust. He learned how walnut and apple smell of their own fruits. How oak lifts its ribs in the pews and chairs of the chapels, and how beech wood feels as soft as the fine powder his mam used on Saturdays.

Learned to work in wood, then, shown by his da. The best apprenticeship, unpaid except in something that is not money. Learned everything about wood, and more. All except for one thing . . .'

Here, the beggar will stop, and sigh. And the listeners, who have forgotten all about the showing, will shake their heads, 'Aww, don't stop now, just the one thing his da kept from him, did he?'

* * *

20

'Just the one thing, and not something his da could have told him, either. Listen. For all the scents of the different woods, and for all the dovetails, butts and mitres, for all the straight grains of beech and the wave-grains of walnut, for all the hidden music in ebony and cherry, for all Icarus learned, that was not enough for his da. Listen to his voice down the years, "When you can make me a feather out of wood, only then are you a real carpenter. This is what your grandfather Thaddeus told me, and who am I to say it is not so? Never, ever done it. You make me a feather that does not only look like a feather, and that is hard enough. But a feather that will float on the slightest up-draught, the air that finds its way through a closed sash ... then you will be a carpenter to make your grandfather proud, and your own da as well."

Then Icarus's da, back there in his workshop, saw, caught on a cobweb in the window, a real feather. The smallest piece of down from the breast of a pigeon preening itself on the roof. Took the feather between finger and thumb, took it through to the middle room, empty that day, the sewing machine still. And the air, still as the machine. Took the feather to the window, to the dance of the dust in a small shaft of sunlight in a middle room up Gylfach Cynon. Then he loosed his finger and thumb and let the feather fall.

Did it fall to the floor? It did not. Fell a hand span, maybe, that feather did, curled like it was sleeping. Fell, hardly at all, from his father's fingers, then it woke, like a hand had passed underneath, invisible, but moving the air enough to play with a single mote of dust. As if that hand held the real feather suspended while Icarus and his da watched, that feather hardly moving, side-slipping slow, lower and lower, to land on that basket by the sewing machine and the pile of insurance men's shirts.'

Ianto Jenkins pauses again. The cinemagoers will shake their heads. 'Can't be done.'

'Not from wood, it can't.'

All except the boy Laddy Merridew, sitting there on the steps of the cinema, the film forgotten, watching the beggar telling his story, as intent as he watched his teacher Icarus Evans in the workshop. Listening, and thinking, and in the end saying nothing at all. And someone gives the beggar another toffee, to carry on.

'And so it started, because Icarus Evans's da said it could. And he said it could be done because his own da, the collier Thaddeus Evans, said so. The boy Icarus Evans went straight to the workshop to find the thinnest piece of wood he could see, and his da nodded, and said: "Ah, not so daft then?" And he watched closely, to see if his son might fathom the secret . . . something he had never managed himself, see?

Icarus picked up a shaving of beech wood from the floor under the workbench. Another of ash. And out the back the boy Icarus went, with those curls of wood and the sharpest blade he could find, out to sit on the step of the brick path that ran up the little garden, and he turned the curls of wood in his fingers to find the best place to begin. And he started to carve.

It is a carving that has lasted for years, for all its smallness. And it is never done, not yet. And soon after, young Icarus's father fell sick with the coughing like so many in the town back then, and he coughed his way into his bed, then into the ground, and that was that.

In the end Icarus learned to work in wood better than anyone else in the valley, and further. And now, he teaches the lads, but he sits there each evening, outside his caravan, to carve the smallest pieces of wood. Still trying to make the perfect wooden feather. Never done it though. The voice of the dead collier Thaddeus Evans his grandfather – it echoes at him, as it did to his da. "When you can make me a feather out of wood, only then are you a real carpenter."

And each year, when he gets the lads into the school workshop, he sets them his own task, and hopes that one day, someone will do it and show him a little piece of magic.'

The boy Laddy Merridew, there on the cinema steps, chews at a nail, and Ianto Jenkins nods, and smiles at him.

'So, for all those feathers, the lads at the school gave him the gift of the name "Icarus" a long time back, and the name has stuck, as names do. But flying anywhere is the last thing he will be doing, until this task is done. Impossible, he says. But he never quite gives up trying.'

Here, the cinemagoers walk away with their heads together to see if they can do the thing that Icarus cannot. Making plans to go home and to find a knife from the drawer in the kitchen, and a sliver of wood from the basket by the front room fire.

But the boy Laddy Merridew does not. After the story is done he does not go home to his gran on the Brychan even though it may be suppertime, but he walks up the track to the farm where there is a house with broken windows, a barn with a good roof still, and a caravan on bricks.

There is no one about. There is not much light in the barn. It smells dusty. Against the wall there are tins of varnish, two ladders, a pile of wood, a workbench. And boxes, more boxes. Like the ones in the workshop at school but these must have been there years. The ones at the bottom collapsing under the weight of the ones above. The cardboard splitting, and spilling onto the floor of the barn curls of wood carved to look like feathers. Thousands of them. Must be every feather that Icarus Evans has ever made, since he was a boy.

Laddy hides where he cannot be seen from the yard, and he watches and waits until the Woodwork Teacher comes down the track on his bike.

Laddy watches Icarus Evans take a plate of something from his caravan to his bench. He watches him eat, and when he has eaten, sees him return to the caravan and come out holding a small cage. He watches as his Woodwork Teacher lets a bird out of the cage and onto the ground, a thin string round its leg, an injured bird that runs in starts and stops to find a berry, a crumb of bread on the earth. And he watches as the bird is put back in its cage, and the cage taken back into the caravan.

Smoke from slow allotment fires drifts across the yard and the boy lifts his face to the scents as Icarus Evans comes out of his caravan with a few wood shavings and a blade. This blade is thin, sharp. He sits on the bench where the boy can see him, and sweeps the blade through the air, and it does not so much as part the smoke layers.

He holds the blade light and flat against the back of his hand, where the veins stream under the skin. He does not move. He lets the pulse of his blood shiver the skin against the blade until the slightest wisp of skin is lifted away. A sliver, membrane-thin, light as a bee's wing and as transparent, which slides off the blade, lifts into the air and disappears. The boy peers to see Icarus's hand where the skin parted, to see if there is blood. And there is not one drop.

Then Icarus holds a woodshaving in his fingers, the wood pale in the evening light. The blade presses itself against the wood, finding its small sinews, waiting for the wood's pulse to work blade and wood together. Slight enough to shiver cross-filaments the thickness of those on a fleck of down from the breast of a wren.

Laddy Merridew watches until Icarus has made a feather this way. Or maybe it is the blade that does it all. Beautiful. A curl of down, but made of wood. And Laddy watches as Icarus Evans inspects the carving, as he stands up, holding the feather between finger and thumb. Then Laddy ducks as Icarus turns to walk across the field, searching the rowans where sparrows roost by the spring, stretching up to find a real feather caught in the twigs.

From where he hides, Laddy can see exactly, as right by the spring his teacher holds up the two feathers, one real, one not, one in each hand. He holds them high over his head, then throws them both into the air, there between the rowan trees.

The newborn wooden cousin falls straight down and lands in the water. It floats for a moment and is carried to the edge of the spring, where the water begins its journey over the lip of the earth to the stream. But then the spring stops. The water goes still and dark. The wooden feather circles slowly towards the centre, and then, silently, it is taken, swallowed, deep into the earth. Icarus turns away, and the boy ducks again but not before he sees the real sparrow's feather float gently and perfectly to the ground.

And not before he in turn is seen by his teacher. 'Who's that? You come out right now.'

Laddy comes out from behind the barn. 'It's me, Mr Evans. Ieuan – Laddy Merridew.'

'Spying on me, are you?'

'No, Mr Evans. Yes, Mr Evans.'

Icarus Evans waves a hand at Laddy as he strides across the yard. 'Go on with you. Get off home. Where are the others?' He looks round. 'Haven't you lot got anything better to do?'

'I'm on my own, Mr Evans.' Laddy's voice is small. 'There aren't any others. I wanted to see . . .'

'See? See what?'

'You, making a feather. Like you said.'

'Can't be done. Impossible. Get off home.'

Laddy pushes his glasses up his nose. 'Sorry. Sorry.' And he makes for the track. But Icarus Evans hasn't finished.

'Come back here.'

'Mr Evans?'

'Wait there . . .' Icarus Evans ducks into the caravan, and comes back out holding the rowan cage.

'Here. Penance for snooping. You can look after this.'

Laddy Merridew's eyes are as bright as the bird's, 'Really?'

Icarus Evans just grunts, 'It's almost mended . . . should be better soon,' and the boy pushes the rowan cage under his jumper and runs off down the track before his teacher can change his mind.

In the Porch of Ebenezer Chapel

THERE ARE PIGEONS ROOSTING in the rafters of the chapel porch. And sometimes, a few feathers will land on the beggar Ianto Passchendaele Jenkins, smiling in his sleep on the stone bench under his newspapers.

Laddy Merridew arrives next morning on his way to school, the bird in its rowan cage held firmly under his jumper and some of his gran's budgie's food in his pocket. He finds Ianto Jenkins still asleep, a pigeon feather caught in his hair. The boy takes something from his other pocket and reaches out to place it inside one of the beggar's boots, but Ianto Jenkins stirs and opens one eye. When he sees Laddy he moves and the newspapers slip to the flagstones with a sigh.

'Sorry, Mr Jenkins. Did I wake you?'

'Only a little.' He speaks quietly, looking up at Laddy's face, as though he sees other questions there.

Laddy hands the something to the beggar. 'Here, your handkerchief. Thank you.'

Ianto Jenkins takes the handkerchief, and something else falls out of the folds. He sits up and examines it. A liquorish Catherine wheel. He raises an eyebrow. Laddy Merridew pushes his glasses back up his nose. 'Breakfast,' he says.

Ianto Jenkins grins. 'Spanish. My favourite . . .'

The boy grins in return. 'Mine too. I like the middles.'

Laddy watches Ianto Jenkins wrapping the Catherine wheel back in his handkerchief, then folding the newspapers that were last night's blankets. He looks round the chapel porch, at the kit bag pushed under the bench, the boots and the watch waiting on the flagstones, old and uneven. At the rafters where two pigeons are grumbling to themselves. And finally, at the double doors of the chapel, their grey paint flaking away from another layer of grey paint, one door wedged open, the wood swollen.

Laddy touches the door, pushes. 'Can I go in?'

'You can indeed, but there's nothing in there,' Ianto Jenkins says, pulling on his boots.

The boy takes the rowan cage from under his jumper, puts it on the flagstones. 'Can I leave this here a minute?' and he disappears into Ebenezer.

Ianto waits, unwrapping the liquorish again, listening. There is not much to hear, but enough. The boy's shoes on the floorboards echoing against the peeling plaster of the walls, stopping now and then as he peers up at the six painted windows each side. He is a while. Finally, he emerges, blinking, 'Nice in there.'

The beggar nods.

'I like the windows.'

'Nice windows indeed.'

Laddy Merridew looks back into the chapel. 'Are they special?'

'I expect.' Ianto Jenkins pulls off a piece of liquorish and puts it in his mouth, 'I keep an eye.' His hair, thin, wispy, is standing up round his head like a dusty halo as he chews his breakfast behind a slow smile, 'Haven't had Spanish since I don't know when . . .'

'The windows. I thought they were meant to be the Twelve Apostles, but they aren't, not properly.'

'No. Not properly. Just twelve ordinary men.'

There is a cough then from one ordinary man standing on the steps of the Savings Bank, Matthew 'Matty' Harris, Deputy Manager, fishing in his pockets for the key. The boy squares his shoulders, sighs. 'I suppose I ought to be off. School.' And he picks up the bird in its rowan cage, slips it back under his jumper and turns to go.

Ianto Jenkins calls him back. 'I don't think I'd take the bird to school? Leave him with me, fetch him after. If you like.'

Laddy Merridew does like, so the bird is handed over and put under the bench. Ianto Jenkins says nothing for a moment or two, unravelling what's left of the Catherine wheel then sticking it together again. Then he nods, 'You remind me very much of my little brother Ifor who I called The Maggot. Look just like him. He had red hair too. Spitting image, you are. If I do call you Maggot by mistake, will that matter?'

Laddy Merridew shakes his head. 'I'm the only one with this colour hair in our house. Dad says I'm a throwback. I'd like to be Maggot . . .' and he's off down the chapel steps, smiling a small smile, off to the High Street and school, where the names they call him are not as kind.

The Halfwit's Tale and the Deputy Bank Manager's Tale

i

AT SUNDOWN, AFTER RAIN, the streetlights spread gold over the tarmac in the High Street until the puddles fizz like a kid's spilt drink. And Jimmy 'Half' Harris, on his way back from the river, will stop outside the cinema in his jumblesale trousers held up with string, and park his old pram filled with pieces of rope, cloth and sticks. He will grin with what teeth he has left in his head, and look up at Ianto Passchendaele Jenkins in khaki, begging on the steps of the cinema, sucking on a toffee. Half Harris will grin and he'll grunt, for he cannot speak, and he may wave one hand in the air as if he's calling down the stars from heaven. Ianto Passchendaele Jenkins will catch the grin like it's been thrown through the air. 'Hiya, Half. Been fishing again?'

Half Harris will catch hold of the pram and rock it like it holds a sleeping child. Then Ianto Jenkins will look up at the windows of the Savings Bank where the Deputy Manager, Matthew 'Matty' Harris, no relation of Half's, may not yet have left for home – instead, he will be standing at the window as his Clerk Tommo Price puts on his coat and says, 'That's it for today then.'

Matty Harris, no relation, will have straightened and straightened his papers that need no straightening at all. He'll have opened and closed the drawers of his desk to hear the small sounds of their importance. Then another sound may join them. The telephone on Matty Harris's desk may ring, and he'll blush and blink and he'll cough and say, 'Best not leave it,' as his hand hovers over the phone like it's a quivering breast all ready and waiting. Tommo Price the Bank Clerk will check his watch and smile, 'New customer, could be,' and his smile will go out of the door and into the street.

Matty Harris will wait, and breathe in deep to lift the phone, then click his tongue when it is only a wrong number. He'll sigh and go to the window and rest his forehead against the glass.

Matty Harris watches the steps of the cinema where Jimmy 'Half' Harris is stopped with his grin and his pram, and sees Tommo Price and Ianto Passchendaele Jenkins stop their walking and their thinking and come to the pram. 'Show us your catch then, Half?'

Half Harris may stand in his jumblesale trousers and bend over his pram to lift his catch into the light. His catch will let fall diamonds onto the road: a rope with its knot still dripping, a length of blue-flowered drowned cotton, a rolled newspaper tied with string dropped from a bridge over Taff Fechan, a mess of sheep's wool, eight assorted lengths of farmer's twine and a broken green bottle.

'Well, there's a grand fisherman you are, Half,' Tommo Price says, and Half Harris, as though he has been given a bright new medal, will grin with tombstone teeth and turn his head to his bony shoulder as Tommo Price walks off up the hill, hands in pockets.

Ianto Passchendaele Jenkins may pat Half on the same bony shoulder as Half lays his catch back to sleep in the pram, neat as anything, pulling the cracked hood up to keep off the drizzle. And Ianto Jenkins will nod to no one in particular as Half Harris goes off pushing his pram, walking round the puddles in the High Street like they were sleeping things not to be disturbed.

A knot of schoolboys will be smoking in the deep doorway of Tutt Bevan the Undertaker's, their backs to his window with its urns and stone doves, and they may wave to Half Harris as he goes by and chorus, 'Hiya, Half,' all except for one who says, 'Who's that then, friend of yours?' and that boy will not be given a second cigarette.

Back at the Savings Bank, Matty Harris, framed in the window, will not nod or smile. He will shake his head, for this is no relation of his with his grunts and his pram and sticks, and he turns away from the window and the High Street to face his wall. On the wall is a white-squared paper calendar on which every day, tomorrow, next week, next month is bare as bones. He will take a thick black pen from his drawer and cross out today with a line as thick as a frown, a nice thick black line to show the day done and complete.

Then he'll take a boiled handkerchief from his pocket and wind it like a grey shroud round his pointing finger, and he'll point and polish his own real treasure ... the new conker-shining mahogany display case on the wall, as empty and yawning as a waiting grave. A display case made special only this week by the Woodwork Teacher Icarus Evans from a few of Tutt Bevan's offcuts. A display case the exact size of a proud and exhausted fish to be caught by a real fisherman in the Taff before too long. And with his shrouded finger he'll buff and buff the already buffed wood, and he'll breathe on the glass to cloud it, and shine it and shine it until he can see his face in it again, and behind him the squinting High Street with its golden river.

And a shiver will run over his hand and he'll stuff the handkerchief deep into his pocket, click his tongue and pull a thread from his sleeve, for he has not brought a change of shoes and must tread the damp and street grime into the hallway of number two Bethesda Mansions where Mrs Eunice Harris – most definitely related, by marriage, to Mr Matty Harris – will be waiting in the dining room, all dark and smelling of onion sauce, tripe and lavender polish, both. She may be reading her own reflection in the top of the dining table with its silver knives glinting like duelling swords, all the while nodded at by the Harris dead high on their brown walls. And she will be readying her tongue to drive cold slivers into Matty Harris's ears, about half-beings and prams and shame.

Matty Harris will feel dry-throated at the very thought and he pulls his coat on, rattles his keys, and is off by the back way to The Cat on the corner of Maerdy Street.

And there, in The Cat, perhaps there will be talk of real fishing in the Taff. Matty Harris may pull at the thread from his sleeve as he watches Maggie the publican's wife in her low dress and her low smile and her low eyes. And he may murmur about eddies and deeps as she leans forward to pull him a half pint.

Philip 'Factual' Philips, Deputy in charge up the Public Library, will dip a finger in a drip of ale on the shining bar top, and he will draw a map, a slow map of a bend in the river where it pauses under the alders before gathering speed to the weir where there is a fish lazing in the shallows. A fish that swims upstream, its scales like mirrors, a fish the size of a yawning new mahogany display case made just this week by Icarus Evans.

And outside The Cat, on the damp pavement, Jimmy 'Half' Harris will park his pram after its journey up the hill with one wheel wobbling for want of a tightened bolt. The door of The Cat will be ajar, the round dark smell of ale and cigarette smoke trickling out down the step, as Half Harris puts his smile round the door and listens for the talk of fishing in the Taff.

'Come in, Half, mun. Don't let the air in, now.'

Half Harris will sidle in, all smiles and no money. Factual Philips may buy him a small glass of lemonade, and Half Harris will stand at the bar holding the lemonade to the light to see the drink send pins of fire into the air. He'll watch the librarian drawing his map on the bar and listen to the talk of the fishing.

'The size of a terrier that fish.'

'A fish and three quarters, look.'

'What I wouldn't give for that fish ...'

'Indeed, and on my wall at the Savings Bank with a little neat metal label ...'

'Duw, yes. A little stamped metal label right enough. *Caught after a two-year honourable campaign by Philip Philips, Deputy Librarian.*'

'That's right, yes. *Assiduous fight* is better though. And *Matthew Harris, Bank Manager.*'

'Can't both be catching it though, now?'

'Indeed. Caught by a Harris that fish will be.'

And Half Harris will have half-drunk his lemonade and be listening with his mouth catching flies, and drawing his own map on the bar in lemonade until the publican's wife lifts her eyes and her voice, 'Will you be off now, Half?'

Matty Harris will say nothing, as there is nothing to say, but Factual Philips smiles and looks at the bar, 'Drawing your own fishing map then, Half?'

And Half Harris will blush and turn his cheek to his bony shoulder and he'll flap his hands all dirty from the river. Off he goes down the steps into the damp and the dusk, followed out of the doors by laughter and the smell of ale, to push his pram home to number eleven Maerdy Street then down the alley to the back.

Old Lillian Harris (no relation, so he says, to Matty Harris), all red-faced from the stove and her hair white as clouds, will smile at her son's homecoming and she'll take a cloth and squeeze a baked potato to check it is done, 'Just in time now. Tea's ready. Wash your hands then.'

Half Harris will take the Pears soap from its tray, put his head on one side and watch the strings of soap saliva glistening into the sink. He'll work up a lather between his palms and blow the bubbles onto the windowpane, where they cling and quiver like there was a beating heart in each. He'll raise his hands to his face and breathe in and sigh. He'll hold the wet soap to the light to see his mam Lillian Harris a golden angel through amber with her plate of ham and potato, butter and beetroot.

Then, over tea at the kitchen table with its cracked oilcloth patterned in faded grapes, lemons, wine bottles and biro lines, they'll talk about the day.

'And how was the fishing, Half? How was the Taff?'

Half Harris will lay down his knife and fork, finish chewing slowly, and swallow. He will lean back in his chair that creaks like a coffin and rock back and forth, back and forth, and in the creaks he tells her his day in the only way he can, while his mam smiles and nods, for this is her son born to be a poet, but he cannot speak.

And the creaks may tell her this, 'Oh Mam, the river was full of coaldust today. Black it was and deep. Like a black snake that's forgotten something, rushing back to the sea in a panic. It's always forgetting things, that river. But it rushed on by with a sigh and an "oh dear", leaving things to be picked up later. I went fishing, Mam. I caught hold of the bending beeches and leaned out over the river, as it left its thoughts caught on low branches. Like this rope, Mam. Caught by the knot between two twigs, and this length of old skirt. What was that doing in the river, now? Tugging and tugging away, the water was, trying to take it all down to the sea as a thank you, I expect. But I leaned out and fished with my sticks, and caught the rope, Mam. It twisted and slipped like a live thing, mind, and oh it was the devil's own job to persuade it onto the bank. But little by little, Mam, I did it. And the cotton too. The river gave them all up with a sigh as it always does, and it went on by without a word. And oh the shining of the road outside the cinema, like gold,

Mam. The silk and satin of the water in the puddles, living gold in the lights. There's beautiful.'

And Lillian Harris may wipe her eyes for she is old. And she will echo to her boy born to be a poet, 'There's beautiful indeed.'

Then together, after tea, they will take the day's catch up to Half Harris's room. The rope with its knot, the length of blue-flowered drowned cotton, the rolled newspaper tied with string dropped from a bridge over Taff Fechan, a mess of sheep's wool and eight assorted lengths of farmer's twine, they will be draped over curtain rods, tacked to picture rails, hung over the high bedstead. And the green glass from a broken bottle will lie on the windowsill to colour the dust green and gold as the streetlights sing through the shards.

The Halfwit's Tale and the
Deputy Bank Manager's Tale

ii

BACK IN THE TOWN, Ianto Passchendaele Jenkins will sigh, and
he will look at his watch with no hands, for it must soon be time
to stop begging. And his watch looks back at him with its face all
blank and hopeful. If he has the time, and if he has the ears to tell
it to, he will stop and tell the story of Half Harris to those who
have followed with their eyes and their questions the man with
his pram as he goes up the hill all mute and smiling at the road,
'Listen with your ears, I have a story for them, see, about Half
Harris who was not born once at all, but twice. It is a story about
cold and ice and water more solid than a marriage vow. But I am
cold, and I am hungry, and stories need fuel they do . . .'

And they who will listen may give him a toffee to suck, and
maybe a coffee with sugar in a cardboard cup, and they will
pull their collars round their ears as they listen to the old story
of Jimmy Half Harris. This story has been carried many times
up to the window of the Savings Bank and into the ears of
Matty Harris, no relation, and he has gone to the window and
banged it shut but can't ever quite manage to keep the words
of Ianto Jenkins out of his office.

* * *

41

'Born twice, Half Harris was, see? Born to young Lillian Harris, who lost her own mam to the consumption when she was small. Then as if that was not enough, she lost her da and her grandfather on a single day – both gone into the dark down Kindly Light pit and never came up alive again. Her da Georgie Harris, collier, and her grandfather Albert Harris, foreman, soon to be promoted, too. And she remembers that day, the bad air in the house. To do with money borrowed by Georgie and not repaid because of forgetting, not malice, but once words are said they can not be unsaid. And the men went to Kindly Light the day of the accident, not together, not speaking, father and son.

And for all this sadness, Lillian lived alone with her grandmother up there in Maerdy Street, wife of Albert Harris who never was promoted after all. Her da's mother, black-skirted Nan Harris. And they were looked down on by those long gone, from their ebony frames all over the walls of that house.

But was this Nan always black? Old Nan Harris? Not at all. But after that day she carried the loss of both son and husband in her heart and she turned black-browed and black-mouthed as well. That day made her into no gentle soul, and perhaps she saw her husband, her son, every single time she looked at Lillian? Who is to say.

You have to have balance, see? Have to bring life into where the dead rule and a little happiness into a dark house, isn't that right? So Lillian, when she grew up, found a little life where she could, and when she could, ignored mostly by that black-skirted Nan. Lillian took a job typing letters in offices. Not good enough for that Nan, of course. And we all need to find a little love somewhere, don't we? Oh yes. Lillian, she was no different.

So then, the grown Lillian was expecting – but who was this child's da? Who indeed? If Lillian Harris did not know, then who could say? But she did not tell that Nan, and hid her belly with strapping, away from her nan and the street, but when she was alone, she rejoiced, for this child was to be a poet. She fed him, unborn, with all the words she could find in books, all the music and the beauty of the valleys. She fed him with words she read to herself silent at night and aloud in the day to make those words as alive as songs. Until she could not hide him any longer, her son, and then oh, she lived in a cold house, and waited for him to be born.

But he did not wait. He was born early and not breathing on a cold night with ice glassing the insides of the windows, the puddles on the pavements frozen, and the water in the cistern solid. A night when the wind shouted to itself under the eaves and covered his mam's cries. Out he slid all glassy as a fish and as silent, into the hands of that Nan in her black skirt all ready to play funeral director, for there was to be no calling of the neighbours. And he was blue and dead, this boy child, and that Nan did not even let his young mam hold him. Instead, she took him away, and left Lillian Harris with her mouth full of tears and his name, "Oh my James, and he was to be a poet . . ."

But then – while the old woman was gone from the room, and while the wind was still howling round the eaves and the thunder beginning to growl, there was born all sudden, there on the floor itself, a second child no one knew was coming at all. And this baby was pink, and healthy and shouting its arrival loud enough for two, which was the rightness of the thing, was it not?

And the young mam, she dealt with this second child herself, and wrapped him in blankets for him to be safe and not seen that night, and held him tight to her breast back in her bed at last, warm and dark.

Meanwhile, the first child who was born dead, he was taken away by that black-skirted black-hearted Nan, fast as she could down the stairs while the dead up on their walls in their ebony frames looked on and rubbed their hands to take him to their bony breasts. And it was a cold cold night with the air as sharp as blades when that Nan carried the child outside, wrapping him round in a torn half-sheet from the linen press, into the dark of the garden.

She dug that child into the soil among the frozen drills all ready for the spring planting when the earth would ring with the green of shallot spikes and the frills of parsley. But now the soil was black as the night. Black as a night scattered with stars, it was, both above and below – for the soil was pointed with ice and it was too cold for the living to stay out of doors long with no coat. And the soil too hard as well for the living to dig deep, and that was both the blessing and the salvation for this child. For look, that Nan dug him shallow for it, and laid him, wrapped only in his half-sheet, in the earth, and only half-covered him, for it was too cold even for foxes, and it would all be better done in the good light of early morning, before the neighbours woke. And then, she took herself back into the house, and to her bed, to worry later about the morning. Did not even look in on that young mam, Lillian Harris, and she left the girl to herself. For it is a dreadful thing to have a child with no ring on your finger and what would she be saying to the street if they knew?

The thunder rolled down from the Beacons that night fit to unearth the dead and to split the river from its frozen banks. A crashing to keep sinners inside for fear of demons pouring from the deep cracks in the mountain. And all the while the boy born second and well slept tight and warm against his mother in the darkness of her bed, as that young mam who could not sleep at all whispered, "I will call you Matthew. Matty Harris, a good name." And her first son slept in the black earth. And that earth did not fill his mouth that night but instead it clasped him round and held him in its arms. So, you see, the first arms to hold him were the cold soil rills, and the first voice to sing to him was the ice creaking round his womb-warm skin.

And the new mam Lillian Harris, half-sleeping from a medicine she found in a drawer, took the thunder into her heart like it was her own alarm. She held her second son Matty, who was born well, and she waited in the warmth of her bed for the other half of sleep to cover the house. And then, putting a finger to her lips to tell the sleeping child he must not waken that woman through the wall, she got out of her bed to find her first son. For she had not held him. Not at all. And all she wanted to do was hold him the once, to speak his name – James, Jimmy Harris – into his mouth as is right.

From room to room she went in that house, quiet as anything, searching in all the small places he might have been left, upstairs and down. But he was nowhere to be found. Nowhere. Until all that was left to be searched were the coal-house outside and the outside lavvy, and maybe, poor love, he was out there?

Out she went in her nightclothes into the throat of the

darkness, and the thunder. And her child was not wrapped in the coalhouse, and on the floor of the lavvy was nothing but sand. But there was a moon that night, shining on the soil in that back garden, and she saw where the soil was freshly dug. She could not shout out, although her breast was bursting with calling for her son. She dug with her bare fingers where the soil was disturbed, and found her first child there, the torn half-sheet over his face.

She took him up out of the earth and held him blue and cold to her breast on that night full of thunder. Is it not a dreadful thing to find your first-born blue, and cold, and alone? So for one night she would take this son, the son she called James, Jimmy Harris, to her bed to be with her, his mother, and his brother for a few hours only. And she did, Lillian Harris carried her child back into the house and to her bed. And there, with the other child quiet and looking after itself and no trouble to anyone, she lay in the warm with her first, breathing his name into his blue mouth, and telling him all the words she could – for he was, after all, her son born to be a poet. But then she was spent, and she went to sleep for the rest of the night, like that.

And in the morning then, oh, the glowering and black-skirted Nan with her dented bucket half-full of water for scrubbing the back door step . . . for the Devil will not cross a scrubbed step. Indeed he won't, for if he lives inside there is no need to cross it, is there? And she found her own black soil on the step, and she shivered to think that soil had come from her own funeral boots in the night – that it was soil from the digging of a child's grave, brought by the Devil, trailing dark-ness. She got down on her knees and scrubbed that step and prayed all the while, until the step was as white as a new grave-stone, and her soul was the same colour as the night before.'

At this very point those listening with their ears and their hearts will go still as glass, and make quiet promises they may not keep. And Ianto Jenkins watches them, nodding, before he continues the story.

'She stood in her kitchen, that black-skirted Nan, and shivered again and again, each time she saw the black soil here, and here, and there on the cracked tiles and the prints of bare toes. She clutched at her old heart to keep it going and she prayed hard as she lifted her feet up the creaking stair, to find what she would find.

And what did she find then, but Lillian, her own grand-daughter, the new young mam, asleep and warm in her bed, and the bedding all scattered with black earth stars like confetti. Curled up and asleep she found her, curled round a new son wrapped in a dirty old half-sheet. A son who was not dead at all that morning, but stretching and yawning instead, telling the world stories with his fists and searching like a kitten with his blind, pink mouth, not making a sound. Then there was a cry from that Nan to see the child she had buried only the night before, alive and mouthing against his mam. Then a second cry, smaller, and one that woke the young mam, finally. A cry from another boy, wound in a blanket and bundled against his mam's back. A second son calling for his first meal.

And all that old black-skirted Nan had to say was, "Aww, my good sheets," for a first and final welcome to them both.'

* * *

47

Ianto Passchendaele Jenkins pauses. And the listeners will forget about the film and their toffees and will shake their heads, 'Aww bless him, bach, bless him, the love.'

'Bless him indeed. Bless them both, then?'

'And he is a poet now, the one?'

And Ianto Jenkins will sigh, and will tap his watch with no hands, and shake his head.

'He is a poet indeed. But he has no voice and no writing either, for he was born twice, wasn't he? Born the once at night with the neighbours sleeping, out of a young mam who filled him unborn with all the words she could find for him to be a poet, and once again out of the earth as black as black and shining with ice and stars.

And the name that chose him out of his mother's mouth when he was dead was James Harris. But later, when they saw his voice was left behind in the earth, they called him Half Harris because before he had lived at all he was dead. And now, before he dies again, look, he is only half-alive, so some say, and it can only be a half-dying he does when his time is ready, after all his living and fishing is done.

But his brother, he is alive as can be. And brought up by that black-skirted Nan herself after all, who left the poet who couldn't speak to his own mother. For who wants a boy who cannot speak? Who cannot walk sometimes? The boy Matty Harris got all the promotions that her husband Albert Harris never had. And she was old, that Nan, and she died, leaving nothing at all to the poet. She left the shell of her house, up there in Maerdy Street, to Lillian. And everything else, she left to Matty, for him to learn his sums, and more sums, and how to wear a suit.'

And Ianto Jenkins will look up at the window of the Savings Bank, where a shadow is crossing the room. 'He does well enough, Matty Harris does, look at him with his suits and his mahogany display case up by there. Deputy Manager of the Savings Bank. And he takes no notice of his older brother by minutes, a poet with no voice, who cannot write neither. Takes no notice, and says he is no relation.'

And the listeners will wipe their eyes and say, 'Aww, bach, bless him, no voice? There's a shame.'

'No voice?' Ianto Passchendaele Jenkins will say. 'No voice? And that is why he wanders with his pram, is it, looking for his voice on the ground? Finding his words on the tips, and in the river water? His mam tells me his words are beautiful — and who am I to give her the lie?'

He will look at his watch with no hands and tap it and sigh, for it looks back at him and tells him just what he wants to hear, that it is time to stop begging and go to sleep. But before he does, he needs to finish the story.

'If Half's words unspoken are beautiful, then the words of his brother who has a voice are not. That brother is "no relation" so he says, and he will have nothing to do with draping rope and string on bedposts, and nothing to do with half-beings who push prams through towns in the halflight.

Works only for money, he does, and married it too, years ago. Eunice, daughter of a solicitor from Swansea who wants nothing to do with her half-brother-in-law either and will not have him spoken about in her house. Matty Harris has not been up to Maerdy Street for years. Ignores them both, his brother and his mam now. Dreadful. There is no love lost in that house in Bethesda Mansions, oh no. Not at all. There was little enough to lose in the first place.'

He looks up at the window of the Savings Bank, to see Matty Harris watching and shutting his ears to words that rise into the evening air and work their way in despite him, like termites burrowing into ebony.

'Always up early, Half is. Pours himself a glass of milk then leaves his old mam one of his notes. Takes an old pencil stub and licks it, and kicks the table-leg with his boot, I shouldn't wonder, to help the writing come out of the pencil where it lives in a black stringball as far as Half is concerned. Sticks his tongue right out to write a single wavy line for the Taff on the back of an old envelope, props it up against a milk bottle for his mam, and he goes out with his pram.

Matty Harris might be unlocking the door of the Savings Bank as Half goes by. I have seen Half looking at Matty, no relation, grunting and patting the pram. I have seen how Matty Harris will cough and straighten his back against the street, and close himself into the Savings Bank.

See, there was a day not long back when I followed Half Harris and his pram all the way to the Taff. Followed him at a count of nineteen, I did, not to be seen, although Half was dancing in the gutter by the factories and tippy-toeing onto the old coal tips, patting the earth and smiling, and he wouldn't have noticed an earthquake happening beneath his boots.

I ducked behind the garages and took my old bones all the way to the Taff. And I watched him, oh yes. Watched him talking to the river, leaning out over the water and catching his old cloths and string from the low branches, then nodding and smiling like the river said thank you or sorry. Watched him nodding and dipping his sticks into the river and catching his fish. Cardboard, sodden. A plastic bag or two, shining and bright and covered in words. Rope with a knot.

A good catch it was, held up to the sunshine, shaken, river water flying like drops from a shaking dog. But I saw something else for you to keep between your ears.

There was more than just Half Harris at the river that day. There he was with his pram and his grunts, and there along the bank were real fishermen. Who else but Matty Harris himself and Philip 'Factual' Philips the Deputy Librarian with their fishing rods all shining, their flasks and stools, their nets all ready to land their catch? And Half Harris saw them the same moment I did, and he was off up the bank, flapping his hands and stamping his boots, and the real fisherman flapped their hands back and waved him away, for he was frightening their fish, see?

Half Harris ran up and down the bank of that river like a dog in a cage, wringing his hands. And then he ran off, back to his pram, and Matty Harris and Factual Philips laughed and went back to casting their flies. And Half got to his pram, and he threw his catch back into the river with great splashes, over and over. Cardboard and sticks flying through the air to land in the water, or in the branches. And the men stood up and shouted at him to be quiet. But Half Harris hadn't finished, had he? No, he had not.

Half Harris pushed along the bank under the trees to the bend where the water runs smooth and slow, and he leaned right out with his sticks and beat the water to a froth. He beat and he beat at his friend the river until the mud was all stirred up and Half Harris waved his sticks and his arms then, and filled the air with his grunts.

A commotion, then, I can tell you. Matty Harris and Factual Philips were shouting, and catching their lines in the trees, and dropping their bags and tipping them up, tins of bait falling into the river and onto the bank and fresh maggots on the mud wriggling for the happiness of the thing. And the shouts telling Half Harris that they did not want the company of halfwits, and he must find another day to bother the river, not theirs.

Three times, I went. Three times I hid, and saw Half Harris beating the river with those sticks to stop the other fishermen catching his fish. Oh yes, I follow the fine fishermen on Saturdays and Sundays with their shining new fishing rods, and their canvas bags, and their chairs, and maybe a bottle or two of ale from The Cat. And I follow Half Harris on the other days of the week. And I cross my fingers for the fish.'

The Halfwit's Tale and the
Deputy Bank Manager's Tale

iii

TODAY, WHEN IT HAS been cold as a sneer for weeks, most unusual for September, and there is even a frost in the mornings like a shroud, and the earth is frozen, Half Harris closes the door to number eleven Maerdy Street as gentle as a feather. And what's in the pram with the sticks but two old blankets from his own bed. He's left a single wavy line in biro on the back of an envelope for Lillian Harris, his old mam, on the kitchen table, propped against a jar of cut-price jam.

His breath makes clouds as he wheels his pram along Maerdy Street. He laughs and walks faster, snapping the clouds between his few teeth. He goes down the hill to town and goes to Ebenezer, and finds Ianto Passchendaele Jenkins asleep in the porch under his newspapers. He creepies up sideways and lays a blanket over, and Ianto Jenkins opens one eye as a thank you, and raises a hand. Half Harris nods.

Today, the road down to the river is frozen and there is ice flashing in the gutter, cold as cold, and in the soil on the coal tips. Half parks the pram and climbs up the tip to the scar where the ice flashes, and he pats the earth.

Then off he goes to the river, under beeches where the ice bends the branches into the water. And the water is not running. The beech trees are tied to the river, unmoving. There are no ropes and knots for Half Harris to catch today and the river is bare as bones, but beautiful. Half smiles at the eddies and deeps caught and silent. He smiles at the shallows where the froth is frozen to the bank, and catches a glimpse of his own face smiling up at him, then it is gone like it was never there. So he pushes his pram out onto the river to look for his face, in case it was him under the ice and he is just a ghost walking on the air.

He pushes his pram right on to the river, and he walks on the water. And the water holds Half Harris in its hand, as flat and weighty as the stilled blood near a stopped heart. Half Harris spreads his arms and lifts his knees, and he dances on his friend the river, solid and shining. He wheels round and round and his coat flies up like the angels' wings in Ebenezer Chapel windows. And in his dance he drops to one knee and raises his eyes to the white trees where heaven shows through the branches.

But then, oh then. He puts one hand on the ice to help him stand, and there, beneath his hand, is a face. He takes the hand away, and peers, to see his own face down there in the river . . . but he does not. He sees the face of a fish, its gills turned to silver, its mouth open and its eye open, that mouth and eye saying sorry and thank you and all the things the rivers say to the sea. And it is looking up straight at Half, and he looks back at the fish, at a small bubble of glass caught on a lip, a fin rippling, and it is beautiful. Half falls back to his knees and rubs at the river with his fingers, painting the river with water, as the fish sends cold questions through the ice.

He goes back to the bank and tries to break a branch from a beech tree, then an alder, but they will not come. And he goes to another and another tree and tries to break branches, reaching up and hanging from them, twisting them where he can, and they will still not come. And he sits by his pram in his boots and wonders. Then he smiles, and finds where the wheel is loose, and undoes a screw – he finds where the pram handle is loose and undoes another screw. But the handle will not come for the rust and the years. And the wheel is just a wheel that skids over the river when he throws it down.

Then, Half Harris pushes the pram onto its side, and he dances on the pram in his boots until the thing splits and gives, and among the things it gives is the handle, made for digging fish out of frozen rivers.

On the ice, Half Harris takes the handle of his pram, and he kneels where the fish is looking up at him, and he hits at the ice and hits it until his eyes are so full of his own river he cannot see.

And then, a little while later, the little while it took to cut into the ice, the fisherman makes for home. The evening shines on Half Harris making his way back to the town, and in his arms, cradled like a baby, wrapped in an old grey blanket and still caught in its bed of river-ice, is the fish.

Half Harris walks back from the river, slowly. Without his pram. Just the bundle in his arms, past the factories, the old tips, into the town. Stopping now and then to peel back the blanket and look at the face of the fish to see if it has moved, but it never does. Up the High Street with the streetlights coming on, the gold glowing on the wet tarmac. He's dragging his feet, peering down at the road like he always does, but not stopping, now, making for home, shaking his head and moving his mouth like he would talk.

He pauses outside the cinema to think, then sits down on the kerb and bows his head over his bundle. And he stays there like that, unmoving, just his shoulders shaking, maybe with the cold, maybe not, and Ianto Passchendaele Jenkins taps his watch and stops his begging. 'What's the matter, Half?'

Half Harris just rocks himself and the fish, and sits on the kerb and the tears are falling from his chin, all salt onto the blanket, his jumblesale trousers, and the road.

The cinemagoers stop their queuing and forget about their decisions regarding toffees or mints, 'What's the matter, Half?'

'No good fishing today, mun?'

'Where's the pram then?' And they look back down the road to look for the pram they have seen every day for years, but it is not there.

Now Half Harris is crying on the kerb, rocking his bundle, and for all the tears, there is no noise in his crying, for this is the man without a voice, born to be a poet. And they crowd round him, the cinemagoers, and Ianto Jenkins, all else forgotten, until the window of the Savings Bank rattles open and the head of Matty Harris, no relation, comes out into the evening and says, 'What's up with Half then?' for in his head he has heard the sound of a child crying, and the rattle of small bones.

Ianto Passchendaele Jenkins asks Half if he may see his bundle, and what is the trouble, and he takes a corner of grey blanket and folds it back. There, clear, crystal, its ripples still folding and dipping, is the river-ice. And in the ice with its mouth open, lying in its bed with its eye, dulling now, fixed up at Half Harris, is the fish.

The voice of Matty Harris, who can't quite see from his window, comes again. 'What's up with Half?'

Ianto Passchendaele Jenkins looks up, 'Don't ask, mun, come down and see. The river's frozen, looks like. . . ?'

The door of the Savings Bank opens and out comes Matty Harris, no relation, to see what there is to see. And what is there to see but half a man rocking a fish?

Then Half Harris closes his eyes, lies down right there on the pavement and curls up round like he was a fish too. And another voice comes, 'Half?'

It is the voice of Philip 'Factual' Philips, Deputy Librarian, on his way back up the High Street from delivering books down in Plymouth Street. 'Half, mun? What's up now? Oh that's no good, that pavement, come here . . .'

And Philip Factual Philips goes to lift Half Harris up. But there is a cough, and another. And an, 'I will take him,' and it is Matty Harris himself who bends down to the kerb instead. And it is Matty Harris Deputy Manager of the Savings Bank who takes up a man who is no relation at all of his, in his own arms, and starts a walk up the hill to Maerdy Street, with Factual Philips following behind, and Ianto Passchendaele Jenkins coming on slowly with a gaggle of the cinemagoers, for there are no films about fish caught in ice, not that they know of.

With Matty Harris carrying Half, and the rest following, they pass the Public Library and the granite statue, its face wet and gold in the drizzle and the streetlights. They pass the dress-maker's with its draped half-figures and Tutt Bevan the Undertaker's, his windows and stone doves all dark now, lights out like a lid's been nailed down.

And on the way up the hill, doors open, and questions are asked, 'What's up with Half, now?'

'What's happened to the pram?'

'What's he got by there, then?'

'The river froze, did it? But it's only September ...'

'Half Harris has caught the fish, bless him, bach, the love.'

When the answers are given and more questions asked, voices pick up the sounds and carry them away. They are carried as far as the ears of Eunice Harris in Bethesda Mansions, wife of Matty Harris, and on the way, to those of Laddy Merridew dawdling along Garibaldi Street on his way back from being on his own down the park. Laddy collected his bird from Ianto Jenkins after school, and the bird is stretch-ing its wings, fluttering against the bars of its rowan cage, under his jumper.

Laddy Merridew runs to the end of Garibaldi Street to see the small procession coming up the hill. He stands behind Mrs Bennie Parrish and her bad leg, which forgot to limp along Garibaldi Street in its rush to see what's what, and Mrs Eunice Harris, who has come out with a curler in, and left her front door open, too.

So that when the procession gets to The Cat on the corner of Maerdy Street, there is a small crowd either side of the road. Maggie, the publican's wife, has stopped pulling pints and has a coat over her shoulders, standing out on the pavement. And there is Tutt Bevan, and there is Tommo Price just popped in for a half, and there is the publican, and there is James Little and his wife Edith out for a small birthday cider, and a draggle of drinkers, not drinking, everyone come out onto the pavement where Half Harris used to park his pram. And on the other side of the road, half the residents of Garibaldi Street and Bethesda Mansions, and a boy in glasses with a bird under his jumper.

Someone at the back by The Cat says, 'No one bringing old sticks home in a pram tonight then?' And someone else says, 'No prams needed, by the look.'

And as Half Harris is carried by in the arms of the Deputy Manager of the Savings Bank, someone with mauve hair and a curler hanging by a thread, says, 'Matthew Harris, what do you think you are doing?'

And Matty Harris, carrying Half as straight-backed as he can, does not stop. Instead, he walks a little slower for people to see what he is carrying, and he smiles, 'I am taking Half Harris home.'

The drabble of drinkers nod and agree, pull their collars up and follow all the way along Maerdy Street to number eleven.

And the ice is melting round the fish in the arms of Half Harris, himself carried in the arms of Matty Harris, who does not go to the front door of number eleven but down the alley to the back, his feet squeaking on cinders, taking his brother home.

Much later, maybe, Ianto Jenkins and Laddy Merridew and all the others who have waited and wondered in the street in the cold night air, will see Half Harris and Matty in Half's bedroom window, smiling the both, holding the fish up for all to see in the streetlights. Maybe as they watch, the fish will turn this way and that and the light will catch its scales, covering the whole small world of Maerdy Street in stars.

And back at the river, the water is flowing again unseen, the branches of the beeches are pulling their leaves out of the last of the ice, for rivers round these parts never freeze in September.

By the Old Sheds at the
End of Maerdy Street

WHEN HALF AND MATTY Harris have gone from Half's bedroom window, and there is no more to see, the watchers may go off home via The Cat on the corner, just to make sure it is still there. But Ianto Jenkins walks towards the other end of Maerdy Street, and the boy Laddy Merridew comes too, to where the houses stop because they cannot go any further. There are sheds instead, built on the old coal tip, where what grass there is holds on tight to the black earth and turns into a steep path, a back way to the town. And at the sheds, they stop, out of the wind. The beggar shivers, 'Cold out here. All well then?'

'Something happened in the park, Mr Jenkins, I took the bird out to feed him, and he flew on his string, like a kite.'

'In that case, it's time to let him go, isn't it?'

'Why?'

'Sounds like he is ready, to me.'

A pause. 'I suppose so.'

And there, on the grass, up behind the old sheds, and away from the streetlights, Laddy Merridew takes the rowan cage from under his jumper, while Ianto Passchendaele Jenkins keeps watch and listens. 'Looks all quiet to me, Maggot.'

Laddy sighs, 'OK then,' and undoes the string tied round the bird's leg. There is the small sound of wings beating on the growing darkness and the bird is gone. Laddy Merridew winds the string round his finger, 'I hope he's OK. I hope he finds his home?'

Ianto Jenkins pulls his jacket tight, 'He will.'

'Gran didn't want him in the house anyway. She's got her budgie.'

'Fight, would they, the budgie and the bird?'

Laddy tries a smile. 'It would have been different if my grandad was still around.'

'He'd have said OK to the bird, would he?'

Laddy Merridew's voice wavers, 'He was fun.' Then he brightens a little. 'They let me see him, before, you know.' He pushes his glasses back up his nose, looks gravely at the beggar. 'Have you seen a dead body, Mr Jenkins?'

For a moment, the beggar says nothing. Then he takes a breath, 'I have, Maggot.'

'It's funny, isn't it? I mean, not funny ha ha but the other sort.'

Ianto Passchendaele Jenkins nods, and the boy keeps talking. 'I didn't really want to, but Mam said he would only look asleep. She was lying. He didn't.'

'No.'

'They'd taken his teeth away. He used to take them out himself to make me laugh ...' Laddy pauses a moment. 'But that was just for me. He'd have really hated not having them in.'

The beggar says nothing.

'I was eight and a half. I went to the church and my mam cried, and Gran didn't. They didn't let me go to the cemetery, though. How old were you when you saw a body?'

'Five, or thereabouts. I forget exactly, now.'

'Did they take their teeth out as well?'

Ianto Passchendaele Jenkins sighs. 'No, Maggot. She was too young. My mam, it was.'

There is a silence. Then the beggar starts talking.

'My mam's name was Hannah, Maggot. I was so young when she died. But I remember some things. I remember her smell – river water and salt. Her clothes were rough sometimes. I remember an apron like a length of sacking, rough when I put my cheek to it, and Mam holding my head and looking down at me. But when I look up . . .' Ianto Jenkins pauses again, his head on one side, 'I cannot see her face.

'But her voice I do remember, better than anything. Telling me stories, stories, always stories. About birds, "the messengers", she called them. Oh, she said there were secrets in everything. I can still hear her telling me how birds are lucky or unlucky, robins especially. "Ianto Jenkins," she said, "always listen. Watch the signs. Robins know things. Bad things. Watch . . ." and I hear my da then, laughing, "Aww Hannah Jenkins, filling the lad's head with your old talk. Been spending too much time with the spinster-women." '

Ianto pauses. As if he is listening. 'Her voice. It is in me, here, and now. She said this over and over, and her voice would change, "Never let a collier go home once he has left for the pit, Ianto. If something is forgotten, and he goes back to fetch it, lock the doors, do not let him out again . . ." And my da, a collier himself, "Hannah Jenkins, what does a boy want with old wives' stories? I will be emptying this bucket over your head soon . . ." and he chased her round the back garden with the bucket that lived over the tap, and she caught her skirt on the rose bush. Da said, "I will be sending you to live with the old spinster-women Watkins if you aren't careful," and I can still hear Mam's laugh. But I try, Maggot . . . and I cannot see her face.'

There is the sound of a car making its way along Maerdy Street, gears crashing. The engine stopping, a door closing. Laddy says, 'Dad used to make my mam laugh a lot, too. Not now though.' He chews a nail. 'Sometimes, I think if I wasn't there, they'd be all right. Maybe that's why I've got to stay with my gran? Just for a bit they said. It's Gran who says I have to go to school. In case.' He stops. Then, 'My grandad had a heart attack. Why did your mam die?'

The beggar does not reply for a moment. Then he sighs. 'Who is to say? Who is to say why anyone dies? Who is to say why anyone lives?'

There is a long pause before he continues.

'My mam was having my brother the other Maggot, and she wasn't well for a long time. I remember being taken up to see her just after he was born. Da said she was rambling, but I am not sure of that. She could not say much. But these words I do remember: "The earth speaks, Ianto." Then she tried to sit up, and Da could not stop her. "Ianto. You must watch after your brother. You must." I think of that now often. I did not know what she meant back then.'

Laddy Merridew interrupts, 'Is that all here, in this town? Did you live here?' But Ianto Jenkins does not reply except to nod. He is silent for a while, then continues.

* * *

'Voices get into your soul and they cannot escape at all even if they'd want to. I can still hear the voices of my da's brother, Uncle Rhys, and Aunt Ann, the day my brother Maggot was born. Aunt Ann brought the Maggot down in a towel to give him a bath on the kitchen table, and all I could see was his hair, red as anything, an amazing sight – and I pulled up a chair to help and climbed up. "No, Ianto, you must not touch, my love, oh he wriggles." I was wondering why I was her love, and watching my new brother the Maggot, his fists flying like he was apprentice to a fighter already. And that silence coming from upstairs, floorboards creaking, then low voices, and Uncle Rhys coming into the kitchen and lifting me down from that chair. That rankled, mind, I could get down myself.

He opened the kitchen door and took me out the back in the morning just coming up, and me wanting to watch the Maggot's first bath. But Uncle Rhys he squatted down on the path and he pushed a finger into the earth where the shallots were coming up in a line, and he asked me who planted them.

"Dada, Uncle Rhys," I said. "Mam helps." And he nodded and took me right on the soil to the end of the row of shallots, where I was not allowed to go. And he held my shoulders and made me squint along the row to see the planting was good and straight. "Straight as a die, see?" he said. "When you help your dada, Ianto, you make sure there are pegs in the ground with string, stretched tight between, in case your da forgets. Will you?"

I went to ask why my da should forget how to plant his own shallots, because Mam would remember all right, but Uncle Rhys kept his hands on my shoulders so I could not see his face. And the yells from the new Maggot in his bowl in the kitchen split the air, and then there was another voice, and I didn't know whose it was, shouting and crying as well until my ears hurt, and then there was someone saying to hush, Ianto, and Da was there, standing on the path, his shirt not buttoned right ...'

Laddy Merridew coughs and pushes his glasses back up his nose. 'So where was your house? And ...'

Ianto Jenkins does not let the second question come out. He waves a hand, 'Away down there and across a little. All gone now, all gone.'

'And your mam, she died?'

Ianto's voice is gentle. 'She did, Maggot, she did. And the next time I did see her, it was just like you seeing your grandfather, I expect. Only I couldn't see her at all at first, just the side of the coffin, I was too small. My da he could see her, mind. He said "Oh, my Hannah." He lifted me up to see her. I remember breathing in to catch her smell and it had gone. Her mouth was open a little, as if she had just said something.'

Laddy Merridew nods, sagely. 'Did you go to the church?'

'The chapel, yes. But I stayed behind at home after with Aunt Ann and the women, and oh I did something bad. I remember now – my brother the baby Maggot was asleep in the other room and I went in and pinched him hard to make him yell again.

I had not thought about what would happen to Mam. I asked later where she was, and when I was told, it was my turn again to do the yelling, "No, my da, no – you cannot leave Mam in the ground ..." And he told me years later how he had to stop me trying to go out to find her.'

66

The beggar's voice is fast, now. 'Ever after that I had bad dreams about the dark. About being under the ground. About the ground falling in on me, where I could not see anything at all, and no air, so I could not breathe. I used to wake . . .'

Laddy Merridew interrupts. 'I don't like the dark, either, Mr Jenkins. I leave a light on. My gran says I'm too old for that . . .' and his voice trails away.

'It's never left me, Maggot. I sleep where there is light, always.'

There is silence again. This time, Laddy Merridew says nothing. There is just a rustle in the grass, then the sound of a television turned up loud a few houses away, a voice, 'Turn that thing down, will you?' and the bang of a door somewhere along Maerdy Street. Ianto stretches and pulls his jacket round tighter.

'And now, Maggot, it is time for your supper.' Laddy Merridew says it must be, and he walks off towards the Brychan and his gran, and Ianto Jenkins makes for the track down the side of the old coal tip, to town, and the chapel porch.

The Baker's Tale

i

AT THE DARK BACK of town there is a small side street that slopes to meet its own stream, a dead end where the houses hold fast to each other as if they might slip into the water. There is a handrail by the kerb, for this is Steep Street, and it is. At the bottom of the street is the stream, Taff Fechan, muttering to itself over stones and half-bricks. And the very last house has a sign above its front window, faded, a sign that can just be read: *Bowen's Bakery.* Underneath, a smaller sign, almost white where the paint has crumbled into powder, blank when the light is good. But when the sun squints low at the end of the day the words will still rise out of the wood: *Maker of Bread, Cakes and Pastries.* And fixed behind the glass of the door, clear as anything in black and white:

Mr Andrew Bowen. Appointments on the half hour, Monday to Wednesday, and *Closed* or *Open,* depending.

One day a year, a September day, early in the morning, Steep Street will ring with voices as people arrive from all over the town. Children will be swinging on the handrail, the little ones hanging by their knees, shirts untucked, laughing as they slide towards the stream. On that day no one will open their front windows just a crack to grumble, 'Be off with you, haven't you got a home to go to, make your old noise somewhere else, will you?'

Instead, out come the householders clutching their collars to their chins and they will make their way down the slope and gather on the path that runs above the stream.

'Been raining up in the Beacons. There's a good swell.'

'Aww yes indeed. A good swell. Carry anything, this will.'

And it will. The branch of a tree is wedged across the rock at the entrance to the tunnel that carries the stream beneath the town. Where there is a metal grille across, to stop branches of trees finding their way to where they might take root and send shoots up through the drains and that would never do.

And when all are gathered on the path, and on the bridge over the stream, one of the children will be sent to knock on the door of that last house, Bowen's Bakery, 'We're all ready, Baker Bowen, can you bring the tray?'

Out Baker Bowen will come, his tie askew and half-tucked into a green knitted waistcoat. He will be carrying a dark and heavy metal tray taken from the back bakery. He will move through the crowd, holding the tray, while from their coat pockets, from paper bags, from school satchels, the townsfolk take bread in all its forms. Slices, rolls, baps and buns, whole loaves even, those who can afford them. There will be a sudden quiet as they reach forward to place their bread on the tray. And a deeper quiet as Baker Bowen, leaning back now under the weight of bread and metal, carries the tray to the bridge and balances it and its load on the parapet.

* * *

With the exception of that special September day, every Monday, Tuesday and Wednesday morning, at a quarter to nine, Baker Bowen will come through his house to the front shop, wiping his mouth of crumbs as he slides the sign to *Open* and unbolts the door to let in the air that rises from the stream. Maybe he will turn and call back into the house, his breath making a brief cloud as he speaks, 'It is a fine day, my love, but cold.'

And there may come a thin voice in reply, from a bedroom somewhere at the back, 'If it is cold, you be careful. It is bad, the cold.'

Baker Bowen will go back inside and straighten a chair in the front shop, still calling to his wife, 'I will be careful, don't you worry. Have you finished with your breakfast tray, my love?'

'Not yet. I still have my egg. Thank you.'

'I will fetch you the paper in a while. Don't forget your tablets.'

There is a small silence. 'Perhaps I shall be better today?'

Baker Bowen may not reply to this last, but he will go back to his front door to watch for his first customer. He will not have to wait long. They come without fail at five minutes to nine, dropped by the bus as it passes at the top of the street, although there is no regular stop up there. The passengers just ask for Baker Bowen's and they sigh as they alight, holding on to the rail as they make their way down the steepest street in the town, complaining as they come, 'Morning, Mr Bowen. There's painful they are today, terrible. I must have done something dreadful to deserve these feet.' The ladies will always say something like that, and the men will do nothing but scowl.

Today it is the turn of Mrs Eunice Harris, come down on the bus after tidying away the silver from breakfast at Bethesda Mansions. Maybe Mrs Harris nodded goodbye to Matty Harris and reminded him to take the briefcase she gave him for Christmas for he may only be a deputy and there may be nothing in it except a packet of sandwiches he made himself, but it is a serious matter being a Deputy Bank Manager's wife and he must not forget it.

She comes limping down the hill and into the front shop, waiting inside the door until the polished counter and the shelves gather themselves towards her out of the gloom. There are no weighing scales in this shop, no baskets on the shelves ready for loaves, no paper bags on string loops waiting for rolls, buns, cakes.

Instead there is a telephone, a pile of papers, a diary open at today. A pile of *National Geographic*s on the counter, more on the chairs. Mrs Harris will sit, unbutton the collar of her good coat, and not take off her hat. And she will sigh with the pleasure of sitting as though it is a year since she did that and the seat on the bus is forgotten, 'A blessing it is.'

She picks up a *National Geographic* from the pile on the next chair while Baker Bowen brushes the last of the crumbs off his knitted waistcoat, takes a white jacket from a peg and goes through to the back, 'I won't be a moment.'

And when that moment is passed – time enough for him to put his head round a far door and to smile and blow a kiss to his wife in her bed – he will call through that he is ready, and Mrs Eunice Harris will sigh and limp through to where Baker Bowen is waiting in the old bakery itself.

* * *

Here are the bread ovens, dark things and heavy. Here are the wooden racks against the wall, the cooling racks, those metal trays, some wooden trays. And here also is the smell of antiseptic and of wool, not yeast. Here is a chair that tips, a high footstool attached. Here there is no bread on the racks and trays – or in the ovens. Instead, the oven doors are open, and shining dully from the shadows are trays of instruments: scissors and tweezers, files and pincers, blades and blade holders, picks and points. The surfaces of metal dishes catch what light comes in and sends it back, until Baker Bowen turns with a smile, 'Righto. Those verrucas any better since last week, Mrs Harris?'

And they will talk about her verrucas with the door ajar to the front shop, and for a while Mrs Harris does not worry about the implications, until Baker Bowen's next customer lets himself in with a jangle from the bell still attached to the door and Mrs Harris asks for the adjoining door to be shut, forgetting to enquire after the health of Mrs Baker Bowen.

The next customer may pick up the *National Geographic* Mrs Harris left open at a photograph of the whirling dervishes of Istanbul, and ponders until it is his turn to go through to the bakery how his left big toe is throbbing like the devil and how the toenails of a whirling dervish must never be ingrown or there would be no whirling done at all.

If it should be a Thursday or a Friday, Baker Bowen will take his instruments out of the ovens, roll them in a canvas wrap and put them in a carpet bag with some bottles of antiseptic and some white linen cloths. He will look in on his wife, 'I am off now, my love. Do you have everything you need?'

'I think I will sleep while you are out.'

He turns the sign on the door to *Closed*, and off he goes, walking up Steep Street then down to the town to make his home visits.

First today is Mr James Little up in Christopher Terrace. Baker Bowen smiles as he rings at the Littles' house, for the appointment will always be made for Mr James Little, but it will be Mrs Edith Little who has her feet tended. The appointment will be conducted in whispers and gestures, 'Not to wake poor James, Mr Bowen, asleep again, I'm sorry . . .' and it will transpire that Mr James Little has been working on his allotment into the night again. 'Mind, the beans this year were marvellous. Not to mention the marrows . . .'

So Baker Bowen does not mention the marrows, as requested, and when Edith Little pays his bill she may add a bag of late tomatoes, autumn raspberries, or the last of the potatoes, 'For your wife, bless her?'

Then, to the Brychan, to see to the corns of Laddy Merridew's gran.

'Corns are trial enough, Mr Bowen. Boys are a trial as well.'

'Are they?'

'They are indeed. They do nothing but get up to things.'

'Such as?'

'Walking about, Mr Bowen, and talking to people. Playing drums, and talking to strangers, and questions, always asking questions . . .'

Baker Bowen can't comment, so he doesn't. Laddy Merridew's gran adds a few questions of her own as he shaves her corns, 'And how is your wife, Mr Bowen? Still poorly? No better?'

Next, perhaps, he is off down the hill to Garibaldi Street, to Mrs Bennie Parrish. Her usual bad leg seems to have slipped downwards from a bad knee to a bad ankle, then it became the bad toes, and the neighbours will smile when she forgets which leg to limp on ... but Mr Baker Bowen was called, justifiably.

When he arrives he will meet Nathan Bartholomew the Piano Tuner on the doorstep, for it is out with the piano tuner and in with Baker Bowen as nice and easy as the single opening of a well-painted front door, with Mrs Bennie Parrish conducting their going out and their coming in.

'Goodbye, Mr Bartholomew and thank you for looking at the piano.'

'I could find nothing awry, Mrs Parrish.'

'Oh yes, I can hear the difference. An acute ear, my husband called it, when he was with us, bless him. And my toes, there's terrible, Mr Bowen.'

'Ah, toes is it, plural? It was just the one, last week?'

'I wish it was just the one, Mr Bowen, I really do, but there are nine more where that one came from and it seems they don't want to be left out of your ministrations.'

And then it is into the middle room they will go, leaving the newly tuned piano in the front room with the nets pulled back for the neighbours to be sure to see Mrs Bennie Parrish's iron upright with the integral candlesticks and a bunch of poppies all inlaid nicely on the front.

'Is it too cold in here, Mr Bowen?'

He says no it is not, and she disappears into the back kitchen to take off her stockings watched only by a smiling photograph of the late Mr Bennie Parrish on the table next to the gas stove. And she goes right up to the photograph waving the stockings rolled in her hand, 'What do you have to smile about, I wonder?'

In the middle room there will be a fire in the grate and a deep chair pulled up just by for Baker Bowen, its antimacassar freshly ironed. He will have taken a white linen cloth from his bag, and spread it on his lap like it was a picnic table, or an altar. Mrs Bennie sits on a cushion placed on a low side table more used to cups of tea and plates of cake than cushions. And indeed it is at just the right height for her to raise a stocking-less foot to the lap of Baker Bowen, deep in the big chair that was her husband's.

'Can you see how bad they are, my toes?'

Then Baker Bowen will take his second pair of glasses from his pocket and peer and peer at the foot of Mrs Bennie Parrish, in his lap, 'Show me where it hurts, I can see nothing.'

And Mrs Parrish will consider, and wave a hand over the foot, 'Here, Mr Bowen, all over.'

And he bends to his bag and takes out the roll of instruments wrapped in their cloth. He opens a bottle of antiseptic and makes the nostrils of Mrs Bennie Parrish twitch. He sets to, to her toes, with his clippers and his files, his tweezers and his picks, until the white cloth is dusted with clippings, and flakes and powder that were until a moment ago all part of Mrs Bennie Parrish.

Then he asks her to remove her foot from his lap and she does, holding her skirt to her knee with one hand and watching his face, but he is putting something in his bag. She watches him take the white cloth from his lap, fold it in two and shake it over the grate, sending her clippings into the fire.

And for all her chatter Mrs Bennie Parrish is quiet while she watches her own body consumed by the flames, and there is a pause maybe, 'A piece of cake and a glass of restorative before you do the other foot, Mr Bowen?'

But Baker Bowen never resorts to cake while he is dealing with the town's feet, and he just asks for the other foot, if she has it nearby.

When the nails are clipped as neat as the Garibaldi Street hedges, he will take his payment and his bag and go out. Then he will pause and turn back, 'Mrs Parrish, I wonder if I might ask a favour? The roses. Might I pick the last one? I have no garden.'

Then he leaves for home, and on his way he may remember he has no bread, and will call in at the General Stores in the High Street to buy a loaf, intending to be quick, not talk. But that is not always possible.

'How is your poor wife, Mr Bowen?'

'As well as can be expected.'

'Is she comfortable?'

'She is. Always cold, mind, now.'

'No pain then, that's grand.'

But what Baker Bowen does not say is that his wife cannot breathe easy some days, for the growing constriction in her throat. That her pain and his is one thing, but if the air cannot reach where it must, their pain is doubled. And fear. But neither she, nor he will speak about fear.

And he will walk slowly back home to Bowen's Bakery at the bottom of Steep Street with his bag and a white rose in one hand, and in the other a loaf of bread all sliced on a machine and wrapped by a machine, in a cold plastic jacket.

The Baker's Tale

ii

BAKER BOWEN MAY NOT have noticed, back in the General Stores, for he was distracted, some neighbours from Steep Street, standing by the sweets and chocolates before going down to the cinema for the late afternoon showing,

'Mints, or fruit drops?'

'I don't mind, either.'

'Yes but which?'

And maybe they waited to pay while the two ladies behind the counter shook their heads at the sadness of it all at Baker Bowen's, and couldn't recall when they last saw Mrs Baker Bowen out and about and it must be a long time now that she is ill.

One neighbour may wonder, for the first time, why a man who has to buy bread is called Baker Bowen, and the only answer that is forthcoming from the other is, 'He is called Baker but is not a baker. Lives in a bakery that is not a bakery, see?'

Later, when they are waiting on the steps of the cinema with their fruit drops and mints, and some toffees, for they were on special, the neighbours may wonder out loud again why there is a name and no job. A bakery and no bread. For they have never thought of it before today.

'Yes, and there is the tipping of bread into the stream. Done that for years but now I can't remember why.'

If they ask it right, and if the questions come to the ears of Ianto Passchendaele Jenkins standing there all hopeful at the sight of a bag of toffees, he will look to the hills at the back of the town, and wheel his arms, tap his watch that has no hands and tell those who will hear, the story of the bakers in Steep Street.

'Listen with your ears, I have a story for them, see – But oh I am partial to a toffee, as anyone knows . . .'

And the cinemagoers will smile and open the packet of toffees they were not going to open until the showing started, and will give one to Ianto Jenkins, who will put it in his pocket, laying a finger on the side of his nose, 'No teeth, last time my tongue looked.' He will sit down on the step with a sigh, and cup his hands round a coffee, and begin.

'Nice and warm, these hands. Maybe this story is not about bakers at all, but about hands? And maybe it starts with the hands belonging to a real baker called William Bowen, grandfather of this Andrew Bowen who still lives in Steep Street with his sick wife, there's the pity.

But this Will Bowen, his grandfather, oh he was a real baker, baking bread every day, the house warmed right through by the heat from the bread ovens. Exactly right, those ovens, and he knew, as he put them in himself. Couldn't afford them, mind. Oh no. What with, a young lad just making his way?

Could never have afforded those ovens, or that house, if it

was not for a friend called Benjamin Lewis. Gave him the money saved for his own wedding and the honeymoon after with the soon-to-be Mrs Susannah Lewis, Benjie Lewis did. Gave him enough for down payment on this house in Steep Street that was nigh on slipping right into the stream, and an old oven. Whatever next!

No baker, this friend. Benjie Lewis was a collier. Both at school together as boys, they were, Will Bowen and Benjie Lewis – the one laughing at the other who stood on a chair to watch his mother bake and loved the feel of bread dough in his hands. And he in his turn laughing at the other who wanted to go into the dark all day to break coal he said, even when he was a lad. Each thinking the other is daft.

Yes, gave him his wedding money, Benjie Lewis did. And helped Will Bowen set up that first bread oven when it came all the way from Shrewsbury, bought second-hand, a good one. And helped to make the house into a bakery – painted the bakery sign themselves too, out the back on a table, Benjie who could draw well enough getting the words drawn right in pencil, *Bowen's Bakery* and *Maker of Bread, Cakes and Pastries* . . . and then it was Will Bowen who fetched a pot of paint and filled in Benjie's letters to make the sign, then there they were both up ladders to fix it to the house, Benjie half-laughing about Susannah, and what she would say when she found the money gone.

Baked every day, Will Bowen did. Loaves and baps, buns and bread plaits for the tables of the big houses who couldn't possibly have their bread in the same shapes as others, indeed not. And the house was filled with the smell of bread, and the warmth of the ovens, for after a while he married as well, and bought a second with his wife's money, this time. Soon enough, among the other sounds in the house were the small voices of Will Bowen's young sons playing at being bakers on the floor in the front shop after hours, with buns made from scraps of dough and pennies cut from brown paper.

And he sold most of the bread from the front room, made into a shop, bread piled high and dusted in flour, loaves and baps, cakes and pastries, all made by the clever hands of Will Bowen. And soon, he was known as the baker in Steep Street, and the word attached itself to his name as words will, given the chance. William Baker Bowen.

And when he had closed up the shop at the end of the day, he took orders round on his bicycle, delivering to all the corners of the town. And it was a funny thing, but always, at the end of the round there would be one loaf and maybe a few rolls, and sometimes a cake left in the bottom of the basket on the bicycle. And another funny thing, for Will Bowen would always happen to find himself down at the far end of town, at a small terraced house on the road leading to the next village and Kindly Light pit, where Benjie Lewis was working.

He would wheel his bike down the alley at the side of the house and lean it against the wall by the back door – you go and look – there is a still a dark mark left on the bricks by the handlebars. And he knocked.

After a little time, the little time it takes for hair to be patted into place in front of a kitchen mirror, and cheeks pinched for the colour to come, Susannah Lewis opened the door. Then Will Bowen held the loaf or the cake behind his back and grinned and said, "I wonder, is there a lady of the house who would like some bread today?" and Susannah Lewis would curtsey, "Best come in and show me your wares ..." she'd say, acting the gentry – and the brown door would close behind Will Bowen as quiet as a stolen kiss.'

Ianto Passchendaele Jenkins the beggar will be doffing his cap and bowing and scraping, and he may take a spare toffee from a cinemagoer, 'Fuel, for later, understand ... stories about bread make me peckish ...' and he's off with the story again.

'But Will Bowen, our Baker Bowen's grandfather, he had to be careful, mind. He had to time it right, for sometimes he found Benjie Lewis washing under the outside tap, Benjie come home after an early shift, and Susannah standing on that doorstep, her arms folded, smiling a smile over poor Benjie's bowed head, "Will Bowen, it is good to see you. Will you come for supper?"

And Will would always wink and say that was kind, but he had to get back to his wife, his boys. But he would be back tomorrow, and would not forget to bring bread, cakes for Susannah, paying Benjie back for the oven. And Benjie not knowing it was not just bread Will Bowen brought for that wife of his.

But then there was one September day when Will Bowen came freewheeling down the hill towards Plymouth Street, near midday, whistling as loud as he could, for Benjie would still be at work – and he did not hear a new sound carried on the wind from down the valley. From the direction of Kindly Light pit.

And he wheeled his bike down the alley as usual, a cake all

ready in his hand, ready to knock on the back door and to say, "I wonder, is there a lady of the house ..." but he never did, for the bike was knocked to the ground by Susannah Lewis who came half-walking half-running away from her house, pulling a coat round her shoulders. She flung the words at him, "It's the mine ... the mine ... something's happened, it's bad ..."

Will Bowen found that back door wide open. He threw the cake onto the table and as he stood there the alarm from Kindly Light came again and blew about the yard. Then he was off back to the bike, but the wheel was buckled and he kicked it aside and ran instead.

"Benjie ...?"

Full pelt then, down the road to join the others running down to Kindly Light.

He heard the noise before he saw the crowd round the pit head, a low noise, the closer crowd, the women, white-faced, huge-eyed, remembering the last words they said that morning to their men, who left them in the morning clean, and came back at shift end smeared always in darkness.

There was Susannah Lewis standing to one side with her hands over her mouth, her hair blown about, shaking her head as if shaking her head now would stop thoughts taking root. And Will Bowen did not like to touch her, not even a hand on her shoulder.

Hours they waited, and then there came the sound of the winding gear, slowly and more slowly. And those it brought up staggered out into the light blinking and shrunken.

And the talking began.

"Seems the roof came down mid-section."

"Seems there was firedamp ..."

"An escape of firedamp caught alight ..."

"A fire all right, explosion behind the collapsed section, mind, not this end ..."

"All right this end, were they?"

"Explosion went right up the ventilation shaft ..."

"I heard it blew two roofs off, brought down some big old wall ..."

"No, not all right this end ... afterdamp."

"Poor buggers."

"Fire that side of the collapse, was it, and afterdamp this side?"

"That's about it."

More hours they waited, as the crowd swelled and diminished, swelled and diminished as though it was a heart or a lung, and Will Bowen did not think to go home, but stayed with the wife of his friend while back at home in Steep Street the bread ovens cooled, and the house went cold.

And then over the next day they brought up the bodies of those who had gone from the afterdamp, the sleeping gas, brought up on planks, on stretchers, a dreadful sight to see them unmoving, even when shaken by a cold hand, "George? My George? Do you hear me? George!" only stopping when a wife, a mother, a sister is pulled away.

But they did not bring up the body of Benjie Lewis, not then, and Susannah Lewis and Will Bowen waited together all night, not touching. She said over and over again, "If he is only all right. Please, he must be all right. I will never see you again. I am sorry, I am sorry, Benjie, I am sorry, if you will only be all right?"

And more talk.

"Digging out the collapse, takes time."

"Can't they get down the ventilation then?"

"Damaged by the blast."

And more waiting.

There was the sound of the winding gear again, as the engine worked the winch to bring up the bodies of the men sent into a deeper dark by the firedamp. Colourless, the gas that lives in the stones and burns like the furies if it meets a spark. And they did say to stand back, for the bodies could not be identified, not yet – but Susannah pushed through as they brought the two things out, and Will Bowen, seeing what they were, pushed her behind him. Two bodies dark with fire and smoke. Fused, their skin black and melted, their arms twisted about each other, fingers stiff and grasping.

Oh the smell. Dreadful it was, and clinging, something that made its way into the heads and minds of those waiting and would not leave, not ever.

And Susannah cried that this was not her Benjie, no not at all, it could not be. But no one listened, for they were calling for help to lift the two bodies down to the ground.

It was the baker Will Bowen standing with the nearest who stretched out his hands to carry the weight of an arm, a leg, a shoulder, where the cloth had burned into the skin, and all was black. Carried the weight of dead flesh, and lowered the thing that was a collier not long since to the ground as carefully as if he was carrying something newborn.

And oh, when he took his hand away it was there, still, just imagine, will you? See, the burned and blackened flesh stuck to his palm and his sleeve like it was part of him. He would never touch her again with that hand, his friend's wife – and he would not wipe his hand on his clothes, for this was perhaps the flesh of his friend.

It was like that, with two blackened palms, that William Baker Bowen walked back – all the way from the mine back through the town, all the way to Plymouth Street with Susannah Lewis, back to the house where in another lifetime, he knocked on a brown door with a loaf behind his back. Down streets that a day or so since had taken no time at all, and which now held his feet from moving like they were in mud.

And it was there, at the tap where his friend washed himself so often, that Will Bowen the baker finally washed the black from his own hands, and took a brush from the stone and scrubbed until his own skin was raw.

He left Susannah asleep, with a neighbour to watch she was all right – then he went back to his bakery in Steep Street, his home. And it was the smell of the bread in the walls of the place, in the front shop and in the back bakery, that made him gag. He stood out on that pavement, held onto the rail, and was sick. It was as though he had been gone for years and not just a day or two.

But then he was back in the house telling his wife in a low voice for the boys not to hear, what had happened, but it did not take much telling, for bad news travels faster than good in a town like this. Then they worked together, Will Bowen and his wife, making up the ovens in the back bakery again, ready for the morning. They made the dough together late into the night, exactly as they always did, and they held each other while they waited for the dough to rise.

And the next day William Baker Bowen was up early, as usual, to set the bread to bake. He filled the loaf tins, and rolled the dough between his palms to make rounds, as he always did. And he waited while it baked. But when it was ready to take from the oven, the bread, the rolls, were flat and hard as the ground. So he set to to collect the ingredients for a fresh batch, and he put a notice up in the window to say there would be no bread today.

But when he went to take the flour, and water, salt and yeast, to set them ready on the slate, he could not touch them. Instead of making dough, for a long while he just looked at his hands. And he cried to the walls, "How can I make bread with these?" For his hands had carried the weight of darkness, the weight of melting flesh.

Will Bowen took the bad bread and heaped it on a tray while he made himself prepare fresh dough again, and while he was waiting for that to rise, he took the tray of bad bread out through the front shop and down to the stream. And there, with only one person to watch, a man up early on his way to his allotment – Will Bowen hefted the bread into the water. And the hard bread sank to join the other stones on the bed of the stream, all tumbled and broken up in the current.

He tried many times, but he was never able to make bread again. Will Bowen took other jobs – painting signs, painting houses. But whatever he did he was always called Baker Bowen by the town.

And his sons, they did not become bakers either. One

trained for a doctor and went to England. The other was a teacher and lived here in the same house in Steep Street, and even he was called Baker Bowen. That teacher's son, today's Andrew Baker Bowen, is a chiropodist. How? Why? Who is to say? We do what we do, and the house has been Bowen's Bakery, to this day. See?

But the bread in the river? The town throws its bread into that stream, once a year now, on the day of the Kindly Light accident. It is become a game, now, where the bad bread sinks as Will Bowen's did, to tumble along in the stones, breaking up as it goes. While the good bread floats on the surface. A gift of sorts maybe? You may know better than me. Throw bread into the stream, bread that is put on the old trays that are still there at the bakery – and watch it get taken by the current, and swept away beneath the town – to join the bigger river down there. They say bread has a better chance of floating if it is thrown from one of those old trays.

I have found good bread on the bank of the Taff as far down as Treforrest, what do you think of that?'

There will be no answer from the listeners, for the showing is forgotten, now, and they may just go to the river where they will walk below the bridges and look at the mud to see if the mud might have once been bread.

The Baker's Tale

iii

TODAY ANDREW BAKER BOWEN visited a customer at the bottom of town, and walked back along Plymouth Street as far as the High Street, then passed the old chapel by the cinema, and heard the beggar Ianto Passchendaele Jenkins talking ... and maybe Baker Bowen stopped to listen and heard sounds that rang in his heart.

There is something in the sunlight that filters down Steep Street at the end of the day, bringing to life the words on the wooden sign above the window of the last house, *Maker of Bread, Cakes and Pastries* as Baker Bowen holds the handrail and approaches his home, ready to find his wife, his ears straining already, to see if they can hear her. In case she is weeping to herself while he is out, and the sound of her weeping is running up the slope with the sound of the stream. As it will only do louder and louder in the days and weeks to come. *Maker of Bread, Cakes and Pastries.*

He opens the door. 'Hello, my love, I'm home. I will bring you a cup of tea, now, and a little sugar, and your tablets. Hang on?'

The sounds stop sudden then, as though she has bitten her

tongue to make them go elsewhere, where they cannot be heard except by their maker.

Maybe Baker Bowen knows that the pain is growing now, every day, and escapes despite her, the pain scratching the wall by her bed with its nails, until the paper is in shreds.

Each day now she tells him she is cold, and he brings a bed jacket from the closet, and then a second borrowed from a neighbour. He puts more blankets on the bed, and he lights the fire in the little grate in the room. But it makes no difference.

'I am still cold, is it winter?'

'Not yet, it is not.'

His wife shivers and says the house's heart feels cold, and why is that? At first he thinks it is the ramble and shudder of the illness, but then he knows it is not. And another thing he knows because his name is Baker Bowen, is that the heart of the place is the old bread ovens in the back bakery.

It is not a difficult thing, in the end, to decide to fire the bread ovens, the great dark ovens that have not been lit for generations. To get his coat again and go out to buy kindling, and coal nuggets, and firelighters from the General Stores in the High Street. Where there is a boy sent down by his gran with her basket, to buy bread and a pot of strawberry jam, and a bottle of milk. A boy called Laddy Merridew who hears the women behind the counter whispering, 'Look at Baker Bowen. There's sad he looks today,' and the boy turns to the man, 'Mr Bowen, please can I ask you something?'

Baker Bowen pauses in his collecting of kindling and firelighters, 'Ask away, lad. I may not have the answers.'

'Bread in the river, Mr Bowen. I have not done that before.

But I was thinking, why does some float and some sink? What is good bread, and what is bad? What is not in bread that makes it not good?'

Baker Bowen shakes his head and says he does not make bread, so he does not have the answer. But the question does not leave his head with the reply. Instead, it echoes and echoes between his ears on his way home. 'What is not in bread that makes it not good?'

Back home, it is not a difficult thing to get on his knees and lay the fire beneath the bread ovens. Then he remembers, with a smile, and takes his instruments out. Piling his scissors and tweezers, his rolls of lint, bottles of antiseptic, anaesthetic ointments on the counter in the front shop, and placing some in his bag, on a chair.

Then he lights the fire, keeping the door ajar with a wedge found at the back of the shelf, to make a draught. And he watches while the fire catches, then as the old gauge on the oven door begins to move, the needle pulling away from where it has been sleeping. He watches until the oven is hot and the bakery is filled with the smell of hot dust, hot lamp-black, and burning cloth – where a scrap was caught at the back of the oven.

Then Baker Bowen washes his hands, black from the coal, black from setting the fire, as warmth begins to spread through the house. And he knows then that his hands are made from the same stuff as those that worked here long ago. That there is memory deep in these hands, in the bones and the flesh. *Maker of Bread, Cakes and Pastries.*

He puts his head round the door of his wife's room, and he finds her asleep. Not as before, restless, her white knuckles clutching the blanket to her chin, but relaxed, her hands open on the coverlet.

While she sleeps, and while the warmth continues to beat through the house, Baker Bowen goes back to the General Stores with a list in his head – strong flour, and yeast. Salt, and milk. And when the ladies behind the counter raise an eyebrow, 'Well, Baker Bowen, what are you doing now? You were here nowjust.'

Baker Bowen just says, 'What is my name?' for an answer.

And then, back at home, his wife still sleeping, he takes the yeast and mixes it with a little milk in a jug, and sets the jug near the oven but not too close. He takes flour, and water, and a little of the yeast, and begins to work on the slate surface, gathering it all together, and pushing it away with the heels of his hands. Until his head is filled with the scents of flour, and of yeast, warm and good. He works and works at the mix, kneading and kneading until his knuckles are red with the effort. And he sets the dough aside in one of his own metal dishes, covered in his own clean white linen cloth, to rise.

And the dough will rise, as dough is made to do. It will be knocked back by the fingers of Andrew Baker Bowen, who has no need of instruction, for it is in him. The dough will be left to rise again as he goes to talk to his wife, awake again, 'How is the pain tonight? Shall I bring you something for it later? Can you smell the oven? I have lit the bread oven. There is dust in the flue.'

Back in the bakery, he divides the dough into portions and shapes them small and uneven between his palms, for in this he is unpractised and thinking too much. He greases one of the metal trays then dusts it with a little flour – a memory held from boyhood, or deeper – and he places the rolls on the tray and slides it into the oven.

While they are baking, Baker Bowen sits with his wife, his head and hers filled with the scent of baking bread made by his own hand. His wife may say it is good for the house to have the bread oven lit for it is the heart of the house after all. And she thinks she is ready to try a little bread, if it is soft.

He will take a tray through, with a pot of tea, two cups, and his first-baked bread rolls. Strange misshapen things, but well-risen, and good for all that, spread with a little butter, a little jam.

And he knows then that his hands will be able, when it is their time, and his wife can not breathe easily any more – to do another good thing. To take from the back of the cupboard a box of white tablets and to grind them into powder. To mix some powder with flour, and a little milk, yeast, and to bake bread again.

He will not question, but will take the rest of the powder and mix it with some sweet jam. And when the rolls are done, he will slide the great tray from the bread oven and set the rolls to cool on the slate. He will mix icing sugar with a little water, and ice them. And when the icing is set, he will spread a little butter. A little jam. Make a pot of tea. And he will take a tray covered in a white lace cloth through to the room he made into a bedroom three years since, and will make sure she eats, and enjoys, and takes her other medicines, to dull the pain and send her to sleep.

He will kiss her and hold her hand, and will sit by her bedside stroking her forehead. And when he has finished his tea, and his wife has fallen asleep, he will draw back the blankets and slide in beside her, hold her as she floats away.

But then maybe he will be woken by shouts from outside, in Steep Street. 'Where are the trays? Where is Baker Bowen?' And he will get up in a little while, and straighten his knitted waistcoat. He will check the calendar, and shake his head, for he forgot the date – a September date – and will go through to the front shop and pull up the blind on the window.

Steep Street will be busy, people coming down the hill, from the bus, from the other houses, young and old, men in suits on their way to offices, lads on their way to school, girls, their hair unbrushed. All going down to the bottom of the hill, to the river and then along the path to the bridge just by there. Among them, the boy Laddy Merridew, who has brought his gran down on the bus from the Brychan, even though she did not really want to come.

Baker Bowen will splash his face with water, run his hands through his hair, and go back to his wife's room to make the bed tidy as she always liked.

And then out he will come in his dark coat, carrying two iron trays from the back bakery. There will come a shout from the crowd, 'Here they come! The trays!'

Then there will be a great pushing and shoving, as the trays are taken to the bridge, balanced on the parapet and loaded, piled high with bread, held steady by Baker Bowen like he's done for years on this day, and like his father did before him and his father before that – keeping them straight while small boys stretch up to place their bread roll up there on the edge.

'Mam?'

'Mam? You will watch for mine now won't you? Will mine be good bread?'

'Aww yes, I can see it for sure.'

Grown men in suits stretching from behind the kiddies to drop bread onto the tray, for not to do it may be bad luck. Laddy Merridew will take a roll from the hands of his gran and reach forward to place that and his own on the tray. And then there will be a single slice of toast thrown, buttered, from somewhere at the back, with a laugh – and it will miss the tray and land on the road – but it will be rescued and placed with the growing pile of bread, everyone staying as close as they can, trying to keep an eye, until the great iron trays are heaped high.

And Baker Bowen will stand back, to wait, a silence in the middle of the noise, to look at the stream as though the answers to everything would be found down there in its little torrent. And when everything is ready, like there is some secret signal, or when the very last bread roll is thrown from the crowd – then it is that Baker Bowen, holding a tray steady with one hand, will fish in his own pocket with the other, take out two iced bread rolls and place them on top.

There may come a shout, 'Never seen that, Baker Bowen, made them yourself?'

The questioner may be laughing but Baker Bowen will not smile, just nod. And as the crowd stands back he will tip the first tray and send the bread falling into Taff Fechan like thick rain, where some will sink and some will float, all taken by the current, bobbing and jostling like the watching crowd on the bridge. Then the second tray, and the water will carry the bread away fast as anything, between the high walls, and off to the tunnels under the town. And among the bread that is floating will be two rolls, white with sugar icing.

The crowd will part, and Baker Bowen will make his way back along the path to Steep Street, carrying his heavy trays. And will he turn up the slope to his door? He will not. Instead, he will stand above the stream watching the play of light on the water, watching the last of this year's bread jostling against the rock in the bed of the stream that divides the flow, some going this way and some going that, according to some indefinable logic.

In the Porch of Ebenezer Chapel

THERE IS BREAD AT the chapel porch the next day, sandwiches brought for the beggar Ianto Passchendaele Jenkins, but not by Mrs Prinny Ellis. White bread, sliced, with Sandwich Spread, wrapped in greaseproof and kept in a school satchel all day by a boy who couldn't tell his gran he doesn't like Sandwich Spread, when she got it in special.

'They are a bit squashed, sorry.'

'Squashed is fine, thank you. Would you like a toffee?'

And there is barter in the chapel porch, a little silence for eating on the bench. Then Laddy Merridew coughs and pushes his glasses up his nose. 'Can I say something?'

'You just did.'

'I think there are funny things happen in this town, Mr Jenkins.'

'Do you now?'

'I do. Gran says that bread is tipped into the river each year, but when I asked her why she said she wasn't sure. Not like you said. She doesn't know anything about your Kindly Light accident, I asked her that as well.'

Ianto Passchendaele Jenkins doesn't say anything for a while, just sits and chews, and thinks. 'I can't help that, Maggot. Just because the clouds are over the Beacons, doesn't mean the Beacons have disappeared, now does it?'

'I said you remembered it like it was only yesterday, and she said she came to live here years afterwards so how can she remember? Then she said it's just your old stories.'

The beggar is quiet again. He looks at his watch with no hands, and taps it, squints at the face. 'It's getting on, mind.' He rubs his eyes. 'And what do you think, Maggot?'

The boy considers for a while. 'I don't know.'

'An honest answer.'

'I like things to be true. I don't like people making things up, not when they are meant to be telling me the truth. I mean, people lying.'

'Who has lied then?'

Laddy Merridew doesn't reply for a moment, then he says in a small voice, 'My mam. She had a boyfriend and didn't tell Dad, or me. I know who it is too and I hate him.' He pauses. 'He's a teacher.'

'Ah.'

'At my school. I was going to be a teacher when I grow up, too. Now I'm not.'

'So what will you do instead?'

Laddy pushes his glasses up his nose again. He grins. 'I'm going to be a pilot.'

'Ah.'

'What did you do? I mean, did you, do something?'

'I did do something. But before that I was going to be a farmer. Up the mountains in the fresh air, a few hens, sheep. I was going to buy a shop in the High Street and sell lamb, mutton, eggs. But I was only twelve, mind. In the end, I was a collier.'

'But you said . . .'

'I said?'

'You said you were afraid of the dark. You had nightmares. Were you just saying that?'

'No, Maggot, I was not just saying that. I never was going to be a collier at all. My da was the collier down Kindly Light pit, off every morning before sun-up with Mr Thomas Edwards from along the way. Mrs Thomas Edwards she looked after the both of us, my brother the Maggot and me while I was small, then she looked after the Maggot every day and brought him home later, when I was bigger, and that was all fine. I was meant to make sure there was a bath ready for my da in the kitchen. But I tell you, that was a source of conflict. Oh yes. My brother the Maggot trying to get to scrub Da's back when that was my job, and him grabbing the cloth, and Da shouting, "Will you stop it the both? There is more water on the kitchen floor than in the bath ..."

There were the days Da was home, and trying to be both Mam and Da to us two, and I was meant to help. He would call up, "Ianto! Get to by here, will you?" and I would mean to go straight away, but I was always thinking and dreaming and could not stop for all the trying. Lying on my bed, I would be, arms behind my head, lost and journeying down the cracks in the ceiling. And enjoying being there on my own for a while, I must admit. So when my da called again, right at the foot of the stairs now, for his voice was louder, "Ianto! You great lump, get to by here," I would tumble off my bed and come thundering down the stairs, "Sorry, Da."

And look. There would be my brother Maggot, pulling himself up on my da's trouser legs, and Da trying to wash his work clothes, his arms covered in soap suds. And for me, the work would be potatoes waiting in the brown basin on the kitchen table for peeling, in water as brown as the basin itself. And Mam's small knife just by, waiting, the one with string she wound round the handle herself to stop her fingers from slipping. But there was no Mam's hand to take up that knife and peel the potatoes any more, so it was my job now.

And I can hear my own voice, "Sorry, Dada." '

Laddy starts to say something, but Ianto has not finished. He flexes his fingers, moves his hand in the air.

'All these years later, Maggot, close my eyes and my fingers are small again, back on that knife-handle, the string warm as though Mam had just put it down to go out the back for a shallot, the blade cool and curved by my da's whetting. And me trying to do as she did when I watched her, me the small boy standing on a chair and her slipping that blade neat under the skin of a potato so the potato never noticed a thing and gave up its coat easy. Moving the knife so fine its coat came away in slivers that fell into the muddy water. Then they would rise and wink at me like fish.'

Ianto Jenkins stops, leans his head back against the wall, eyes nearly closed. 'I am rambling, Maggot. Rambling . . .'

Laddy Merridew interrupts. 'So how come you were a collier as well? Did your da know you were frightened? Did he make you go?'

The beggar shakes his head.

'I did not tell him about the bad dreams I had, not at first. There was enough to worry about in our house anyway. And always something happening down the pit. Little things.

"There's always trouble down Kindly Light," Da used to say. "Plenty of good steam coal down there, but the mountain does not want us to have it."

Then one little thing happened down Kindly Light. A little bit of roof fell in before the supports were done in one of the new roadways. A little bit of roof that only caught one man, crushed my da's leg bad and it never healed after at all. Being a collier was finished. For my da, it was finished, see? I was twelve. And suddenly, Ianto Jenkins was the one who needed boots, and water bottles, and all the neighbours knew, and Mr Thomas Edwards was being asked if he would keep an eye on me when I was below ... and Da, he never asked me.' Ianto's voice falls away. 'He never asked ...'

Then the beggar shakes his head. 'I can tell you about my boots though. About my boots and the getting of them from a real dead collier.'

'Who?'

'... so listen, Maggot?'

And the story of the getting of the boots begins.

'Up until then I had shared boots often with my snoring brother Ifor, who I also called Maggot, and his toes were the ones that had room to dance down there, not mine! Oh shoes were easy. My brother the Maggot had my old ones, and I had different ones from the boys along the street usually. But boots were a different matter. Hard to come by. I had often asked why I didn't have my own boots, and the answer from my da came always unchanging, "Ianto, it is still growing you are, and whatever is the point of your own boots when it is your young bones that will be piercing good leather full of holes? For that way your feet may as well be walking on the ground."That was the trouble with my da, for there was no arguing with that.

But those boots that were all mine in the end were very big, and there was no danger at all of my bones piercing these for years. For they had belonged on the feet of a grown man, a hewer called Ernest Ellis who lived just along the terrace. And Mr Ellis had no need of boots where he was gone, taking his coughing with him, for whoever heard of an angel with harp and hobnailed boots?

"Ianto! Mr Ellis is gone, look, and has left his boots for a draw . . ."

That was Mrs Jones from along the terrace, whose son Geraint Jones was already a collier and married and much older than me, nearly twenty, but who needed boots as well. I was sorry for him for his da died down the pit when he was a boy.

And oh I did not want to go down, Maggot. Afraid of being under the ground, although I would never admit it to my da. Afraid of the weight of stone above, and of the darkness, and I could think of little else . . . "Ianto! Go and pick one piece of coal from Mrs Ellis's hands, will you?"

That was my da who told me over and over that I was too much of a thinker and it was colliers that were wanted now in this family, not thinkers. And he was in his bed with his leg which would not get better.

Oh, but drawing lots for the boots of a hewer who would not be needing them any more was an uncomfortable thing and I said so to Da, and of course he told me I was thinking again and please would I stop or all this thinking would be causing it to rain. "Ianto! Did you hear me? Go with Geraint

Jones and pick one piece of coal from Mrs Ellis, will you?" And there was me hoping I would not get the boots, for then, maybe I would not have to go down at all . . .

See, it was getting dark when this Ianto Jenkins and the young collier Geraint Jones went and drew pieces of coal from Mrs Ellis's hand, for those boots. One piece of the two would have a cross cut into it with a knife. And Mrs Ernest Ellis was saying Divine Intervention itself would be guiding the coal with the cross to the fingers of the one who was most deserving of the boots of dead Mr Ellis. There was no arguing with Divine Intervention either. Divine Intervention was worse than Da. And I had my fingers crossed behind my back that Divine Intervention would please please please give those boots to Geraint Jones so I would not have to go . . .

But oh it was gloomy in that kitchen. It all smelled of embrocation and polish and dust, like Ebenezer Chapel on a Sunday when the minister has a chest. I kept thinking that the house was still ringing with the last air breathed out by Mr Ellis. That had me thinking about the world being full of the last air of everyone who has lived, and trying to work out where new air might come from, and whether . . .

"Ianto! Get to by here will you?" I heard my da's voice in my head then. But then Mrs Ellis came out of the shadows in the middle room carrying dead Mr Ellis's boots, moving all slow like someone had tied a bag of potatoes to her skirts. And she set the boots on a piece of newspaper on the kitchen table where they stood together and looked at us. She patted them, "Here you are, boys, and they are good boots."

Oh and it was all dreadful still from upstairs too. So still and the quiet beating loud in my ears, and I could hear it, the silence. And I was thinking then, that maybe when someone stops breathing it leaves a bigger noise in the air than all the years when they were alive? I was thinking about my mam, and being under the ground, and that if I raised my eyes to the kitchen ceiling maybe dead Mr Ernest Ellis might push his ghostly hand through to fetch his boots from us. Weighed the place down, that did.

"Make your choice," Mrs Ellis said, holding two pieces of coal behind her back, and she said this as though there was something dark and swelling behind the walls. I shivered. Geraint Jones looked at me and he shivered too, and neither of us wanted to touch her fingers at all. And me, I was think-ing about those fingers touching dead Mr Ellis last . . . And all the time there were those boots on the table set just like he was standing there looking down at us. We went forward and half-snatched our pieces of coal, and Mrs Ellis said, "Who has the one with the cross then?"

And then I was saying nothing but feeling sick to my stom-ach and reaching over to pick up the boots. I was cursing Divine Intervention beneath my breath, and Geraint Jones he was looking crestfallen all right.

I remember getting home with those boots and there was my brother the Maggot in the kitchen, and me showing off those boots when only a moment before I had been hoping Divine Intervention would give them to Geraint Jones. "You need to be a collier to have boots like these," I said, and I put them on our own table to polish them a little, making sure to have them where he could see them. Make them truly mine and the Maggot my brother truly jealous. "Serious boots for serious men's feet, Maggot. Not daft old things like your little boots ..." and no Da downstairs to stop me taunting him, was there?'

The beggar Ianto Passchendaele Jenkins stops, and looks at Laddy Merridew, who is looking at Ianto Jenkins's old boots.

Laddy frowns. 'Are those the same boots?'

The beggar smiles. 'No, Maggot, they are not. There have been many pairs of boots on these feet since then.' And he sighs, taps the face of his watch with no hands, and yawns.

Laddy Merridew gets up from the bench. 'I suppose it's time I went back to Gran's?'

And as he wanders off up the High Street, Ianto Passchendaele Jenkins stretches out on his bench to have a rest before the cinemagoers start arriving for the evening showing.

The Deputy Librarian's Tale
and the Undertaker's Tale

i

IN THE NIGHT, THE breeze finds a sheet of newspaper dropped when someone was taking fresh covers to Ianto Passchendaele Jenkins down at Ebenezer. It slides the newspaper along the pavement for it to come to rest against the kerb, by a drain. The breeze may stop too, to have a read, then it lifts the paper into the air and wraps it with care round the leg of the town statue.

The first bus of the morning will stop outside the Public Library and the driver will nod to the only passenger to get off, 'Nice morning, Phil,' but there may be no reply.

The same passenger will get off the first bus here every morning. Philip 'Factual' Philips, Deputy Librarian, a man in the same suit for weeks, his shirt collar curling. In his pocket a packet of ham and tomato on white made by his wife.

'Sandwich again, Phil. That all right?'

'Nancy? Do you know how old wheat is?'

'Tell me.'

'Eleven thousand years.'

'Not this, Phil. This was grown more recent.'

* * *

Factual Philips starts work early, well before Laddy Merridew's gran arrives to clean, before she sweeps up the sweet papers and polishes the two red dragons at the foot of the library's marble staircase. He will come down from the bus carrying a bag of books taken home the night before and pored over even while eating his steak and kidney pie.

'Aww Phil, you and your books. Talk to me will you?'

'Yes Nance, look, Euclid says here that a line is a straight curve, and straight lines are infinite, unless they stop, of course . . .'

'Good for Euclid. Jelly and condensed for afters?'

'Did you know Marco Polo used condensed milk?'

'On his jelly?'

Factual Philips will let himself into the library, pick up the papers and the post from the mat that says *Welcome to a Place of Silence* and take it all through to the Reading Room. He will leave it on one of the tables while he goes down the steps to his office in the basement and puts his jacket on the back of his chair. Then he will fetch a kettle out of a cupboard, and while it boils he may take a large book from the back of the kettle's cupboard, and sit and read closely, making notes. *The Collected Adventures of Sherlock Holmes*. Then he will make his morning Instant, tuck *Sherlock Holmes* under his arm and go back up to the Reading Room, where one of the strip lights will be flickering and buzzing like a caught wasp.

South Wales Echo, Western News, Guardian, Daily Mirror . . . he will thread them onto their wooden sticks, snapping the elastic into place, and leave them on the tables ready.

'Now the post.'

Factual will open the envelopes addressed to himself and puts the ones for *Mrs Z. Cadwalladr, Chief Librarian* to one side. He may unfold a couple of posters for pinning up on the library noticeboard, please. *Save Our Playgrounds. Public Meeting on Friday*, and *Interested in Starting a Toy Library? Phone Shirley at the following* . . . and will take them nowhere near a noticeboard, but tear them up instead and throw them in the wastepaper basket. Then, with half an hour at least before opening – Factual Philips, Deputy Librarian, will go back to *The Collected Adventures* and his coffee.

In his office down below ground, there are no windows, for views out of windows are distractions. The walls are covered with maps, diagrams, lists. On one wall a map of the world with flags in all the capital cities, lists of mountains and their heights, the names of rivers. On another wall all numbers. Tables and formulae, equations and graphs, geometric shapes, angles and circles, diameters and radii. On another, lists of dates, battles, kings and queens, inventions, countries conquered and lost. And pinned on the back of the door in the form of complicated diagrams, each spidering across unused pieces of bedroom wallpaper from home all sellotaped together, reaching right to the floor, every mystery ever solved by Sherlock Holmes, read twenty times over, at least, and new things discovered each visit. Every clue, every red herring and solution, an ever-growing list of minute detective detail. And a hole cut strategically, for the doorknob.

Before anyone else arrives, Factual Philips will finally leave Sherlock in the basement and check the library's shelves, running his fingers along the spines. He may be upstairs this morning in the Reference Room, in an alcove by the window. Local History, where he will take down one or two books and read the back covers, 'I read you three years back. And you.'

And he moves on to the next alcove, where he tries to shut the window, but it will not close. A book is still open on the table from yesterday. Factual Philips taps his nose. 'I deduce . . .' and he goes to close it to put it back on the shelf. But then he looks to see what it is, stops and replaces it on the table, open, exactly as he found it. 'I deduce indeed. Waiting for Tutt Bevan, you are . . .'

While the newspaper is still wrapped round the leg of the statue, and Factual Philips is looking at local history, the breeze may make its way under the back door of 1, Owain Terrace, a little way behind the High Street, and into the house of the Undertaker Simon 'Tutt' Bevan, who will be tutting to himself even as he washes a plate in the sink. There will always be a few unpaid bills for wood and brass-headed screws next to some pencils, forks, knives, lined up neat as matchsticks on the kitchen table. Tutt Bevan will dry his hands on a striped tea towel, hunch his shoulders and tut again as he feels the draught round his neck, then he may turn to see the breeze sliding one of the bills off the table and onto the tiles. He catches hold of the table to bend down, then he places the bill exactly right, weighing it down with a fork. He will fetch his cap and his jacket, his keys from their hooks, and he almost shuts the door, then remembers he has forgotten something. For the third time that morning he tuts, louder this time, and fetches a walking stick from its place behind the door. Then Tutt Bevan the Undertaker will leave the house to go out into the early morning.

Outside his door he turns to face along the terrace, pointing his stick in front, and he squints along it as though it was a rifle.

Back at the Public Library Reference Room, Factual Philips may have finished trying to shut a window that never will shut, and gone back to his office to read. Outside, up the red stone walls the breeze climbs, searching for the gaps, teasing away the things that cling. A single grey hair caught on a small roughness. Small flecks of down from the breasts of the pigeons that preen themselves on the slates. On up the wall it goes, past the foundation stone, the plaques and their important names, all forgotten now. Past the secret initials of stone-masons hidden in the window niches. It inspects the windows all carefully shut, their metal blinds down in case someone may wish to peer in and worry the sleeping books. And finally, it finds one where the blind has been raised already, one with a gap where window meets frame, and the breeze may slip through the gap in the window the Deputy Librarian could not shut, and into the Reference Room.

'A perfect straight line,' Tutt Bevan the Undertaker may say, and he will follow his stick past the cracked tarmac of an old car park where the only things parked are nettles and broken bottles and old tin cans. Skirting the brick wall and the bins behind the laundry, the wooden walls of sheds whose keys cannot be found, and into the alleyway that leads to the High Street. He may lift his stick into the air now and then, and point it towards the light at the end of the alley. And he follows it until he comes out of the shadows onto the High Street. Opposite the Public Library, on the pavement, his head on one side, listening.

'Morning, Tutt.' The voice of Peter Edwards, deep. He will not wait for a hello, but will run in his old collier's boots across the High Street, dodging the cars, running to where the pavement widens in front of the library. He unwraps the newspaper from the statue's leg, screws it into a ball and pushes it into his pocket then sits down on the steps.

Tutt Bevan will wait to cross, tutting at the traffic. Then there may come another voice, smaller, 'Want to cross over?' And a hand on his sleeve, Laddy Merridew on his way to school.

Tutt Bevan tuts and nods, and Laddy Merridew waits, holding the frayed sleeve of a jacket bound with leather as Tutt points his stick straight at the Public Library.

'Ready?' and Laddy Merridew walks across with Tutt, waiting for him to step up on to the pavement the other side. The exact spot Tutt crosses every day.

Then the boy squeezes the man's arm by way of goodbye and off he goes towards the school. Tutt Bevan will not move from his place on the pavement and he will watch the shape of Laddy Merridew growing smaller and fainter then disappearing down the High Street. And in his mind's eye the boy carries on down the hill, one foot on the kerb and one foot in the gutter, following the curves of the High Street as it rides down the hill on its way to the river. Past the chapel and its beggar dozing in the porch he goes, past the cinema, and the Savings Bank to the school, where he turns off the road. But the road goes on without him down past the factories on the edge of town, then to the river, where it becomes a bridge leading to the other side and to the hills.

Tutt Bevan sighs, and points his stick at the library doors. And he follows it towards the statue and Peter Edwards sitting there on the step, where he stops. 'Morning. It is a good one?'

'As good as they may be.'

'Still no work then?'

Peter Edwards squints up at Tutt Bevan and shrugs. 'Don't you start. The wife's bad enough . . .'

Then without shifting from his line, Tutt will go straight to the library steps, where he rings the bell for the place is not open yet.

It doesn't matter who opens the door. Maybe Laddy Merridew's gran who has arrived to clean, wearing her blue wrap-around pinny with its rickrack braid coming adrift over her slippers. Or Factual Philips, on his way to the basement to fill the kettle again. Tutt Bevan will raise his cap, and salute whoever it is. He will take his stick, and when the door is wide, raise it and look along it, the stick pointing straight at the marble staircase. There are the two dragons guarding the way, one with a cigarette butt deep in its throat where the lads stick them for a laugh; Laddy's gran finds ash on the steps, and butts left in the sand bucket where the dragons stub the things out.

Up the stairs he goes, to the first landing, to the Reference Room, and an alcove by a window, its sign saying 'Maps' next to the one saying 'Local History'. And on a table beneath the window is an open book, a few of its pages in the air, unde-cided whether to fall this way or that. The book Factual Philips did not put away, for he knew Tutt Bevan would want it first thing. A book the breeze is playing with as he watches, playing tricks on the Undertaker, hiding his maps.

Maps of the town, earliest to latest. The pages rising and falling as the breeze plays with them; the town changing as the pages move. A new street here, a terrace there. More houses here, less houses there, a row of shops appears, then a hall, a building that becomes a warehouse, a tenement, a warehouse again. A chapel. Two chapels, three, four, then three again. This decade, that decade. A bridge over the river marked, then gone. No bridges at all. Then three. No railway then a spider's web of tracks at the valley floor, marshalling yards. They appear and disappear as the pages flicker. Streets built and unbuilt hanging in the air over a pale oak library table marked with ink blots, scratches. A name or two, shadowy. And, where only fingers can read the words, *Simon Bevan loves Blodwen* carved neat under the lip.

Simon loves Blodwen, indeed, and Tutt will put his cap and his stick down on the table, run his hand under the lip to feel the shape of the words with his fingertips. Words carved when Simon Tutt Bevan was a boy, and whoever Blodwen was all forgotten now except in the carving.

Then he will pick up the book of maps, and go over to the window to look out over the roof tiles, the alleys, backyards and bins, holding the book up close to his face. There are no annotations, no hills to give direction. Only the ribbon of the river running through the town is unchanging, even when they made new bridges when the old were swept away in flash floods. He matches the page to this view, or tries. Matches this line to that alley, this space to that park. Then he finds the river laughing at him for the page is upside down.

Tutt Bevan leaves the walking stick pointing at the window and waits for the door to open again, listening for footfall on the parquet, in case the feet come over this way, towards the map section. And the feet will come. The feet of Factual Philips, Deputy Librarian, who is only come to look up the name of the Minister who buried Fancy Philips, his grandfather, or a union official who led a march once.

But Tutt says, 'Can you help me, if you have time? I can't quite see if this street is this one here? Do you know?' and he tuts as he points to the map and to the town, the back yards and the bins.

Factual Philips, who knows every street in the town like the back and the front of his hand, every alley, frowns, 'Where?'

'Here. And here. See? This one?'

Tutt points the map at the windowpane as if he was persuading the book to ask the window a question. But the window will just shimmer back instead of saying anything useful. And Tutt asks again, 'Are they the same? Could they be?'

For once Factual Philips is stumped. Stumped by his own town. For the river makes a reference point, but which way up is the river? Which hill did the mapmaker choose a long time back as a high place where he must sit with a sharp pencil and paper, looking down at the valley? And for all that the early name of the town is on the spine of the book, it is as though the pages have at some point fallen away from the binding, then been put back wrong. For whichever way the book is held, what it says remains the same. And where the houses may be now that were shown by careful pencil squares on map after map is a matter for conjecture.

For the first time in a long while Factual takes a deep breath before he says, 'I'm sorry, Tutt, I can't help you.' And with a face as long as a week without newspapers, he goes off down the stairs.

Coming up, panting, his glasses slipped down his nose, is Laddy Merridew. 'Are you Mr Philips? I forgot, I need a book on coal mines for school this morning,' and Factual Philips, on solid ground once more, will show the boy the Reference Room and Local History, and leave him there.

As he rounds the corner of the stairs to the hallway with its black and white tiles, he may see a couple of lads left there to play whilst their mam is choosing a book. One lad on tiptoe on the bottom step, reaching up to put his spent chewing gum into the mouth of the dragon on the right. And the other lad trying to cross the hallway without standing on a black tile, 'Or the dragons will get me, Kev, look. And there's a ditch full of fire in the corners!'

Factual Philips, Deputy Librarian, brings all his importance with him down the stairs, 'I'll give you dragons and ditches of fire, you two. Take your old silliness outside. And your chewing gum as well.' He points to the mat by the doors. '*Welcome to a Place of Silence* – know what that means?'

And the lads laugh as their mam comes out from reception, putting her book in her bag, 'Aww, they were only playing.'

Factual Philips frowns. 'Playing? Whatever good did that do for anyone, now?' and he catches sight of Laddy Merridew coming back down the stairs, a book on coal mines under his arm, and waves a triumphant hand, 'See? There's a boy who is going somewhere.'

Laddy Merridew may wonder where somewhere might be, but he doesn't ask, and goes to put the book on the school ticket. Factual Philips sees off the dragon slayers and their mam, and he disappears down into the basement, muttering, 'Teach them a few facts. That will count for something. Boundaries. That is what lads need, mark my words . . .' and he slams a cupboard door by way of punctuation.

The Deputy Librarian's Tale
and the Undertaker's Tale

ii

THIS MORNING, MATTY HARRIS, Deputy Manager of the Savings Bank, called by the Public Library to consult a map of Belgium, for Eunice Harris is planning a holiday somewhere exotic. Tutt Bevan asked him to check the book of town maps against the town itself . . . and he did, with Tutt looking over his shoulder, tutting like the devil. Matty checked all the rooftops outside the window, the parks, the railway, the river, and turned the book this way and that. He got no further in his interpretation than Factual Philips, and Tutt Bevan left without a word of thanks.

And as he put the book away, Matty Harris wondered why the Undertaker tuts to himself all the time, and why the sound has made itself into his own name. And while he was thinking about it, why does Tutt Bevan follow his stick in a straight line lately, never turning a corner unless he has to? And what is he looking for in the maps? Matty Harris's head was so full of these questions there was no room for his own thoughts, let alone the whole of Belgium. And off he went down the staircase behind a red-haired boy in glasses, the questions all talking to each other in his head, until he passed Factual Philips scolding lads in the hallway of the library, growling, 'Playing? What good did playing ever do anyone?' And Matty's head made room for a few more questions, for he's heard Factual Philips telling lads off before. 'Boundaries. That's what boys need. Boundaries.'

And later in the day, when Matty Harris finishes at the Savings Bank he will leave his Clerk Tommo Price to lock up for the night. He will not go the back way up the hill for a pint at The Cat at the corner of Maerdy Street, not yet, but instead he will cross the square to the cinema, where he may find the beggar Ianto Passchendaele Jenkins leaning against the wall as the queue builds up for the six o'clock showing. Matty joins the back of the queue with no intention of seeing the film, and when he can, he puts a coin in the beggar's cap. 'Why does Tutt Bevan make his old noises? And why is he following that stick everywhere of a sudden? And what is wrong with Factual Philips? Why doesn't he like kids playing? Enjoys fishing, and isn't that playing, of sorts? . . .'

Ianto Jenkins the beggar will smile and sigh and tap his watch with no hands. 'One at a time, probably, is that right? Why indeed. I will tell you about Factual Philips first, and Tutt Bevan after, and you will get two stories for the price of one.'

Someone may ask how much stories are, and the beggar will smile and shake his head.

'My stories cost nothing for one, and twice as much for two. So here is the first, the story of our Deputy Librarian, the boy who was not allowed to play. We shall go back to a day when his own grandfather was working on the railway, taking the steam coal down to Cardiff. Known as Fancy Philips, his grandfather, known as that for his pigeons, in a loft in his back garden. One little lad he had, Little Phil, who would later be our Factual Philips's da. And there you are, this Little Phil adored his da, went with him once when the foreman was on holiday to Barry, for his da to show him the engine, and to cook the lad's breakfast egg at work. On the coal shovel in the cab while they were firing the engine – leaving the shovel in the fire and then cracking an egg for the boy to see it spitting and whitening faster than he could watch. Oh yes, close as anything, that Fancy Philips and his son Little Phil.

Fancy Philips used to catch that lad up on his shoulders when he got home at the end of the day, warm with the smell of hot oil and smoke and sweat, his face covered in smuts and his eyes red from the smoke. Lift him high in the air, then run around the house, pretending the low doorways were the openings to tunnels. Playing at being a train. Charging at the doorways so the boy screamed that he would hit his head, then ducking at the last minute, and outside to rush around the back yard, until the boy was weak with laughing and his mam would put her pinny over her face, laughing too, "Put him down, the lad will be ill!" Then Fancy would take the lad to check on his birds, take him to the loft out the back and take out the birds, one by one, call them his lovelies, and let the lad do the same, "Careful, Phil. Gently . . ."

But then there came a day when the Kindly Light alarm echoed down the valley and the street was filled with people, running down to the pit. Women running with fear, and men running to see if they could help, hearts in their mouths. And the men on the railway left what they were doing to help. But Fancy Philips hung back, and stopped.

Fancy did not go up to Kindly Light that day to help after all, or the next, or the day after . . . for there would be plenty of men up there already, wouldn't there? Of course there would. He would only get in the way, and there would not be anything for him to do in any case. It was done.

But that first day he just went home, and sat at the kitchen table with his hands jammed over his ears to block out the alarm sounds, knowing he should have gone, and he had not. And every moment that passed making it more impossible to go and more impossible to not.

And it was then that Little Phil – the father of our Deputy Librarian, remember – was waiting for him, hiding behind the door in the front room, and when his da did not come to find him to swing him up in the air, and play at being a train, as he always did, little Phil crept through to the kitchen and under the table to grab a hold of his father's leg for a surprise and to cry, "Play with me, Da! Be a train!"

The little lad was dancing round Fancy Philips, and pulling at his jacket, making the sounds of a train, a high whistle, and more huffing and puffing, a scream, almost – "Come on, my Da! Be a train . . ."

And all his father could do was push the boy out of his way, harder than he would have if he had been thinking, and he sent the boy reeling back to knock himself against the door jamb and onto the floor, "Go away and stay away!" But the lad did not stay away. This was just another game, for he was not bad hurt, oh no. And he picked himself up and rubbed his shoulder to show his da that that was a little bit hard but he was a big lad after all . . . and he came straight back to his da, now sitting with his head in his hands – straight back to the man who was kind and gentle, and who played trains with him and made him laugh. And maybe his voice was a little smaller now, "Play, my Dada? Shall we hold the birds now?"

And instead of playing, or taking him to the birds, Fancy Philips swung his fist. He caught his son on the side of the head and knocked him flying a second time, harder – then he knelt in his own kitchen and wept . . . and did not see his little son picking himself up and running out of the kitchen door.

The little lad was not found then for hours, and his mam went frantic from house to house, "Have you seen my boy, Little Phil?" But a boy who has run off because of a beating was not much to worry about, not now that there was the accident up Kindly Light, and the neighbours just said, "He'll come home when he's ready and he should spare a thought for those who won't be coming home at all . . ." So, it was not until after dark that they found him, Little Phil, curled up in the coal shed of a house three streets away, and not asleep. Shaking still, and cowering away, and had to be pulled out by the leg, crying "No, no . . ."

And that might have been an end to it, but for the funeral, then. It is only the men of the house have to go to the funerals, even now –

"Aww, not Phil, he is too young?" See, Little Phil's mam, she knew he was too small for these things, but his father would not have it, for he would not have it said that his family did not do their bit. And he took the little lad with him, not on his shoulders this time, and no laughter. In a stiff collar and borrowed trousers that scratched, to sit in silence in Ebenezer, just by here, to see and hear the last goodbyes to fathers, sons, uncles and brothers. Little Phil never forgot the darkness of that day.

And that was not the end of it. For when Fancy Philips came home after that funeral, he did not even take off his dark suit, but went straight to that pigeon loft and opened up all the cages, shouting at the birds to get out of there, and hitting out at the ones who tried to come back in. Until eventually, they did not try to go back into the loft at all but sat on the roof of the house for a while, and then a few days later, they all flew off and never came back.

Neither Fancy Philips nor Little Phil his son played at trains after, or anything else, come to that.

And yes, Little Phil, Factual Philips's father, grew up without playing at all. As serious as anyone could be, reading his school books like a good boy and nothing else, learning his words and his numbers. He did well, and became a serious lawyer down in Cardiff in no time at all and married a fine upstanding member of the Women's Institute. And his own son is our Philip Philips, that is called "Factual" and who works down the library.'

And maybe Matty Harris, who asked all the questions, will shake his head and say, 'But all children play. What happened to stop our Factual Philips the librarian playing then?' And the beggar Ianto Passchendaele Jenkins will sigh, and suck on a toffee before replying.

'He did, oh yes. He used to play when he was a lad, but away from his father the lawyer, all serious in his study, who brought his boy up to study his books like he did himself, and who thought his boy was reading in his room ... but oh yes, boys will be boys, and young Factual Philips was not in his room at all but was out in the street playing a game with his friends, when his father heard their screeching and hoots. For young Factual's friends had taught him to play at being a train.

Just like his grandfather and father played once, a long time ago. There they were, chugging down the street, all in a line the one behind the other, holding each other by their jumpers, the pace set by the one in front and the whole train pulled back by the boy in the rear, the guards van – sometimes running and trying to catch up, acting just like the trucks clanking on their chains in the marshalling yards. And maybe the laughs and the hoots brought back that bad time when he was a lad himself, who knows? But out he went, that lawyer, and hauled his son in from the street and told him that playing never served any purpose. But he had something better for him to do – "A thousand lines. You will write a thousand times, *Playing games never did anyone any good.*"

So there he was, our young Factual Philips, left in his father's dark study with pencil, and paper, and a thousand lines to write, sitting at his father's great desk, while all around and above, watching him, books and more books, glowering great law books in gloomy leather bindings, on shelves right up to the ceiling. And Factual began to write, slowly and carefully, because his father the lawyer would be checking every word soon enough, *Playing games never did anyone any good. Playing games never did anyone any good. Playing games ...* over and over until his hand was aching with the effort. So he stopped and stretched, and that is when he saw, glowing up in the shadows, right up there on the top shelf, different bindings, a whole shelf of red books. Pulled the chair over, climbed up, and brought a book down. A strange law book, this: *The Adventures of* . . .

But there were footsteps outside the study door. His father, come to see how Factual was getting on, and the door opened halfway but Factual's father was not looking, he was talking to someone back there in the hallway, Factual's mother perhaps, "Don't worry, Audrey. Boys need boundaries. Oh yes, boundaries . . ." and that gave Factual a chance to sit on *The Adventures of* . . . and to pick up his pencil and write the next line, head bowed over the paper, *Playing games never did* . . .

His father the lawyer closed the door again. "He's fine, Audrey. Concentrating hard. This will do Philip a lot of good, you mark my words."

Young Factual waited until his father's footsteps had faded, and took out *The Adventures of* . . . and started to read.

Sherlock Holmes, that's what that book was. And the others too, all Sherlock Holmes, adventure after adventure. So, yes, Factual Philips was stopped playing trains right then, and he had to write his lines, and that was not the last time, either. But strangely, writing lines was something that Factual seemed not to mind, after a while. A thousand. Two thousand. Three . . . helped along by those red books from the top shelf.

And in the end playing stopped altogether. And that is why Factual Philips does not like others having fun, see? Seems such a waste of time. Maybe it is? Who is to say? But detective books, now there's another thing. He was even going to be a policeman himself once. Talked to real detectives in Cardiff, friends of his da's. Even signed up once, for the training, but quit because they had to play at being policemen and he didn't fancy that. So because he loved books, he's a librarian. Like that. And in the cupboard where he keeps the kettle, he has the Public Library's only copy of *The Complete Adventures of Sherlock Holmes*, reads it over and over, finding new facts every time. And behind his desk, Agatha Christie whodunnits in alphabetical order, too, for when he needs a rest.'

The beggar stops his story, folds his arms, and says he will say no more until someone fetches him a cup of tea and a Welshcake . . .

The Deputy Librarian's Tale
and the Undertaker's Tale

iii

If it is not time for a snack then there must be something wrong, that is all Ianto Jenkins can say. But before too long his arms are wheeling again as if they are drawing down words from the wind, and the beggar is looking up the High Street towards the Public Library and the alley opposite, where the Undertaker lives, and his second story is beginning.

'Listen with your ears, the ones that ask "why" and will never stop asking it until the day they are laid to rest. Why does Tutt Bevan the Undertaker make his sounds? Why does he walk as he does, now, in a straight line following his stick? And why is he looking every morning at maps of the town, turning them this way and that, looking out at the real town through the window? Looking for something for certain, he is. And it was Tutt Bevan's own mam, Rosie, who started it. Another child who hid on that day, the day of the accident down Kindly Light.

See, what looks like an empty kitchen, a back door flung wide and a chair knocked over. And mud on the floor. A good china cup in pieces, not picked up.

But the kitchen was not empty. Oh no. Look – there in the corner, in the cupboard under the stairs, see? A cupboard used as a pantry, all dark and smelling of yeast and old apples ... a small girl was hiding, watching her mam cry. A small girl called Rosie Brightwell, the girl who would be Tutt Bevan's mam one day, watching and wondering what has happened, and sure indeed she must have done something wrong, worse than playing in the ash in the middle room grate. For her mam was crying so hard and not for cutting onions.

Rosie came into the kitchen nowjust and there she was, her mam, with some ladies from the street, who didn't usually come to this house – her mam holding on to someone's hand with her knuckles all white. And the child slipped beneath the kitchen table with no one noticing, then to the pantry cupboard under the stairs and pulled the door almost shut so she could see out and no one could see her.

And then she saw her mam taken away crying by old Mrs Watkins from up the road, that Mrs Watkins who wore slippers all day and had two spinster daughters and who now had her arm round Rosie's mam, saying, "Come with me, Mrs Brightwell, my love?"

And oh the child Rosie was there in the pantry surrounded by the smell of apples she did not dare eat in case that too was wrong. Hungry and sick at the same time, and wondering what it was she must have done, and she tutted to herself just as her mam tutted when things were not quite right, the good knives and forks not straight at the table, or a plate chipped.

Rosie crouched in the shadows watching the kitchen door

for a long time, knowing what it is like to be forgotten. Maybe she too cried a bit, but she did not cry easy, this child. Oh no. Went to sleep on the floor, waking only when there was the sound of boots on the sill. Only the boots. The man wearing them was silent.

Her da, come home early from the ironworks, a da who usually came home noisy, flung his bag down on the table no matter how neat it may be laid – and called out, "My Margie, I am here! Is Gareth home yet and where's that Rosie?"

But today he did none of that. Her da just put his bag down on the floor like the bag weighed a hundredweight. He stood there as though he was counting to one hundred, then over he went to the table and picked up a plate. He lifted it to his nose and sniffed at it, then he sat down at the table and howled, holding that plate over his face as his little daughter watched from her cupboard. And the back door open for everyone to hear.

"Oh Da!" But the child did not say this loud, only whispered it, "Oh Da," for no, Gareth was not home yet, her big brother who worked down a pit with a pretty name, digging the coal, and who usually came home and pretended to be a lion, on all fours. Swept the girl off her feet, roaring like a lion roars, and carried her round the house on his back until their mam would shout to come and eat and leave the lass alone not to excite her before bedtime?

A late child, Tutt's mam Rosie Brightwell was, see? Her da old enough to stop working, and her big brother Gareth Brightwell not married yet but almost. Been courting Lily

Rees up Dowlais, been saving up to get married and finally had just enough for Lily Rees up Dowlais's mam and da not to complain. Not too much, anyway.

The child watched her da from the shadows, her lovely da with a plate over his face, his shoulders heaving like he was laughing. But he was not.

She watched him get up from the table and take the chair fallen to the floor, and he pushed it in all neat, like her mam said to. And then there was a shadow on the doorway and it was that Mrs Zacharia from next door with the white whiskers on her chin and no sweets in her pinny pocket today, no smiles, "Mr Brightwell? We have Mrs Brightwell with us now, see, and she is a little better. Up at number eighteen, she is, with the Watkins. Shall you come and fetch her? Your Rosie is gone somewhere, I think. Out playing?"

Watching as her da waved Mrs Zacharia away, then sitting at the table, and picking his lunch box off the floor, opening it. Untouched, the lunch, Rosie could see that. And she watched her da take out some sandwiches made only that morning by her mam, at the counter over there, slicing the bread level, and singing, then putting the top slice for herself, the "dry slice" she called it, to be eaten after Gareth and her man had gone to work. Those sandwiches her mam made were still in the box, slices of bread spread with a little margarine, a little cold cut of lamb, a little beetroot. Almost nothing at all.

And the child in the cupboard saw her da taking out a lamb sandwich and putting it on a plate, holding it in his hands still dirty from the tram ride home, the day at the ironworks done almost, and he patted the sandwich with two fingers, over and over.

Somewhere inside the child knew that her da was crying because the slices of bread were not whole. That they were cut. And the other halves had gone this morning with Gareth to his work. Her own big brother's lunch to be eaten under the ground. Watching through a gap in the cupboard door now, where the wood had split in the kitchen heat. She saw her da get up and cross to the window, where he held on to the kitchen sink as though he could not stand any longer by himself. And he took the sandwich, and bit into it, and began to chew. And at the same time, tears were running down his face and onto the sandwich, dampening the bread, and he was eating his own tears. But her da found it hard to swallow, and he coughed a little, and took a white cup from the draining board and filled it, took a mouthful, and chewed it all slowly, the bread and the water and the lamb.

Then her da went back over to the table all laid neat for four, and he pulled the chair out, the chair he just tucked away. He carried the chair out of the kitchen to the middle room, where the child could not see him any more. But she heard him right enough, moving another chair, to fit this one by the dresser. And something that sounded like a cough coming again. Then she heard the creak of the staircase over her head, his feet going up, and turning to her own room, and she felt her da placing the chair in her own room, and that was not a good thing. The child pushed herself out of the cupboard then, ran through to the stairs, and stood in the shadows of the hallway to talk to her da, but she did not know which voice to use – a loud voice was wrong, a soft voice was wrong, "Oh my Da, I do not want the chair."

And her da listened, see, and sure enough, after a pause, back down the stairs he came carrying the chair, and said nothing to the child, but went out to the yard where he found the axe for firewood from the back of the privvy, and he set about that good chair with the axe. Bending over it, his arm rising and falling and the sound like a hand beating at a locked door. Until the chair came to splinters, her da silent, the birds taking fright, and the child, Rosie, who would be Tutt Bevan's mam, flat against the garden wall as though she would be swallowed by the bricks, making one sound only for she would not cry.

"Tut, Dada. Tut."'

The cinemagoers will sigh. 'Aww, waste of a good chair,' one will say, and another will tell him to be quiet for it was never about the chair at all. Then Matty Harris, still leaning against the cinema wall, listening, and not quite satisfied with the stories, not yet, for they have not answered all his questions, frowns, 'But what is this to do with walking in a straight line then?'

The beggar pauses. 'Ah. Loss takes people in strange ways, it does. Look. For a while all was almost the same in that house, except for only three chairs round the table, now. And the child's mam no longer making everything neat and tidy, but instead forgetting to lay the table at all, and it is the small child Rosie who did it, tutting to herself, trying to make it right. She dropped things sometimes, and her mam did not even notice, but the child did, for she wanted things nice and straight. And the meals were always as neat as she could make them. But silent.

Then there came the day that her da did not come home from work himself. And there had been no accidents, oh no. And when they asked they found he had not been to work at all, and he was nowhere to be found in the town. A mystery. Rosie's da disappeared for more than a week. Then he was found, and where? In the town? In another? Not at all. He was found miles away, not anywhere near a town.'

Ianto Jenkins stops again, and asks for a drink of water. He waits for a while, then he clears his throat and continues.

'There is a place to the north, on very edge of this country, where a river runs into the sea, spreading its skirts over the valley until the water is hardly deep enough to carry a single fish. There are beaches in the river, shingle banks, stones brought down all the way from the mountains. Stones that were once rocks, tossed about in the water, falling and sliding against themselves for years until they became pebbles, small, rounded. On their journey to the sea, to become sand, then dust. They found him there, in the middle of the river. On that shingle bank they found him, just standing at the end of the day, looking out to sea. A grey end of day when mist knits the sea and the sky together and there is no horizon. No shadows. Standing facing the sea, staring west in his shirtsleeves, his trousers wet all where the water had climbed up the cloth. And no boots. His feet white on the stones like they were stone themselves. His hands hanging by his sides, empty.

"Where are your boots?" they called across the river – the men who came to find him. He did not reply at first, then came his voice, soft, carried over the water's noise, "Left them, must have."

And it seems this is the last thing he said to anyone. A strange journey indeed. It was pieced together finally from snippets told in pubs a long way from this town. Something like this but the actual is never known. Near enough.

First, there were two tickets bought on two buses, going north, where he sat hunched in his seat twisting his hands, not speaking to anyone, except one young lad who asked if he was going somewhere nice.

"Going for a bit of a walk."

And then a ride in a Welsh Hills lorry from the Rhondda to a place on the border of two countries. A side road where the Welsh Hills driver stopped for his sandwiches near a field where on the maps, the border runs through, dividing grass from the same seed, in the same small patch of mud, into two nations. Seen here, he was, later, by the side of the road, just standing by a gate. Looking at his watch, someone said, and thought he was waiting for a lift. But he must have waited until it was past noon, someone said, for the sun to drop in front. Kept watching the sky, looking at the light, and keeping his shadow behind him. That was the first day.

On the second day he was seen again, some miles away, after lunchtime, walking through a hamlet, away from his shadow again. And as hamlets are, grown round a crossing point on a stream, or a crossroads, maybe a place where animals were driven? And so the road curved, as roads will – and he did not go with the road but stopped.

He stopped because in front of him rose a wall, right across his path. And what did he do, go round the wall to find another path? Oh no. He was seen climbing that wall, and dropping into a garden. Someone who saw him went to peer over the wall, to see what he was doing, in case he was up to no good. But he was doing nothing more than walking away between the flower beds, under two old apple trees where he bent and picked up some apples from the grass.

The householder took up the tale when asked, because further on in that garden is a small pond, a natural thing where the groundwater wells up, and there are reeds, king-cups growing. And indeed, his wife, watching from her kitchen window, was about to shout, to come out with a wooden spoon raised as though it was a stick, when her husband stopped her, "Watch . . ."

They saw their visitor get as far as the edge of the pond and stop when it barred his way. He did not skirt the pond, but removed his boots, then waded in. He pressed on, knee deep through the flowers, stepped out the other side and sat on the lawn to put his boots back on. A dog barked and the man looked up, puzzled, as though he was waking from a sleep, and made straight for the wall on the other side of the plot. Stepped carefully onto the border among the shrubs, until he was facing an old climbing rose. And he seemed to ignore the thorns, but grasped the stems, climbed it and was gone over the wall.

Then a stranger was seen near sundown on the next day, further on by a half-finished stone wall dividing a field. Seen standing alongside the wall, not moving, as though he was waiting for something or someone. Eating apples from his pockets, facing to the west. Seen by the man making the wall, who thought he was going to take some of the stones away, he was so close. But in the end all he did was lift a few new stones to the top, place them carefully and correctly, then he continued on his way, walking alongside, one hand on the top, until he disappeared into the trees at the edge of the field. And that was the third day.

He was not seen the next. But after, when the word had spread, there were found places he had slept. A woodshed, a barn, alongside another garden wall. He had always left something as a thank you, mind. A clean and folded handkerchief by a place where the leaves were flattened, the stub of a pencil wrapped in a note written on a scrap of paper bag, "For my place of sleep, thank you."

On the fifth day, he must have gone right through a great estate, where there is a house bigger than this chapel, this cinema, this Savings Bank, all built together, the land greater than half this town itself. Must have walked right through the woodland where they breed birds to be shot. And maybe there was no need for him to wait for his shadow to fall behind him at midday, for there are no shadows like that beneath the trees.

A gamekeeper caught the noise of his pheasants and fetched his gun for it was probably the fox again. And for all the searching that gamekeeper did, all he heard were a few twigs snapping in the distance, and all he saw move were the starlings that peck at the pheasant's corn rising dark and singing above the wood. And he knew there must have been an intruder, but no one was seen, and nothing was taken save maybe a handful of the corn. But perhaps someone slept beside the pheasants' hut, for the warmth?

When the traveller crossed the boundary of that great estate he had almost crossed a whole country then, hardly shifting from his line.

And a woman said she found him the next day standing in her kitchen without his boots. Barefoot on her cold floor, she said. The last house before the edge of the country, not far from the river that runs straight down to the sea, wide and shallow. Come straight in through the open back door. Standing there, he was, by the kitchen table, his hand on the back of a chair, smiling down at the single place laid for tea as though there was someone sitting there. And that smile chased away whatever fear she may have had, she said. He looked up and smiled at the woman who thought maybe he had come to find food. "Will you need something to eat?"

But he shook his head, and left her kitchen by the inner door, and went into the house. Then to the hallway and made to leave by the front door. But it was locked, she said. He was just standing in his bare feet with one hand on the door, and never said a word, did not turn round. The woman said she went into her front room and fetched the key from the bowl on the table, and she unlocked and unbolted the door for him.

Not without a worry, oh no – for isn't the front door of a house only opened twice – first to let in a bride and groom, and then again to let them out, but for their last journeys? And she stood on the step, pushing a bramble aside with one hand to watch him walk away from her house across the lawn, then through a gate into the field where there were ewes. She saw him cross the field in the direction of the river in front, only stopping to take some wool from a wire fence. She thought he may have played with it in his hands as he walked away.

And the last day he was found, in the cold of the evening, standing on his island at the mouth of the river, on pebbles and shingle brought down from the mountains. Standing there in his shirtsleeves, his trousers rolled up to his knees like it was the start of a holiday, an outing from the iron-works. Staring straight out to sea, he was, straight at the horizon. His feet white on the stones like they were stone themselves. His hands hanging by his sides, empty.

"Where are your boots?" they called across to him.

"Left them, must have."

And they went to him, calling, "Come away in now, it is cold. They will all be waiting ..."

But he did not turn his head, or speak. And it was not until someone said the only thing to do was to go to him if he would not come to them, that anyone moved. And this man waded through the current, calling to him all the while, "Come on, mun, we are cold enough ..."

But when he reached him, and stood next to him, and put a hand on his arm, he felt how cold that arm was, how cold the shoulder. How solid and stiff his body was, standing there in the water, the eyes fixed and clouding. And they knew then he could not have spoken to anyone about his boots ...'

* * *

140

Here the cinemagoers will shake their heads. 'Walked for seven days? But he went nowhere at all.'

Ianto Passchendaele Jenkins shakes his head in return. 'Nowhere? They saw where he walked. In a perfect straight line, from one side of the country to the other. Walking in the afternoons only, his shadow only ever behind him, walking towards the sea.

And sometimes, we can ask why and there is no answer, but it is right all the same. His journey was finished.

And who is to say, but his grandson Simon Tutt Bevan, decides to help people sort out the loss of the people they love. He does it well, and gently. And he tuts, for things are never straight as he would like. Tuts when there is something adrift. Like his mother did, and her mother before her.

Nearly too old to work now, he is, but besides that, his eyes are not what they were. Hence the stick, see? Won't tell anyone that, oh no. But all he sees now are bright lights and shadows. And before they fade, he will be walking across the town, in a straight line. For the granda he never knew.'

Ianto Passchendaele Jenkins will stop and shake his head. He takes an old handkerchief out of his pocket and may be going to wipe his eyes, or blow his nose. But he looks up instead and catches Laddy Merridew watching him, Laddy Merridew who wasn't here when the story began, but must have arrived in the middle – so he just polishes the face of his watch with no hands, and pushes it back in his pocket.

And the cinemagoers will walk away, some putting one foot in front of the other, as they have seen the Undertaker do.

But they meet the wall of the chapel, or the steps, or the curve of the road, and they stop, laughing, and go off home. But there is one man left, the Deputy Librarian Philip Factual Philips, who stood there at the back as he was passing, to hear a little about history. And now, as Ianto Passchendaele Jenkins turns away to go back to his bench, Factual Philips leans against the wall – and where his mouth is, a smile begins.

The Deputy Librarian's Tale
and the Undertaker's Tale

iv

Today, Mrs Cadwalladr the Chief Librarian has an afternoon off, gone up to Brecon to see the sister with the goitre. She went off after lunch, leaving instructions with Factual Philips about rearranging a rearrangement of books he did last week. And after she went, there was the sight of Factual running up the stairs to the Reference Room two at a time, the door closing and the sound of two men's voices, low. Then another sight – Factual Philips talking to every person in the library, those choosing books, those standing reading, those tearing the adverts out of the daily papers in the Reading Room, 'I am sorry, you'll have to stop that now. The library is closing for the afternoon. Unforeseen circumstances.'

There are those who will say he was smiling, but then that could always have been a mistake, and they were not there, after all, to hear the conversation upstairs. But it must have gone something like this, when Factual Philips, who for the very first time was not able to answer a question asked in his library – and him with every book in the place read and digested too – left his office in the basement and went up to the map section to find Tutt Bevan the Undertaker, back again, still turning the book of maps this way and that, muttering to himself, 'Things were built, see. The straight paths have all gone.' He shakes his head. And here Tutt Bevan shows Factual Philips one old map with a straight track from one side of the town to the other, hidden between the little patches that are houses, following alleys and side paths from one hill through the valley to the next. 'I don't know. All I need is this one little thing before I go myself, a journey like my grandfather Brightwell did, before he went? And what a going that was. Marvellous. Marvellous.'

And there is something then. Maybe it is the echo of a boy making the sound of a train whistle between his fingers, or the memory of a boy shut in a father's study, lost in the red books from the top shelf, and the mouth of Factual Philips finds itself smiling again, and saying, 'I played a game once . . .'

So now the double doors of the Public Library have been locked, and the staff sent home. It is only twelve noon, and if Mrs Bennie Parrish comes to change her books she will go home sucking her teeth and muttering about impropriety.

Two men, one with a stick, his arm held by the other, have walked together straight up the hill up from the town to The Cat on the corner of Maerdy Street and waited for it to open for the lunchtime drinkers. Factual Philips has been talking to himself all the way up the hill, 'Now, I just have to remember how it went . . .' And a little later there they were inside The Cat, sitting together below a display case filled with a shining fish, its little brass plaque saying *Caught by James Harris, fisherman* shining in the lights of the bar.

Now there they are, Tutt Bevan and Factual Philips cradling two half pints, whispering, their heads together like boys plotting adventures. Waiting for the bar to fill, for the smoke to rise, for the sound of beer-filled talk to ring through the room.

The Deputy Librarian goes back to the bar. 'Two more halves, thank you, Maggie.'

'Not like you to be here in the day. Library burned down, is it?'

Slowly, The Cat fills as the Librarian and the Undertaker have their second half pint. Factual Philips gets up and stretches, then makes for the smallest room at the back of the pub. Tutt Bevan waits a few moments, then does the same. And while the older man with a walking stick holds it against the door and keeps watch, the other climbs up and balances on the toilet seat like he did years ago, when he was a lad. Before he was caught by his father and given a thousand lines each time he was found playing. He reaches up and pushes at the window, sealed with dust and rust and the gifts of spiders.

Then he's knocking at the window with his fist, 'Diawl. It will not open, it sticks.'

And the Undertaker, one hand against the door, 'Maybe it's best we give up?'

'Rubbish . . .' for the librarian knows, Sherlock Holmes never gave up, did he?

After a while the window opens, scattering rust and more than a few flakes of paint. And the air comes in, and with it the sounds of the town, the hum and the shouts and the barking of dogs while Factual looks down the years into the yard of The Cat Public House.

As before, there are empty barrels. There is the alley running behind Maerdy Street, and the wall where he dropped down after his friends years back, ferns now growing where it joins the wall of The Cat.

There is a hand-drawn trailer propped in the yard, some old boxes in a corner, slumping all damp from this morning's rain. Scents rising, beckoning – damp afternoon air, damp coal dust, old beer and barrels. And over it all, smoke from the chimneys of Maerdy Street and Mary Street, whose gardens stretch away from him like a chain, their washing lines hanging slack, their walls sagging, the gates into the back alley hanging open, forgotten now behind the garden sheds.

Factual Philips pulls himself up to lean on the windowsill and peers out at the narrow wall, the green duckweed growing on the old cinders, and nettles where the walls meet the earth. He looks back at the old man by the door. 'Too far down, can't see us doing this now.'

Tutt tuts. 'Impossible. I said it would be.'

But Factual leans out further just to see, and below there is another window right above the alley half-hidden behind a fan of ivy and a rusty metal grille. So he climbs back down into the smallest room brushing himself free from cobwebs and dust, and he smiles. Beneath The Cat is a cellar, and not all underground.

Factual Philips straightens his shoulders. 'Righto, back to the bar, Watson. 'On't give up quite yet, eh?' And back they go to find their table taken and the fish in its case winking at them. And when Tutt Bevan asks who Watson might be, the only reply is a grin.

'Another half, is it?' says Maggie the publican's wife, resting herself on the mahogany top. And so it is another half indeed, while they check the door just there, behind the bar, behind Maggie, smiling at them. 'Surveying the place, are we?'

So they wait. Then the telephone rings, and Maggie sighs and opens the door, reaches into the hallway for the phone and pulls it on its wire back into the bar, where she talks into it, 'Helloo, Matty, it's you then?' her voice all soft, and one or two drinkers wink and smile and play with their money on the counter top. But through the door is the stairs. Factual and Tutt can see that. Up to the bedroom. And where there is a stairs going up, Factual Philips deduces, there may also be one going down.

'I have to go, Matty,' Maggie says to the telephone. 'Can't talk for long. Have to fetch some bottles.'

And Factual Philips is brave now, made courageous by the fish he did not catch, and by the almost three half pints in his stomach. 'Bottles, you said? Heavy. Bottles are no job for a lady now, Maggie. Where do we fetch them for you?'

'There's kind,' she says and points with a red nail. 'Down the stairs.'

Tutt Bevan points his stick at the cellar steps, and she frowns, 'Doesn't take two of you, does it?'

'Oh yes, when one has a bad back,' says Factual, and they are gone.

There is a single bulb on the stairs and no door at the bottom, a cellar room of barrels and pipes and pallets and boxes against the walls, crates of small bottles, and packets of crisps and scratchings. A broken chair from the bar, thrown at the wall during a fight, but all four legs seem solid enough. And there is the window, half-blocked from the outside by ivy, that metal grille.

'Easy!' Factual Philips drags the chair across and stands on it, but Tutt says, 'Let me?' So it is Simon Tutt Bevan who leaves his stick against a barrel. And Simon Tutt Bevan who has not climbed onto a chair for decades climbs onto one now with a steadying hand from the Librarian, and he peers at the window. Dark with dust and grime, the glass cracked across one corner, the frame unpainted for years, peeling and cracking onto the sill.

There is a draught where the window doesn't quite fit, the breeze from the afternoon coming through into the cellar, damp into damp. Tutt Bevan tamps round the window for the catch, feels the draught where the frame has buckled. The catch is stiff, but he puts his weight against it and with a push or nine it opens outwards, taking the ivy with it, then a tenth push sets the grille swinging back against the outside wall. 'Rusted through. Easy, it is easy.'

Factual Philips, the younger, climbs out first, ready to reach up and help Tutt Bevan, who half-climbs, half-falls down into the alley with his stick.

And there it is, the alley between the Maerdy Street back yards and those belonging to Mary Street, running away from them straight as a ruler, at least until the bend in the distance where the street follows the valley. Behind them is The Cat. And behind that the hill they have climbed up from the town.

'Here we are.' Factual is grinning like a small boy. 'See, behind us it's all a straight line to the hill. And in front, we just go like we are on rails. A train. Don't do corners too well, trains ...'

Tutt Bevan frowns, leans against The Cat and raises his stick. Peers along it towards the bulk of the hill, and the stick points down the alley and at the wall where it bends. 'But there are walls, and houses, look, down there?'

'Leave it to me, I'm the driver.' And Factual, brushing the knees and elbows of his library suit, and wiping dust from the windowsill over his face, grins again and straightens his shoulders, facing down the alley.

Then there they are, two grown men all ready to play at being a train, and no voices shouting from the window like years ago. Just a little pool of silence, the rustle of something small in the nettles at the base of the wall. And there is Tutt Bevan, one hand on the wall, one hand on his stick, not really certain.

'Nothing to it. Follow me.'

They walk the length of the alley in silence, one behind the other. Factual in front, Tutt Bevan and his stick following, and they try to keep straight but have to skirt an old wire trolley, a rusted tricycle with no front wheel and a symposium of old beer cans.

Then, they get to the bend, so they stop. Tutt sees that the gap through which he saw the hill is there because some of the houses in Mary Street have been pulled down. There is a space, like a row of lost teeth. The house straight ahead is buttressed, waiting for the fall. There is a gate, hanging, what was a back garden once, now planted with weeds, and broken bricks, and a few old rose bushes still straggling up through the mess.

Tutt puts a hand on the gatepost. 'We can still go to the left, a bit by there? Straight through the building site. Then back on track in Mary Street?'

But Factual shakes his head, pointing at the buttressed house where the back door gapes and a dark kitchen does not welcome. 'Here. We can go through the house.' And the train continues on its rails, two abreast now, one man holding the elbow of the other as the train pushes aside the old roses and picks its way over the bricks, down the garden, down three broken steps to an old privvy with weeds growing round a seatless pan, the door nowhere to be seen. A cat, running low then up and over a wall. The coalbunker, its sliding door raised, nothing there but black. And through the gape of a door they go, into the creak of damp floorboards, the smell of piss and dust. Tutt goes to lean against the wall and there is the clang of metal, a kitchen tap suspended in the air on its pipe, brick pillars waiting to hold a kitchen sink stolen a long time back. A mess of twigs where a bird has made a nest on a high shelf over the dark brick scar of an old range while the ghosts of brass plates and candlesticks dance in the gloom.

Then the deeper gloom of the middle room, the men whispering about staying in a straight line, as much as they can. The roll of a bottle kicked across the floor and a thud as it falls into the gap where the boards are ripped up for firewood. The smell of their burning still in the air, faint, and dark metal hooks on the picture rail, holding nothing. A damp cardboard box behind the door, papers stuck with mildew. Receipts, orders, bills, picked up by Factual Philips, held to what light there is drifting in through the window, 'Look at this. Bullseyes. Toffees. Penny chews. A sweet shop . . .'

And Tutt Bevan nods, 'Daley's, this is. Remember? Used to

run through here, stole bullseyes from the boxes under the stairs. It smelled wonderful . . .' and he is sniffing at the dust and the darkness, lifting his face now, shutting his eyes, and smiling, 'Bullseyes, oh yes. And sherbet. Those toffees wrapped in paper and twists of cherry pips.'

He moves his hand in the air – walks towards the door to the narrow hallway and sniffs the air again. 'It's stronger here. Look, liquorish. Spanish. The stuff that made our tongues black as the devil. Do they still . . . through here?' Tutt stumbles over a loose floorboard, and Factual catches his elbow. 'Steady, mun.'

The two of them stand among the bricks in the front shop, and Tutt remembers what has gone. There are no white paper bags on a string for a quarter of mintoes ready for Morgan Ddu from number twenty-one. Or two ounces of sherbet, or a couple of silver-wrapped toffees to suck for Mrs Pym with no teeth at number eight. There are the white-grey patches on the floorboards in the corner, below the hook in the ceiling where a budgie's cage once hung. And the holes in the plaster where the shop blind has been pulled off the wall. A front doorway and no front door.

It is in remembering that the shop is remade, the shelves filled with glass jars reflecting the single bulb in the shop, the one in the hallway. That the mahogany counter is replaced at the height of a small boy's eye, the weighing pans shiny and gold, on the base of one some chewing gum stuck by mistake. That his fingers move despite themselves, clutching at the memory of warm pennies ready to trade for a quarter of Spanish Catherine wheels or penny chews, fruit salad squares in striped paper, pink prawns and blackjacks.

'Aniseed balls, Phil. Acid drops. Do you remember?'

Factual nods, 'I do indeed. And pear drops . . .'

On the other side of Mary Street is the allotment, and it is easy to walk across, the two men, sheepish now, waving to the gardeners, who scratch their heads and wonder at these two walking out from a derelict house and right through the rows of onions and potatoes and where are they going and why not use the pavements? The soil is black, the weeds bright and hopeful.

Then the ground falls away and the allotments end at a wall, a drop to the road. Tutt stands at the top of the wall, and shakes his head. 'What does a train do here?'

Factual shakes his head as well. 'Jumped, back then, if I remember right. Straight down, dodged across into the park . . . nearly got hit by a bus once . . .'

And the best they can do now is pick their way along the allotment wall to the steps, and down to the road that way, and back to the point below the wall, no pavement here, where they wait for the traffic, and in a space, there is Tutt Bevan tutting as the Librarian holds his elbow. And in this way they go across and through the gates of the park, and there is the tarmac drive sloping away gently, and the hill right there in front still, so a straight line is easy, past the old trees that drop silver leaves in autumn, not red and brown. Past the twin benches of the Watkins sisters, spinsters both, and on down the drive across the park. Not noticing the boy, Laddy Merridew, sitting on Gwynneth Watkins with a late lunch sandwich, skipping school because it is mathematics this afternoon and mathematics hasn't come to terms with Laddy Merridew yet. He is sitting there, hunched over, writing something in a notebook, new, the price written on the cover in biro. He looks up when he sees Tutt Bevan and Factual Philips, closes the notebook and stuffs it in his pocket. He half-raises a hand to say hello, but it is as though the two men do not even see him there, so he stays put and watches as they walk together over the grass, straight towards the kiddies' playground and its new sign, *For no person over the age of ten.*

Through the little gate they go, past the metal legs of the swings that lift themselves out of the tarmac as if they would like to walk away – and over there the see-saw plank shows its wood through the paint, the handles rubbed brass and blue.

Straight in front is the old iron rocking horse, with room for a football team of lads on its back, its nostrils flaring, its eye dark and fixed. Tutt shakes his head, 'Still here? Strange old thing,' and he climbs on and sits behind its head, thinking. Factual Philips climbs on a way behind him, and sits thinking too, and before either of them know how it happens, the horse is moving slowly back and forth. Squeak squeak it goes, squeak squeak, its head straining forward, nostrils red as blood, or warpaint.

And then to the see-saw, the two men climbing astride, the long legs of the Undertaker folding and stretching beneath him, the shorter legs of the Librarian finding the tarmac with a thump of his shoe, remembering how easy it is to stop the thing, and send your partner off balance, bumping the old plank in the air, both men clutching at the blue and brass handles to stop falling, laughing suddenly like schoolboys, and Tutt's stick falling to the ground as if it has forgotten what it is there for at all.

Until suddenly a small voice, 'Mam? What are those men doing?' and a stern-faced mam just mentioning, please, it is only for children this playground, not for great lumps like them. Two red-faced men climb off the see-saw and the child climbs on, his small battle won, while back there on his bench, Laddy Merridew takes out his notebook and biro and writes something down, not to forget.

Tutt Bevan and Factual Philips continue on their way through the park, keeping to the tarmac drive except where it does a circle round the rhododendron bushes where the boys go to smoke cigarettes after school, straight to the gates the other side, crossing the road, and on down the alley between the wall of the launderette and the working men's club, down the hill towards the High Street.

The alley comes out at the car park behind the shopping precinct, there is the deliveries entrance to Woolworth's straight ahead, and the train goes through that entrance to the storage area at the back of the shop.

'What are you doing here, Mr Bevan?' and it is the manager of Woolworth's come to find a box of Imperial Leather and the last of the Pond's Cold Cream for the toiletries counter, and finding instead the undertaker who buried the manager's own uncle last week, a lovely funeral too, solid oak. There is a short conversation about train sets, and a holiday soon on discount, to Majorca as well, for the manager, before he shows them the way into the shop.

Then Tutt and Factual are walking straight down the aisle between toiletries and children's T-shirts, and out of the side door of the shop past the ladies leaning on their counters, 'Where did those two come from, Gwlad?'

But to some questions there come no answers and the side door closes.

Outside, the journeyers are faced with a high red stone wall. Factual Philips sighs, 'The Public Library is right in the way, I am sorry, nothing I can do about that . . .' and Factual is right. There is the side wall of the library, its red stones rising over their heads, and not a single window this side for them to climb through even if they had a ladder.

Tutt Bevan sighs as well, 'Aww. Never mind, we've come a good distance.'

But Factual Philips is not in the mood for giving up, and anyway their line will be waiting for them on the other side of the wall, won't it? 'We aren't done yet, mun . . .'

Then it is round the wall to the wide pavement right in front of the library, to find Peter Edwards sitting on the steps of the statue. 'What is going on? You left here nowjust?'

'Just going for a walk, nothing much,' and the High Street is a gentle curve down to the square, with the wall of Ebenezer Chapel to stop them next in their line, but it is an easy thing to skirt the chapel, to cross the square and pass by the Savings Bank and the cinema, past the entrance to the school, then carry on down the High Street towards the river. Passing the station, over the railway line, and down to the river where the road bridge is not quite aligned but it is better than walking downriver to the footbridge. And then straight up the hill, taking it slowly, through one new estate and another, then some older houses, following the alders, then the road becomes a track that follows an old stone wall and only goes to the little cemetery at the top of the hill overlooking the town. Just below the ridge and the trees bent by the wind as though they would tip forwards and run back down to the valley floor.

And later, the travellers stand, tired now, at the top of the hill by the graves in the little Kindly Light cemetery, at its centre a tall granite memorial stone. And they turn to look back. Factual Philips sits on the wall, gazing down at the town, 'Look where we've come,' and Tutt joins him.

They see the river running at the lowest point, following the contours as the terraces do, each making its own way, dictated by the valley. They point, and seek out the way they have come through the town, and Tutt Bevan tries to see, or remember, the alleyways and streets, houses and parks on the other side of the valley. They see the chapel, the library, the school, where their path turned an angle, but where they continued like ants following some ancient walkway through a wood.

Factual Philips smiles for it has been a good day with clues found and followed and paths walked, and he turns to Tutt Bevan, sitting there with his chin on his stick, looking back over the town, 'Done well, I reckon.'

There is no reply but the usual and a shake of the head, from Tutt Bevan. He does not see their path as straight. He sees only the places where the path was wrong, the corners they had to turn round solid walls too high for men to climb. He remembers the library and the chapel standing square across their path, the blank walls of the cinema and the school building. Locked gates. Then the road bridge at an angle over the river, resting on stone stanchions built into the banks, the foundation of rocks beneath the surface not quite in line with the road, so the road was moved to fit. He sees the walls he could not cross and the misaligned bridge rising into the air, becoming insurmountable, his own mistakes, dreadful. For a long time he sits there, unspeaking, grim. And he tuts. And he stands up to point out to Factual the places they could not go.

But even as he stretches out his arm to point the sun warms their backs and throws their shadows along the grass and down the slope of the hill. Shadows which are joined by another, tall and regular. The granite memorial, carved with the names of the Kindly Light lost. And the three shadows grow longer and darker as the sun sinks behind them, until they merge into a single shaft as straight as a compass needle, running down the hillside and over the river at no crossing point at all, due east. Not stopped by tree, earth, water or stone. The Undertaker and the Librarian watch as the shadow flows on over the town, straight and strong, until it touches the top of the opposite hill and disappears on its own infinite and unplanned trajectory into the evening sky.

In the Park, on the Bench Dedicated to Miss Gwynneth Watkins

LADDY MERRIDEW HAS INVENTED a dentist's appointment as that is preferable to mathematics, and he is spending his appointment in the park, as he was before, writing in his notebook. He's half-listening for the bell on Ebenezer Chapel to sound a muffled half past something calling him back to school for geography, which is not so bad. But he is concentrating so hard on the words coming out of his biro that he does not hear the boots of Ianto Passchendaele Jenkins coming towards him on the path. Nor does he hear a hello as Ianto Jenkins sits next to him on the bench. Or a cough. 'Morning, Maggot.' It is only after a while that the boy looks up, and jumps.

Ianto Jenkins smiles, 'Sorry, did I wake you?'

The boy smiles, closes his notebook and hands Ianto a piece of chewing gum. The beggar hands it back. 'Never got on with chewing gum, myself. You don't have any toffee, do you?'

Laddy shakes his head.

'What you are writing?'

Laddy reddens. 'Nothing much,' then he changes his mind. 'Your stories. Is that all right?' He puts one hand over the words. 'There's nothing else to do at Gran's. She doesn't like me playing my drum.'

Ianto Passchendaele Jenkins thinks for a moment. 'No school today?'

'No. I mean yes. But I'm not going this morning.'

The beggar says nothing, just raises an eyebrow.

'I don't like maths, I'm no good at it. I get it all wrong, and they laugh. Anyway I'm not there for long, so there's no point.' He is quiet for a while, bites his thumbnail. 'Mam rang last night. You know when people are too nice, and you know there's something else, but they aren't saying?'

Ianto Jenkins nods, slowly, as if he doesn't really.

'It was nice to talk to her. But the thing is, I don't know if she's telling me the truth, do I? Not now I know she's lied to me sometimes.'

Ianto nods again, as if this time, he does know.

Laddy Merridew clicks his biro on off on off. 'Dad's ringing tonight.'

The two sit in silence for a while. A silence that is broken by the arrival of a yellow dog who stands and barks at nothing and a shout from across the grass for the dog to get back there, and fast. So it does. Laddy watches it go. 'My dad is too nice.' He thinks for a moment, then asks, 'What was your dad like?'

Ianto Passchendaele Jenkins takes a deep breath before answering.

'My da? He was nice too. For years until pain stopped that. And he was deaf, mostly, although his ears seemed to get better just when my brother the Maggot and I did not want him to be hearing and that was nothing short of amazing. Mind, some of the noise Maggot made was hard not to hear – beating the pans in the kitchen with wooden spoons until

160

the walls shuddered – "I am being a band, listen!" Oh yes, a band all right. But Da was deaf enough for normal things, like most of the other colliers I knew, and that was due to the noise down below, he said.

'My da used to put his hand up to his bad ear when he wanted to hear. He would cup his hand behind it like he was tending a bird. But I noticed that, for all he used to tell me to listen in chapel, he did not always help his ear to hear the sermons, and that was a strange thing. The hand he brought up to his ear in chapel was his right hand, another strange thing, for when he was not in chapel it was his left he used.

'But he did not write with his left hand. He did not write much at all, for there was no call for it he said, but when he did have to write, it was with his right and done very slowly. He told me that when he was at school he was not given permission to write with his left hand, which is how he would have written, if he'd been allowed to. For if he did it would be the Devil himself doing the writing, they said at school, and there was no telling what might come out onto the slate. So all those who had the inclination to write like that had their left hands tied behind their backs for them to learn to write the other way. My da said that was the reason for his stuttering a little bit now and again.'

Laddy, holding his biro in his left hand, frowns, 'I don't stutter,' and the beggar says something about things moving on, as things must, right-handed, left-handed, it makes no difference, now.

Laddy shakes his head. 'I wish you'd tell the teachers down the school that. They say they can't read my writing.'

'In that case their eyes must try harder,' Ianto Jenkins says. 'But hands ... Da's hands were black under the skin and it did not matter how much he scrubbed it was always there, like it was part of the body itself. And he had a cough. Mind you, Maggot, I did not know any collier who did not. My da took peppermints down for his throat, and it made the cough a bit better. Not like dead Mr Ernest Ellis whose boots I had, mind, who was now gone and his cough with him ... his cough was so bad the neighbours could not sleep next door.'

Laddy Merridew smiles. 'We're meant to be doing coal mines in history.'

'History, now, is it?'

'They make it boring though. Not like your stories. You make it like it is still happening, in your head anyway.'

And the beggar shakes that head, 'It is. And sometimes, Maggot, I wish it wasn't.' He pauses. Then asks, 'Will you write about Ianto Jenkins in your notebook?'

Laddy thinks for a while. 'I think so ...'

'And why is that? Only "think so"?'

'I don't know.' He points to the path. 'Did you see Mr Bevan and Mr Philips from the library walking everywhere in straight lines yesterday? I tried this morning, from Gran's to here. I reckon it's impossible.'

'Maybe it is.'

'So why did they try then?'

'Because they had to.'

'Why?'

'Seems to me they had to, anyway. That journey started a long time back, when they were boys, maybe even further.'

Laddy Merridew sits and thinks for a moment, clicking his biro.

'Am I on a journey then?'

'You are, indeed.'

'I might try again.'

'Did you look at a map? Would you look at a map next time?'

'No – I just followed my nose.'

'And did your nose know where to go?'

The boy shakes his head.

'Ah well. Maybe it is all to do with where you start and where you finish. Sometimes, all maps do is stop us finding new places. And sometimes . . .' he stops.

'What?'

'Sometimes, maps make places different to how they are in our heads.'

'How?'

'Questions . . . well, Maggot. I had a map once, drawn special. It made me less frightened of going down the pit, but it came after something bad . . .' and he taps the face of his watch with no hands just to check if there is time before the chapel bell calls Laddy back down to the school. And there is, so Ianto Passchendaele Jenkins begins his own story again.

'It was a few nights before I was to go down Kindly Light and I could not sleep for being frightened. I must have woken my brother the Maggot as well with my tossing and turning, for he was up and walking about the place in the dark wearing dead Mr Ernest Ellis's boots, looking such a charlie – "I shall come and be a collier with you, Ianto . . ."

"You will not, my Maggot," I said, "You are too small. Have to be big and strong, to go down there. In a hundred years, little brother . . ." and I told him none too gently to take them off for they were mine, and to shut up and get back into bed, or we would be waking Da and that was a bad thing for he was not well.

And he was not well. My da's leg that was crushed down the pit was not healing right at all, and the wrappings had to be changed every day, and that leg smelled something bad. Some days he was staying in bed for hours, just sleeping, and that was not like my da at all.

But I must have gone back to sleep after that and oh, I had some bad dreams again that night, I remember. I have never forgotten them. I dreamed that men with white faces were lowered into the darkness at the beginning of a day, then men with darkness on their faces came up at the end of the day. And in my dream they were changed under the ground but exactly how I didn't know and neither did they. I knew then that I would be changed myself when I went below ground, whether I wanted it or not. It was terrible. I woke again, wet with sweat, and cold, for my brother the Maggot had rolled right away and was as far from me as possible. And I was suddenly so lonely, and I missed my mam, and it was as if for all those years I had not been missing her properly and now I was and there was not room in my heart for all the missing. There was a weight on my heart as though the ground had fallen on me, and I could not breathe. And I rolled out of bed and went along to my da's room and I went in and shook him awake. He was facing the wall.

"Who is it?"

"Me, Ianto, Dada."

"What?"

"I am frightened, Dada."

My da did not turn over. "And I am tired, and my leg hurts like the devil and now thanks to you I shall not get back to sleep . . ."

Then the words came out too fast, "Dada, I am frightened of going below. I am frightened of the dark, and of the ground and the stones falling – Dada, I am frightened . . . please don't make me go?"

He turned over then to look at me and the bedclothes moved, and his leg hurt him and he breathed in sharp through his teeth and the smell was bad again, "Get back to your bed."

And I had not heard my da speak in that voice before, and I had been lonely when I came in and the floorboards were cold and I was lonelier than before and I must have started to cry, even though I was twelve, and big, and nearly grown, and he just lay back on his pillow and did not look at me any more. And then his voice was shaking, he kept it low not to wake the Maggot, "I will not have a coward for a son. Go away."

I did go away. I went back to bed, but I did not sleep.'

Laddy Merridew stops him. 'But being frightened of something, really frightened, isn't the same, is it?' Ianto Jenkins shakes his head and there is a pause before he continues.

'My da made me the map that next day, sitting up in bed. Maybe he knew he had said something hard. He did not say it again, but what he said could not be unsaid, could it? Perhaps to make things easier, he drew me a map of Kindly Light pit as I watched, and it was an extraordinary thing to see. It was drawn on a hymn sheet brought away from Ebenezer Chapel without thinking, and that name was written at the top. My da added the words "Kindly Light". I had to bring a book for him to lean on, and I brought the Bible for it was the right size. He smiled and said that was appropriate.

The pencil was so small in his hand. His tongue licked at his moustache now and again like he was just a small boy concentrating on his sums. I remember thinking he was a boy once and that was something new to consider later.

My da's map started with a few little squares signifying the village houses near the pit, right up by the first lines of "O Iesu Mawr", which is still not my best hymn for it is such a slow one and a dirge. Then it grew to show all the roads below, all the tunnels, the pit head and pit bottom, all labelled neat. It covered the whole hymn sheet in the end and even turned onto the back for the furthest places and the ventilation shaft.

And it did look very strange, Maggot, with the words of those chapel hymns appearing in the tunnels like angels or devils were to read them below, and instructions for singing light or soft – for the minister he liked his singing to be well – in the down-draught. My head found itself doing two things now. First of all it found the map a funny thing, and I was smiling to myself to see this small city appearing over the hymns. And then it became a frightening thing, for although Da had told me about Kindly Light in words many times, and drawn it for me in my head . . . now that I could see it spidering all over Ebenezer's words I saw how big it all was. I could not quite keep it all in my head.

In a few places he put directions next to the tunnels that

said how long it would take to walk from pit bottom to coal face: "26 minutes or 39 minutes", he wrote along one of the roads, "42 minutes or 60 minutes" along another. The smaller is the time it would take to walk at the beginning of the day with a good sleep and a good breakfast inside. The longer number was the same walk at shift end with your legs aching and your stomach howling, and your poor tongue stuck to the roof of your mouth with dust, for you finished your water hours ago.

Seeing it all and learning it all – for he told me I must do that, not to be any more of a burden than the new lads are anyway – I wondered if there was really singing down there, because it all felt dark and looming, to me. He said there certainly was singing sometimes, especially early, and if the air down there was damped well and truly and throats were not yet dried over by the dust, and if it was a holiday the next day, and if the pay was to go up. And then too, at the end of the day there was also singing, and sometimes it was hymns like those on the map, and they echoed along the tunnels.

But it was not always hymns they were singing. Da said there were songs that would get them thrown out of chapel for a month and that was a fact. And he said this with a laugh as if he had forgotten last night and what he had said. I asked him once if he could sing a little for he still had a voice on him despite the dust . . . but he would shake his head and say there was always time for singing later. He sang a lot before Mam died, Maggot. And after? I do not remember.

But I do remember my brother the Maggot playing with an old wind-up train on the bottom stair, and holding his hand out asking to see that map, and me saying no, it was too important – and Da's voice all sharp from upstairs, "Ianto, show your brother the map, will you?" then calling me back upstairs . . .

"Yes Dada?"

"You are not kind to your brother. He worships you, that boy does."

And me leaning in the doorway of Da's bedroom, the smell of his bad leg in the air, "I never asked to be worshipped . . ."

But I was very glad indeed to have that hymn sheet map, for now I knew where I was going. I was glad it had hymns on it as well, and I would be keeping it folded small in my pocket. And do you know something, Maggot?'

The beggar stops, and Laddy Merridew looks at him. 'What?'

'That little piece of paper did one big thing. It changed where I was going from a bad dream into a real city underground. And I was almost looking forward to seeing it, just the once – but I did not tell myself that out loud.'

'I don't suppose you still have that map, do you, Mr Jenkins?'

'To stick in that notebook of yours, is it? No, Maggot. It is lost down there.' He is quiet for a while, and just as Laddy Merridew is about to ask another question, he says, 'And now – what is that sound I hear?'

The muffled bell of the chapel clock is sounding the half hour. The beggar gets up and stretches. 'You need to go to school, and I have work to do.'

Laddy Merridew pushes his notebook into his pocket, and walks off down the path.

The Piano Tuner's Tale

i

SOMETIMES THE WIND WILL lose its voice in the noises of the town. Then it finds it again in the alders that line the river where Half Harris catches his cloths and sticks, and in the rose bushes that straggle over the garden walls in Tredegar Terrace. It whistles down the dark alleyways between the houses. It hoooos low notes through the old railway tunnel near the Brychan, and it sings in the wires that carry men's voices out of the valley. Then Ianto Passchendaele Jenkins will stop his begging on the steps of the cinema and raise a finger into the air, 'Will you listen to that?' and the cinemagoers will listen to the singing as each wire carries its note steady as a bell until the streets of the town are filled with music. 'Oh there's beautiful, listen ...'

And the wind tries to sing in the other wire that grows thick round the old Kindly Light buildings down the valley, rusty and barbed as brambles. But all the wind learns to say here is, 'Keep Out. Danger.'

At The Cat Public House on the corner of Maerdy Street the doors will be closed for the night now, and bolted. The publican is taking boxes of empty bottles down the cellar steps, and Maggie the publican's wife has stopped leaning on the bar in her low dress and smiling. She has taken off her high heels and gone upstairs, barefoot. The last of the night's drinkers left thirty minutes since, gone off to see if their homes are still there in Gwilym Terrace and Mary Street, Garibaldi Street and Highland View. Most will be. And most of the drinkers will have been let in by now and a few sent straight back out under the stars to sleep anywhere they like.

'Mind you keep that old singing in your head, Caruso ...'

But The Cat is not quiet for all that it is almost empty. Sound is spilling into the street out of an open window and from under the door. A single broken note from the piano in the bar, an old iron upright that leaned against the wall for a rest a long time back and never moved again, too heavy to shift for new wallpaper or a lick of paint. Tuneless, the one note played over and over, flailing away from the wood and the wires, its echo breaking against the tobacco-stained walls while the player of the note reminds the piano how to sing.

Nathan Bartholomew the Piano Tuner, who says not much to other people but gazes into their faces as if he is searching for something. Who speaks softly to his pianos as he tunes them, reciting whole poems, verses of hymns, resting on the sounds and inflections. The 'm's, 'n's and 'l's drawn out as he holds them steady while the notes of the piano waver among them and settle. He perches on stools that are far too small, his legs bent, knees almost touching the keys, his long narrow feet in thin-soled shoes planted flat on the floorboards. Or if the floorboards are hidden by a carpet, those shoes will be placed together at the side of the stool, socks rolled neatly inside and the feet pressed to the floor, the bones showing pale under skin as thin as sheets.

Nathan Bartholomew has no home in this town but a rented room at The Cat. He arrived a few weeks back with a single suitcase, ordered half a cider and sat at the old piano with his back to the room, and did not lift the lid.

Matty Harris, Deputy Bank Manager, standing at the bar, finishing his third half pint, his eyes never leaving Maggie the publican's wife, 'No good trying to play that one, mun.' And Philip Factual Philips, Deputy Librarian, drawing a map of the river on the bar with one finger in a drop of spilled beer, 'Sounds like someone's strangling a cat, that thing . . .'

Then the newcomer reached down and put his glass on the carpet. He sat for a while saying nothing, running his fingers over the scratches and stains on the piano lid, playing scales on the wood, turned to no one in particular and said he'd heard there was a room. 'For a month or two? I tune pianos. Are there any need seeing in the town?'

And the Librarian turned from his artwork, and Matty Harris had a think. And others as well.

'Aww Duw, yes. That thing in the school hall calls itself a piano.'

'And there's the one at Penuel Chapel. Mind, I think they keep it bad so you have to sing over?'

'And Mrs Bennie Parrish, she's still got Mr Bennie Parrish's old piano. She was telling me only nowjust it is all silent now he's dead and gone.'

And Maggie, the publican's wife, watching Nathan Bartholomew from behind the bar, 'Then there is ours. That thing. Past repairing though, isn't it? Good for nothing, really? Too late.'

Nathan looked up, his hand stroking the piano lid, 'It is never too late.'

And there were pianos in the town. The old walnut grand in the corner of the school assembly hall, the ivory picked off, one leg pinned with metal, its lid stacked with books and old exam papers with the names of scholars who left last year, the year before. Its notes, hoarse and short, echoing against the floor-boards and the walls then stopping at the hall doors as though they had not the strength to run along the corridors. And upstairs, in their airless and tiny rooms, the pianos for lessons, for practice, with graffiti in the veneer: *Barry hates Mozart.*

There were ebony uprights in the chapels, polished once, now dull as shadows. Penuel and Bethel's pianos – their chords rising into the tight air on Sundays to drop down the cracks between the flagstones. Pianos in the houses, many, used as sideboards in the middle rooms, lamps and doilies on the lids, photographs and more photographs. Ashtrays. Budgies.

'They've forgotten why they are here at all . . .'

Maybe Nathan Bartholomew started work a day or two after, at the house of Mrs Bennie Parrish, whose piano is never played now Mr Bennie has gone, but she likes it right all the same. Sometimes her leg plays up so badly the neighbour's twin boys who are saving for roller skates call to take her books back to the library for a coin or two, and they did when Nathan was at her house. They stopped to peer into the front room and whisper, 'Look – he's taken off his shoes!'

And there was the Piano Tuner sitting on the stool, his feet bare on her carpet. He knelt slowly as if he would ask the piano to marry him, his ear to the wood, tapping a key over and over again. Then reaching up a hand in a cotton glove, stroking the strings. All the while talking to the piano about music being the food of love, and looking at the photos of a smiling Mr Bennie Parrish in his silver frames on the wall just by. And the boys didn't quite stifle their laughter and Nathan Bartholomew stopped in his talking and listening and looked up.

Mrs Bennie Parrish limped through from the middle room, 'Leave the poor man alone, will you and fetch my books . . .'

She listened for the stamp of their feet going up the stairs and gave them a coin when they came down carrying four books, two each. And when they had gone, she went back to the middle room and settled herself in the deep chair by the fire to listen to the sound of the Piano Tuner's voice and the notes of her late husband's piano playing through it.

Later, she made a pot of tea and knocked on the front room door to take it through with a slice of lardy cake. 'How is my piano?'

He poured his tea into the saucer and blew on it, and she watched an Adam's apple in a thin neck rise and fall as he swallowed her cake before he said, 'Almost right now. Almost . . . .' and he played a final arpeggio, humming with the piano as it played, tapping his foot. And what he meant was, 'Almost right. As good as I can get it.'

But it sounded fine to Mrs Bennie Parrish, and that was all that mattered.

So now, he will spend a little time each evening in the bar of The Cat with the old iron upright when the drinkers have gone off home and The Cat is getting ready for the night. He sits on a wooden chair for the piano stool is lost a long time ago, ridden on its three wheels for a bet down the hill once, late at night. He sits on the edge of that chair as though he may stand up and leave, but the sounds keep bringing him back as he taps at a key as yellow and pitted as a last tooth. Tapping the same key with the forefinger of his right hand over and over again, feeling it stick against the next where there have been pints and half pints spilled into the dust over the years. His left hand in its cotton glove resting on his knee. The front panel of the piano is against the wall, propped on a carpet the colour of cigarettes. And behind a coat of cobwebs, strings that are as rusted as the barbed wire round Kindly Light pit shudder as he touches the keys. And he hums the note as it should be, and talks low, poetry, hymns. Then he puts a gloved finger up to the strings and holds them, feeling them trembling almost against his skin.

'Give us a tune, mun?' The muffled voice of the publican calling from the cellar, where he has found an old chair pushed underneath an open window and a broken grille to mend. 'Lads. Did anyone see lads down here?'

But Nathan Bartholomew saw no lads at all, and shakes his head as though the publican can see him, still tapping at the same note over and over again. And he replies, but quietly, 'Tune? When did this play tunes, last, then?'

He feels the sounds running from the wires through the wood to his fingerbones, then feels them leave, carried on the stale air to the window. Sounds that are as raw as scratches from brambles. And the dust rises and flakes of rust tremble off the wires into the body of the old piano. Plays his note again, and hums, brushing his gloved finger up and down the wires, dislodging more dust, and rust, until the publican shouts to him to stop because the piano is past worrying about. 'Use it to sit on they do, not play the thing. Give it a rest then? I'm going up to bed nowjust.' And he ducks behind the bar, grumbling.

Nathan Bartholomew gets up from the piano and stretches. He takes off his glove and shakes it, then pushes it deep into a pocket, replaces the piano's front panel with its half-gone inlay harp and drum in the veneer, its graffiti.

'Right, out it is. Constitutional. Don't you be locking me out, now?'

There is no answer at first from down in the cellar as the Piano Tuner unbolts the door, but then the publican's voice behind him, 'Lock up when you get back then. Except Wednesdays. Out playing cards for money, Wednesdays.'

Nathan crosses the road to take a walk down Garibaldi Street. Past Matty Harris, Deputy Manager of the Savings Bank he goes, kneeling to do up a shoelace on the pavement opposite The Cat. Matty says to no one in particular but especially Nathan Bartholomew, '. . . just off home . . .'

Nathan says nothing and with hands firmly in pockets he disappears down Garibaldi Street. He walks right to the end and into the little roads beyond, meeting no one, hearing nothing at all except the rush of the town on the night air and the barking of a dog. And after a while he turns to go back to The Cat. But when he gets to the end of the street he stops, for there on the pavement, kneeling still, but not for a shoelace, is Matty Harris the Deputy Manager of the Savings Bank, gazing at The Cat as though it held the answer to every question in the world.

Up in a window with only a net drawn across, a woman is moving against the light like a shadow caught in a box. Her skin is smooth, her hair dark, catching the light then losing it. Dancing to no music they can hear in the street, naked as a baby. Graceful, twisting her fingers in her hair, lifting it and letting it fall back to her shoulders. She sways and turns, her skin heavy and glowing in the streetlights, then she pauses, shadows playing on her dark places.

Two men watching from the street, one kneeling, the other not. The one seeing her every move, wondering what it would be like to put his hand just there, for his wife has never danced like that in all the years . . . and the other hearing sounds in his head. The cry of a violin when she raises her arms and the moan of an oboe when she sways and turns her face away. And when she lifts her breasts, both men hear different drumbeats tapping against the night.

Then, there is the square shadow of the publican crossing the stage, and recrossing it, raising his fists to pull the curtains. The dancer is gone, and the window is just a window after all.

Matty Harris gets up and leans for a while against the wall before he walks off down the hill towards Bethesda Mansions, where there is precious little dancing to be had. The Piano Tuner waits for him to be gone, crosses the road to The Cat, and bolts the door for it is not a Wednesday. Then he pauses, listening, before sitting at the old iron piano, putting his hand on the lid. Hums a note, and fancies he hears an answer, but the two sounds are not the same. Not at all.

And, because sometimes it is important not to make sounds, he takes off his shoes and stands on the carpet at the foot of the stairs in the half-dark, feeling the years of smoke and laughter and shouts beneath his feet. Up the stairs he goes, carrying his shoes, and forgets the third step after all that, and it creaks under his weight.

He pauses on the landing with its single bulb, outside the publican's bedroom where fingers of light escape under the door and reach for his toes. He hears nothing except the slow tick of the clock on the shelf at the bottom of the stairs.

In his room, he readies himself for bed, then slides open the sash. He lies and watches the yellow of the streetlights striping the ceiling through the curtain rings. And when he closes his eyes the sounds begin, as they always do, the light singing like the strings of a harp brushed by a passing cat, the air vibrating. The pillow and its scents of wood shavings and saliva brings dryness to his mouth, and Nathan cannot move, for every movement is sound. Every breath is sound, every heartbeat. The smallest echo of a drum played in another house, in another street. Another town.

As he listens to the knocking of his heart there comes the dead march of a bedhead banging against the wall. No voices in the dark, no laughter. And as quick as it begins it stops. The silence it leaves is the colour of the walls in a room that has not been painted for years, and the Piano Tuner turns away in his own bed, his hands over his ears, to keep in his own sounds.

Maybe it is the movement of the earth beneath a house in Garibaldi Street that untunes the piano belonging to Mrs

Bennie Parrish, and maybe again it is her knotty fingers removing the front panel, lifting it down to the carpet. Those fingers then working at the nuts that hold the piano strings and turning them, just a little, but enough for Nathan Bartholomew to be called again and for another loaf of lardy cake to be baked, ready.

The Piano Tuner plays a few scales and the piano laughs back at him. Then he takes off the front panel and sees scratches on the wood that may not have been there before. He peers at the strings and raises an eyebrow. Mrs Bennie Parrish stands in the doorway hearing the question he has not made yet into words, 'Perhaps. It does not sound quite right to me. And would you like your tea and cake?'

Nathan Bartholomew runs his fingers over the strings and says he does not understand it but he will try again. Then he waves a hand for her to shut the door, and as she does so, she finds something to look at on the wallpaper, and says, 'You can call me Lavender . . .' but he is not listening, and when she glances back she sees him slipping off his shoes and socks and placing his feet, bare, on the rug.

Mrs Bennie Parrish goes through to the middle room and rearranges slices of cake on a plate, and clatters two cups together on a tray, and when the tuning is done, she carries the tray through to the front room and sits on an upright chair in the corner to take the weight off her bad leg. 'It must be the weather . . .' she says, not knowing whether she means her leg, her heart or the piano, and she watches the Piano Tuner pouring his tea into his saucer and sipping it, his lips making the small sounds of a cat lapping milk. And for some reason it does not cross her mind that she used to stop Mr

Bennie Parrish from doing the very same thing in case the neighbours minded.

The next patient is up the Brychan, Laddy Merridew's gran, who has come back from the library early, special. There is a budgie in a cage and her piano is speckled with husks of birdseed, and feathers. 'Sorry, Mr Bartholomew. Should have swept this lot,' and she lifts the cage and places it on the floor where last week when he called by to see what was what, there was a drum. The Piano Tuner smiles, 'Your drum gone, now, has it?' for when he asked if she played the drum last week, she said no she most certainly did not play the drum, and it belonged to Laddy her grandson who was living with her for the moment, and it drove her to distraction it did with all its noise and gave her a dreadful headache. And last week, it was waiting for the ladies from the Women's Institute to come by and fetch it with the rest of the jumble, for the sale next week.

Laddy Merridew's gran shakes her head. 'There's a naughty boy he is. Hid that drum, and when the ladies from the Institute came to fetch it, there it wasn't. And they came in a car as well. There's embarrassing. Won't tell me where he's put it, neither. Boys need boundaries, they do.' And she echoes the words used by Factual Philips, Deputy Librarian, so often, but come to think of it she hasn't heard him say these for a while.

Nathan Bartholomew mumbles, 'And drums. Boys need drums, as well . . .'

And when she asks him to repeat that for she is a little deaf, the Piano Tuner smiles, and says he said thumbs. All fingers and thumbs today. And then she leaves him to the tuning, and the budgie, and the birdseed husks.

A little later, when Nathan Bartholomew leaves the house, there is Laddy Merridew sitting on the step.

'It is a good thing to do, looking after pianos, Mr Bartholomew?'

The Piano Tuner says it is.

'And I looked after my drum, Mr Bartholomew, as well.'

The Piano Tuner says he is sure he did. And that was a good thing too.

The boy looks at the front path for a bit, concrete slabs, a dandelion. 'How do you mend pianos?'

The Piano Tuner takes a breath to talk for a while about keys and hammers and strings and sounding boards, and the boy listens. 'And what happens if a drum is broken?'

The boy is looking up at the Piano Tuner now. Nathan stops his talk of keys and hammers. 'Does your drum need mending then?'

Laddy Merridew nods. 'The top got broken, by mistake.'

'The skin?'

'Oh it's not real skin, Mr Bartholomew. Only plastic. It's cracked.'

The Piano Tuner thinks for a while. 'How big is this drum?'

And the boy holds his hands apart the space that fits his drum. Not much more than the span of his two hands held out together. 'My best one it was too.'

Nathan Bartholomew, who knows it was the boy's only one, asks, 'And where do you play your drum now? Not at your gran's any more with her headaches?'

The boy squints up at him. 'It's a secret.'

The Piano Tuner smiles, and picks up his bag. 'A secret, is it? Well, maybe I will think and find something to mend your drum.' And he walks away through the Brychan leaving the boy sitting on the step.

And then there will be telephone calls made from the dark hallway of The Cat Public House, with Maggie the publican's wife on the landing, unseen and listening. Telephone calls on a telephone that needs feeding with money, and between the fall of coins there is the voice of a Piano Tuner asking for the number of a sheep farmer up near the Beacons, then a second call, and more coins, and a farmer in for his tea, and a request made for the skin of a sheep, or even a goat for that would be better. Yes, a goat. And the farmer coughing and saying no that is not possible, not at all – 'but what about the abbatoy down in the town then? Down Brecon, the abbatoy with that old lorry that comes on Wednesdays to collect – and takes the devil's own time to get up the track too and demands payment to the driver?'

And it is another call then in that dark hall, and the fall of more coins, and the securing of the skin of a goat who lived its life on a hillside above Brecon, for the drum of a boy.

Coming down the stairs in her bare feet is the publican's wife, who has heard every word, who asks, 'Why do you need the skin of a goat, Nathan?'

When he tells her, she smiles at him and lays her hand on his sleeve, 'There's nice you are.'

And it is not long before there is the skin of a goat delivered to The Cat and stretched over a biscuit tin on the table in the back kitchen for it to be scraped until there is nothing left to scrape. Then Nathan is laying it flat on the table and the knife is whetted until it is razor-sharp, and thongs cut from the edges, straight, ribbons, as long as he can. And a rough circle cut from the best of it. And when he is discovered, not such polite requests to take that thing out of here from the publican, and then there is the sight of the Piano Tuner taking a parcel under his arm and leaving The Cat, followed by Maggie the publican's wife, pulling a cardigan round her shoulders, 'I will come too, for the walk, just?'

Then it is the two of them walking up to the Brychan to wait on the corner by the turning to the farm now owned by Icarus Evans the Woodwork Teacher, for a boy on his way home from the school. Nathan Bartholomew hands him the parcel. 'To mend your drum.'

And as Maggie listens, the Piano Tuner tells Laddy Merridew about the skin, and the ties, and how to stretch and tie the skin over the drum. 'And do it quickly. And let it all dry somewhere safe. And when it dries, it will tighten, and the sound will be good. Better than plastic.' Then, leaving the boy round-eyed with his parcel, they walk back down the hill. And as they do so, the publican's wife tucks her hand under the Piano Tuner's arm.

The Piano Tuner's Tale

ii

PIANO TUNERS WHO TALK to pianos, who search people's faces as if there is something hidden there, do not come to this town every day. Later, much later, down in the chapel porch the beggar on his stone bench will smile in his sleep and wonder if tomorrow will come questions.

And they do come, the questions, 'Who is Nathan Bartholomew, then? What is he here for? What is he looking for? And why . . .'

And when the questions reach the ears of Ianto Passchendaele Jenkins, he will sigh and tap his watch with no hands, and he will say he does not have much time for stories today, mind . . .

'It is not an easy story, this one, not at all. It is dark, and to do with how a child can be hurt even before he is born. And how the hurting is done unwittingly for all that.'

Here Ianto Passchendaele Jenkins sighs, and shuts his eyes and he wheels his arms again, pulling the story down from the air. And it is only Peter Edwards, the Collier who is no longer that, who may cross to the other side of the street not to hear this or any of Ianto Jenkins's stories, and instead will shove his hands deep in his pockets and move his feet a little faster to the statue outside the library where he waits and waits for something and nothing.

'This is the story of Eve, Nathan Bartholomew's grandmother, and her son Edward Bartholomew who will be father to Nathan. But stories need fuel as they always do and it is a long time before my dinner.'

The cinemagoers will laugh and someone will go to the ticket office and get a coffee with two sugars from Prinny Ellis, who is at her knitting, and someone may have a bag of bullseyes ready and Ianto Jenkins will wrap one in a scrap of newspaper taken from his bed and kept in a pocket for the purpose. He will look over to the chapel porch, and he will sigh, 'Lovely weddings there have been in that chapel . . .' and the listeners may wonder why he is talking about weddings when this is a story about darkness, but he waves their questions away and begins.

'This story of Eve Bartholomew and her son begins almost but not quite on a wedding day. Oh yes. Eve's own wedding.' He stops and taps the wall behind him, 'She lived up Mary Street, once, with her mam, all on their own, for her da had left them a while back. He still sent money once a week for the rent, mind, delivered by the coalman like clockwork, but that money would stop, he said, when Eve was twenty-one. Went to work on the ships, and never came home again, but some said he was living with a black-haired singer in Swansea called Bessie. Eve's mam, a strange one, was not working at all, but spending more and more time in her room, in front of her mirror and talking to herself, saying over and over, "I am not ready yet, how is my hair?"

No place for a girl, not at all. And Eve was only nineteen, and learning the sewing trade at the dressmaker's in the High Street. She was to be given a proper position when she learned enough to be a good seamstress – and that was almost. Eve was about to get married and be a Missis, and the dressmaker liked that for it would look well on the card in the window. Here, she lived after, too, just here, after the rent money stopped coming . . .'

Ianto Passchendaele Jenkins will tap the wall and point at the steps where the cinemagoers are sitting. At the cinema doors, the posters, the red carpet where Laddy Merridew and his gran are talking, come down as a treat to see *Where Eagles Dare* because his gran likes eagles . . .

The cinemagoers shake their heads, 'Here? They lived here?'

And the beggar nods. 'Just here. There was a row of old houses here once, all forgotten and rotten, and maybe there still are – under these stones, to be found one day when all this is gone.'

He nods at Laddy and his gran by way of a hello.

'But the wedding. I am forgetting, getting old, see. Terrible thing. The girl Eve was making her own dress. Not living here, back then, oh no. That nice house up Mary Street, it was, where she sewed her dress at night looking out at the hill called Black Mountain across the roofs of the town and the glow of the ironworks. Sewed at night, then hid the dress in an old box under her bed. No one could see that wedding dress before she walked down the hill to the chapel wearing it, and if they did it would bring bad luck.'

There is a laugh, then, and Ianto Jenkins raises a hand. 'Bad luck is real enough, believe me. There will be no laughing at bad luck here, or there will be no more of the story . . .' and the miscreant will cough and be silent, so the beggar just frowns and continues.

'And who was she marrying, this girl, Eve? One of the Bartholomew brothers, Edward, the youngest, and it was three years they had been together. A lovely couple, everyone said, a real lady and a gentleman walking out. And so much of a gentleman he would not touch Eve before their wedding night. But his voice was no gentleman, oh no. Best shut your ears.'

The cinemagoers smile and shift in their shoes, and there is Laddy Merridew's gran telling her grandson to go and fetch some chips, for he must be hungry mustn't he and here is the money and get plenty of vinegar if he is bringing some back for her as well. But to take his time.

'Aww, Gran?' but Ianto Passchendaele Jenkins has stopped talking, and it seems he is inspecting the old wall for cracks, so Laddy shuffles off up the High Street, dragging his feet and the beggar does not speak again until the boy is quite gone round the corner.

'So, Edward Bartholomew told the girl, Eve, everything they would do on their wedding night. Whispered it close under her hair as they walked home in the dark, pressing his fingers against her dress.

"I will touch you, my Evie, here, light as anything, and here. And here. Touch you and stroke you until you are crying with it all. Soft my fingers will be, so you can hardly feel them, and you will reach out for them with your skin. Like this . . ."

And he would kiss her against the wall of the old schoolhouse, then pull away so she had to reach for his lips in the shadows. He leaned his cheek against hers, "My face against yours, my Evie," and he pulled at her hand, laughing, "Feel me, Evie?" and she turned her head away, red as fire.

He kissed her with his tongue by that wall and pressed his length against her until she was weak, feeling him through her dress, afraid to touch him, but wanting to touch him, so weak with wanting she might have melted into the stones. It would be soon now, their wedding night . . .

And she made her wedding dress sitting up at night in her room. For each button she sewed she felt him loosening them slowly, the dress slipping off her shoulders. For each ribbon she felt the dress falling to the floor. And as she fixed a lace edge taken from a borrowed handkerchief to the hem of the veil she felt his eyes on her as they would be, for sure.

But it never happened quite as she imagined, bless the girl, oh no.

It was a September day, only a few days before the wedding and the streets of this town were filled with dreadful things, the alarm sounding, the cries of women, the shouts of men, bringing what they may to help where no help could be given.

Only a few little days and Kindly Light pit took Edward Bartholomew's fingers, and hands, and hair and mouth. And all her mother said when Eve went crying to her for comfort was, "Tell me, how is my hair?"

And what happened then? Did Eve put away that dress, never to look at it again? Did she sell it to be worn by someone luckier than herself? She did not. Instead, she sat up that very night and the next, to finish the dress, the curtains closed and only a small lamp to work by.'

'Poor thing, the love,'

'What was the dress for now, then?'

'Shhh, don't ask questions. Listen to the story . . .'

The storyteller continues. 'It was evening, a day or so later. And next day was to be the funerals of those men killed down Kindly Light. Remember? But it was also going to have been Eve's wedding day . . .

That evening, there was Mrs Fairlight next door bringing in her washing and she saw Eve coming out into the little garden behind the house, wearing her nightdress even though it was not yet night. The nightdress was dirty, and looked as though it had been worn all day and maybe the day before as well. Down Eve went to the end of the garden where there was a rose planted years ago by her father, when all was well. A tangle of thorns that never gave more than a few old white roses on the thinnest of stems. Mrs Fairlight next door saw Eve pick two ragged late roses, and she asked, "Eve? It is all right then?" but there was no reply from the girl who smiled as though there was nothing but sweet things in the air.

Mrs Fairlight stood on a brick in her slippers to look over the wall better and she saw Eve, barefoot on damp ground, scissors in her hand. She saw Eve taking the flowers back into the house, and Mrs Fairlight said later she thought Eve was picking them for the funeral. For her Edward.

The next day should have been her wedding day, the house full of laughter and friends and good food, even if there was a mother upstairs looking at her hair in the mirror when by now there was no hair to see at all.

Maybe Eve rubbed her hands with a little salt and oil to make them smooth. Maybe she tied the flowers together with some pale ribbon left over from the dress upstairs, hanging now behind a door . . . maybe she put a little scent behind her ears. Maybe she did her hair, pinned it up as best she could, but the pins fell out, some. And maybe she asked her mother for help with her hair, "Mam? I don't know how . . ."

But all her Mam did was ask if her own was lovely.

Eve went to her room, then, all quiet, and put on her wedding dress, and the veil, covering her face so when she looked in the mirror she only saw a white shape, like a ghost come in the night to herself.

She fetched the flowers from the kitchen, and went out into the street, looking from side to side, all shy. And down the pavement she walked, head high, holding her roses, and a few children called out to her, "Can we play too?" until their mams called them inside for this was no time for children to be out. And one of the mams might have gone to her, caught her by the arm, and said, "Eve? There's lovely you look . . . let's go in by here, shall we, and wait a bit?"

But Eve would not wait. This was her wedding day, and for the first time she heard laughter in her head, and singing, voices of friends, and there were the neighbours wishing her well as she walked by. When all the doors were closed for the end of the day.

Past the dressmaker's she went, past the window with the ribbons and the fastenings, and the white canvas body waiting for a new dress to cover itself with. And she caught sight of herself in window after window as she went down the High Street, and she was beautiful, her veil waving about her head in the breeze like weed in water.

She looked at herself in all the windows. A ghost on her way down the High Street, carrying her roses. All the way down to the chapel. This chapel. Ebenezer. Just by there.'

And here Ianto Jenkins will point to his own porch and shake his head. His bench. The cinemagoers look, and say nothing. Laddy Merridew's gran is busy shaking her head too, and she misses her grandson coming back from the chip shop, standing at the back to listen.

'Eve paused outside these very doors, her veil catching on the flagstones in the porch, just there, see, as if to say, "Do not go in."

She stood with her head on one side, listening – and she heard what she wanted to hear. The hum of voices inside the chapel. A clearing of throats ready for the singing. The scrape of chairs as Mrs Fairlight, who must have come down another way, pushed into her place. Then the notes of the bellows organ making music for her, playing the hymns they chose, she and Edward Bartholomew only two weeks since, him stroking the back of her hand under the table in the minister's dark office. And she put her fingers on the handle of the door, her veil still caught on the flagstones, pulling her back, *Do not go in.*

But she did not listen to the stones. Instead, she pushed open the heavy doors and in she went. There was her chapel filled with people, all in their places, waiting, hushed, and Edward in his place with the minister. And her da come up special from Swansea. With his fancy woman Bessie, and her mam with a hat, all fine and smiling. Eve started her walk, blushing, her head low, watched only by the windows, and the dust on the chairs, and the ghosts.

Stood in the chapel by there, right where the minister stands, and she looked the ghosts in the eye, and gave her vows to Edward Bartholomew just as if he was standing there beside her. "For richer or poorer," she said, clear as anything, and "until death us do part" as if that had not already happened. Ignoring the darkness of the chapel. The empty chairs. The black books and sheets set out all ready for that funeral tomorrow. Hearing his voice and the voice of the minister, and the choir singing and the hymns belling about her head.

And that singing only stopped when the doors opened again to let in someone setting the chairs out for tomorrow's funeral . . . who asked what she thought she was doing and there came no answer from Eve except a smile.

Then she came out of the doors into the dark, as Eve Bartholomew, for that was her name now, was it not, if she had just married Edward Bartholomew? Waited for a while in the porch, smiling and bowing a little, one hand at her side as if she was holding the fingers of someone beside her. Then she walked, slowly, mind, for there were people watching and waving, and she heard them, didn't she? Back up the hill towards the room they were to have tonight, the room up The Cat Public House, over the bar, rented for one night.

Past the dressmaker's where there was not enough light to see herself reflected now, and on up the hill. Where her man must have gone on ahead, as she always knew he would. Making things ready for her, turning back the bed and laughing at his friends down there on the pavement shouting up, "Got the instruction book, Eddie?"

Still carrying her two roses. Eve's veil torn where it caught on the flagstones, and again on the kerbs, dirt on the hem of her skirt, and a shoe lost a heel. All ready for her wedding night.

She found him not far away, in an alley, her soft-tongued man, tasting of drink, leaning against the wall, the same wall where Edward pressed her against the stones for her to feel his hardness through her dress. Waiting for her, and smiling, and saying nice things, and she went to him and lifted her skirts.

It was Edward who pressed her against the wall again, only rougher, like that, still in her wedding dress, his fingers on her and in her and telling her, when she asked, that he loved her. And he showed her. Wasn't that what Edward Bartholomew was going to do? Lift her dress and put his hands on her and tell her she was beautiful? It was Edward she heard, his voice like it always was going to be. Edward she felt, his hands, his fingers, his hair, his mouth, his body.

It was not as she imagined. But she was new to this. It would get better.

And it did not stop there, oh no. All a man had to do was tell Eve Bartholomew that she was beautiful, and she would let him lift her skirt. And after a while he did not even have to tell her she was beautiful, just give her money. And after another while she did not feel the roughness of men's hands and the lack in their kisses, but instead she heard the soft voice of her man telling her again that he would be touching her soon. Here. Like that. And he did, then, see? Over and over, in her head. Every man she went with was her Edward, and no one else, and there was no shame in that now was there?

But the townsfolk do not know what happens in the heads of others, now do they? They saw Evie who slept with men for money, and they called her shameless to her face as well as behind her back.

"Dirty it is. Ych y fi."

And when she had a child coming, the words did not get softer. "Look at that Evie now, expecting. Shameless."

"Whose is it I wonder?"

"Expect she doesn't know herself."

"Aww, maybe it's Tom's."

"Or Harry's."

"Or Dick's . . . bound to be."

But of course she knew whose baby it was. Her Edward's, of course, as natural as anything and when her boy was born she would call him Edward Bartholomew for his father. And when the women shook their heads at her in the street, she told those who would listen not to worry. For all will be well.

But then all was not well, see, for the men she went with had given their Evie more than just their money. That gift was called syphilis. The child was born dead.

Eve asked if she might hold him, and if she might call the small dead thing Edward Bartholomew. But the woman just wiped her hands on her apron and took the little body away in her bag for it to be buried with no marker, no kind words said.

Eve did not stop then. She found her Edward Bartholomew down every alley, and then she found him in the little upstairs room in the old house just here, where she lived in a few rooms with her mother, strange always, after the money stopped coming from Swansea. She had more children, children who died at birth one after the other. All boys, and all called Edward after their father, until finally, one lived. Another boy, another Edward Bartholomew, born weak and sickly but who thrived after a fashion, never to be a healthy child at all. His eyes were soon filled with clouds and he was only able to see for a short time before the darkness fell absolutely and he was blind for the rest of his life. But those early years of sight he remembered.'

The cinemagoers nod, and mutter, 'Dreadful thing. Dreadful,' and one will ask, 'That boy, the young Edward Bartholomew – that would be Nathan Bartholomew's father then?'

And Ianto Passchendaele Jenkins nods.

'When her mother died, Eve took her blind boy away from the town and no one knew where they went. Maybe no one cared. But then, many years later, someone heard that Evie Bartholomew had gone properly herself now, died of her disease, and that her blind son was working as a piano tuner in

England. A successful one too, by all accounts, at all the great houses. Told always by Eve his mother, that he must use the name Bartholomew and nothing else. And he had married a woman who was also blind, and they had one son. And that son is called Nathan.'

'Aww, that is a good ending after all then,' someone will say.

'But look, look what happened. That Edward Bartholomew, Nathan's father, he worked with sounds, always sounds, pianos, voices, and with touch, feeling words, faces, all things. But he was not blind from birth and he remembered seeing.

He remembered a yellow dog running down a wet street, and he told his son. He remembered the thrashing of trees in the wind and washing on the lines and he told his son. He remembered an old dress, dirty, hanging on a hook in a small room where he played on the floor, in a small house where his mam sent him to play in the back when a man friend called for her with his hand in his pocket and a grin on his mouth, and he told all this to his son. And he remembered an old woman with no hair who sat her life away in front of a mirror, light shining on her head like a halo.

But Edward Bartholomew and his wife, they knew, didn't they, what it was made him blind. And that was love and madness, both the same thing, perhaps? So, their son Nathan was taught, perhaps knowingly, perhaps not – that love is an unclean thing, and that good is to be found in sounds, for only they can be perfect. And Nathan too becomes a piano tuner, searching to make pianos sing just right, and hearing sounds in his head sometimes, as though touch and sound are muddled and mixed in him, and come from everywhere.

Eve's son Edward Bartholomew never returned to the town

where he saw the yellow dog run down a golden street. But his own son, Nathan, now a man in middle age who has never married, nor been with anyone, he has come back. And he searches the faces of people he meets in this town, to find something to recognise. The shape of a nose, a hairline, a smile.'

The Piano Tuner's Tale

iii

TODAY, THIS VERY DAY, the piano in the school assembly hall is being tuned. The books and papers are gone from the lid, and the dust dusted away, the surface polished, the scratches not as clear. The broken leg of the piano limping in its metal brace was noted, and a message sent from the headmaster to the Woodwork Teacher Icarus Evans in the workshop, to come and see. And he came to the hall and saw the piano, its lid raised up like a great wooden wing, and he took measurements, nodding at Nathan Bartholomew, who was tapping the keys with one hand, the other in its cotton glove reaching for the strings inside the piano's body.

And later, as the piano is almost making the sounds it was made to make, and as the school day is ending, the Piano Tuner sees, waiting in the shadows in the corner of the hall, a boy in glasses.

'Laddy Merridew?'

'Oh Mr Bartholomew, the drum. I came to tell you. It is a beautiful sound now.'

Nathan Bartholomew packs his bag. 'I am glad. I am very glad.'

'I wish you could hear it.'

'I will have to imagine. So, play it well.'

There is a pause, the boy chewing his lip. 'Shall I show you where I play? Will you tell my gran?'

The Piano Tuner maybe remembers what it was like to be a boy with a secret, and he smiles. 'No, it might make her headaches worse. Show me where you play?'

And it is then that the Piano Tuner and the boy walk together through the school yard, across the playground and down to the High Street and on down to the river, and they turn onto the footpath and follow the river out of the town and past the railway, the factories, the rubbish dumps, and on towards the next village, passing close to the old Kindly Light workings all overgrown with brambles and barbed wire, the gates rusted and padlocked for twenty years or more now, buildings closed up and their doors nailed shut, windows barred.

Laddy Merridew stops, turns, and smiles, 'In here.' He crosses to the wire, rusted and loose. 'In here,' and he ducks underneath, then lifts it high as it will go for Nathan Bartholomew to thread himself beneath, through the gap, past the sign that says, *Danger, no entry.*

'Here,' the boy says, running across cracked concrete towards the buildings, closed, blank-windowed and dark. More signs saying, *Lamp room* and *Baths.*

'Here,' the boy says pushing aside a corrugated iron sheet that swings on its fixings, brushing the rust off his fingers onto his school trousers. Ducking under and in through a low doorway, where planks are hanging from their nails.

Through other doorways, deeper and deeper into the maze,

away from the wire, pushing through more brambles then standing on a fall of bricks to climb through a broken window that catches hold of Nathan's sleeve and says stop. But he does not stop, he climbs through after the boy and stands there, his sleeve still caught by the glass, deep among the Kindly Light buildings where the dust in the air and stones in the walls still hold the rush of the winding gear and the shouts of men. Listening to the boy's footfall echoing and fading among the darknesses of long-gone machinery that rise over Nathan's head as his eyes magnify what light there is and conjure dead metal fingers playing the shadows.

Then, out of the darkness comes the sound of a drum. Slow beats, even, soft and gentle. Then becoming stronger, stronger, but never harsh. Round sounds that echo off the walls. Rounder and rounder grow the beats, deeper and deeper, each within its own echo. Simple, the sound, as though the whole place was only a chamber in a great heart, and the old mine buildings and the tunnels beneath them nothing but the workings of a vast body.

And the boy does not stop, and the drum plays. 'Do you hear it, Mr Bartholomew?' Laddy Merridew's voice, high above the drum, away over there among the stones, the machinery ghosts. 'Do you hear them, the sounds?'

Nathan hears everything. He hears every touch of the boy's hand on that drum, the scurry of mice in the corners, the scrabble of sparrows. He hears the drumbeats playing on the staleness in the air, on the chill of the fallen stone walls and on their own echoes. He hears the hum of the earth below him.

It is as though each sound has slipped into the gaps in the

rubble poured decades ago into the old mine shafts. It is as though they are swallowed by an earth parched of sound. As though they then find their way over older and deeper falls of stone into the forgotten tunnels as water will, reverberating against each surface until the ground beneath them is singing with the sound made by a boy's hand meeting the skin of a goat from a farm on the hills above Brecon, stretched tight over the body of an old drum.

And when he can, Nathan Bartholomew, still standing by the broken window, says, 'Yes, I hear it.'

Later, the Piano Tuner leaves young Laddy playing his drum to Kindly Light in the short hour left between school and night and he walks slowly back along the river to the town. Along the riverbank where his grandfather, whosoever he be, may have played, once. Stopping at a broken bridge that grandfather may have crossed, reaching out over the river, the stones of its stanchions square and solid. Listening to the wind in the alders, their branches bending to the water and playing in the current, wondering if it is this tree or that his own father remembers seeing before his blindness fell.

Past the old factories then, and the lorry parks on the edge of the town, the dark shapes of old coal tips with their covering of thin grass, along the High Street past the turning to the school, the chapel and its sleeping beggar, past Tommo Price the Bank Clerk as he leaves for home, 'Nathan Bartholomew, your piano's waiting . . .' Past the cinema, the library and on up the hill to The Cat.

But he does not sit at the piano when he gets back to The Cat on the corner of Maerdy Street. He goes through the bar where the tables are half-empty, a few drinkers playing with Icarus Evans's dominoes, a couple leaning at the bar and talking, and behind the bar, her hair backlit against the gold and green and silver of bottles and labels and glasses, Maggie the publican's wife, who raises a hand and a smile for him as she puts down a pint.

Up the stairs to the landing, and past the publican's bedroom to his own, where Nathan kicks off his shoes and lies on his bed in his clothes to think about the sound of an old drum played over mine shafts. About this town where his father was born, and maybe his grandfather before him, and certainly the man for whom his father was named. And he falls asleep like that, on his bed in his shirt and trousers, and dreams about the earth singing. He does not hear the last orders, and the voices raised, 'Aww, time for one more, surely?'

Nor does he hear the drinkers leaving, the singing in the street, nor The Cat closing up for the night, the door of the bar closing. Nor the publican leaving a little later to play cards for money on a Wednesday in a room above the Savings Bank, for Nathan Bartholomew is too busy making dreams of a yellow dog running down a wet street.

Later, the Piano Tuner wakes thinking of the boy and his drum and the mine and the trees moving over the water, and he cannot sleep any more. He gets up and goes softly down the stairs to the bar, stepping over the third stair. He draws up a chair to the piano and lifts the lid. He touches the keys, one by one, light as anything, not even pressing them down, just running his fingertips over the ivory chipped and pitted where cigarettes were left to burn. And in his head there are sounds, the notes of the piano as they should have always been, round and perfect, singing to him through his fingers, and he plays scales and arpeggios, hearing the notes, the runs and rills, sometimes hearing the wrong note when his fingers miss a key, going back to play it right. Then he stretches his fingers, leans back in the chair, shuts his eyes and pretends to play. Brahms. A Bach sonata. Schubert. Mendelssohn. Songs without words.

His head is bowed over the keys, and he is wondering how this piano would sound if he took it to the mine and played it in that space where Laddy Merridew played his drum. Wondering if he could wheel it all the way there, through these streets and along the river. All the while the notes in his ears, the perfect pitch of a concert piano, and the only other sounds his own breathing, his heartbeat, the dripping of the tap behind the bar.

A hand on his shoulder, 'I thought I heard something.' Maggie the publican's wife standing barefoot on the old carpet beside the piano, a nightdress only, 'Play it again?'

Nathan Bartholomew just shakes his head, 'I was playing nothing.' He does not look at her straight, but shows her how he was only running his fingers over the keys, not playing the notes at all. And she keeps her hand on his shoulder, her warmth through his shirt. 'But I hear it, Nathan. Don't stop.'

So Nathan continues to touch the keys, and as he does, she moves her fingers on his shoulder in time to the tune his fingers do not play. And as her fingers move, the notes echo, double, in Nathan's head while she stands behind him and plays his shoulders through the thin cotton of his shirt. Her fingers find the skin of his neck and they play on, running round and under his hair as he leans back into her, her fingers moving round to find the skin at his throat where they rest, and her breath is warm against his ear. She strokes his Adam's apple and down until her fingers are playing along his collar bone, moving slowly, and on down his chest as he touches the piano keys, listening to the sounds in his head, 'You really hear it?'

And she laughs and does not answer and leans against him, moving her hands down his body, her skin against his, playing him. Telling him not to move, to carry on playing his piano as she moves round him, her hair brushing his face, she breathing into his mouth, opening his shirt and his skin singing with it all, and the sound of the *Lieder* in his head. Maggie the publican's wife leans against the old piano in the bar of The Cat with its air full of old beer and cigarettes, her hair against his face smelling of smoke and of spice, her skin of soap and of sugar, and her hands moving here, and there.

Finding him then, and holding him then, her fingers as warm and as soft as the lapping of a tongue.

Her nightdress spreads over the piano keys, and when he touches the keys through the cotton the sounds still come to him. Notes come through his fingers with the warmth of her body, and her nightdress riding up over her thighs, and the scent of her rising into the scent of beer and smoke. And she smiles and watches his face, then closes her eyes, 'I hear it still. Do you?'

And this time it is Nathan who does not answer, who stands and holds her, his face in her hair, breathing in the smoke, her scalp smelling of sawn wood, her breasts heavy under his hands. Then he lifts her up against the piano. Lowers her slowly as he kisses her, as she laughs into his shoulder, her fingers playing down his spine, until she is sitting on the piano keys and pulling him between her thighs, the toes of one bare foot resting on the chair, and the other behind him, holding him.

And the broken chords of the old piano in the bar of The Cat rise into the air as raw as bramble scratches, and they echo and echo against the walls.

On the Old Footbridge over the Taff

NO ONE WAS WALKING on the path that passes by the old Kindly Light workings this morning, early, but if they had been, they might have heard Laddy Merridew's drum beating again, beating deep in the ruined buildings and yards. They might have heard it echoing far below their feet, reaching north as far as the High Street where the echoes might have been heard in the chimneys if anyone was listening for them. But they weren't. Only Ianto Passchendaele Jenkins heard the sounds beneath the flagstones of Ebenezer Chapel porch, and left his bench early as a result.

Now, Laddy is making his way back along the path by the river, his drum under one arm, dragging the toes of his shoes one after the other on the ground. He doesn't notice Ianto Passchendaele Jenkins leaning on the rail of the old footbridge over the Taff, watching the water, until the beggar says, 'Leather against stone. No contest if you ask me.'

The boy puts the drum down on the footbridge and takes half a bar of toffee from his pocket. 'I'm not hungry.'

The beggar smiles and reaches for the toffee, bends and re-bends the bar until a piece softens and pulls away, leaving a thread no bigger than a hair curling in the air. He grins. 'Lovely.'

And for a while the beggar and the boy lean on the rail of the footbridge and say not a lot while they watch the water flowing grey as iron towards them from the town.

Laddy Merridew clears his throat. 'Mr Jenkins, can I ask a question?'

'You just did.'

'No. I mean, if you need to make your mind up about something, how do you do it?'

'I don't make many decisions these days, Maggot.'

'It's just that Gran keeps talking about me having to make decisions.' He spits into the water, then crosses to the other rail and watches the bubbles disappear downriver. 'Can't do that only when the water's flat.' And he's quiet for a while, leaning over the rail, the river curving away in the distance under the overhanging trees, and disappearing. 'I can't see what to do. It's like the lights have all gone out and I can't see.'

Ianto Jenkins nods. 'I understand that.'

Laddy nods too. 'Sometimes, I think the dark's easier when there's noise. Sometimes, just being in the quiet is scary, isn't it?'

Ianto Jenkins thinks for a moment. 'Is that why you've been banging that drum at old Kindly Light?'

Laddy looks at the beggar, maybe expecting him to say something about watching out for the old buildings, or dogs, or old shafts that might open up and they ought to do something about the place – but Ianto does not. Just says, quietly, 'I haven't been that way for a long time now.'

'It's great, Mr Jenkins.' Laddy is not looking at the beggar any more, but down at the river, as though it might be listening, understanding. 'Maybe it's because there's holes in the ground, so sounds are bigger?' He pauses, then squares his shoulders. 'I made one decision, anyway. I'm not going back to that school any more.' He pushes his glasses up his nose. 'I expect they will say something to my gran. But I'm not going back.'

'And why's that?'

'No point. They still call me those old names. The teachers are hopeless. Apart from Mr Evans. He's OK. History some-times, I liked the coal mines stuff. Sometimes. But I won't be here long, anyway.'

'Going back home soon then?'

There is no answer. Laddy just spits into the water again, and again. Then he picks up his drum, hugs it. 'That's the problem. I don't know which home to go back to.'

There is a conversation then, with only the river listening in, the boy and the beggar leaning on the rail, watching the water flowing as quiet as the air – about arguments heard through floorboards when boys are thought to be asleep. About the boy lying there, worrying the arguments were his fault. And if he wasn't here then maybe they wouldn't have anything to argue about. About coming to stay for a while with his gran and packing his own case, and getting that wrong like everything else. About phone calls from his mam and dad to his gran late at night when he is upstairs. About that teacher at home, the one Laddy knows but doesn't like at all moving in with his mam. His dad moving out. About talking with his mam the other night. And Dad phoning last night, and saying he's trying to find another house but it isn't easy, and Laddy having to decide who he wants to live with most of the time. And

Gran saying of course he will be with his mam, that's where he belongs, but Laddy doesn't know any more, 'That's what I mean – they keep talking about decisions, Mr Jenkins.'

The beggar shakes his head. 'I wish I could help, Maggot. I'm not much good at those.'

'I wish home could just be like it was before.'

'Before?'

'When they didn't fight.'

'I suppose everything has to change, some time.'

'That's what Dad said. He said it will be like starting again, but that's scary.'

'It is. Maybe new things are?'

Laddy sighs. 'That's like all the lights have gone out as well. Does everyone find new things scary? Or is it just me?'

'Oh no, Maggot. It is not just you, believe me. Whether they say so, or not. Ebenezer won't be there for ever, and what will I do then? Whatever it is, I can't see it and that's a worry. And I can tell you, being dropped into the dark down Kindly Light that first time was very scary. My stomach still jumps when I think about it.'

Laddy almost smiles, 'What was it like?' and the beggar taps the rail of the footbridge as both he and his stomach remember.

'New lads were fair game, that's what everyone said. When there was a new lad, the banksmen let the gear run so fast you left your guts up top while you dropped – the men laughing when the cage rattled like the devil passing the other coming up, and the sound of the hawsers singing. Fast and singing into blackness, apart from the lights at pit bottom to welcome boys who heaved their breakfast bread and jam onto the ground and had to go hungry then. That's what they said. I was so worried about that. Didn't want to look stupid, not in front of Da's friends . . .'

Ianto Passchendaele Jenkins gazes away down the valley. 'Sometimes, they'd slam on the brakes when the cage was halfway down the shaft, just for a laugh. I tell you – I was so scared about that first ride it kept me awake the night before. Then when I did get to sleep, the worrying woke me, early.

The boots that were once Mr Ernest Ellis's were beside the bed that morning, dropped any old how by Maggot. Like great boats they were. So I would have some of Da's old wool socks over my own and some rag to wrap round so my feet did not slip about. All laid out on the floor ready. My da had a word with Mr Thomas Edwards from along the way, a friend, and a hewer as well, and Mr Thomas Edwards was to watch out for me, Da said. Be my butty while I was learning. I was hoping to goodness Da hadn't told him I was frightened.

Lying there, I was, Maggot still asleep and snoring, listening to the old robin scolding to himself in the early hours. Must have been the one from over the way, telling off the other birds who came close. And the sound was like a beam of light. I don't remember much of my mam, Maggot, she seemed so very far away. But when I heard that bird I remembered her telling me about birds and their signs, and my da laughing at her. But this sound of his singing, it was sharp, breaking the darkness.

I could hear a stream. I could always hear that stream in the night if the wind was in the east and the babies not crying in the houses up the street. And if the wind is in the east – even now the railway tunnel up by the Brychan sounds loud and ghostly, calling out to the town that's its time to get up even when it isn't.'

The beggar stops talking, and the boy smiles. 'Kept me awake when I was smaller, staying with Gran, that tunnel. Not now. I'm used to it.' He hugs his drum. 'I used to be afraid of the old lady up there – Batty Annie – but I'm not now. I wonder what time it is?'

Ianto Passchendaele Jenkins taps his watch with no hands, 'It doesn't matter what the time is, if you've nowhere to go. It is a beautiful thing, that is.' And he continues the story.

'It was before five in the morning that first day, and I was up and dressed, those boots on my feet, standing there in the bedroom with the Maggot lying in the bed, half-awake, "Bring me something back, Ianto?" and I said something like, "Bring you something back? What do you expect there is down there? Diamonds?" and he shifted over to my place in the bed nearest the wall, and he curled up in the warm spot, and pulled the covers round his ears.

I was going to the stairs and my da called from his room, "You do everything they tell you, mind, and don't you be a nuisance to anyone." And I knew what he was thinking, that I would make a fool of him, and I would not be a good collier, but there was nothing I could do about what he was thinking.

Downstairs, I drank some water from the kitchen tap, and I washed my face. There was a mirror just there, on a nail, an old mirror all speckled and dark, my da's shaving mirror. I looked at myself. The marks in the glass made my face dim as anything and I was no longer a boy in that mirror but an old man, shadows creeping down his face. I filled Da's water bottle, and cut two slices of bread, spread them with some jam, and I wrapped them in a handkerchief like Da had told me – in case the men played games with the cage . . .

And then there was Mr Thomas Edwards outside the back door, stamping his feet, "Ready, young man?" and I looked round the kitchen in case it would disappear if I didn't, and I took Da's cap from its nail and put it on my head, and went out into the morning.

I remember too, as soon as I was outside, my bootlace came undone, or the sock inside slipped, so I put my water bottle on the wall to fix my boot. And I was just about to walk down the alley when Mr Thomas Edwards coughed, and I turned, and there he was grinning and holding my bottle out, "You'll need this . . ."'

Laddy Merridew bites a nail. 'He sounds nice. Did they make the cage do things?'

'He was, and no, they didn't. Maybe because I was my da's boy, who knows?'

'And what was it like down there? Was it dark like you thought? Were there horses?'

'Questions . . . just like my brother the Maggot, you are, and not just the way you look, either. I will tell you, but not today. Got work to do, remember?' Ianto Jenkins taps his watch with no hands. 'Time you were off, I'd say.' He taps the rail again as well. 'I could take a walk down to Kindly Light. Haven't been there in a long while.'

Laddy steps off the footbridge. 'Thanks, Mr Jenkins.' He walks a short way, then turns back, holds out the drum.

'Can I leave this at Ebenezer? Maybe I could play it there sometimes? It's a long way down to the pit every time.'

The beggar changes his mind about going to Kindly Light for his legs are tired, and he and the boy walk back to the town together, up to Ebenezer Chapel, to find a somewhere, an old cupboard perhaps, or a place the floorboards are loose, to hide a drum.

The Window Cleaner's Tale

i

WHEN THE WIND IS in the north it lifts the sweet wrappers from the gutters and whisks them through the rusted gates of the park, over grass that is not kept off despite the signs but is pitted and mud-puddled now under the old conker trees. Judah Jones will be cleaning windows up his ladder and the wind will send cold fingers round his anklebones. Then it may leave Judah Jones's ankles to themselves, as if calling by at all was a mistake. It will set the last geraniums nodding and dropping red petals in their beds, and test the leaves of a tree by the park gate. And wherever he is in the town, the Window Cleaner will pause and raise a licked finger into the wind, 'Leaves for Judah Jones, is it?'

These leaves are not the burned leaves of autumn, no, not at all. They are pale and bloodless leaves, silvered. They are hanging by thread-stalks, twisting like milk-teeth on their last rootlets . . . until they drop and chatter over the grass. Off they go, dancing with the sweet wrappers, to pile in late confetti against the twin metal benches of Gwendolyn and Gwynneth Watkins, spinsters both.

Judah Jones may appear in his flat cap and his fingerless gloves pushing his bicycle through the park, his window-cleaning ladder tied against the spine of the bike. He will rest the bike gentle against one of the Miss Watkins and he'll pat her cold bones. He will take his bucket from the handlebars and bend to pick up the leaves by the handful, all pale and crisping. He will pull out the sweet wrappers, the silver paper and the bright red of a Kit Kat's coat. And he will drop the leaves into the bucket.

Tutt Bevan the Undertaker and his stick short-cutting through the park, maybe retracing his steps from the other day, may wave, 'Evening, Judah, chill in the air today?' but Judah Jones will be so caught up with the collecting of the leaves that all Tutt Bevan hears in reply is, 'Perfect.'

As he goes home via a few last windows in Maerdy Street, Judah Jones imagines all the windows of the town mosaiced with autumn leaves. Leaves that still rustle when the wind blows. And the people in the street no longer able to peer into the houses, and the people in their front rooms in Bethesda Mansions, Plymouth Street and Maerdy Street able to get away with anything and no one would have to know. But it is not like that.

As he pushes his bike towards The Cat on the corner of Mary Street he thinks of the rooms in the houses, the rooms he sees when he is cleaning windows, fires warm in their front-room grates and budgies dozing in cages, dining tables with velveteen skirts, and cups of tea with plates to match, on trays with slices of lardy cake and butter. Dusty bedrooms with working trousers over bedside chairs, thrown with a petticoat, one stocking, the other curled on the carpet. And lumpen pillows on unmade beds, their dips and valleys as familiar as songs.

* * *

He will round the corner by The Cat all ready to go down the hill home to Plymouth Terrace. And he will find Peter Edwards and the men waiting outside The Cat for the door to open and let them in, colliers who are not colliers now for there is no longer any call for them to do what they do . . . and they have left their sitting and scowling on the steps of the statue outside the Library, and instead here they are and they have not seen Judah and his bike.

Judah Jones will stop all sudden. He will creep back unseen, back round the corner where his bike and himself will be leaned against the brick wall, and where he listens to the voices of the men, colliers from Deep Pit up the valley, once. Among them there is one that rings in his ears like bells wheedling him to prayer. The voice of Peter Edwards rippling and deep as dreams. But not talking to him, oh no indeed.

'Here you are boys, money in my cap, if you please.'

There is a laugh. 'I w-w-will be shot, m-mun.'

'That's right is it, Twp Two Two Shoes? And who will be doing the shooting of a great lump like Twp then? Not that slip of a wife?'

'This is one coin only for a p-p-p-pint of milk to f-f-fetch home,'

'Shut up, Twp. In the cap. Drop it in by here,'

And there is a small sound, a coin dropping into a cap, onto another, another . . . and Peter Edwards's voice again: 'You can tell her now . . . tell her you dropped your money . . . and you have, see, without a word of a lie. Grand. That will do us two pints between five . . .'

Judah Jones has to stay where he is, and he turns and presses his forehead against the bricks. In his head he sees a man. In the dark, skin gleaming like he's still deep underground, black gold in the shadows, the muscles moving under his skin, alive and swelling. Judah smells the living sweat of that skin, and the coaldust, and salt, and tobacco, and he sees his own hand reaching out in the dark, his washed white fingers reaching for the man's arm, all solid and warm and glistening . . . he spreads his fingers to brush the skin, the hair, and his fingers meet nothing but a wall of bricks.

He's lucky perhaps, because the door of The Cat opens, he hears it open, and he hears that voice, 'About time, waiting until Doomsday we'll be soon enough . . .' and then those voices fading, 'Two pints, Maggie, there's a love . . .'

Then the voices fade completely, to let Judah Jones collect himself together, and peer round the corner, then carry on pushing his bike past The Cat with its closed door, and on down the hill to Plymouth Terrace.

And in Plymouth Terrace is there a fire waiting in the grate? Is there washing left on the line to be collected in with the evening and a kiss by the back door? There is not. The grate is empty and as cold as his bed, and the back door is put on a chain once he is inside. There are no petticoats over bedside chairs, nor stockings curled like mice on the carpet, and there never have been. And nor has there ever been the beauty of black streaks from under the nails of a collier called Peter Edwards on the pale soap in the dish by the kitchen sink.

He has been seen, Judah Jones has, in the park in the early morning collecting his buckets of leaves. Seen by those who are up while the mist still lies on the grass like a shroud. The mist parting and gathering round Judah's boots as he walks, his footsteps leaving small whirlpools that eddy and waver then close up slow behind him when he's not looking. And by the gate, a small boy pulled along by the hand may look back and ask, 'Mam? What is he doing then? Mam? Can we go on the swings?'

His mam may cough and say there's no time for that when all the way down the hill she was saying there was plenty. And this morning, the old iron rocking horse on its square of tarmac will go unridden and the swings on their brown chains will go unswung. 'But Mam?' There will be no reply. And the boy will not know if it is his mam or the man collecting leaves is to blame for his disappointment.

Later, when the mist has gone, when he has gathered all the pale leaves he can find today on the grass, Judah Jones will carry on cleaning his windows. He will not push his bicycle up the hill to the rows of houses in Garibaldi Street, Maerdy Street and Tredegar Street, not today, oh no, not today, not tomorrow, or the next day. Not while those silver leaves are coming down off the tree by the old park gates, helped by the wind.

Instead he will go down the hill to the High Street and set up his ladder against the stone walls of the shops, and knock and set the bells ringing on their springs to ask for warm water. And he will take his cloths and clean the windows of the General Stores and the sweet shop, the chip shop, the Public Library and the Undertaker's, where he will wait until Tutt Bevan is out for a while not to hear the sound of his annoyance at a coffin lid that will not shut. He will knock at the door of the dressmaker's and shine the glass so the cards of buttons, the lace ribbons, the petersham and the unfinished blouse on its canvas body can see out proper. Next it will be the Savings

Bank, and Tommo Price may answer his ring at the door, and Judah Jones will ask if they want their windows done, and Tommo Price will agree, and for an hour or so all the windows that watch over the ledgers will be sudded and polished, but it will make no difference at all to the figures on those pages. And all the while there is a bucket of leaves over the handle-bars of his bike where it waits all patient against the wall.

After the Savings Bank Judah Jones pushes his bike past the cinemagoers waiting on the cinema steps, and there may be a few who notice the bucket of leaves, and they pull at the sleeves of those standing next to them to ask did they notice that as well. And Judah Jones will go over to where his soul has been waiting to go all day. The grey and square-stoned chapel called Ebenezer, empty these twenty years.

At Ebenezer Chapel, he will lean the bike against the wall in the chapel porch where the beggar Ianto Passchendaele Jenkins sleeps at night under newspapers. If Ianto is there, Judah Jones will raise a finger to his cap, 'A lot to do, a lot to do, mind . . .' and the beggar will agree, lying on his bench, his hands behind his head. 'Indeed.'

Judah Jones begins to wash the windows, just like anywhere else, outside, going up and down his ladder and polishing the glass with his cloths, fetching water from the Savings Bank, the cinema. And when they are done, does he go home? Does he take his ladder and tie it to his bicycle and go home to Plymouth Terrace? He does not. At Ebenezer Chapel he cleans the windows once a year, not only from the outside where they collect the street grime and dust like everywhere else, but from the inside, to clean off them whatever collects on windows in empty chapels.

Judah Jones will stand for a while outside the chapel and wait with his head on one side, listening for sound, but there will be none. He will enter all quiet with his buckets, the one holding a little clean water, the other leaves, and he will tug the doors to behind him.

He will wait for his eyes to accustom themselves, and his feet will echo on the old floorboards. He will clean the grime from the images: Thomas and Thaddeus frowning, Matthew counting his coins. And the rest. He will clean them all with water and a cloth, all except one right at the back of the chapel, waiting in the halflight.

Judah Jones will go to that one window at the back and gaze up at the figure on the glass. Then, after a long while, he will take from his jacket pocket a twist of paper filled with salt, and pour some into the bucket of leaves. He will take the bucket of clean water and sprinkle a little over the leaves and the salt – and wait a few moments. Then he picks a handful of damp leaves from his bucket, and reaches up to brush them gentle over the glass, rubbing at it until the leaves crumble, fall to dust and rain onto the flagstones beneath. Handful after handful he takes until his leaves are all gone, and he will do this every day while there are leaves from the tree near the park gate still tumbling over the grass to pile against the cold benches. And all the while he looks up at the half-figure caught in the window, and in the eyes of the Window Cleaner there is something more than praise.

The Window Cleaner's Tale

ii

AND MAYBE THE CINEMAGOERS, later in the day, all bundled on the steps of the cinema, their breath rising from their mouths like souls that have forgotten something, will want to know about the Window Cleaner who carries an old bucket of autumn leaves into chapel. Who adds water and salt, and wipes them over a window.

And if they ask it right, and if they rustle a toffee bag deep in a pocket, and if the rustle comes to the ears of the old man begging there, he will lean against the peeling wall and shake his head, maybe at the questioner and maybe not. He will smile at the boy Laddy Merridew slipping into the queue then changing his mind and sitting on the steps to listen, and will begin.

'Listen with your ears, I have a story for them, see, about little Meggie Jones who came before Judah and who started something that only Judah Jones will finish.

A long while back this is, mind . . . and little Meggie was living with her new husband Geraint Jones in their rented house in Plymouth Terrace, wed only a six-month and Meggie carrying their first child already. Her Geraint put his arms round her every morning in the kitchen before he left for work as a collier, to look into her face so close she would laugh.

"My Meggie, don't do that, don't push me away . . ." for he looked into her face to take the shine of her eyes down to the dark of Kindly Light pit where he was a hewer.

A beautiful man he was, mind, that Geraint Jones, gone down when he was just a lad to work in Kindly Light a few years since – alongside an experienced collier, Billy Price, a neighbour old enough to be his own father. Treated Geraint like a son, Billy Price did. And he had his own son, too – but wouldn't let him be a collier, not at all. But that is a different story. So Billy Price was like Geraint's own father then, and treated Meggie Jones like his own daughter.

And there came a day when the mountain rebelled, and there was a great fall of stone in that pit under the mountain, and a clashing of rocks, and a small terrible spark and gas that found a handful of black dust . . . an explosion then, racing its fire along the roadways. And the force of it all, the smoke and the dust billowed from the shafts to hang over Kindly Light and up the valley towards the town, like a message no one wanted to open.

And then, round the pit head, waiting, the women, the wives and the mothers all whitefaced and practising being lonely in their hearts, waiting for their men to come up.

Some men did come up. Some were brought up alive and they staggered out into the light all shrunken somehow. And later they brought up those men who had gone, and their friends carried them through the waiting women, who looked at the faces of the men all dark and sleeping to find their own. "Is it my George?"

"Aww, my Harry …"

Later still they brought up the men who were burned down there. And some – oh, terrible – no one could tell who they were at all. The searching for a name was too much.

And as they all came up into an air they would not have a use for, not now, their bodies were carried through the crowd and laid on the floor of the lamp room, their women following to gather round the doors, waiting to be let in to find the man they slept with not two nights since.

With each rise of the cages, little Meggie Jones's heart beat a little faster for it was just possible that her man was hidden, and asleep, or that he had not gone down at all today, but had gone to another place, and was in the next valley, walking, perhaps, dreaming, forgetting to come home.

But this was dreaming indeed. He was not in the next valley, and he was not found anywhere, not among the men who held each other like brothers as they died … not down there at all. Not at all … he was never found despite the looking and the looking, not brought up to the lamp room. Ever. He was truly lost under the mountain and Billy Price as well, gone together. Maybe lost under the falls of stone? Maybe crept together into a gap that seemed safe, "Here, Geraint, follow me …" only for that space to collapse a little later? Who is to say? Never found at all. And what did Meggie Jones have left to do but go back home, to creep into a cold bed and turn her face to the wall?

A few little days later, in Ebenezer Chapel just here, they gathered to sing for the dead, and most of those dead were in their boxes, their faces covered for the last time. Meggie Jones sat at the back in her good coat that would not close now because of the baby coming, and she watched the other wives with their men all boxed and neat and named ready for the ground, but she had no one . . . even like that, in their boxes.

At that very moment, the sunlight found its way through the chapel window above her head and shone onto her, onto her hand where her ring shone back in reply . . . and she looked up, and what did she see but the shadow of a man looking down on her, watching her with a half-smile. And he was beautiful.

It was as though the window was speaking to her, right deep inside . . . where only she could hear it. And when she came to, the chapel was empty, all the others gone off to bury their men, leaving her in the dark. Meggie Jones had no one to bury, so she stayed there, stayed in her chair, raising her eyes to that window above her head where she thought to have seen a man.

She wanted to see him. She had to see. And she climbed up with her baby all heavy inside her, and stood on that old chair to reach up to her window, and with a nail she scratched in the dust, in one corner. And right there the light shone through the dirt of ages, and that light was green and gold.

And little Meggie Jones thought she should clean the glass to see the colours, the image, the man – and she climbed down and searched the dark and closed chapel to find a cloth, to find how to do this, her task, while the other wives had their husbands to bury.

But she found no cloths nor water, and out she went into the evening light, thinking to go home, back to Plymouth Terrace, to the house she didn't even know if she could stay in now, to fetch a cloth from the yard . . . but there was no need for her to go all that way at all. For in the chapel porch, piled on the flagstones, the wind had brought leaves.

Leaves from the wild cherry trees on the hills perhaps. Bright and shining, reds and golds, flat and perfect . . . and to Meggie Jones they would do fine to wipe the grime from that window, and she took the leaves, and brought them into the chapel. She took a chair and set it right under the window. And the man in the window that was and was not her husband looked down at her as she climbed onto the chair and began to clean the glass with a handful of leaves the colour of blood.

She stood on that chair with her unborn child, and she cleaned that window, not raising her eyes to the glass, not properly, for this was hallowed. She only rubbed a small circle down in the corner of the glass covered with its grey coat of dust. Then with a single leaf she made the letters of her own name. But now . . . in that first little circle, where Meggie Jones thought to find words, maybe a verse, instead, she found grass as soft as hair, each blade as real as tears. She found buttercups and whinberries where the gold shone through her name. The things she knew from places deep in the folds of the hills where perhaps she lay with her man and where maybe her child was begun.

But oh look – back on the ground among the grass and the flowers, see? There among the flowers of the Beacons, were the feet of her Geraint overgrown with ivy fronds, his skin brown from the sun, the nails square and naked and strong.

And little Meggie Jones ran her fingers over those toes and cried for the first time that day, remembering her man and knowing finally that she would not see his toes again . . . and she wiped her eyes with a handful of fresh leaves before going back to her task.

So you see it was with tears that she washed the window,

and it was her tears and those leaves that worked away at the glass, taking away the grime of years, until she saw her man standing there, her collier Geraint Jones after all, come back from under the ground in his working clothes and dark with coal but barefoot, his face as beautiful as it ever was.

And little Meggie Jones found not only her man under candlewax and dust, and not only flowers, oh no. Her leaves set free the birds from the Beacons ... a merlin and its mate, tumbling in the grey sky. Crows catching the wind. A buzzard, heavy as her child, floating on the up-draught.'

At this point the cinemagoers, who will have forgotten all about the showing, and who have been looking past the story-teller, looking at the chapel just there, with its porch and its bench all tidy, are thinking perhaps they will go and see, for the door is open, and what is Judah doing now?

But the story is only half done, the storyteller has stopped and is back begging, holding out his cap to the new arrivals, so the listeners have to send someone off to fetch him a coffee with two sugars, and they wheedle like children, 'Aww, stop your begging now, and tell us about the buzzards? Was there really buzzards in chapel then?'

Ianto Passchendaele Jenkins will sigh and he will stop his begging and sit on the step,

'Buzzards, now who was talking about buzzards? I was talking about windows, and leaves, and in the end, I was talking about a man. For little Meggie Jones found all sorts in that window, she did indeed, and it is very true that there were buzzards, but there was also a man.

See, under all that blanket of dust there was a man as sure as there was a man in her bed a few days back, and as sure as that man's child was pushing at her now. She ran those wild cherry leaves down his thighs, their rough trews all transparent in the glass, and as she cleaned them of their dust she could see the town through those thighs, the houses, the High Street, the square, the shops, the men and women now coming back down from the new cemetery on the hillside, walking in knots, arms round, and through his jacket she saw boys playing again in the street.

But his face. It is his face that really mattered, for here was this window that had been in Ebenezer Chapel for years, and in that face what did Meggie Jones see, as she wiped it clear of its dust with her leaves? She saw her Geraint's cheek, unshaven. A hollow where her man bit the inside of that cheek for fear. A bruise all purple over his cheekbone where the mountain hit him. The birds were gone, and the hill, the flowers and the grass. All gone. What there was in the end was just the dark of coal seams, the shine of water dripping, the shine of black dust in candlelight, and a man unshaven with the face of her Geraint, looking out of the window straight into the face of his wife and the mother of his child. But he was alone, see? Alone in the dark, and under a mountain, in memory of all colliers who do not come back.'

Ianto Passchendaele Jenkins stops for a moment, shaking his head. Then he sighs. 'And that is nearly the end, except for one thing. That if you have love to give it has to go somewhere, for it cannot go nowhere. So little Meggie Jones gave her love to a window. I understand that, even if you don't. Her man was lost and alone under the mountain and he came back to her in a window.

So she looked after the windows then. Proper, all tidy. But whenever the wild cherry trees dropped their leaves, she took them, and she cleaned that window with them like they were the softest of cloths. Her child does the same. And her child is old now – the Window Cleaner Judah Jones. And maybe, like his mam, he sees who he needs to see. Who is to say? Who is to say, indeed.'

The cinemagoers will sigh and say, 'Aww, there's lovely,' and make plans to go maybe now and maybe later to the chapel to see the window. And they will ask if Judah Jones is doing the same and if his leaves are letting the window breathe and become warm under his touch ... the beggar just sighs and says nothing.

The Window Cleaner's Tale

iii

TODAY, JUDAH JONES HAS pushed his bicycle through the park and the wind has blown the leaves from the trees near the gate, leaves that glint like silver coins. It has sent them scuttling over the grass to wait for Judah, piled against the benches of the Misses Watkins. And when he arrives, he smiles for no one in particular, 'Leaves for Judah Jones, is it?'

Maybe this very day a miracle will happen. Maybe today the man might stir in the window and a muscle will move under the painted cloth of his shirt. Maybe the fingers will flex to send blood to the tips. And maybe the chin will tilt, the head turn a little and the eyes will gaze straight into those of the old Window Cleaner.

So Judah Jones has taken the silver leaves and filled his bucket. He has said he is sorry to the houses in Maerdy Street and Tredegar Terrace, and will come back in a day or two. And he has gone to the High Street, cleaned the windows of the General Stores, the chip shop and the dressmaker's, the Undertaker's and the Savings Bank, and he has leaned his bike against the stone bench in Ebenezer Chapel porch and washed the outside of the chapel windows.

Now he is inside the chapel and has washed most of the windows of their grime. He has dampened the leaves with clean water and a little salt, just like Meggie Jones's tears before him, and he has waited for a while in the gloom. And now, he is reaching up to his window to wipe it with leaves.

Over time, the window to Judah has grown more beautiful, the face shining in the halflight glistening as though it has pores and sweat, the chin dark as though there is a beard coming. He reaches up to touch the man's cheek and wonders if the glass is cold still, or whether today there will be warmth under his fingers.

But Judah Jones has cleaned that window with his leaves every year for so long that the glass is as thin as a thought. The face of the man on the glass is as beautiful as a thought as well, every brushstroke. Every part of the painting transparent, delicate. Every flower, every stone on the hills. Light as a small shell on the beaches, the nail of a baby, the membrane inside the egg of a wren. So full of beauty in its transparency that Judah Jones is crying as he rubs his leaves over the body of his collier.

Is he fading then, the collier in the window, so like Peter Edwards? Does Judah Jones see that and stop? Does he feel the tremble in the thinnest of glass? He does not. The leaves brought the man to life for little Meggie Jones and they will do so for Judah. They will.

It is not long before the leaves are brittle and crumbling again, and they fall to the floor of the chapel in silver rain. The painting is so faint now that he can only see his man if he moves from side to side and catches the light exactly . . . and Judah wonders if this is the miracle starting, that there will be nothing before there is something . . . for now he can just see him, the hands of his collier square and strong, his feet bare on the grass, and the flowers of the Beacons that were bright with colour are now ghost flowers below two silver merlins tumbling in a silver sky.

This very day something is happening as Judah always knew it would, and he shuts his eyes and brushes his man with silver leaves, and dreams of being held by those arms, just once.

He shuts his eyes and runs his fingers down the arms of his collier, to feel the muscles of Peter Edwards taut under the skin. And the thighs, he feels them tremble as his own are trembling now. And he moves his fingers to the face, and feels the chin, the lips, the nose, the fluttering of closed eyelids, and back to the mouth, and Judah sighs, for the glass is warm at last, the lips have parted. He feels the beat of a pulse and the warmth of breath on his fingers. Then he opens his eyes.

But there is only empty glass. There are no flowers, no trees, no merlins tumbling ghostly in a pale sky. No wild cherry trees on the hills. No cliffs of coal. No man.

Judah puts his hand to the window and it is warm, as though it is fed with veins, unseen, running in spiders' webs through the glass. He stands on his chair to put his face close to where his man was, to turn his head from side to side for there must be the shadow of a man, a trace of his breath in the chapel air, the indents made by a single hair imbedded in the window. But there is not. And Judah Jones rests his forehead against the window, where the face of the collier was . . . and he places his mouth so gently where the mouth of the collier was, but his lips meet only glass.

He presses and presses, thinking maybe, deep in the layers,

the man is there ... but the window is no thicker than the membrane inside that wren's egg. It can no longer bear the weight of a kiss. And it shatters.

All that is left is a Window Cleaner called Judah Jones, standing on an old chair in an empty chapel, a window broken. The evening breeze lifting his hair, tender as breathing. He has not noticed yet, but his lip is cut, and down his chin is running a thin stream of blood, living, bright and perfect.

Through the broken window all there is to see is the High Street, its tarmac and gutters, shop fronts and grey roofs. The people going home to their fires. And the cinema. A boy in glasses standing there, Laddy Merridew come down to talk to Ianto Passchendaele Jenkins, looking up at the window and holding his breath. While on the steps of the cinema Ianto Jenkins himself is nodding and nodding.

In the Park, on the Bench Dedicated to Miss Gwynneth Watkins

THE NEXT DAY, IN the afternoon, the cinema is closed while someone talks to the machinery, and the wind blows the beggar Ianto Passchendaele Jenkins up the High Street and down again, then all the way up the hill behind the shops to the park. He has his lunch in his pocket, lamb and beetroot on white, to eat later.

There in the park is Laddy Merridew, sitting on Gwynneth Watkins again, his school satchel thrown open on the grass, his notebook and pencil forgotten on the seat. Laddy is hunched over, reading a letter that looks as though it has been taken out of its envelope, folded and unfolded and read a hundred times. He does not notice the beggar sitting down beside him on the bench, until Ianto Passchendaele Jenkins takes his sandwich out of his pocket and unwraps it. Laddy looks up, 'Where did you come from, Mr Jenkins?'

'Who knows? Now, you mean, or then?'

Laddy folds the letter up and stuffs it in its envelope, then back in his pocket. He does not answer the question. 'I missed your story today. What was it?' He picks up his notebook.

'Nothing, Maggot. There wasn't one. Nobody asked.'

Laddy examines his hands carefully and bites a nail that has already been bitten well and truly. 'My dad came to see me.'

Then he stops. 'How come you live in the porch? I mean, why not live inside?'

'Why?'

'I was wondering, how much it matters where you live, after all?'

'Did your dad talk about things, then?'

'No, not exactly. He drove all the way here after work, that was nice. I think he'd talked to Gran before I got there. Then he had to drive back. It's a long way he came.' He pats his pocket. 'He left this when he went.' Laddy is quiet for a while. 'He's leaving, Mr Jenkins – I mean, he's going to live some-where else. Manchester, I think. This letter is meant to explain but it doesn't. He said he couldn't explain, because he didn't understand it all himself, and wasn't going to make things up. He won't lie to me, that's what he says. Look . . .', and he starts to pull the letter out of his pocket.

Ianto Jenkins stops him. 'No, Maggot. That's private, it's just for you, isn't it?'

There is silence for a while. A few leaves skitter over the grass, and Laddy pulls his coat round. Then, he clears his throat. 'But I like it that he won't make things up.' He pushes his glasses back up his nose. 'What about that window in the chapel?'

The beggar nods. 'Icarus Evans came this morning to board it up.'

'What will happen?'

'Nothing much, I shouldn't think.'

'Why?'

'Ebenezer won't be there for ever, Maggot.'

'What do you mean?'

'I expect there are plans. They keep saying they are going to pull it down.'

Laddy frowns, says nothing. Then, 'You didn't answer my question. Why do you stay out in the porch, Mr Jenkins? Why not live inside where it's warmer?'

'And darker. The dark still reminds me too much.'

'What was it like down there, Mr Jenkins? You said you'd tell me, the other day. Can you remember?'

'Oh Maggot. Can I remember? It is a better question to ask me if there is room for much else in my head sometimes. I remember it like it was yesterday – I remember him asking me too, over and over again, to tell him what it was like – the other Maggot, my brother, and I tried to tell him more than once. It wasn't easy.'

Laddy says nothing. So Ianto Jenkins clears his throat, hands Laddy Merridew a liquorish Catherine wheel and tries again to explain.

'Like a great cathedral it was, Maggot, down there. But this was a cathedral with few lamps except what the men brought, and almost no windows.

For there were windows, down there. Probably still are, too. There were the tunnel openings leading off every so often all blank and empty. Part of the wall and not part of it. Letting the outside be seen but not felt from inside, and letting the inside be seen and not felt from outside, and that is the strangest thing.

There were pillars too, Maggot, down there, holding up the roof. Black and solid. And as I moved my lamp from side to side the light came back at me from the surfaces like so many black and blank mirrors until I was almost dazzled and Thomas Edwards laughed at me, I remember, "Ianto Jenkins, will you stop looking at the walls? You will be seeing the Devil himself . . ."

But I had to keep looking. And listening, as well, for it was the noisiest place I had been in my life. And each noise did not just come at you once, but twice, three times, echoes, echoes, see? Shouts, for the voices of the colliers never seemed to be just talking. The horses . . .

Kindly Light was dark, it was indeed. It was full of things dreadful too – that first day I saw a horse fall as it strained to pull a load of coal to pit bottom, and it chose a place where the roadway was not level and the truck carried on and ran the poor horse down, breaking its back. I will not forget the screams then, believe me.

But for all that, and it is a strange thing to say, now, it was the beauty of the place that rose up above the rest. There was no other word for it, Maggot, a deep, swelling, black as night beauty that was heavy as the whole world.

The floor was dangerous though, and with dead Mr Ernest Ellis's boots being too big I was always tripping up, until Mr Thomas Edwards my butty said I would be better off with no boots at all, but I was not having that. Mind you, Maggot, the floor of this great underground cathedral was pitted and running with water, and that water turned the lamplight into a great carpet of stars . . . but Mr Ellis's boots saw off the water something wonderful.

The roof down there was low and frowning – so low that Thomas Edwards had to bend and hunch forwards to walk down the tunnels for he was too tall, his lamp sent shadows flying along the walls – and sometimes, he knocked his hat on the roof and it fell forward over his eyes and there was such a roaring then. Oh and I learned some choice words in those few days.

I said all this and I asked my brother the other Maggot if he could see it all in his own head now I had tried to draw it for him, but all I got was a snore in return.

In the dark with the rain beating against the bedroom window it was hard to stop thoughts . . . they are like the wild ponies on the hills. I carried on thinking about cathedrals and the sound of singing from the tunnels as Da said it would be, but always above the singing and shouting there was the creaking of the wood lining the tunnel walls and now and again a loud crack as one piece of wood protested against the weight of the mountain. As I would do. I had not expected that.

And also there were shouts and yells from far away, and the sound of picks and hammers and drilling, and the trundling of the trucks on the rails. And above all these sounds there was another that I heard, insistent, and high, the hiss and thud, the beat of the great engines, or there again, it may just have been the mountain breathing.

And the smells down there too . . . well, that was not really like the great cathedral above, there was the stink of the horses and there was coal dust and not just the dust on the pews and the prayer books. That dust does not have to be dampened before it is safe, does it? And in the above ground cathedral there is never the smell of pigs, just faint . . . so you lifted your nose to it and snuffled like the pigs themselves – then it was gone.'

* * *

237

Ianto Passchendaele Jenkins stops, as Laddy Merridew has fallen asleep, his head on the beggar's shoulder.

'Ah, but I must be losing my touch.' He puts a hand on Laddy's shoulder, to wake him. 'I sent you to sleep.'

The boy shakes his head, slowly. 'No, I don't think so . . . I didn't sleep much last night. I was worrying.'

'I'm sorry.'

'It's not your fault. I was worrying that people lie all the time. But you don't, at least, I don't think.'

'Thank you for that.'

There is a pause, as if Laddy is not sure, after all. 'You were talking about Ebenezer Chapel?'

'No.' Ianto Jenkins stands up and looks down over the town.

Laddy stretches. 'What will happen if it is pulled down? It's your home, Mr Jenkins.'

'Only for a while.'

'Where will you go?'

'Who knows? Who knows, indeed.'

Laddy Merridew picks up his schoolbag, pats his pocket to make sure his letter is still there. 'Maybe see you tomorrow, then.' He starts to walk away, then turns to wave, but Ianto Jenkins has already gone.

The Clerk's Tale

i

WHEN THE WIND IS in the east, coming just steady over the coal tips, the tunnel near the Brychan sings like an empty pop bottle. The sound bells about the soot and bricks as if it's caught in the throat of a Dowlais tenor, coaldust and all, then it spills out and flows down the valley to the town. It settles in the alleys between the houses, seeps through the gaps in the windows; a hooooooing that has children crying there's ghosts in the chimney.

Then Ianto Passchendaele Jenkins, in khaki, will stop his begging on the steps of the cinema and lifts a finger into the air, like he's conducting. And he will look up at the windows of the Savings Bank, waiting for Tommo Price to move. And Batty Annie, her hair like string, leaves the door of the old linesman's hut swinging on its one hinge, and stumbles, bent, along the tracks in her slippers waving a shrimping net that's full of nothing but holes. She's fetching her son home. 'Wait for me, Lovely Boy?'

If the wind is stronger, it will set the big old iron rocking horse going on its tarmac square in the park above the High Street, and it squeaks, squeaks, squeaks like there's a football team of little lads astride, some standing. The swings on their brown chains swing with no hands to push. Back, forth. Squeak, squeak. And sheets of newspaper will blow across the streets, swirling with bus tickets and sweet wrappers, piling against the doors of Ebenezer Chapel to make work for no minister now, just the beggar who will have to bend his old bones to pick them all up.

When he hears the hooing of the tunnel, Tommo Price, wearing a suit, looks out of his window at the Savings Bank, as if instead of the High Street he can see all the way to the Brychan on the very edge of town, as if he can see Batty Annie bent into the wind, disappearing behind the houses on her way up the old coal line on her way to the tunnel, 'Wait for me, Lovely Boy.'

Tommo will shake his head before going back to his ledgers. And the figures on the paper will be blown about as he watches. Tommo will push his chair back, call across to Matty Harris, Deputy Manager, that he has to go out. Matty Harris will nod slowly and carry on pulling a thread from his sleeve as he talks to Maggie from The Cat on the telephone one last time, 'I just wanted to hear it from you, Maggie . . .'

By the time Tommo gets to the tunnel, Annie will be inside, her slippers soft on the moss and stones. He'll breathe shallow at the stink of piss. He will see nothing at all as the light is gone, taken by the wind. He will feel it, cold on his face, as he hunches his shoulders, coughs. 'Annie? Come away now . . .'

Tommo will hear her breathing, sharp, each intake like a sob. He'll hear the scritching of her net against the bricks, a scuttle of tiny claws, the damp velvet dark pressing on his ears. And the sound. The hooooing of the wind, louder now. And if Tommo puts his hand on the wall, presses his fingers into the grease and soot, he can feel the wall trembling, still. As if the coal train is coming. 'Annie? I will make you a cup of black tea with sugar?'

Slowly, Tommo's eyes will find Annie, just a shape in the darkness. She will come to Tommo like a bat, holding out the shrimping net, 'Aww, Tommo, can you reach up by there? Just there. I can see him, Tommo . . .' And he will hold her hand and scritch the net across the roof of the tunnel. The dirt will fall onto Annie's upturned face, her threadbare donkey jacket. Dirt, soot, brickdust will all collect in Tommo's hair for he does not look up, oh no.

Maybe the wind will die down a little. The air in the tunnel will settle. Tommo will feel it, the air, it prickles, and the hairs on his neck rise to meet it. 'Come on, love?'

They'll walk back to her hut, Tommo's arm round her shoulders. Annie will have both hands on the net like twin crabs, holding it to her heart.

And when they reach the hut, she will go straight to the little fire just alive in the hearth. She will take the net from her breast, holding it closed with one hand. She will hold it out until it is right where the smoke is rising, right under the chimney open to the sky, and she will take her hand away, shake it, shake it. She will sit on the stool by the warm, and smile. 'My boy's in the chimney, Tommo, fetch the cup of water.'

And Tommo fetches the thin white porcelain cup from the basket in the corner and fills it with water from the outside tap that rattles and chugs against the wall. And he gives it to Annie, not to drink, not at all; but to hold under the chimney for a mirror.

'Is it going to be a moon tonight, Tommo? Will I see my boy?'

Always happens, it does, regular as the clock on the Town Hall sticking at ten past the hour because of a nail. Then, Tommo Price, in his suit, walks back down the hill to the Savings Bank, brushing the dirt from his hair, and leaves Annie talking to her chimney.

He passes by the steps of the cinema under posters with red lips, nods at Ianto Passchendaele Jenkins, the beggar older than the century, and chucks him a penny.

Ianto Passchendaele Jenkins picks the penny out of his cap, holds it right up to his nose and squints at the head on the penny to see if it's a king. It isn't, none of those around now. Only a queen.

He shakes that penny at Tommo like it's a fist because he remembers the day Batty Annie's living son went to play Squash the King in the railway tunnel, skipping school with a friend who didn't believe it could be done, and the tunnel still alive and yawning.

The Clerk's Tale

ii

FOR A COIN OR a toffee, Ianto Passchendaele Jenkins will sell his soul again and tell it to the cinemagoers, counting Annie's son out like he's done a thousand times, wheeling his arms like the true Juggernaut and tapping the face of a watch that has no hands . . .

'Listen with your ears. I have a story for them, see? About Batty Annie who lives in the linesman's hut up on the old coal line. And her living son, Dai, only seven years old, mind, back then. And his best friend, a young lad called Tommo Price, a man now – who still does not believe anything he is told, unless he sees it for himself.

Making the bread in their house in Plymouth Street Annie was, all those years ago, when her son had six minutes left only. Standing on a stool in the kitchen, reaching for the flour, they reckon, and her husband Evan coughing his guts out upstairs – but he still alive, just. And she thinking her Dai was at school, his dinnerpennies given in to the teacher, doing his sums to be a famous lawyer.

But he was not at school. Oh no. Tucked their satchels they

had, behind the railway brickwork, him and his friend Tommo Price, and only a shout or two away from his mother in her kitchen, if the wind is right, there's the shame.

And she with the flour over the table, and the water, and the flour over her hands, and the water over her hands, and the softness of the bread gathering together, and the smell of the yeast, making bread for her men, him only seven and his da who coughs under the blankets at night until Mrs Pym next door rolls over Mr Pym in her curlers and bangs the wall and cries, "Is there no sleep to be had?"

See them now, the boys, Batty Annie's Dai and his best friend Tommo Price, sitting on the rail near the tunnel, eating cherry pip sweeties bought with Tommo Price's dinnerpennies, sticking their tongues out blood red down the middle. Their shoes fresh polished and shining like conkers for there was to be a singing for the real dead king at Ebenezer. Nice boys, both, in their school jumpers all tidy and straight. The one jumper machine-new and bought with money, the other made by Annie, full of love and knots.

Five minutes to go and they reckon Annie was up to the elbows in flour, softness under her nails, gathering it all together and rolling it away with her palms. And Dai was talking about pennies. "I can squash the king, Tommo."

"No, you can't . . ."

"I can so, now then."

And Tommo was pushing him, "Nah, liar, you can't so there . . ."

"I can, so now . . ."

And Dai poked Tommo in the side and he fell off his rail, laughing . . . then they were up and running, the pair of them, along the tracks, jumping the sleepers, hooooing like ghosts. Hooooooo into the mouth of the tunnel, and it just went hooooo back at them, stretching like a waking dragon.

Four minutes and the coal train pulled out of Clydach, wheels spinning and sparking. With thirty trucks of steam coal. And the boys' shirts were all untucked, and their socks were round their ankles, and their shoes were dusty, and Annie's hair had fallen in her eyes and she brushed it away with the back of a hand, and there was a streak of flour over her forehead like a message.

And her boy Dai had fallen on the stones, he'd hurt his knee all bleeding, his dinnerpennies fallen out of his pocket in the halflight. But he wouldn't cry, oh no, with his da coughing at night and all and quite enough for his mam to be going on with thank you.

"I can squash the king, I can . . ."

But his best friend Tommo Price didn't believe him. "I don't believe you," his best friend said, and oh, it mattered. Dai had his pennies in his hand now, off the ground where they were glinting.

Three minutes and Dai, who had never squashed the king said, "The rails shift, see . . ." because he'd heard the big boys talking in the street . . . "The rails shift when the train's coming, Tommo. Up and down they go. Put the penny there too soon, it falls off . . ." And he thought he sounded so knowledgeable. Like an engineer. "Have to wait, see. Have to wait 'til the train's nearly there . . ."

But Tommo Price said, "Nah. You're scared . . . nah, the king won't squash like that. He won't."

They reckon it was two minutes when Annie saw Mrs Pym

in the window opposite, waved, called her in to say sorry about the coughing with a cup of tea ... a bit of hot water in the kettle and she put it on the gas, high. She could try Evan with one, give him two sugars for a treat. Went to the door in her pinny, stood talking ... when her boy started his walk back into the tunnel.

"I will do it, Tommo Price, you'll see ..."

And Tommo Price put his hands on the brick wall and the bricks were trembling. "You will not ..."

And Annie said to Mrs Pym that she'd go up to fetch a cardigan in a minute. "Cold as the grave it is," she said.

One minute and the rails were singing. The train was coming and its sound filled the tunnel and Tommo could not see the boy for the sound and the dark and he shouted to his friend, "Come out ..." But the tunnel was so full of the sound of the train, the grinding and rattling, the screeching and roaring, that his words were swallowed.'

Ianto Passchendaele Jenkins will stop wheeling his arms and hug himself and he'll look at his watch with no hands, tap it and hold it to his ear where it ticks and ticks like a death watch beetle and never tells him anything other than that. 'And him only seven, mind ...'

Then the cinemagoers who have listened with their ears and their eyes – for they have followed the arms wheeling and the head rolling, and the eyes glancing up at the windows of the Savings Bank – want to finish the story.

'Did he squash the king, bach, bless him?'

'Aww, did they find the penny then?'

But the storyteller is off now, back begging he is, as the two o'clock is coming out all smiles and toffees. But he is not finished, and will not be until he tells the other half of the story, about Tommo Price, who never believed what his friend told him.

'You never told us about Tommo . . .' And the cinemagoers look up at the window of the Savings Bank to see Tommo Price duck out of the way fast, maybe to pick up a dropped pencil. Maybe not. And the storyteller continues.

'Listen with those ears then, if you still have them. And let them hear the story of Billy Price, Tommo Price's grandfather. Let them hear the sound of his spade digging the back garden on a day off his work as a collier down Kindly Light pit, and the voice of the widow Ivy Jones next door coming over the wall, "Mr Price, can I have a word?" all formal and careful.

And Billy Price leaning on his spade, glad of the rest, wiping his brow with a handkerchief, "Morning, Ivy. How's this for a busman's holiday? How's that young son of yours?"

"Not so young, Mr Price. Geraint is starting down Kindly Light Monday week."

"Is he now? Well. Make a fine collier too."

"I would be so grateful, Mr Price, if you would watch Geraint for me?"

And Billy Price, who has a son of his own, and who knows Geraint is her only one, "I will, Mrs Jones. I will watch out for Geraint. Not that he'll need it, mind. Safe as houses . . . don't you worry . . ." and they talk for a while after, as well.

Billy Price's son was still at school – a clever boy too and not going to be a collier if his da could help it.

* * *

But that Geraint Jones was the very same one that would be wed only a few years later to little Meggie, remember? That Billy Price was old enough indeed to be his own da. And he did watch for him as he promised his neighbour Ivy Jones, acted as Geraint Jones's butty for a bit, then they were workmates, then friends, despite the years between. Worked alongside each other when they could, Billy Price like the father young Geraint Jones lost when he was a boy.

Worked together, and died together, they reckon. On the day the mountain fell at Kindly Light, Billy Price and Geraint Jones were working on the level that disappeared, as though the mountain was closing up all our roadways, all our little animal tunnels. Their bodies were never found for all the searching. Ivy Jones, bless her, she had no Geraint brought back to her kitchen on a stretcher, like the other mams who lost sons. And Mrs Price, Billy's wife, there was no man carried slow along the street for her, either.

In the chapel by here, at the funeral later – some of those never found had coffins complete with their names. Inside, just a few lumps of coal wrapped in cloth to weigh them down. Geraint Jones and Billy Price had no coffins.

And for Billy Price's family, his wife, his son – there was no body found, so Billy Price may not be dead. His wife, Mrs Price, she would not go to the funeral at all. "Bring me his body. Then I will know."

It was a simple thing. He may have just gone, disappeared as some men do, or he may have been drunk under a hedge not knowing who he was, or the records may be wrong saying he was down the level that collapsed.

And the Price son was the same. The son who was good at numbers, and would not be a collier at all, not if his da could help it – the son who would be Tommo Price's own father, see? If there was no proof then there was no certainty – and maybe that was why he worked afterwards with numbers? Who is to say? And Tommo Price is no different. He has to have proof that things are what they are. Always has. Even when he was a small boy, he would never believe anything unless he could be shown.

And I can tell you this, as well. When Tommo Price was small, a year or two before the death of Annie's son, mind, his grandmother, old Mrs Price, she died herself. Still asking for the body of her husband Billy, too. And there she was, all laid out in her coffin on the table in the front room, her mouth held shut with a black ribbon tied below her chin. And young Tommo – her grandson, only five – he waited until the talking stopped, the watchers gone for their supper, and he crept in with two small glass marbles in his pockets. Pushed those marbles one after the other right up his grandmother's nose, then stood back waiting for her to sit up, and sneeze, and for the marbles to knock on the tabletop. But she never did.'

And the cinemagoers walk away slowly, shaking their heads.

The Clerk's Tale

iii

THE WIND CAN BE in any direction it likes and old Ianto Passchendaele Jenkins in khaki will always be begging on the steps of the cinema. 'Film good, was it? And the toffees? Oh that I had the teeth for a Callard and Bowser, now.'

Mrs Prinny Ellis who takes the ticket money brings him a sandwich with beetroot. A Welshcake. Yesterday's paper. 'He has no bones, Ianto Passchendaele hasn't, mind, or he'd be stiff. No bones under them trousers . . .'

Tommo Price can see Ianto Jenkins from his window at the Savings Bank like God above who can do nothing once he's let his creation loose. He watches when people come out of the midday showing and stand with the beggar for aeons with him wheeling his arms and tapping his watch, and Tommo turns away and goes back to his ledgers. He drinks his tea from a thick cup and he fixes his eyes on his ledgers where the numbers stay still and solid and if he concentrates hard he only half-hears his name,

'Tommo Price it was. Tommo Price . . .'

Tommo passes Ianto Passchendaele Jenkins later on his way home from the Savings Bank and sometimes if he has the devil on his shoulder, Ianto Jenkins waves a penny at him and hoooooooos like the wind. Or a train.

'Annie's son's in the chimney again, Tommo?'

But of course there are no boys in chimneys, or in tunnels, and Tommo Price goes home to his wife Sarah Price, who makes white fish for tea with white buttered bread and serves it silent. Lardy-faced, she is, and secrets slide from her like dropped bullseyes on a frozen puddle.

'Aww. Off to Annie's now, is it? There's a shame the fish is eaten all.'

'Shame indeed . . .'

'You can tell me what she says, Tommo. I wouldn't breathe . . .'

'Indeed you wouldn't, my love . . .'

Every evening after tea Tommo Price goes up through the Brychan to the old coal line, to Batty Annie's hut, just to make sure. Even when he is tired to the grave, like tonight, with watching the figures on the paper, and watching Ianto Passchendaele Jenkins on the cinema steps, looking up and watching him in return. Tommo Price pulls his jacket round as he walks past the houses, past Laddy Merridew sitting on the front step of his gran's, biting his nails.

Tonight the wind is blowing from the east and Tommo thinks to go straight to the tunnel where Annie will be as sure as eggs with her net. And she is not. It is past seven and the light is fading, and the tunnel is hoooooing soft and in waves.

For a bit Tommo waits there, because she will come stumbling along any minute with her net. And he thinks of Annie there, waiting. The Annie who held him tighter once than his own mam, and stroked and stroked his school jumper and left little dabs of bread flour and soft dough clinging to the wool and said it was not his fault.

But tonight, this very night, she doesn't come with her net. Tommo walks along the tracks to her linesman's hut and taps. 'Annie?'

'Aww, Tommo, there's a thing and I'm not very well . . .'

And she is lying in the corner in her donkey jacket, not in the bed Tommo brought in pieces up the hill and nailed together again. Not under the blankets from his own cupboard.

'Where's the coal, Annie? I will make you a nice fire, now, and some black tea with sugar.'

'Will you fetch my boy, Tommo? I can hear him.'

And Tommo gets Batty Annie onto the bed in her coat. He makes up the fire, small, and sets the kettle on the coals, sighs and takes the shrimping net from up against the wall. Out he goes to the tunnel but he stands in the entrance out of the smell of piss and counts to one hundred swinging the net like a pendulum. And he goes back to the hut.

'Where is he, my boy?'

'Here, Annie, in the net . . .'

Batty Annie listens. 'He is not there, Tommo. You don't have him, you don't, my Lovely Boy . . .'

So Tommo Price who is tired from his day bent over his ledgers, and his white fish and his white wife and finding Batty Annie ill . . . he goes back to the tunnel. And it's not like going back to stand in the tunnel with a net, but it's like going back to look for the penny like he did, over and over and not finding it, and kicking the stones around and piling them against the bricks, and clearing the ground to the mud and finding nothing at all. Because there was nothing to find. And he knew it. All it ever was, was a boy who never squashed the king, killed by a train.

Tommo stands inside the tunnel and listens to the hoooing and does not lift the net. But he goes back tired to the hut, holding the net like Annie does. Clasping it to his breast. 'Here he is, Annie.'

But she turns her face to the wall.

He's back in the tunnel, inside this time, inside the sound of the wind, inside the throat. There are blacknesses in the dark. And like he does for Annie, Tommo begins to scritch the net across the roof where the blacknesses are. Scritch scritch, and the old soot and the brickdust falls onto his face – for this time he is looking up.

And he can smell the piss in the tunnel, and the damp and the dark, which smells like metal.

The dark smells like metal. Like the warm damp fingers of a boy who's been clutching his dinnerpennies, hard. And it smells of sugar. Of cherry pips. And Tommo can taste cherry pips on his tongue like he hasn't for years, and knows that if he stuck his tongue out it would be red down the middle. And the soot and dust falls like black rain in the dark, a black rain that falls into the net and is heavier than dust.

Tommo feels in the net and finds that which is not dust. He holds it up in the halflight, sees the face, and the face is flat, and he cries. He pushes it deep in his suit pocket and he cries. He scritches the net across the roof, fills the holes with darkness and the smell of pennies, and he cries.

Then Tommo Price holds his best friend to his breast, keeping the net shut against the closing night. But there's a moon up there, and it shines steady and unblinking down on the town and on Tommo Price taking Dai along the old coal line, home to Annie.

Tommo takes the net to the linesman's hut, straight to the hearth, and holds it out, right where the thin smoke is rising, right under the chimney, and he takes his hand away and shakes it, shakes it.

Then he takes the penny from his pocket and closes Annie's fingers round but he can't find the words to go with it. And she puts the penny to her cheek, soft as a kiss, and closes her eyes.

Tommo takes the white porcelain cup from the basket and fills it from the outside tap that rattles and chugs against the wall of the hut. He gives Annie to drink a little, slowly, holding the cup to her lips like it was a chalice. He takes a sip himself, then, knowing what he will see reflected in the water, he sits by the warm, leans forward, holds the cup out under the chimney and waits for the kettle to boil.

In the Porch of Ebenezer Chapel

THERE IS NO LADDY Merridew for a few days. No toffees, or Spanish Catherine wheels, with or without the jelly bits.

When Ianto Jenkins does see Laddy, it is in the High Street, outside the library. Laddy Merridew is leaning against the library wall, surrounded by other lads. They are talking, he is not. He looks up as Ianto comes by to check the bus times and the beggar raises a hand, but the boy looks away as the lads' laughter rings against the air, 'Stinker's friend. Stinker's friend.'

Later, the boy is alone, still leaning against the wall, and when Ianto says hello he does not answer.

Later, Laddy Merridew comes to the chapel porch between showings, and finds the beggar winding his watch. He stands on the steps, biting his nails, saying nothing, until Ianto Passchendaele Jenkins inspects the watch and says, 'Must be almost time.'

'Don't be daft. Got no hands, that watch.'

The beggar considers for a moment. 'And who says a watch needs hands? It's still working, inside.'

'That's what I mean. It's daft.'

'Oh I see.'

'Everything is just your old stories. Nothing you say is true.'

The beggar takes off his cap and scratches his head. 'Why do you think that, Maggot?'

Laddy Merridew doesn't reply. He glowers at Ianto. 'I'm fed up of people lying to me.' He shifts his bones. Then he says, 'I am not Maggot either. I am Laddy. Not Maggot. But . . .'

'But what, Maggot?'

Laddy pushes his fists into his pockets. 'That tunnel up near Gran's . . .'

'What about it?'

'I went in there. They said I wouldn't, the others. Right to the middle where it is really dark.'

'And why did you do that?'

'They said if I did, they'd give me a cigarette to try.'

'And did they?'

'They waited for me to get right into the darkest bit, then they ran off.' There is a pause. 'They lied.'

'Ah.'

'They laughed as well.'

Ianto Passchendaele Jenkins nods. 'Was that them this morning?'

Laddy nods.

'Not nice, being lied to. Or laughed at.'

'No.' Laddy chews a nail. Then he seems to brighten. 'But the scratches on the walls of the tunnel. I saw those, at least, I think I did. Is that story really how they got there?'

'Scratches get on walls in all sorts of ways.'

'My gran says there's no such thing as ghosts. And if there were they wouldn't live in bricks.'

'I never said they did. Chimneys, now, that's a different

thing, oh yes. Ghosts need a way in and a way out, after all. Like tunnels . . .'

'I'll tell her you said that.'

'I wouldn't if I was you.'

The boy almost smiles, 'I'm sorry about this morning.'

Ianto Jenkins shrugs.

'But Mr Jenkins – your stories. How do I know they are really real?'

The beggar sighs.

'So, how do I know . . .'

This time Ianto Jenkins frowns. 'Maggot, you will listen now. Here . . .' Ianto Jenkins points at the bench, 'Sit here, or not. It doesn't matter. And you tell me if this is real or not. I would have told this to my brother Maggot, afterwards. After – but I could not.'

Laddy goes to say something but Ianto Jenkins holds up a hand to stop him.

'It was raining now for two whole days, and I was a collier down Kindly Light for those same two days. After the first day it was not only raining above the ground. Oh no. It was raining below sure as eggs. It drip dripped from the ceiling. First it was those single drips that are down there always . . . then it was more, and more until there were so many they could not be separated. On the second day, it rained down there until the tunnel floor was inches deep in water despite the engines and the pumps. The engines up top going full pelt all day and all night to work the pumps that sucked the rain out of the mountain, to make Kindly Light "fit for walking in, fit for working in", so said my da's friend, Thomas Edwards, who was helping me.

And on the day before, my second day, I could hear the sound of the engines all the time in my ears even though I was hundreds of feet below them, and knew I could not possibly be hearing them really. I think I heard them because I knew they were there, not because I have good ears at all. Believe me, I was going deaf already with the noise down there.

I am following the other colliers and Thomas Edwards down one of the roadways where there are great pillars left in the coal to hold up the mountain. I am careful not to trip on the rails, but it is hard to see where they are. It is then I am standing in water almost above dead Mr Ernest Ellis's boots, in a dip between these two great pillars of coal. Then Thomas Edwards stops to look at something. "The pillars are to come down soon, and timbers will be there instead," he says. I feel sorry for the pillars, then. I am looking up, and when his back is turned I take my penknife and scrape my initials quickly in the side of the pillar, for there is something about leaving your name under a mountain when only you and the mountain know it is there ... but I am too slow, and Thomas Edwards sees and he roars with laughter, a great roar that echoes down the roadway, and he shakes his head and walks off and says, "Am I given a collier to work with, or is it philosophers and sculptors they are taking below now?" ... and all the time I can hear the rain falling in the tunnel like someone saying hush, and I hear the great creaking and breathing in and out of the mountain over the noise of men and animals, and it hasn't made me frightened before and now it does. Thomas Edwards has gone ahead of me into the darkness which has closed round him like someone has drawn a curtain between me and him, and I am left by the pillars – close to the one that has my name, and I am hearing all the sounds of the mountain and Mr Edwards shouting over the noise, "Come on, Ianto Jenkins, and stop your dreaming," and there is still the engine in my head beating and beating and getting louder and louder until I can hardly breathe . . . and the coal pillar is massive like a great arm stretching through the floor and rising up above my head and oh, I cannot stop the thinking and the noise too, and the engine it beats and beats and I am right next to the pillar, and I go up close and put my hands on it and it is wet and cold, but beating too. I wonder if it is beating with the sound of the engine from above, and I have to hear for myself – to do that I must take off my cap for it is in the way and I need to get my ear right against the coal. I have my ear pressed against the coal and my eyes closed not to hear Mr Edwards's shouts, and there is a sound in the pillar, Maggot. A noise I hear in my heart, not my ears, a deep swelling hum like a thousand swarms of bees saying "Get out . . ." And then there is a roar down the roadway, and for half a second I think it is a roar to Ianto Jenkins to get on with it – but it is not, it is a roar unlike any other. It is Thomas Edwards's voice roaring and it is not anger in that roar, but it is fear, and I have not heard that before but I know it. And his is the last voice I hear for a while, oh but what a while. Then it is dreadful, Maggot. It is dreadful and noise. And it is dust and the rush of no air, and flying rocks, and it is the world and the whole mountain tipped about and I am thrown over when the ground tips and I am just a handful of stones thrown into Taff Fechan from the bridge, and I hear my brother Maggot laughing, and the shouts of men and the screaming and screaming of horses. I am the stones in the river, tumbling fast over rocks, I am tumbled about breathless and I can't breathe. Then something cracks me on the head, and the river swirls under the bridge and my head splits and I see fountains of sparks in the water . . . and I want to stop and think how strange it is, but something loud stops my thinking. I have no memory of things or thinking for a while after that.

I do dream though, of a fire, and I do dream of men black by that fire, and one running down the roadway with the fire at his back like a monkey. I do dream that I close my eyes but the fire will not leave my eyes and is burned into them and comes back and back and the monkey screams. I do dream I am caught up by Thomas Edwards, who has his arms about me like my own da, and being bundled between men in the dark right into a space where I am thrown against a wall and the bodies of men cover me over and hide me from the dark. I can't breathe easy, Maggot, my face all stuffed into Thomas Edwards's jacket, but I try and he smells of tobacco. And I have lost my water bottle from my pocket. And I am so tired, Maggot. I cannot breathe deep for the weight of men, so I breathe shallow and slow. And I do dream about a sleep that falls after and heavy, and men yawning, although I cannot see them yawn.

And the tunnels, the little roadways of Kindly Light are not able to carry the weight of the stretching mountain, and it is collapsing in on itself . . . and how small we are. How small. Caught up in it all, and crushed. But it is not the fault of the mountain at all, neither the fall of stone, the fire gas, and the sleep. It is not the fault of my mountain at all that men are caught down there. But oh my Maggots both, I know whose fault it is that there are men below at all. Good men and boys.'

* * *

Ianto Passchendaele Jenkins stops. There is a quiet, broken only by the cooing of a pigeon up in the rafters. Laddy Merridew is silent.

'Good men and boys. Gone. And I am brought up into the light again, much later, days later maybe – oh, but what light. A dark light that is in the faces of the women waiting silent, and in a second I had the knowledge that the waiting would not go away now at all but would be under their nails whenever they looked at their hands. I heard the voice of a woman and I do not know which one, "It is only a boy."

And then I don't want to remember more after that. Not now.'

Ianto Jenkins is up from his bench, leaning his head against the wall, his back to the boy. Laddy Merridew starts to say something, but the beggar stops him.

'Go home, Maggot. I am tired.'

The Gas Meter Emptier's Tale

i

WHEN THE TOWN IS asleep, the breeze steals in under the doors when the walls are not watching. It plays round the sleeping necks of Mrs Bennie Parrish and Nathan Bartholomew the Piano Tuner, and they will pull the covers up in their different rooms, different houses. Down the stairs it goes in Judah Jones's house, to play round the wheels of his bicycle parked in the dark hallway and it blows the ash from the grates in the town's front rooms and covers the trinkets on the mantelpieces in another layer of dust.

At the Adam's Acre allotments, opposite the row of new houses called Christopher Terrace after both the town planner and the owner of the big house now pulled down, everything is quiet, all the rows of onions and carrots are sleeping above ground and below. The wooden sheds will be padlocked against the night, and the spades and forks and trowels are lying ready for the morning, in their wheelbarrows.

All is dark, all the gardeners in their houses, sleeping, and planning in their dreams what potatoes they will dig up tomorrow, and what prize marrows they will grow next year.

The night conversations are done a long time ago,

'Did you put out the cat, Evan?'

'I did, Gwladys.'

'And did you remember to put the porridge in the range for the morning, Evan?'

'I did, Gwladys.'

'And did you lock the front door, Evan?'

'I did, Gwladys.'

'Are you sure? For the paper is full of nothing but burglaries these days, Evan.'

'Goodnight, Gwlad.'

All asleep, except for one. Over by the old wall, where the slope of the hill takes Adam's Acre lower and lower towards the valley floor, a small light may be moving among the rows. The light of an oil lamp swinging as it is now held high, now low, the small shadow who holds the lamp lifting it to see if the last apples are ready for picking on the tree by that wall, then lowering it to check the snails are not taking his last shoots. Then the light stops moving as the night gardener puts the lamp down to run his fingers round the roots of his plants, loosening the earth, helping them to stretch up and out.

James Little, the man who for years collected the shillings from the town's gas meters in their hallway cupboards or under the stairs, hidden away behind suitcases and jars of pickle, bottles of home brew and trays of apples. Coins that were saved for the gas in jamjars on mantelpieces in back kitchens, no money for sweets, or new shoes, 'And it is tripe only for supper tonight, the shillings are all in the meter.'

Retired now, this James Little, given a clock with a painted face as a thank you and left someone else to collect the money from the houses where he called each week for years for the gas company. Years of cups of tea and slices of cake, while people asked if he really had to take all their coins away, '. . . for it is not payday until the end of the week and gas is only air . . .?'

Tea he would have, and said thank you for the cake but would never eat it there, wrapping it instead in a square of greaseproof paper put in his pocket by Edith, his wife. James Little would always shake his head at the pleas for money back, but sometimes, as he left, he would drop a shilling from his own pocket on the front step by mistake.

And when he got home at the end of the day, his bag heavy with coins and his pockets even heavier with cake, he would kiss his wife at the door, 'No need to get cake from the bakery this week, Edith. Look, eighteen slices and two ginger biscuits . . .'

James Little will finish checking his winter cabbages are well, his carrots are fine in their earth and his parsnips can breathe. He stands, stretching his aching shoulders, lifts the lamp and looks at his watch. Half past one in the morning. 'Almost time.'

Over to his shed with its two padlocks on the door, and the single window well blanketed with a square of old oilcloth cut by Edith when it was too big for their kitchen table. And he puts his gardening tools away, neat against the wall in their metal clips. He takes off his wellington boots and stands them by the same wall, and puts on instead a pair of plimsolls. He hangs his old coat on its peg, then takes down another jacket, dark, with deep pockets, left over from his job as a collector of gas meter coins. But there are no squares of greaseproof in the pocket now.

He finds his bag, an old school satchel from a son long since left home, checks the contents and sees it is securely buckled. Then he leaves his shed, making sure the window is covered, and both padlocks locked. He walks back up to the road, stepping over onion sets and rows of potatoes, round clumps of chrysanths smelling strange and green in the night air.

When he gets to the road, to Christopher Terrace, James Little will stop outside number eighteen, his own home, but he will not go in. He stands on the pavement looking up at the bedroom window where the curtains are drawn and Edith will be muttering in her sleep, her teeth in a glass. And he will blow her a kiss before walking in the direction of Maerdy Street.

It is dark crossing the old tip, with a few old ponies for company. He can smell them, hear their breath snuffing in the night, just shadows among greater shadows. Then the grass changes to tarmac under his shoes, and he is past the old sheds and out under the streetlights at the end of Maerdy Street, its houses shut up for the night. And he pauses, looking down the empty street, waiting for movement, but none comes.

James Little walks back to the old tip and round to the alley behind the houses, walking carefully, not to squeak the cinders under his soles, into the shadows where the streetlights do not reach. Down the alley, tapping the wall with his fingers as he goes, the bricks, the small gates, the brambles. Counting the gates, some latched, some tied shut with string. Some gone, just gaps in the wall, taken for firewood maybe, or just gone back into the ground.

Then an old gate, rotten, held up by nettles, no latch at all, rusted away, and James Little's fingers stop. A gate that opens into a small garden, through more nettles, and down a few crumbling steps to the back of the house, a yard, an outside toilet. A bucket hanging over the tap by the back door, an old cloth over the bucket. And the front door not closed. Open a few inches only, a shoe holding it open, forgotten perhaps when the owner went up to bed a few hours since. An old house, with old owners, deaf probably, and asleep. James Little simply pushes the door open and is inside, carrying his bag.

A short while later he is back on Maerdy Street, his bag back over his shoulder. He counts the houses under his breath as he goes, in case he can't see the numbers on the front doors, '27, 25, 23 . . . 15, 13, 11. Here we are.'

James Little looks up and down Maerdy Street. All is quiet. But upstairs at number eleven there is one window open, no curtains, and the streetlights are playing on some glass thing on the sill, sending green and yellow reflections dancing up the walls. And over the curtain rail there is some old cloth hanging, a strip of flowered material only. No good being here in front if there is a window open.

He goes down the side alley to find the iron gate into the back yard of number eleven. They are not good at night, iron gates. And he reaches into a pocket and brings out a small tin of oil, and he oils both hinges just in case. He waits a few moments for the oil to talk to the rust in the joints, then he lifts the latch, wedges the gate open with a half-brick and he is swallowed into the shadows behind the houses.

His feet in their plimsolls make no sound on the back yard flagstones. And there is the back door, positioned where they all are, the kitchen window and the window of the middle room. This window is open a little at the top, the sash dropped an inch or two. And this is a good thing because the back door is locked when he tries the handle.

James Little sighs, for he is not getting any younger, and he searches for something to stand on. And there is the wooden block used for chopping kindling, waiting patiently by the tap outside the back door, and if he is quiet . . .

He rolls the wooden block to beneath the middle room window from its circle of moss beneath the tap, stands on it and can just reach the top of the sash. A drop or two of oil each side, and the window opens. And James Little, giving thanks that he was not born to grow very tall, and also giving thanks that it was Edith who ate most of the cake slices that rode home in these pockets over the years, climbs into the middle room of number eleven Maerdy Street, where old Lillian Harris and her son Jimmy who they call Half Harris, are fast asleep.

It is not quite dark in there. There is a light left on, on the landing. The streetlights shine in through the stained glass transom, and the hallway over there is purple and yellow as an old bruise. James Little goes to the foot of the stairs and stands there, listening. There is a pram parked here, a newish one to replace another that was broken – its hood up, a few sticks in the body. It smells of damp already, and earth. He smiles, one hand on the pram handle, listening for sounds from upstairs, but there is nothing but a faint snoring.

Back in the middle room there is a dresser, two drawers and cupboard doors below, open shelves full of china above. Toby jugs, bowls, plates, a glass cakestand, and a pair of brass candlesticks. That might be hopeful. And out in the kitchen a mantelpiece with two brass plates polished almost flat, a figurine of a balloon-seller, one balloon missing, more candlesticks and a handleless mug. He fetches down the mug and it holds nothing but a pencil, a few pound notes rolled in a rubber band, some coins, a dead lipstick and a Kirby grip. There is a table laid for breakfast, a marmalade pot with an old teaspoon inserted through the gap in a cracked lid, two plates, a pile of used envelopes on an oilcloth decorated in lemons and biro-marks, and the stub of a pencil sharpened roughly with a knife.

James Little opens the door to the pantry and takes in the half-rusted tins marked *Tea, Coffee, Sugar* and *Flour* on the middle shelf. It smells of mice in here. He puts down his bag on the kitchen floor and opens it, goes back to the pantry and pulls down the tin marked *Tea*. He takes the handleless mug off the mantelpiece in the kitchen, with its roll of pound notes. In the middle room, he opens the cupboard doors, and crouches down. More china, thin porcelain, white with yellow roses. A sewing box. And in the drawers, papers. Bills, certificates, all neat in a file, and envelopes, hundreds of the things, all used, the backs covered with wavy lines drawn in biro, pencil, sometimes both. He takes the sewing box and carries it through to the kitchen.

Later again, James Little is back out on Maerdy Street, the window of number eleven closed to just an inch or so from the top, as it was, the chopping block rolled back to its exact circle of moss by the tap, the iron gate closed behind him carefully and silently, the half-brick pushed back against the wall of the house, and he is off across the old coal tip to Adam's Acre.

Back to his shed, where he lights the lamp, changes back into his Wellington boots and his gardening coat, and hangs his bag on its hook.

And just as he is about to lock up, turn away and step carefully over the onion sets and rows of cabbages, back up to Christopher Terrace and home, he sees something glinting in the soil. Something between his last beans and his parsnips. He smiles and kneels on the earth, to dig with his fingers. Just a little, for it does not take much, to unearth a small spoon out of the soil, a silver spoon, which with a little wipe and a polish, will be perfect. He yawns, puts the spoon with a pile of others on a shelf in the shed, next to a bunch of dried rosemary, locks up and goes home to catch some sleep before Edith wakes.

But James Little is tired after a good night's work, and does not see the door of number twenty-six opening, and the Deputy Librarian Philip 'Factual' Philips coming out into the morning. He has to catch the first bus to town to get the library tidy, for Mrs Cadwalladr the Librarian will be in at seven for a meeting. Factual Philips stands in his doorway and watches James Little yawning then disappearing round the back to number eighteen in his wellingtons and old gardening coat. And Factual squares his shoulders, checks his watch and frowns.

He is not the only one. There are others who notice James Little going late to Adam's Acre, staying until last, not going home with the other gardeners.

'Arrives just as I am packing up, he does, and sometimes there is no light at all to garden by.'

'Must see in the dark.'

'Maybe his mam was a cat, then?'

'Nah, serious. Carries an old oil lamp. I've seen him, forgot some cut flowers for my Dorrie once, went back to fetch them. Saw him. Does his digging by lamplight.'

'Doesn't have a home to go to, maybe?'

And the milkman, who has his own allotment against the old wall, may join in here, 'Oh yes, I see him now and again, going home in his wellingtons, five in the morning ... strange, that ...'

The Gas Meter Emptier's Tale

ii

QUESTIONS ARE ASKED, AS questions will always be. And if they come to the ears of Ianto Passchendaele Jenkins the beggar, begging there on the steps of the cinema, he will wheel his arms and look up towards Adam's Acre,

'Listen with your ears, I have a story for them see, a story this time about thieving, about a piece of ground, about a child. But it is not what you think. And as always, stories need fuel they do, and I have not had a toffee for at least an hour.'

Two come forward with bags of toffees, and the beggar considers for a moment, his head on one side. 'Best not disappoint, eh?' And he takes two, and pushes them into his jacket pocket for later, and begins again.

'Let me start with a question? What do you do if you have nothing, nothing at all. If you have a family to feed and no money to buy food?'

Someone shouts, 'Get a job?'

And there is a laugh, 'Right enough, you never worked a day in your life, mun.'

Ianto Passchendaele Jenkins smiles, 'So, this is the story of

James Little's grandfather, Walter Little, who lost his twin brother William down Kindly Light pit. Both hewers together, they were indeed. And Walter with a broken wrist from tripping over one of his kiddie's toys on the floor, so he missed going down on that day. Yes, Walter Little, a gentle man he was too. Lost that twin brother he named his own son for – and would not go down any pit after that accident, for real fear. I know what that is.

His son was William Little, called after the twin – but Walter never called him William again not to remind him too much of Kindly Light, but just Billy Little, instead.

Now Walter, Billy Little's da, was perfectly capable of working, but there was no work, see, other than down the pit. And Walter Little had a wife and two more kiddies to feed, and another one coming soon and no money coming in to buy coal.

And this Billy Little too, Walter's son – he was afraid of the pit as well, as children will be if they catch fear from their elders. Maybe he listened too often to one of the old spinster sisters, Gwynneth Watkins, who used to stand in her doorway yabbering, that old biddy Watkins who saw things in her tea leaves, and watched the way you walked for that told her your secrets. She watched Billy Little playing in the street, and she called him over, wagging her finger: "I see darkness for you, Billy Little. I see you in such a dark place, oh a dreadful dark place where you are alone and no one there to help you. Aww, do you hear the sounds, too? Listen, Billy Little, there are sounds echoing off the wet walls, and it is the shouts of others in the same place as you, and the terrible music of men crying in the dark."

Well, no question but that must be the pit, Kindly Light, mustn't it? For the accident, it happened not long since. And Billy Little was at his wits' end for his da and for himself. They must not go down the pit ever, must they? But they still needed coal, didn't they? And no money coming in to buy it.

Well, where there's a will there's a way, as they say, and Walter Little got coal for his family as many did in those times, going out at night to take it from the drifts over the valley. Walter Little and his son Billy Little, both together, walking these streets at night, pushing the pram that carried all the family's babies. Over to the other side of the river they went with many men and boys from the town, to the slopes of the place they still call the Black Mountain. They took lamps but kept them covered with rags so they would just shine a little on the ground so they might see what they were doing. And they dug out what coal they could from the old drift mines, and made new ones, the men of the town, at night. Their boys were not in their beds at all but helping their das, bringing out the coal on kitchen trays, and in saucepans, for their mams to ask them the next day what had they been doing with the pots then?

And what did they call this but dark gardening? When the word went out that there was a spot of dark gardening to be done tonight over the way, everyone knew what that meant and they just nodded and touched their fingers to their noses. Like this . . .'

And Ianto Passchendaele Jenkins will tap the side of his nose, and smile.

* * *

'And when there was a moon they didn't need their lamps at all to find the coal as it shone up at them out of the hillside, uncovered by the digging of rabbits and foxes. But then a moon was also a bad thing, for those who owned the hillsides paid men to keep watch over their land, their coal. Just you imagine the journey back to the town with that old pram, brimful of coal dug from the hillside with garden spades and trays from the kitchen, tucked in to sleep covered by an old blanket. Walter Little and his son Billy who had precious little to laugh about, finding a little as they walked home together through the empty streets. Enough coal to keep the range alight a few days, that is all, and look at the size of the whole mountain, look over there . . .'

The beggar will point and the cinemagoers may mutter that it is a fine world we live in if men can own whole mountains, but they stop when the story continues.

'Then there was the night that finished it all, a night when the landowner's bullyboys lay in wait in an alley, three of them, ready to teach those who steal a lesson. And who did they catch that night but Walter Little and Billy, pushing the pram together up that hill by there, going home to their beds.

"Well well, will you be looking here. Taking the baby out for a little air, are we?"

And they pushed Walter Little into the road, and one held the boy back while the others hit his da to the ground, Billy Little pulling at a jacket and shouting, "My da! Leave my da alone!" hoping someone would come out to help, but no one dared . . . until the man shut the boy's mouth with his arm. And when Walter Little tried to get up with his fists ready, "Hit a little boy, would you?" they kicked him in the stomach with their boots until he retched and could not get up by himself any more, and tried to say something about three kids and a baby coming and no heat in the house, "and only a bit of spare coal no one will miss . . . ?" But they hauled him to standing and one held him against the alley wall while the others took turns until his face could not be recognised as a face.

"Can't look after a baby like that now, can you? We'll give the thing a little air . . ."

And then they took the pram full of coal and tipped it into the gutter. They pissed on the coal the three of them, and they broke the pram to pieces, the boy Billy Little shouting, "No! leave my da alone. Leave our pram alone. That's my mam's pram, that is . . ."

As they went, they shouted back to the boy, Billy Little, "You go off home to your mam, and tell her to come and fetch her thieving husband. She can heat her house with piss."

And the lad went running to his mam, crying, "Mam, the pram is broke, and so is Da, and you must come . . ."

But you see, then there was no one to fetch anything for a while, while Walter Little was getting better from his beating. There was not enough to eat in the house, and it was always cold. Billy Little was the eldest of the children, and it was up to him to fetch, wasn't it? Down the town to see if the shops had anything left at the end of the day and they almost never did, or there were other boys there before him, or there were fights over the stale bread, and the apples half-rotten. It was hard to walk back up the hill to the house with nothing in your stomach to help your legs, and to tell your mam, standing waiting with the young ones at her skirts, "I am sorry, Mam, I found nothing . . ."

And then the day came when Billy Little was walking back up that hill and he was not well at all, and sat down on the step of a house, feeling faint and sick to his stomach, his empty stomach. Where he was taken in and given a glass of milk and a biscuit, in a kitchen all warm, with a fire, full of the smell of cooking, and even that smell was more than they had at home.

While he was in that kitchen, someone came to the front door, and the lady with the biscuits left her kitchen to go to see who it was. There were voices in the hallway for a while, and a longer while. Billy Little had nothing to do but finish his biscuit and look round. On the kitchen shelf he saw a tin, its lid not quite on, the sort of tin his mam had, where she used to keep coins, when she had any. And he got up and looked in the tin and there were indeed coins there. And before Billy knew what his fingers were doing they were in the tin taking out a shilling and whisking it into his pocket. Easy. Not a thought. It was not Billy's fault if the woman with the biscuits had the smells of cooking in the air when there were none at Billy Little's house, and too many coins in her tin. Easy. "Look, Mam – found this in the gutter . . ."

And see, it was not far from a lump of coal taken from a mountainside to a single coin taken from a tin, to more coins taken from tills and then whole purses taken from ladies' handbags . . . and it was not far from purses taken from handbags to looking for windows left open and helping himself to things from houses. Small things at first, then bigger. And that's what he did as he grew up, see. Then he was not looking for open windows but helping the windows to open, stealing silver and jewellery, and then it was not far to getting caught again and again, and then being sent away for it.

And of course, that spinster woman Gwynneth Watkins was right after all. For Billy Little was in prison. In a dark cell with wet walls, all on his own with no one to help, where he heard the shouts of men in the dark, and sometimes the dreadful sound of men crying at night. But it did not stop him, and after that he was in and out of prison like it was his own home, even when he had a child of his own later. That child is James Little, who now tends his allotment at night, and walks the streets in the early hours with a bag over his shoulder.

But it is a dreadful thing to know your father is a thief, and that is what the boy James Little had to grow up with. The taunts at school,

"My da is a minister,"

"My da is a fishmonger,"

"Your da is a thief..."

Taunts that followed him from boy to man, taunts he could not escape. Even when he is tending his allotment he hears, "Aww. Wonder where he found those plants... that spade... that wheelbarrow? That is James Little, the son of Billy Little, you know? Half his life in jail he spent, Billy did..."

And it is shame that started him tending his allotment at night, away from the taunts, and it is not surprising maybe, that even though James Little was trusted to collect the coins for the gas board for years and years, and was given a clock with a painted face as a thank you, there are still those who wonder. That wouldn't be you, now would it ... ?'

Ianto Passchendaele Jenkins will look round at the listeners, and the cinemagoers just shuffle their feet and will not reply.

The Gas Meter Emptier's Tale

iii

FOR A WEEK, THE morning meetings at the library have been somewhat problematic. Factual Philips is getting more and more tired thanks to his detective work, and he has tried to take the minutes whilst at the same time making notes about James Little on the back of the minute pad:

1. *Time of comings and goings.*
2. *Make note of any changes of clothes.*
3. *What is in that bag?*
4. *

There is a large star by '4' and its creation was accompanied by a loud cough from the Librarian, who adjusted her bosom and announced the passing of an important initiative that boils down to putting the same books on different shelves. 'Yes, and it was not minuted was it, Mr Philips? You look tired, Mr Philips?'

'Nothing that a good night's sleep won't cure, Mrs Cadwalladr.'

But a good night's sleep is not easy to come by. For Factual Philips has not been sleeping, but collecting facts. He catnaps now, sitting in his front window watching out for James Little, playing detective at last.

* * *

Factual Philips, Deputy Librarian Detective, writes notes about seeing James Little night after night leaving his house at midnight in his wellingtons, buttoning his gardening coat. They will all be clues, no doubt about that. Seeing him walk under the streetlights along Christopher Terrace to Adam's Acre and cross the road, disappearing into the darkness of the allotments. Seeing a small light then, the oil lamp moving about, and around the light the small mysterious shadow of James Little.

Factual Philips, Deputy Librarian Detective, has seen the shadow work at his digging, weeding his ground, tying onions in bunches, picking apples. And sometimes it looks as though he is not only working his own allotment, but digging at others.

The Deputy Librarian Detective shakes his head. 'Digging up their potatoes? Taking their beans, peas? Pulling up their onions for himself?'

And, then, at half past one in the morning, sharp, the lamp wavers along the rows and disappears.

'Right, now he is in his shed . . .' and Factual Philips watches the street then, to see if James Little comes home to Christopher Terrace, back to number eighteen. And yes, after a while, there he is, stepping over the other allotments on his way back to the street. And sometimes, he goes back to his house. But twice this week, Factual has seen him do things differently, and has made a note of the occurrences in his notebook.

1. *Wearing different clothes to the ones he went to his shed in. Different shoes.*

2. *Carries a bag over his shoulder.*

For he sees James Little is wearing another jacket, dark, pulled tight round and buttoned. The collar up round his ears.

3. *Suspicious garb.*

No Wellington boots, now, but instead, a pair of black plimsolls. And over James Little's shoulder is an old school satchel, looks like, and he does not go to his house except to blow a suspicious kiss at a window, walks to the end of the street and disappears.

Twice, Factual Philips sees this, and it is not right at all. The third time, the Detective is ready himself, in his coat, ready to leave the house. And he does, waits for James Little to walk away and when there is a safe distance, he follows. Across the old tip and along Maerdy Street, James Little's plimsolls making no sound on the pavement, Factual Philips cursing under his breath and having to walk on tiptoe not to make a sound himself, keeping his distance, ready to duck against the wall if James Little turns round.

The first time, Factual sees James Little going down Garibaldi Street, looking round to check no one is watching and slipping down the alley behind Mrs Bennie Parrish's house. And Factual knows that house is full of nice things, it has a piano, and photographs in silver frames as well as a lamp dressed like a Spanish Lady with gold earrings. Mr Bennie Parrish had money, oh yes. Factual knows this, he took enough books up for Mr Bennie when he was ill, didn't he? And he had to eat slices of cake he didn't like, while she watched, in that front room. Silver cake forks too. And a real painting above the fireplace.

He cannot follow into the house but makes a note of the

address and the time, and waits along the street, leaning against a cold wall, until James Little creeps back out twenty minutes later, his bag over his shoulder.

The next day, Mrs Bennie Parrish comes down to the library.

'Good morning, Mrs Parrish. And is everything quite right up in Garibaldi Street this morning?'

'Aww, my leg it is playing up something dreadful. It does it good to walk to town but it will kill me soon enough. I will take out Dylan Thomas today.'

'I am sorry to hear that, Mrs Parrish.'

'Why? What is wrong with Dylan Thomas?'

'Nothing indeed. The leg, I am sorry about the leg. But there is nothing else amiss? You are quite sure?'

And Mrs Bennie Parrish puts Dylan Thomas in her basket and goes off down the High Street complaining that Mr Philips at the library is having a funny turn.

And then, two nights later, Factual Philips, Deputy Librarian Detective and his notebook follow James Little again, and this time James Little goes up the hill to the house of Matty and Eunice Harris, double-fronted as befits the Deputy Manager of the Savings Bank and his lady wife.

There is a front garden with a high hedge, and James Little disappears behind. There is the smallest sound of a sash window sliding, oiled wood on wood, only enough for Factual to hear because he is waiting for the sound, not enough to wake anyone sleeping upstairs. Factual Philips waits a moment, then peers round the hedge, and there is the window open, and no sign of James Little, and through the front window Factual Philips can see a mahogany dining table shining in the light from the street, laid with silver knives, and spoons, and forks, a silver candlestick. And as he watches, there is James Little coming back into the room, bending over the table, one hand in the bag hanging over his shoulder. Factual Philips, Deputy Librarian Detective, has seen enough, thank you very much.

And so, when James Little goes back to Adam's Acre, there is someone waiting for him, someone who got back ahead of him, someone waiting in the darkness behind his shed, a Detective who grabs James Little by the elbow before he has a chance to open the padlocks, 'Right. Got you. I'll take that.'

It is Detective Factual Philips, grabbing the old satchel from James Little's shoulder and striding away before he has a chance to speak. Jumping across the other allotments up to Christopher Terrace, calling over his shoulder that the contents of this bag will be of interest to the police, and to Matty Harris. 'Like father like son, a terrible thing. You are discovered, Mr Little.'

Lights are going on in the upstairs rooms of Christopher Terrace, and there is the small shadow of James Little following the Deputy Librarian up to the street, shaking his head. James Little in his dark jacket and his soft shoes all muddy from climbing too fast over the earth, while in the pool of light below a streetlamp, Factual Philips opens the satchel. And it is absolutely empty.

James Little, out of breath, 'It is not what it seems . . .'

But Detective Factual Philips is insisting it is exactly what it seems, and what has he done with the stolen property, must have dumped it in a front garden, or somewhere on the old tip? 'And let's have a look in that shed of yours.'

By this time the noise has woken the neighbours, and Edith Little, 'James? Are you late home again?'

And as the dawn is coming up over the allotments, the residents of Christopher Terrace accompany the protesting James Little and Edith in her curlers, to his shed. 'The son of a burglar, he is. Didn't you know?'

'No, new here only. Terrible. So he is a burglar as well? Who has he burgled?'

'Mind my sprouts, will you?'

The Deputy Librarian Detective is frogmarching James Little down to his shed, and telling him to open the padlocks, and the residents are looking at the window and the door, and nodding to each other for if proof was needed there it is, in a square of oilcloth and two padlocks from the ironmongers. And James Little says nothing, but opens the door, and as the early sun shines into the gloom, it falls on a pile of silver spoons on a shelf. A silver dish holding a ball of green string, and a pair of silver candlesticks sitting on a box of fertiliser . . .

'Told you.'

'There.'

'Whose are those?'

'Don't know, never seen them before.'

'Told you. Like father, like son.'

'Fetch the police.'

They look at James Little, standing there in his old gas coin collector's jacket, and his old plimsolls, to see what he will do. And he does nothing, except hold on to the shelf with one hand as if to steady himself, suddenly looking old and small. And Edith pulls her dressing gown round tight, and stands next to him, facing the Christopher Terrace neighbours and the Deputy Librarian Detective who has forgotten all about his books for this morning.

Everyone speaking at once then, about the police, and about minding the onions for they were only planted a week since, and how about getting your feet off my new raspberry canes, and where has he hidden the loot from tonight, and no one is listening to anyone else.

And in the middle of it all the small voice of James Little, 'I am not a thief. I am not.' But no one is listening, still. Until he points to Factual Philips and says, 'I have been to your house. Is there anything missing? And I've been to those living to the left and right of number eighteen. And the next houses. All Christopher Terrace. I have been to all your houses. Is there anything missing?'

'That's terrible. There must be something gone.'

'What? My wedding band is not gone and I leave it every night on the draining board.'

'My father's medals are in the middle room, he polishes them before bed. They aren't gone.'

'Because I have taken nothing, see?'

But here, Factual Philips coughs loudly and holds aloft a matching pair of candlesticks for the residents to see, from James Little's shed. 'So what are these? Facts, that's what these are. I rest my case.' He turns to James Little, 'And where did you get these then? Grew them from seed, did you?'

Here, James Little hangs his head. And there, by a shed on an allotment with people in their pyjamas listening, James Little tries to tell his side of things, but he is shaking so much the words won't come . . .

Factual Philips laughs. 'Evidence! Fetch the police,' and he waves a candlestick.

But the residents don't necessarily agree. 'Aww, someone go and fetch Ianto Jenkins. He'll tell it all right?'

And two men are sent down the town, still in their pyjamas, and they come back with a bleary-eyed Ianto Passchendaele Jenkins.

'For my breakfast? I will tell a story for breakfast? An egg. How about a nice egg?' And the beggar sits on the cracked concrete slabs by the shed, yawns, and begins.

'Listen with your ears then, if they are awake, I have a story for them see, a story about gardening . . .' but the Deputy Librarian Detective snorts, 'What about a story of skulduggery instead, thieving, and plotting? What about prisons, and padlocks, and penitence and p-p-porridge?' but then he runs out of 'p's and the beggar stands up, not smiling.

For the first time, Ianto Jenkins raises his voice, 'Listen! Listen, will you? This is wrong. Mr Little has done nothing . . .'

There is a final bluster from Factual Philips, a shout from somewhere near the back of the small crowd, 'Listen, will you?' and after a moment the beggar continues the story.

'Perfect. When James Little was a little lad, his da Billy Little used to take him to a park where he was the gardener. A beautiful park with a big house right in the middle. And high gates and benches made from wrought iron – and never anyone about. He took young James for the boy to carry his bag. Billy

Little said it cost money for people to get into this park, and they were lucky he had a job, and knew the special places. Sometimes the owners must have forgotten they were coming, and they locked the gates so Billy Little and his lad had to climb over the big brick wall to get in. Imagine. Billy Little told his son to get on and play well away from the house, as he had things to do being the gardener and he must be left alone. Important job, this. So young James did as he was told. Used to play, and dream, watching the trees. They had no garden at home, see. And his da Billy Little was not at home much, and these trips to the park were special.'

And here there is a laugh, 'And we all know where he went, oh yes . . .' until someone says to shut up and listen. And Ianto Jenkins continues.

'Billy Little, his da, had work to do, as he said. He had digging to do, in the old vegetable garden right over by the brick wall where true enough the earth had been left to go hard, and where nothing had grown for years, and it was all overgrown. And he dug under the old apple trees that hung over the wall. James Little remembers that. And he also remembers his da going away again and again, but never knew why until he went to school.

"My da is a minister."

"My da is a teacher."

"My da is a hewer."

"Your da is a thief."

And in the end his da went away and did not come back at all. Remember that? Billy Little who died of the consumption in prison, miles away, and no visits from his wife allowed? All people remember is that he was a thief. But he was also James Little's da. Who took his lad to the park. See?'

The residents of Christopher Terrace say nothing. James Little turns away for a moment, and they let him, and it is only his wife, Edith Little, who puts her arm round his shoulders, as the beggar's voice goes on.

'But of course, it was not a park at all, he knows that now. It was the garden of the big house. And the big house then pulled down and Christopher Terrace built instead, and where the vegetable garden was, and the apple trees alongside the brick wall, it was all made into allotments. Adam's Acre. Here.'

And the sun is up now, the Christopher Terrace residents looking at the old wall, the bricks red in the sunlight and the last apples of the season hanging there, all innocent.

'But Billy Little's gardening. "A good gardener always digs deep," he said. And he would dig for a long time leaving his lad to play, and would come back and fetch him when he had finished, and young James would help carry his bags home. Bags were always lighter than when they arrived, see?'

Ianto Jenkins looks round. 'Oh yes, fine soil these allotments. Fine for the beans, good for potatoes, chives, onions and parsley. Chrysanthemums. But especially good for silver spoons, knives, dishes, candlesticks. Years of them, stolen from not just this town but all over, and all dug deep by Billy Little, who never came back to fetch them.

They are everywhere, the things he left, deep in this soil. James Little has dug them up for years. His patch and other people's, too, were full of things . . . used to dig them at night. Must have been hundreds of spoons, knives, forks, little things, easy to carry.'

Here, someone says, 'And what did you do with them, then, James Little? Sell them?'

James Little smiles, and shakes his head, and carries on with the story himself, with a nod from the beggar. 'No, I put them back. That's all. The man who collected the coins from the meters for years, he knows where the meter cupboard is, knows where the windows are, where the other cupboards are, drawers, where the mugs are on the mantelpieces. Knows all sorts. I just put them back, a spoon or two here, a dish there. Left them in places where spoons might live, not to be really noticed, see? In a tea caddy. Or on the mantelpiece, in a dish. The big house is long gone, I don't know whose anything is, so I give bits back to everyone.'

He looks round at the crowd, shifting in their dressing gowns. 'Mr Philips . . . you have six matching soup spoons in the top drawer of your dresser, at the back. And a silver dish or two in the kitchen, at the back of the cupboard by the stove.'

Another voice, Nancy, Factual Philips's wife, come down to see what the fuss is about. 'Aww well. Lovely little things, those dishes. And there was me thinking you'd got me an anniversary present, Phil . . .'

There is silence from the Deputy Librarian Detective, and James Little continues.

'Last night I put three solid silver pie slices on the table in Mr Harris's house, left them on the table in the front room. And

Mrs Bennie Parrish, I left her another two photograph frames, in a drawer for her to find. See, people don't know what they have half the time. Think it's just something they forgot.'

Then there is a voice from the back, a man in striped pyjamas, his dressing gown held tight round: 'It's true enough, I reckon. Well, well I never. Look, there's my sister Bertha up Twynyrodyn, found a silver dish at the back of the dresser a long time ago. Nice little thing it was too, Georgian, and she swore she hadn't seen it before, ever. Paid for singing lessons for my nephew Darren, that did. And he's singing in a choir now in France. All posh songs, classical. Would never have done that without that dish.'

And another, 'Well, I know someone in Garibaldi Street sold a silver butter knife she never knew she had, bought a china jug with the money. And in the jug was old newspaper rolled up, and she went to throw it away to wash the jug, and there was a ring inside. Gold and all.'

And a small voice, a boy in glasses who couldn't sleep at all in his gran's house up the Brychan, who saw the crowd and wondered, and just came picking his way over the earth to find out: 'And my gran, it's silver snuffboxes. Found three so far. One in the hall cupboard and two in the kitchen, in the bread tin ...'

James Little smiles. 'That's nice. And now, I am tired, and I need my bed. But I must shut up the shed first.'

Ianto Jenkins stretches, fishes in his pocket, then holds up a small silver spoon in the morning sunlight. 'Well, that's that. Now, where's that egg for my breakfast?'

And then there is the sight of the residents of Christopher Terrace making their way up the Adam's Acre allotments back to their homes, to their dressers, their cupboards, their mantel-pieces, to find what silver James Little might have left for them. And the boy Laddy Merridew wanders off towards the park.

Factual Philips puts his notebook away for another time and waits behind with James Little, maybe to mumble, redfaced, that he is sorry, maybe to help him pack up for the morning. James Little nods, and goes into his shed to change out of his plimsolls and his jacket. Then, just as he is about to lock the padlocks, and leave, to step carefully over the onion sets and rows of cabbages, back up to Christopher Terrace and home, he sees something glinting in the soil over there on the earth. He catches the Deputy Librarian's sleeve, and points, for there is something between his chrysanths and his shallots.

Factual Philips kneels on the earth and digs with his fingers in James Little's allotment. Just a bit, for it does not take much, to unearth a small silver button hook out of the soil, which with a wipe and a polish will be perfect. And he hands it to James Little, who yawns again, puts it with a pile of others on a shelf in the shed, next to a bunch of onions, and locks the door.

By the Cemetery on the Hill
they Call Black Mountain

THE NEXT DAY LADDY Merridew arrives, panting, at Ebenezer Chapel porch, earth black under his nails, and even blacker across his cheek.

'Mr Jenkins?'

Ianto Passchendaele Jenkins is lying on his bench, arms behind his head and his khaki cap over his eyes. He squints at Laddy from beneath the cap, 'Morning. Been digging?'

Laddy nods. 'But that was after Gran found more of these in the biscuit tin.' He fishes three silver snuffboxes from his pocket. 'And Mrs Davies next door found a soup ladle behind her coal scuttle.'

'Well there you are.' The beggar sits up and stretches.

'But I've been at Adam's Acre and dug, just a bit – didn't find anything though. There's loads of people on the allotments with spades and forks.'

'And have they found anything?'

The boy pauses. 'Well, no, not yet . . .'

'Maybe the things aren't theirs to find?'

And there is no answer to that, so Laddy Merridew sits down beside Ianto Jenkins and is quiet for a while. Then he says, 'That story is real, isn't it. Because the things are there. Mr Little did dig them up, and he did put them in the houses?'

Ianto Jenkins looks at Laddy. 'And the other stories are still not real?'

Laddy says nothing.

'Not even my story? The accident?'

Laddy pushes the snuffboxes back in his pocket. And Ianto Passchendaele Jenkins gets up. 'Must be time for a sandwich . . . Got time for a walk?'

And it is surprising how easy it is to come by a sandwich from Mrs Prinny Ellis over at the cinema, almost as if she makes them special. And a flask of coffee this time, with sugar as well, 'Don't you worry, Ianto, there's more where that came from . . .'

And then there is the sight of a young boy and an old beggar walking out of town, following the river for a while, stopping for the beggar to rest his bones, until they get to the footbridge, where they stop. And maybe Laddy Merridew is going to say something about making decisions, but then by the bridge, standing on the concrete of the bank where no alders can grow, there is Half Harris, his pram waiting on the kerb, his boots slipping near the water's edge, where it runs fast and deep. Balancing there with a stick, dipping it into the river, flicking the drops into the air and watching them fall.

Laddy Merridew and Ianto Jenkins stop on the footbridge to watch. 'You making it rain, now, Half? There's lovely.'

Half looks up and slips again and lands on his behind on the concrete, and grins, waving the stick. On the end is nothing yet but water.

'Good luck, Half, good luck with the fishing.'

And it is a strange thing, but all Laddy's thoughts of decisions disappear downriver with the rain.

On over the footbridge, following the road through the houses on the other side of the river, on and out through the new estates to the hillside beyond, scrub, sheep-pitted grass, dips and scars of old drifts. The beggar stopping every now and again to catch his breath, 'Oh, my old bones ...' before continuing. Past tumbledown walls. On to the track that runs up the hillside, following one such wall, where they meet the Woodwork Teacher Icarus Evans on his way down, an armful of rough wood, bark peeling, trails of lichen. Laddy Merridew stops this time.

'Is that for the boat, Mr Evans?'

Icarus Evans looks hard at Laddy. 'What's that got to do with anyone?'

'Nothing, Mr Evans ...'

'Well, there you are then ...' and he goes on down the hill.

Ianto has to stop more and more often to catch his breath. On up that track they go, beggar and boy, until at a turn of the wall they are at the old cemetery on the hillside, the low wall, the few stones lined up like they might get up and march back to the town. The memorial. And on the ridge that runs away to the right, old trees bent by the wind, tangled.

Ianto Jenkins sits on the wall and after a while, pours himself a coffee from the flask. Laddy says nothing, but goes through the gate that hangs open on one hinge, held there by nettles. It is not a large cemetery. Laddy walks round the stones, peering at the names, taking off his glasses now and then to polish them. Reading the names aloud. 'Edward Bartholomew ... Thomas Edwards ... William Little ... Thaddeus Evans ... Benjamin Lewis ... Gareth Brightwell ... Charlie Harris ... George Harris

'. . . I know these names, Mr Jenkins. I know them. And there are others, Ernest Pritchard . . . Ernest Williams . . .'

Ianto Jenkins does not turn round. 'Families long gone. My neighbours, Mrs Pritchard, Mrs Williams. And more. Long gone. But look on the memorial, Laddy. Those who were never found.'

Laddy crosses to the memorial. 'Billy Price . . . Geraint Jones . . .' And then he walks across to the far corner, where there is a stone fallen, fallen onto its face, pushed by the wind. No name visible. 'Mr Jenkins, whose is this stone?'

There is no reply, and the boy looks up, but the beggar is not listening. He has walked along the wall to the gate and is inside the graveyard, standing on the old flags, looking at the straggle of grass and weeds and nettles against the stones. Where the rabbits have dug and troubled the turf, and where sheep have come and lain against the wall for shelter, making smooth pits in the earth. There is the constant clank from the marshalling yards carried up on the wind, and the smaller more insistent sounds made by a few brown leaves tumbling along the path, coming to rest against the stones. And Ianto Passchendaele Jenkins starts talking,

'There was trees, all over, then, Maggot. I still hear them. And a different sound, deeper. Do you hear it?'

The boy listens. 'I don't think so, Mr Jenkins. All I can hear is the trains.'

The beggar looks down the slope towards the town, down there in its valley, going about its business.

'I came up here, when I could, after that day, Maggot. After Kindly Light. When I was well enough. I had some days in and out of sleep, I remember that. Just up by there on the ridge I came. But it was a strange thing indeed. I was the same Ianto Jenkins that had walked here a thousand times and maybe more, and it was also the same mountain. And yet where my feet joined the ground it was not the same at all. I stand here now with the sun behind me, and look at the ground, at my shadow. Take that away and how do I really know I am here at all?

I was sent below to Kindly Light where it was all shadows, and perhaps I disappeared in those shadows? That is what it felt like, Maggot. But then, in the next breath, I was walking up here, on my mountain.

But it was not easy to come up here that day. There was something made me wait until school had started and most people had gone to work. For the school bell to stop ringing, at least. For sounds like that, men going to work – they only served to let me know another place where I did not belong any more.

The doctor who came – and I must thank the colliery bosses for that – said I must not do too much too soon. That I could walk as much as these legs wanted to and no more. He said the cough would be with me for some time yet, and he was right. It used to wake me in the night.

That day, I sat on the bed and reached for my boots. And my fingers and feet did not want the boots of dead Mr Ernest Ellis, standing there on the rug. They wanted the small boots I had shared with my brother the Maggot. The ones that pinched and raised blisters. I wanted those – and I could not find them. On my hands and knees, I was, searching under the bed, but they were not there. The Maggot was not there. Maybe he had gone out before I was awake? I could not think. His pillow was on the bed next to mine. The dent where his head was – I put my hand there, and it was cold. He must have gone out an hour since, and I could not remember if he shook me and said, "Shall we play, Ianto?" I dare say he could not sleep with me tossing around in the bed. I dare say my brother the Maggot who looked so like you – he may have gone to stay with neighbours for the moment – and I did not blame him, or them for taking him away. I would have done the same. I was not right, not for a long while. And could not look after myself properly let alone a Maggot. I put on dead Mr Ernest Ellis's boots after a bit, and walked down to the end of our street with my feet heavy on the end of my legs. So it was me and Mr Ellis's boots that walked out of the town, and I remember thinking I was closer to dead Mr Ellis than I was the day I won his boots in the drawing of the coal.'

Laddy Merridew interrupts. 'Sorry, Mr Jenkins. But couldn't your da look after your brother?'

There is a silence, broken only by the wind playing with the leaves on the path. And Ianto Jenkins sighs. 'No, Maggot. He was too ill to look after himself, let alone his son. I said, his leg wouldn't heal. I don't know about these things, mind. And it wasn't long after that . . .'

Laddy says nothing, and after a pause, Ianto Jenkins continues, his voice heavier.

'But that day, as I walked along our street the silence from behind the doors came out somehow, dark and swelling. And that same silence hung over the whole place. Not even Middy Pritchard from number five shouting to her children to come by here. No trucks and engines on the railway at the bottom of the town. No clanking and hissing, no rattling, shouts and whistles carried up here on the wind.

The day was good and fine and it had no business being fine at all. I went down to the river, to the hollow where the robin's old nest was perched in the rowans. I went to it, to see something whole. And it was gone, broken up, the place where it was perched all pulled about and smashed. There had not been a flood, and it must have been lads who did it. But for a moment I felt like it was me who took the nest away.

And then I shook myself, "Now Ianto. Just like a girl you are. Snap out of it will you? You have taken no nests."

Dead Mr Ellis's boots were so heavy on the end of these legs. I took them off and left them under the bank by the stream, and I walked on barefoot.

And then I was walking on a different mountain than the one before. The grass was cold and wiry, still. The places where moss grew on the stones were soft as before, like walking on a bed on the ground, or a cloth. But no matter how wiry the grass, how soft that moss, below it the ground was harder than before, and I am sure it was telling me something, something I am not able to explain.'

The beggar stops talking for a while, then he gets down from the wall and stands by the memorial. Then he looks down at the town in its valley. 'See, Maggot, I did not feel I was a boy any more, that day, walking up by here. The fact of Ianto

Jenkins the boy had been left below and there is no more to be said about that. But what was I then? Was I grown into a man in the space of a day or so in the dark? I do not think so.

I was sitting here on the mountain without dead Mr Ellis's boots on my feet and I pinched my toes one by one until they turned white, and the white remained long after my fingers had left off the pressing. It is true that those toes looked the same as Ianto Jenkins's toes from before and they felt the same . . . so it had to be something else of Ianto Jenkins that had changed and not the feet of Ianto Jenkins . . . And I was thinking then, Maggot, in which bit of my body did Ianto Jenkins live before the accident? And in which bit was he living now, then? Because it was not the same place at all.

I had no wish to be going back down to home, not yet anyway. I had no wish to walk back past the houses and hear the voices coming after me like they had before, the voices that got into my head then, and have been there ever since . . .

"No right to be here, he hasn't . . ."

"No right at all, quite right . . ."

"Should be one of the men . . ."

"His fault. His fault."

"Said it himself. Done something, that boy did."

"He did, mark my words . . ."

And the women turning their backs on me to go into their houses, and one, her hair all over, and a small boy all bewildered and dirty hanging on her skirts, her voice ringing, "Why are you still here? Where is my husband? What did you do? What will I do?"

They had no need to say the words after that but those are

the words I heard in my head and still do, "How come you are out at all?"

Why was I here at all? Why *am* I here at all? That was and is something I can't answer.

When I got back to the house, I half expected it to be just as it was before, with Da handing out orders and my brother the Maggot at some mischief in the back. But it was quiet. There was no one. And it was hard to be alone. I wanted to see someone, and looked for a reason. Then there was a reason – there were still some eggs in the cupboard and I had no stomach for them, but perhaps someone else would. Maybe Mrs Thomas Edwards along the way. Whose husband was my butty. My da's friend. Or her son, David.

Oh Maggot. I went along and round the back of number eighteen as I always did before the accident. And like things always were, it was all quiet, and the kitchen door wide open.

She was sitting by the empty grate. Mrs Edwards. Mrs Thomas Edwards, who was the wife of my butty. Mrs Thomas Edwards, who had looked after me when I was smaller, and the Maggot she was a mam to right enough. And wife of that Mr Thomas Edwards who pushed me behind him in the tunnel. Whose arm lay across my face. There she was, just sitting on a stool in the cold. There was no sign of her son, young David. And the funny thing was, that on the drying rack above the range there was a single white shirt, all stiff, the arms hanging down, the cuffs open, waiting to be buttoned. The arms were so white in the kitchen where it was so dark. And Mrs Edwards, she heard me come in, and she lifted her head and there was such a light in her eyes, a hand went up to her throat and her mouth opened.

But when she saw it was only Ianto Jenkins, the light in her eyes went out straight away, and her hand fell back into her lap.

I held up the bag of eggs, "I have brought you some eggs, Mrs Edwards?"

But she said nothing at all, just turned her head away slowly, and no words at all came out of her mouth.

So I just put the eggs down, careful, in an empty bowl on the windowsill and I left her by the range. And when I went back out I was thinking how white that shirt was, and how she must have worked so hard to get it white like that for Mr Thomas Edwards. And now she would not be doing that any more. And as I was going away down the alley it seemed to me that the sleeves of that shirt were reaching down to touch her cheek.

And then their son came back, David Edwards, younger than me but strong for all that, pushing his way past me, banging me into a wall, "Where is my da? What did you do to my da?" and a voice inside me said that Kindly Light may have happened a short while since, but it would echo and echo for more years than I could think of in one thought, and that is a fact.

And it was later, Maggot, a lot later, the names began. They called me all sorts, for Kindly Light was my fault. They gave me the name Passchendaele, later still, for being a coward. I can hear them, Maggot. "Wouldn't have lasted five minutes at Passchendaele, that Ianto Jenkins." '

Laddy interrupts, 'But Mr Jenkins. It was an accident, wasn't it? It wasn't your fault, was it? You were a boy, that's all.'

Ianto Passchendaele Jenkins twists his hands, looks at his watch. 'I was a boy indeed.' He stops. Looks at Laddy. 'I was a boy, like you, a little older. It's been my fault now for so long . . .'

Ianto Passchendaele Jenkins shivers and goes to the nearest gravestone. Thomas Edwards. 'I was always afraid of the dark, Maggot. Afraid of going below the ground.' He puts a hand on the stone and is quiet for a moment. 'Now, what else do I have to look forward to?'

Laddy Merridew does not reply, for sometimes, things are too much for words. But he holds the beggar's arm as they start their walk in silence back down the track to the town, and that walk takes a long, long time.

The Collier's Tale

i

IF IT RAINS ON the town when the sun is bright over Black Mountain, Batty Annie says it will be a fox's wedding. Lillian Harris will set an enamel saucepan on the floor of the back bedroom at number eleven Maerdy Street to catch the drips from the ceiling, and Mrs Eunice Harris will push a rolled newspaper under the kitchen door not to let the rain interfere with her clean floor. Then she turns the key so that Matty Harris and his wet shoes will have to wheedle through the keyhole to be let in.

And the rain makes to glower all the stones of the town. Even the bricks in the old back yards transform themselves into something dark, the stormclouds stain the slates as black as ink, and the walls of the privvies, now used as coal sheds and places for the lads to play hide and seek, weep and remember the warmth and stink of distant piss.

Outside the library the rain drips off the hair of the town statue, and onto his boots. He stands and looks at his hands, and the men sitting on the statue's steps will pull their collars up against the rain and tug their caps over their ears. They will still be wearing their colliers' boots, although the feet inside are no longer colliers' feet. Those boots have been polished and tidy now for months since Deep Pit closed. Look, the raindrops collect on the toes like glass bubbles, then join and run off the leather in streams. For it may be raining still under the Black Mountain, but the pumps are not working any more and the water levels have risen as high as the kneecaps of six-foot men.

Peter Edwards will be there, sitting on the wet step in his flat cap and letting the rain wash his boots. They are not polished, like the others, these boots. The rain splashes on the old leather and seeps into the cracks, trickles into the eyelets and soaks into his socks what black they can find on the way. There is coal caught like ants in the stitching, there is coal in the folds and creases that no water or rubbing will get rid, while both man and statue wait in the rain for something to happen.

Peter Edwards may grumble, 'It is raining inside my shirt . . .' He will look down to button his jacket and his cap will be whipped off his head from behind. And in return he will swat the other, who falls sideways off the step into a puddle, then they are both up and grinning like cats on a wall, cap-fighting.

Mrs Bennie Parrish may get off the bus with her basket and limps towards the library, 'Great lumps of men, look. Have you nothing better to do?' and their grins will fade and they will sit back down and look at their hands, while the rain wanders off down the High Street to play in the gutter and sit on the windowsills of the shops.

* * *

The rain washes the windows better than Judah Jones ever does up his ladders. But it did not always do this. Not long back the rain was heavy with coaldust and left dirty finger-prints on the windows and doors, for the old women with their pinnies and buckets to complain over low brick walls: 'Ych y fi ... aww, what's the point now in cleaning if the weather will be dirtying my house again?'

Peter Edwards hears in his head the voice of Bella his wife following him out of his house every morning since the pit was closed, 'When will you be getting new work then?' and his reply to her every morning, 'When the coal is gone from my hands I will get a job. And not before.'

In a while the Public Library will open, and the men will get up to go –

'Righto. We're off then.'

'Coming to the library, Peter Edwards?'

'Nah. He 'on't go into no libraries. Too many words ...'

'Go on, break the habit of a lifetime? Catch your death, mun, you will ...'

But they know it's no good telling him where they are going for he will not come too, not into a library.

Peter will shrug his shoulders against the rain and the turning of the world and look at his hands. He'll spread them palm-up to see the skin between his fingers and turn them palm-down to see the nails. In every crack there is darkness, his skin holding coal dust deep in itself. Dark as the shadows where the coal seams run under the skin of mountains, it has seeped into his pores over time, taking the place of the sweat he paid for it with. Blue-black as a bruise in the scar tissue on his fingers and on the backs of his hands.

The men who are no longer colliers will close the heavy library doors behind them. They will wipe their feet none too careful on *Welcome to a Place of Silence* while Mrs Bennie Parrish tuts at the reception desk for she wants to borrow *The Collected Adventures of Sherlock Holmes* and it is not to be found anywhere, and Laddy Merridew's gran leans on her mop and sighs at the bootprints on her floor in the entrance hall.

They will take off their caps and go through to the Reading Room with its polished benches and its newspapers wound all neat on their sticks. They will lay their caps on the tables for them to breathe a little damp on the polish and they will talk in whispers for there is a sign that says to be quiet although there is no one else to mind.

One of the men gestures with a thumb out of the door, for Mrs Cadwalladr the Chief Librarian's office is shut, and there is a notice to say she is out today on a conference.

Down past the reception desk there are the stairs to the basement and the small office of Factual Philips. There will be mugs all ready and waiting, regulation library mugs with the town crest important in black and *I cannot live without books* underneath, and there will be Instant from the cupboard, and a jamjar of sugar. Soon the men will go down the stairs, leaving their flat caps to read the newspapers all by themselves.

'Duw. Kettle's on . . .'

'There's a surprise.'

'Morning, lads! Come a little in?'

And they go into the office and take a mug and make plans to go back up and read the Situations Vacant. Sometime soon.

Factual Philips will take another mug from a drawer in his desk, a mug with no writing on at all, and he makes another coffee and takes it outside to Peter Edwards still sitting in the rain on the steps of the statue.

'Come inside, mun, in the warm?'

But Peter shakes his head, and when the Deputy Librarian is gone he turns his back on the library and warms his hands round the mug. The rain finds its way down under the frayed collar of his shirt and meets itself coming through the button-holes on his jacket.

Maybe he hears his wife Bella's voice again, as she watched him from by the gas stove to make sure he used hot water and soap and a brush to scrub at his hands, 'When will you be getting work then?' and his reply, 'When the coal is gone from my hands I will get a job. Not until.' And he looks at those hands round the mug of coffee, smiling a little at the skin still black as black in the creases.

When he has finished his coffee he leaves the mug by the library doors, and he walks back to the statue, his hands in his pockets. And are his hands alone in those pockets, with just an old bus ticket or a sweet paper? Indeed they are not. For in each pocket Peter Edwards keeps nuggets of coal, taken from the pit on his last day down. As he walks he turns the nuggets against each other for their dust to be taken into his skin to replace the coal washed away each morning while Bella his wife watched, wringing her hands, knowing the insurance man was coming later in his car, to collect their money.

If it stops raining later, the men will come back to the steps of the statue for a change. And maybe Laddy Merridew will pass by, kicking a stone in the gutter, and he will stop to watch the men doing nothing. He may have just come up from the cinema where the beggar Ianto Passchendaele Jenkins is tapping his watch with no hands, and wheeling his arms, telling his stories. Maybe Laddy stopped to hear the beggar, 'Tommo Price, it was, Tommo Price,' or, 'Listen to the story of little Meggie Jones,' or, 'A story of dark and diamonds, it is, and a half-born man that was born twice . . .'

Laddy may pause and say to no one in particular, 'He's off telling stories again, that Ianto Jenkins . . .' The men will look at one another, 'Well, that's better than sitting here waiting for the world to turn,' and they start down the High Street towards the cinema.

'Peter Edwards, you coming then?'

Peter will shake his head, 'No indeed. Stories is bubbles,' and he just sits there and goes on searching the maps on his hands for coal seams. His face will cloud over, and he will not shift from the step, as if he is his own coalface and cannot be moved. He'll just hold his bits of coal and watch the men go round the corner of the High Street and he'll listen to the talk as they disappear,

'I like stories, me.'

'Me too. Nothing like a good story to pass the time . . .'

And then they are gone.

Peter Edwards will lean back against the statue and close his eyes. He will forget about the steps, the High Street, the library. And in the darkness of the coal in his pockets a deeper darkness will be growing. A darkness that speaks of damp and fertile ground beneath tall trees. Warmth. Peter breathes the darkness, the scents from an earth long gone, vapours from strange flowers high in the canopy. He hears the cracking of fallen branches trodden by creatures past, their footprints left in mulch. He hears the buzz of insects and the drip of rain off leaves a thousand years dead.

The Collier's Tale

ii

IN HIS CHAPEL PORCH, the beggar Ianto Passchendaele Jenkins is waiting for someone to bring him a nice warm coffee, with two sugars. Or for Mrs Prinny Ellis to find him a sandwich with beetroot from her greaseproof packet. Mrs Ellis came down with her basket a while since, opened the ticket office of the cinema, and is knitting a red jersey while she waits to sell tickets for the two-thirty showing.

The cinemagoers will see the men who once were colliers coming down from the library, all together, ready for a story. But no Peter Edwards.

'Why isn't Peter here then?'

'Poor man. Why leave him out there on his own?'

And the men will try to say that they ask him to come too. But it is not easy.

'Has a mind of his own, he has.'

Someone will have watched Peter Edwards sitting by the statue. Seen him holding his hands up and turning them this way and that, then pushing them deep in the pockets of his jacket, sitting there, scowling. Then looking at those hands again and the funny thing is, they were blacker than when they went in –

'Why?'

And Ianto Jenkins may say, 'I am old, today. Maybe I can't remember now. Ask him, will you?'

But the miners know not to ask that Peter Edwards. 'Not interested in stories, listening or telling. Why is that?'

Then Ianto Passchendaele Jenkins will look up the High Street as if he can see past the slow bend in the road, past the shops and see the library, the statue, the man sitting there on his own, and he will sigh. Then he will stand and stretch himself and yawn a deep yawn – and tap the face of his watch that has no hands and he will shrug his shoulders and begin.

'Listen with your ears, I have a story for them, see, about a small boy called Peter Edwards, the very same Peter who sits up there, and will not go into the library to keep warm.

'But you go and find me the plaque that used to belong on that old statue, will you? Go and find it in the lake where the lads threw it years back, and if it is not too far gone you will still see the names engraved there. And if not see them, you will be able to feel them with your fingers. All the names of the men killed down Kindly Light one September day a long time back. Among them, one man called Thomas Edwards, hewer. A good man, he was. A good butty.'

Ianto Jenkins will stop for a moment, then shake his head as if he is waking after a sleep.

'Thomas Edwards, hewer. A good man. Grandfather of Peter Edwards. I tell you, look again at the face of Peter Edwards, and at the face of the statue. There is something the same, a kindness about the eyes or the frown, maybe – like both of them are asking the other questions.

But yes, Thomas Edwards was killed down Kindly Light, that September day. On that last morning before leaving for the pit, he opened the door of the room where his son David was sleeping, and kissed him goodbye. He had never done that before, not that his lad could remember, and David pretended to be asleep not to spoil the pleasure of it – the rasp of his da's cheek against his own, his smell, his work clothes smelling all of dust and darkness, and the smell of his mam's soap on his da's hands. David felt his da Thomas Edwards pull the covers up and tuck them round, then he was gone – just the back door closing, a cough from the back yard and the rattle of a bicycle chain against the mudguard his da was always going to fix.

You just imagine that son when his da did not come back. And how he would not listen when they tried to tell him, gently, but slapped his hands over his ears, and shouted anything that came, words and no words. Noise to cover the words he did not want to let in. Stayed for days by the window, watching, it seems, until finally he heard the sound of that bike again. The unmistakable rattle of that chain against the mudguard. Listen! Coming down the street, clear as anything. And it must all have been a mistake, mustn't it? The son David ran out of the house and into the street to fling his arms round his da ... but the smell was wrong, the jacket ... and he looked up to see the face of the man and it was just a neighbour bringing the bike back down home from the pit. Smiling, "Hello young man ..."

His da was dead. Killed by Kindly Light. And David swore he would never work in that place.

But here's the worst. When he grew, what jobs could he do? That boy could do nothing else but work in the place that killed his own father, because there was nothing else – unless you had book learning, and he did not. Worked as hard as he could, though, to earn for his own two boys, when they came along, enough to pay for a good schooling. One of those boys was Peter. David Edwards swore they would not have to go down the pit, like he did. No they wouldn't. He would see to that. They would work at their books and get to the good school. To Cyfarthfa.

Oh children are like water in the Taff, flowing along nice and solid enough, until it meets a rock in the bed of the stream, see. At the rock, the water in the stream divides. Some flows this side, all deep and smooth and steady, and the rest flows where the bed is stony and the water is shallow and rough. You look next time you walk down by the river up near that Baker Bowen's, will you? Look to see if the water flows together again on the downstream side of a rock? It does not. Where water divides itself it never meets properly again, but instead is kept apart by itself, invisible.

The two Edwards boys were like that. One son did his bookwork just right. And the other son, Peter, his head was as full of as many questions as any boy. But books?

Oh, his mam and da tried. Indeed, yes, they tried to get him to learn his letters, and his numbers . . . but they would not go into his head and stay there. Instead, the young Peter Edwards was more interested in picking up stones. He would turn over stones, fill his pockets with them, bring them into the house, lay them in lines on the lino, put them on the windowsills, marvel at them. But black letters, numbers on inked pages?

They would never stay still on the paper. They slid and slipped about when Peter looked at them, just like they wanted to be somewhere else.

Then one day, David Edwards came home from the pit and found Peter at his book in the kitchen, not trying to write and to copy the shapes on the paper as he was told, but dreaming instead, clicking stones in his pockets.

David Edwards undid his belt. "I'll give you learning your letters!" The book fell to the floor, Peter scrambled to hide beneath the table, but it was no good. His own da laid about him with that belt, hitting under the table as he cried, "No, my Dada!" until the boy's good woollen jersey was torn on the shoulder.

"You will learn your letters, my boy, or it will be the belt, every time. We will start with 'A'."

Twenty-six times, Peter was beaten with that belt. Twenty-six times, once for each letter. But they still would not roost between his ears.

And his brother, did he help? Oh he tried to. "Look, Peter," he said, at night, when they were supposed to be asleep. "Learn your letters and there will be stories . . . learn your letters and here, in this book, and that book, journeys with pirate ships, and camel trains over sand, read them with me? And cowboys, and Indians and planets . . ." But Peter, for all the trying and all the beating never found his way into words. Never found his way into books. Or stories.'

Here, the cinemagoers will shake their heads and pass round a bag of fruit drops, and maybe remember the lad down their street who still can't read and he is ten next Monday. Or the man who sells newspapers down by the bridge from a stand – he can't read the papers either, just reads the photos – and still seems to know what's going on so what's the problem?

Ianto Passchendaele Jenkins says he is thirsty, and could do with a little something, and someone finds him a coffee, with two sugars, and someone else opens a bag of toffees wrapped in gold paper, and he tucks one in his pocket, 'No teeth, but never mind.' And the story continues.

'Now. Peter never learned to read for all the hurt his father did him with that belt. And one day, when he was a little older, seven maybe, or eight, he walked out of the house after a beating and did not stop. All the way to the edge of town with no one asking where he was going. On, out up to the hills to let the hills smooth his bruises. And he thought maybe to dip his hands in a stream, for it to wash away the blood he was licking from a cut done by that belt.

He knew a place where there was a good stream, steep-sided and deep where it cut into the earth. Near where he found sheep's bones, once. The chalky bones of a ewe caught in the wire – close by it the small skull of a lamb, its own bones now nothing but pale fragments scattered over the banks. Their skulls touching, and violets growing between the yellowed teeth of the old ewe, her bones picked clean by foxes and crows.

And this boy Peter he tumbled and slipped down the slope to the stream, bringing with him small cascades of earth and stones. He thought to look for more lamb's bones in the grass, or the pitted grey shanks of dead sheep in the stream, hanks of damp wool on the overhanging branches.

He thought to kick off his boots and dip his feet into the water then to lie on the mud with his hands in the stream, feeling the cold tumble over his fingers. So that is what the lad did. And when the hurt was gone, more or less, taken downstream by the cold, he just lay there watching the sky being the sky and a branch over his head being a branch. To watch the grass on the bank being grass and to hear the bubble of the water by his ear being just that.

He let the mud ooze between his fingers like they were the roots of trees. And like roots, his fingers met small stones in the mud. Peter wheedled those stones out of the mud, played with them then threw them, sent them spinning from where he lay, unthinking. Spinning them to reach the other bank.

Stone after stone, his fingers reaching beside him and he not looking at what they were finding. Feeling them hardly at all, just sending them spinning into rowans misshapen by wind and water, on the other side. Stone after stone. Until something changed – maybe a cloud ran across the sun, and he turned his head? Peter lifted the next little stone, and went to throw it, but it felt different. Hardly at all, but perhaps there was something in the feel of it that spoke to his skin, still bruised but not hurting? Just alive and feeling?

Something in a shape, a surface, a ridge instead of smoothness, an edge, a ledge where his finger rested? A dip in the stone where the ball of his thumb was pillowed?'

Ianto Jenkins will raise his arms and looks up at his hands, and he stands there a moment while the people watch . . .

* * *

'Peter Edwards lay on that bank and lifted his hand into the air to see this stone, this misshapen thing that came out of the mud by his head. He looked. He sat up and looked again. This was no pebble. He dipped what he had found into the water to wash away its coat of silt.

It was no stone at all, but a bone-fossil, black and solid, brought down from deep in the mountains. A bone now resting in the hand of a living boy as sure as it was in the spine of a beast before boys walked these valleys.

Peter knelt by the stream with that bone in his hand. And something happened . . . he felt not just the hardness of a stone in his palm, but instead, he felt inside himself the snouting of a beast deep in the years, foraging among tree roots long gone. The bone told him all that in the wink of the boy's eye, and he tucked it in his pocket, found another stone and held that too, did not throw it across the stream. And this stone told his fingers what it was to be a mountain. And another, what it was to be made a valley by wind and water.

Later, he walked home, his pockets full of stones, his special bone-stone deepest, where his fingers turned it over and over for it to tell them its story. He found his mam alone in the kitchen, spreading bread with margarine for their supper and setting it on the table with boiled potatoes and ham. "So where've you been then all day?"

Peter smiled and told her about the stream and the black bone-stone and its stories, and he held it out for her to see, just as his da David Edwards came in, slamming the door back on its hinges. Been up The Cat and drunk half his Friday wage, "Learned his letters, the boy, has he? Going to read to his old da finally then?"

He pulled out a wage packet, torn, and held it out to Peter to read what was written on the brown envelope. And his mam stood between them both, "Leave him, will you?"

But the drink pushed her aside and the boy Peter held out the bone-stone to his father, "This. I found this, and Mam says . . ."

"Mam says, does she?" that David Edwards wheedled. "Mam says, does she? What does Mam say then?" looking at his wife, who said nothing at all, white round the lips. And the boy was frightened for his mam then, and it was his turn to stand between them,

"No Da – listen – I've been up on the hills and I've found this, and there are stories inside it . . ."

He held out the black bone, hearing it speak, things about snouting animals and the climbing of spidery limbs up tall trees, but his da had the drink noising in his ears. "Get you and your stones to the devil!" and he lunged at his son and swept the bone from his hand – and with the boy grabbing and grabbing at his jacket, "No, Da!" out he went to the front step, pulled back his arm and threw as hard as he could, sending the little bone sailing away and over the houses in Mary Street.

And then, with Peter pushing himself between the kitchen chair and the wall, and his mam out in the yard not daring to speak, that da David Edwards and his drink came back in, unbuckling that old belt. "To the devil, I say. This will learn you your stories."

Later, limping down Mary Street, Peter Edwards saw pieces of coal in the gutter, fallen off the coalman's lorry when its wheel ran into a drain. All he did was bend and pick up a little piece, and he sat on the kerbstone turning it in his fingers – and the stories came.

Stories of what it is to be a forest, tall and dark, dripping. What it is to have beasts foraging at your feet and birds building in your topmost branches. What it is to hear all the sounds of the forest, and to smell the damp smells rising at dawn, rising more at dusk. And what it is to die as a tree, to stand tall, held by your neighbours who will not let you fall.

The boy Peter Edwards knew what it was to be alive back then. On that kerb, holding that coal, he was the drip of rain off leaves and the fall of trees onto damp earth. The growing of plants long dead and the ooze of mud, the flow of rock and of river and the rise of mountain. Only jolting back to Mary Street when a neighbour came by with a pram and said to get out of her way.

So, did Peter Edwards ever learn to read words on pages? To make sense of black ink on white paper or signs in chalk on board? He did not. When his brother went off to the Castle School, Peter went to his own place, and skipped school more than he stayed – and when the brother left for the college in the city, to learn about cold offices, numbers on pages, and how to write words that people read because they must, Peter Edwards went to work among the stones he loves. Down the pit to be with his coal's stories.

But does he tell anyone this? He does not. And now all he has left are those pieces of coal in his pockets, for him to hear the story still.

Of course he will not go into that old library, a place where there is nothing but words he cannot read, words for whom he was beaten, for whom he still has scars under his shirt. And of course he does not want to listen to stories. He has no need to – they are in his head and in his skin, with the black of the coal his fingers keep finding in his pockets.

But look, look what has happened. His wife Bella has watched him every day, waiting for his hands to be clean. She was there when he came home at night, to watch him standing by the sink scrubbing at his hands with an old nail-brush, scrubbing his nails and knuckles. She asked him over and over when was he going to get a job of work to keep her in that house? And his answer was always, "When the coal is gone from my hands, then I will get a job – and it is not quite gone, see. Not yet." Holding his hands out for her to see, like a child, turning them in the halflight, the black deep in his skin, and her watching them dripping soap onto the tiles. For Peter Edwards has spent months holding coal just to keep the black in his skin, leaving his words and intentions in the air of the kitchen.

So now. Go up to Maerdy Street. The house at the end. Is Bella in the front room, waiting for Peter to move a chair or set the fire? Is she waiting by the front door to say it is warped in the rain and what will he do about that? She is not.

Is she waiting for him to bluster onto the kitchen rug and stand there with his arms wide, in one hand an envelope? A letter of engagement from the factory down by the Taff, or the garage up on the Tredegar Road wanting a strong man for occasional duties, or a blotted note from a hill farm wanting help to rebuild a barn?

She is not. Just left the back door open when she left, and did not look back to pull it to. Only the one suitcase, I am told.

Picked up in a shiny black car by the insurance man, his hands as clean as new money – and a job that won't run out at the end of a seam.

Told nobody, Peter hasn't. For to tell it means telling a story. And that would never do, would it now?'

The cinemagoers will shake their heads and say that is a shame. They may say life is like that. And they may sigh and make plans to hold nuggets of coal themselves, when they can, to see what happens. And to wash their hands after of course, just in case. Just to see in those seconds whether it speaks to them too.

The Collier's Tale

LATER, IANTO JENKINS TAKES the packet of sandwiches left by Prinny Ellis and leaves the chapel porch. He makes his way slowly past the Savings Bank and up the High Street, stopping now and again to catch his breath, until he comes to the pavement outside the Public Library. On the Town Hall the hands on the clock are still stuck at ten past always because of a nail, or another accident. And the muffled bell on Ebenezer, its clapper wound with a rag, is trying to tell the town it is one of the hours but it doesn't know which.

Peter Edwards, his hands deep in his pockets, is alone and asleep on the steps of the Kindly Light statue, their faces almost mirrors the one of the other. Ianto Jenkins sits beside Peter and waits as the streetlights flicker on and chase the evening away up the hill.

Peter stirs, finally, stretches, and fixes his frown on the beggar. 'What are you doing here?'

'Fancied a walk, that's all. I could ask the same.'

'The bailiffs came today, took everything, the bed even.'

'There's a shame. Where will you go?'

Peter Edwards rests his head against the statue again. 'I don't want to talk about that.'

But the beggar will not stop. He takes out the lamb sandwiches, 'You will share my supper?'

Peter does not reply, watching the streetlight outside the library, the crack in its glass cover, the flicker of the loose bulb, and the dance of light on library wall. The beggar watches for a while then smiles, 'That reminds me . . .'

'Got a story about that and all?' Peter's voice is hard.

'Maybe.' Then Ianto says, quickly, 'Catch hold?' and as he says 'catch hold' he tosses something else to Peter, something from his pocket. Peter Edwards catches it, and turns it in his fingers. A small lump of coal.

The light flickers and flickers on the library wall. Peter frowns and he mutters, 'That reminds me as well, I suppose. There's kids still play up on the ridge above the cemetery with bits of broken mirror, flashing the sun.' He pauses. 'Doesn't seem that long ago I was up there myself, skipping school. Always hated school.'

Then he stops and waits for the beggar to say something, but he does not. Just listens, and nods. So Peter goes on, still playing with the lump of coal, speaking slowly, as if the words are weighty, 'Used to find bits of broken bottle, stole my mam's old compact mirror once, to make the light dance on the graves up the main graveyard. Anything to get out of the house. My da was a terror.'

He checks his hands, the black of the coaldust on his fingers. His voice lifts, the words come faster, 'Or, we'd be the Welsh against the Romans, sending the sun flashing down from our fort, on to their shields below. Dustbin lids. Marvellous sight, whole Roman legions – the Ellis boys from Plymouth Street, Prinny's boys, all three of them. Marvellous.'

The beggar nods again. 'Good game, that one. We played at making ghosts, being ghosts, my brother the Maggot and me. Best when the sun is low, isn't it? Catches the glass just right.'

Peter Edwards is standing now, one hand raised towards the streetlight and the wall, 'The soil was that colour – there, the colour of rust. I remember there was an old ousel that came searching for grubs in the grass. I wonder if it's still there, or its children? I wonder if that ousel is one of the Roman legions, now, those Ellis boys who took their dustbin lids for shields? They dropped slugs down the girls' necks. Got called all the names under the sun by the girls. Hated them then, mind – went and married them later.'

Then he stops. The lads from the Brychan have arrived and they are sniggering, leaning against the library wall to listen. One shakes his head. 'I won't be marrying no girls.'

Another nods. 'Nor me. That's a good game, though ...'

Peter says no more, waves them away, waits for them to be gone, but they stay, just go on leaning against that wall as though it might fall down if they stopped. There is more low talking, and sniggering, as if they know something no one else does.

Peter shrugs and goes back to the statue, puts the coal down on the step and sits, hands pushed deep in his pockets again. Ianto Jenkins hands Peter a sandwich, and the two take their supper together in silence, cold lamb and beetroot on white made by Mrs Prinny Ellis.

When they have finished, Ianto Passchendaele Jenkins looks at his boots. Then he pushes the lump of coal back towards Peter Edwards. 'Here. There will be more ...'

Peter shakes his head, 'Got plenty of my own ...' and Ianto

Jenkins says nothing, just leaves the small black stone alone on the step. After a while Peter takes it and turns it over in fingers still greasy from the lamb and the butter.

For a few minutes they sit there together, not speaking, then Peter shakes his head. Shakes it hard as though a bee has entered his ear. Shakes it as though that bee is buzzing against the drum, filling his head with sound – the hooter at Kindly Light echoing on the wind, as it used to, calling the colliers to work. But different, deeper. The sound of boots on a road. Voices.

The double beat of boots that are too big for the wearer, loose over the feet inside them. Walking fast. The feet of a boy, perhaps, little more. A heart beating, not Peter's, but another, smaller, younger, faster. A voice, a boy's voice not broken yet, breathless, talking low, as if to be heard only by the speaker, 'Today I go down Kindly Light by myself.'

This is what he hears. Peter puts that piece of coal back down on the step fast and the sounds are gone, as though the wind has blown them away. He shakes his head again, says nothing. And there is the boy Laddy Merridew coming up the High Street, an old shopping basket by his side, 'Hello . . .'

The lads leaning against the wall of the library laugh, 'Hello, Stinker, shopping for soap at last, was it?'

Then a few of the colliers that are no longer colliers arrive to waste some time before going home,

'Good grief. Will you look at that?'

'Is that Peter Edwards, telling stories?'

But that piece of coal is in Peter Edwards's fingers again, and it is as though he is in another place, and his voice rises, fills that place, becomes stronger. 'Listen . . . I hear this. Third day at work down the pit for a boy. A boy who has stuffed rags in the toes of his boots for the boots are too big.' He pauses. 'Not any boy. This boy is Ianto Jenkins . . .'

Peter looks at the beggar leaning back against the statue, at the beggar's face pale in the streetlight. The lads have stopped their sniggering when one of them hissed, 'Shh, will you?' and there is Laddy putting his basket down, 'Mr Jenkins?' but the beggar does not reply.

Then there is Eunice Harris come to find the bus, and Judah Jones pushing his old bike on his way down to Plymouth Street, stopping to listen when he hears Peter Edwards's voice. There is Maggie come down to find a box of crisps for The Cat on the corner of Maerdy Street, and Tommo Price coming up from the Savings Bank, 'A story about Ianto Jenkins? Well, there's a first . . .' and Matty Harris, standing close to Maggie and saying nothing at all. But Peter Edwards does not seem to notice, and goes on playing with the piece of coal. 'Listen,' he says. 'Listen . . .' as if he is telling himself to listen harder.

'Listen. Those boots on the road, again. Now they stop. The boy Ianto has stopped to pat his pocket. He has brought his breakfast with him, in case he is sick from the drop of the cage. And he pats the other pocket, where his water bottle should be. It is not there. The boy has left his water bottle on the wall outside the back door where he knelt to do up a bootlace.

He's thinking fast. It's raining too. Can he go a day without water down below? One little day. Can he go to one of the men, Mr Thomas Edwards, maybe, and ask if he can be sharing his water for he has gone and left his bottle on an old wall back home? But this is only Ianto Jenkins's third day, he is a man now, a man of twelve, almost thirteen, mind, and he will soon be riding down to Kindly Light in the cage on his own and what man takes water from another collier?

But Ianto remembers his mam's voice, "Never let a collier go home once he has left for the pit ..." He knows that is bad luck. So it is a choice between a little bad luck and going thirsty all day and coughing so much the men will be laughing and telling him he is making a dreadful fuss? "Here, bachgennyn, should have brought a baby's bottle down after all?" And what will the bad luck be? His da being cross with him like he seems to be these days? Ianto can cope with that.

He runs back home. He creeps up the alley as much as those boots can creep, and he takes the tin bottle from where it is waiting on the wall, stuffs it in his jacket pocket.'

As he says this Peter Edwards looks across at Ianto Passchendaele Jenkins, all shrunken and grey now on the steps of the statue, his eyes great in his head.

Peter frowns, 'Bad luck that was.'

There are echoes from the colliers who are no longer colliers. 'Terrible bad luck, that.'

'Yes. Terrible ...'

Ianto Jenkins looks away, pushes his hands deeper into his pockets. The lump of coal turns faster and faster in Peter's fingers.

'But Ianto Jenkins does not creep back quietly enough, does he? I hear a window opening upstairs, see the head of a younger boy at the window, a little lad with red hair all in his eyes, sleepy, saying, "Ianto? Shall we play after?" but his big brother is not looking up. Not answering. Just walking away.

And the boy Ianto, he is a collier walking down to Kindly

Light then. And someone is speaking to him. Thomas Edwards – he pats his shoulder, this boy who is to be a man today, and says, "You'll get used to it soon enough, young man," and Ianto Jenkins is ducking angry away from that hand, and scowling, muttering under his breath, "I am not a baby." '

Peter stops then. 'My own grandfather, that Thomas Edwards was. Must be. But listen. There is a thorn tree by the side of the road to Kindly Light, in a hollow. The boy Ianto knows there was a robin's nest in that tree in the spring, where the lads couldn't get at it. But he also knows this. For a collier to see a robin at the mine is worse luck than a collier going home to fetch something forgot.

Ianto keeps his eyes on the road, the gutter, on the end of a cigarette in that gutter, on a place where a man has spat, all black and glistening in the damp. Keeps his eyes down, on the toes of his own boots, on the heels of the man in front. Tries to walk faster. He pushes past some colliers, friends of his da's, and Mr Thomas Edwards again, who laughs, "How many days is it now, young Ianto?"

"Two and then three today, Mr Edwards."

"That much is it? Well don't be overdoing it now, will you? Be growing out of those boots nowjust . . ."

And is it because they are his da's friends, who have helped him on his first days, especially Thomas Edwards, or is it because he is being a man today, that when he sees a flash of red in the rowans on the other side of the road, he says nothing. Nothing at all. And then, it might not be the robin – it is September after all, and maybe it is just the light on the rowan berries? It might just be an old wren with the light catching it just right, the russet on its wings? Sometimes, they can look red in the light?'

The beggar speaks then, and just says one word. 'Sometimes.' And some of the listeners shake their heads, 'What's wrong with that?' and no one answers. Peter's voice rises again.

'But the bird must be flying alongside, dipping between the huts, the walls, because the boy Ianto sees it again, up and over the roof of the building on the corner where Kindly Light watchman waits at the window with his china mug – a flash flying low across the path. And he hears that sound, the same one he hears at night, or in the early morning, tick tick tick like his brother the Maggot winding up that toy train of his. And the boy Ianto looks about him to see if the men have heard it, through the noise and the clatter of doors and boots, and shouts and machines, and knockings and bangings, and rattlings. But there is no other collier, no real man, stopping to say, "Wait. A robin . . ." and the bird is up there clear as anything, there for everyone to see.'

Peter stops yet again. Laddy Merridew is sitting close by Ianto Passchendaele Jenkins, the lads from the Brychan are still leaning against the library wall and they are not laughing any more. And the small group of townsfolk has grown. There is Nathan Bartholomew standing next to Maggie the publican's wife. Baker Bowen on his way back from General Stores with a bag of strong flour. Icarus Evans and his bike and trailer of offcuts from Tutt Bevan the Undertaker, Tutt Bevan himself on his way home via the library, off to meet

Factual Philips after work. James and Edith Little on their way back from a visit. All gathered now to listen. And Peter, frowning at his hands, at the coal, real enough, tests it on the step where it leaves a mark as black as black, but on his fingers, precious little.

Laddy asks then in a small voice . . . 'Was that the day of the accident, Mr Jenkins?'

And there is another silence for the question is not asked for an answer at all. But the boy does not stop. 'Mr Jenkins?'

The beggar is quiet. And in the hush a voice from the small crowd says, 'Bad luck, to see a robin by a pit. I know that. Everyone knows that, don't they?'

And another says no they didn't and who says and there is a small argument, who knows more about these things than others – and the argument brings Philip Factual Philips out from the Public Library. 'What's the fuss?' and when he is asked about red-breasted birds seen near pits, and colliers who return home to fetch something forgotten . . . his facts are there for all to hear. 'Bad luck the both. Always were at any pit. Why?'

But the voice of Peter Edwards comes again, 'It is not any pit, is it? It is Kindly Light.' And it is a moment before he continues.

'Listen now, will you? It is three days later. Three days after the accident, it is – and they have brought up those who are burned from the ventilation shaft end. They have cleared enough of the mid-section to find the men who died there. They have brought up several caught by the afterdamp . . . and the message comes, "A boy, alive . . ." A boy beneath the bodies of colliers, behind the body of Mr Thomas Edwards. As if they are sleeping. But it is only the boy who wakes as he is moved, and when he hears the sound of a voice that says, "It is only a boy."

And they bring him up, this boy. They bring him up into the light just after the body of Mr Thomas Edwards my grandfather. The boy comes out of the cage, held by the shoulders, and out into the light – he staggers and looks round at the crowd as though he has never seen people before – sniffing at the air like an animal.

There is a man comes forward then, who has been charged with making a list of the men who come up alive. "What is your name?"

And the boy says nothing, just shakes his head. He is asked more times. "What is your name?" But the boy is looking round as if he is in a place he does not know. And his head is filled with horrors. Not only the collapse of the mountain over Kindly Light, the fire, the afterdamp – but the things that happened before, just before, signs he should have known, listened to. And the words of his own da a few days back only, "I will not have a coward for a son."

So the boy stands up as straight as he can in those boots that are still too big – and he says the thing that a man would say. The words that will hang round his neck for a lifetime. With the women listening, the men listening, what children there are listening, the mine man listening, his da's friends listening, he turns to the name-taker, "My name is Ianto Jenkins. I am a coward."

And as if that is not enough, he says for all to hear, "It is my fault." '

* * *

Peter Edwards stops and shakes his head. There is not a sound then. Even the traffic in the High Street seems to have stopped. There are no buses. No voices. No dogs to bark. Not even the breeze. Peter pushes the coal into his pocket and looks down at the old beggar Ianto Jenkins there on the steps, looking somewhere past Peter's shoulder, into the air. And Peter says nothing.

One of the women listening by the bus stop, and missing her bus twice now, asks, 'Is that right? Is that how it was?'

Peter will turn away then, not to look at the face of Ianto Jenkins as the beggar gets up slowly from the step, 'That is how it was. And they asked why I was here at all, after.' And he starts down the High Street towards his bench, the chapel porch, but Laddy Merridew calls him back.

'Mr Jenkins?'

'Yes.'

'I don't care what anyone says. Kindly Light wasn't your fault.'

Ianto Jenkins sighs. 'I am glad of that, Maggot. But in the end, who is to say? Not the men who went down in the cage with me that day . . .' and he takes a deep breath. His voice is quiet now, and the listeners move closer to catch what he says.

'I can still hear them, as the gates are shutting, Maggot. Geraint Jones and Benjie Lewis talking loudest, both going to be fathers for the first time. Geraint Jones with only a couple of months to go, "Won't be out for a drink, Saturday, only water . . ." and Benjie Lewis, his first child due a little later – "Saving, we are, Susannah and me . . ." Billy Price laughing, " 'On't last long, lads. A couple of sleepless nights and you'll be back drowning your sorrows with the best ..." and the newest collier apart from me, Gareth Brightwell, dropping his things on the floor, and William Little bending, handing them back, "Here, not to worry ..." then the bell sounding and before I know it, there is lightness below me, and dead Mr Ernest Ellis's boots fall away with the world, and me with them, down and away into the pit. The cage dropping fast and my stomach left up top, the dark closing round us like a fist and the wind flying past my face, the earth breathing out. The cage stopping all sudden, hanging, bouncing, and the voice of Thomas Edwards coming to me loud in the darkness, "Playing with the emergency brakes, don't you worry," and we are bobbing up and down in the shaft, wild as anything, everyone holding on to whatever they can and then the final drop fast to pit bottom, the sudden slowing, my stomach left up there again. The gates rattling open, and Eddie Bartholomew who's getting married at the weekend out first, and the colliers shouting – "Want a loan of the instruction book, Eddie? Want a lesson, Eddie?" And the language getting stronger and Thomas Edwards grinning across at me, "You shut your ears, young Ianto ..." and another collier, a man called Thaddeus Evans who I don't know really, saying something about his son carving feathers from wood, but that makes no sense to me. And there's another father and son, the Harrises, saying nothing at all, all the way down, not even looking at each other, and getting out and going to work in silence. The older man not even putting out a hand when his son trips across the rails. Maybe they had an argument? And I look back on that now, and see what a dreadful thing that was, not to be talking that day.'

* * *

He stops, takes another deep breath. 'All gone, every one.'

The silence that follows is broken by the Woodwork Teacher Icarus Evans, arms folded, his voice strong. 'Thaddeus Evans. Well. Took that old secret down with him, didn't he?' And Mrs Prinny Ellis on her way to find where everyone may have gone for there is no queue at all down the cinema and no beggar either, and the technician has packed up and gone home for a quick tea, 'Ernest Ellis's boots? Is that Ernie Ellis my grandfather, went of the consumption?'

The beggar says again, 'All good men, every one.' And he turns to go. But Laddy Merridew stops him, 'No, Mr Jenkins, don't go. It was not your fault.'

The beggar sighs and sits down again on the statue's steps. 'I don't know any more, Maggot. All I know is, I am going to work with Thomas Edwards, and he has to bend to walk, and I can just stand upright, but still knock my head now and again. I am walking along in a tunnel. I am afraid, still. I am just a boy in a dark tunnel, and the air is warm. The air is dark, and it is warm, and the smell is rank with coal and piss and the stink of the horses.

The only lights are those from lamps. The walls glow at me. There is a draught and the light licks over a pile of mud, wet and gleaming. The rocks are alive, and in the walls I do see shapes, like they are in the flames of a good fire at home. I see my house and my mam who is under the ground, hanging a sheet to dry again and smiling, and the wind is blowing her hair over her face so I cannot quite ... and I say "Mam?" and the word just echoes back at me, over, over. I feel Thomas Edwards move a little closer.

I hear her voice again, Maggot, then. I do. "The earth speaks, Ianto. If we listen." '

Ianto Jenkins is not looking at Laddy Merridew or the rest, now, but out over the town towards the dark rise of Black Mountain.

'In those tunnels under the mountain, I heard her voice, and I saw the whole town as if from far away, above or below, the houses all through a mist, and the chapel, and the stone bench that would be my home. Everything so small, and the hills so high they were become true mountains. Clouds passing over the sun sending great black shadows over the town. And if I tried to look closely the pictures faded like water fades when the sun warms wet stone. It was dreadful, terrible. Beautiful.

I saw these hills, all transparent. I saw the rocks living and breathing to a different rhythm, with a heartbeat like our own but sounding deep and slow. I saw the stomach of the mountain moving against the mountain's heart and ribs, and beneath the mountain's skin there were rivers of light that glowed under the grass. I heard the groaning of stone on stone as the mountain settled and stretched. And the drip and rush of water. I saw the fall of stone, and fire. I knew air that would not refresh but bring sleep. I saw men burning, smelt their flesh, I felt the crying of their wives, their mothers, their sons, their sons' sons. I saw it. See?

I saw it all, before it happened. I knew and I said nothing. Do you understand?'

* * *

And he gets up to go, but Laddy Merridew is catching him by the sleeve, 'But Mr Jenkins, it was not your fault. It was not . . .' He turns to the others, 'Tell him. You tell him.'

For a moment no one speaks. It is as though they are all waiting for someone else to speak first. And it is Ianto Jenkins himself who does. His voice changes, becomes paler.

'I saw many things, didn't I? But there was one thing I did not see. I did not see a boy called Ifor Jenkins, my little brother who I called the Maggot, leaving our house after I had come back for the water bottle and woken him, my little brother who put his head out of the bedroom window and asked "Shall we play, Ianto, after?" and I did not answer him as I was grown up now and too busy going to work in dead Mr Ellis's boots. My little brother who I had told all about Kindly Light – how dark and beautiful it all was – who I laughed at saying he must leave important things to those who were more grown than him. I did not see him putting on the boots we had shared until a few days past, maybe thinking he would need boots where he was going . . . or taking two slices of bread and not even finding any jam. I did not see him putting the bread in his pocket. I did not see him running down our street, and waving to Mrs Pritchard who shook her head at him, "Should be at school, you should . . ." walking down the same streets I had walked not half an hour since, down to the road that runs with the river, down the valley to Kindly Light. I did not see him waiting a while on the road, playing in the bushes, eating his bread, finding a handful of water from the stream, wiping his mouth on his sleeve.

If I had seen him, would I have taken him back home? I don't know.

But I did not see him. Did not see him dodging back into the bushes when a teacher from the school came walking to work. I did not see him a while later arriving at the gates of Kindly Light, where a friend of our da's was standing, "Another young Jenkins sent out to work, is it? Whatever will that dada of yours think of next?" I did not see him wheedling at the man on the gates to let him just come in and see where his big brother worked, that he would be no trouble and do as he was told. I did not see the man on the gate telling him this was no place for a kiddie, and my Maggot stamping his boot, "I am nearly eight!" I did not see the man on the gate call over to another about to take over from the banksman, "Here, a new recruit ... show him the shaft, just quick, will you?" And the banksman laughing and scratching his head. "Jenkins's young-est. Well, well." I might have seen him led past the lamp room, taken quickly to the pit head, shown the cages, the winding house, might have seen him wrinkling his nose at the smell, and I might have heard the banksman going off duty, "Can't stay here, young'un, dangerous place. Got time to walk down to another shaft then?" and Maggot chattering, half-running behind, questions questions all the way as they walked through Kindly Light all the way to the ventilation shaft, to let Maggot see that, with its high walls round, and maybe it is when I am by the pillars below, and think I hear him laughing, saying my name, "Shall we play after, Ianto?" – maybe I do hear him after all? I do know that when the mountain fell, and there was the explosion, it happened back there. Between the fall and the ventilation shaft. Went up that shaft, they said, ripping the roofs from two buildings up top. And it left the shaft almost untouched – just the blast rushing up and the thing escaping

339

from under the mountain. The roofs taken off, and that was all, apart from two walls crashing down, where the mortar could not hold the big old stones. A wall where a boy had run for safety, frightened by the noise, a little lad with red hair, a boy called Ifor Jenkins, my Maggot, who a moment before was asking his old questions of a banksman who by rights should have been on his way home. A banksman who never went home at all. And the boy, my brother the Maggot, found after, when someone remembered the younger Jenkins boy came visiting. Dead beneath the stones.'

And then there are questions from all directions, but the beggar does not reply. He is walking slowly away under the streetlights and this time, Laddy lets him go.

The voices start: 'Terrible. Terrible to lose a brother like that.'

'A boy himself, that Ianto Jenkins.'

'So, his fault, was it?'

'He said so, himself.'

'But he was just a boy. How could it be his fault?'

And Laddy Merridew, picking up his gran's basket, 'It was not Mr Jenkins's fault. But he thinks it was. He's always thought it was.'

And Peter Edwards, still holding the piece of coal, 'It all comes down to a forgotten water bottle, and bad luck after for the boy, maybe.'

'Bad luck all right, living in that old porch since I don't know when . . .'

'And when's that?'

'But the other things, the birds? The noises?'

Peter Edwards pushes the coal into his pocket. 'They were there to be seen and heard by everyone, not just a new lad.'

Factual Philips nods. 'Right enough. And there were inspections, and more inspections. Got all the records in the Reference section, not to be taken away. It would have happened anyway.'

'Happened anyway?'

'Divine Intervention, was it, then?'

'That's right.'

'No it isn't. Intervention maybe, nothing divine about it.'

And there is argument and counter-argument as there always is, stopped only by the bus arriving, ready for those who were meaning to go up the hill a while ago. Some of the arguers get on the bus with their bags, their questions, and their talk about it all being old stories, and there's no logic around these days, not in this town, and that's a fact.

The lads propping up the library wall have gone now, and slowly, the rest of the crowd thins, then disappears leaving just the boy, Laddy Merridew, and Peter Edwards. Laddy stands there holding his basket, and Peter sits for a while on the step of the town statue, flicking the little lump of coal over and over in his fingers. Laddy breaks the silence. 'Please, will you tell Mr Jenkins it was not his fault?'

'I will indeed. Tomorrow, now.'

'And will you tell him he is not a coward?'

'I will. Mind you, I can't stop him thinking that.'

'We can try though,' and Laddy wanders away towards Ebenezer.

Peter looks up at the Kindly Light statue, the shadows of its face deeper in the streetlights. He thinks of a father who beat a boy for not knowing his letters, and a boy who grew thinking all written words were bad and stories too. He leans back and holds up the lump of coal. When he does, and when the flicker of the streetlight catches the fingers that have just been playing with the coal and were black as anything, he sees they are now as white as a lady's, clean as those of a scrubbed child.

And others, those ordinary men whose stories were told by the beggar over and over, who have often wondered why and whose business was it of his anyway . . . as they go off home they may walk a little slower for the thoughts in their heads weigh them down – and they may not go to bed straight away for they have more thinking to do when they get there. And Sarah Price, Eunice Harris, Edith Little and Nancy Philips will just have to go up first and warm the beds.

There is not just thinking to do but remembering as well. The remembering of snips of conversation from years back, from when the ordinary men were boys, or from further back, stories recounted by parents and aunts and uncles over cups of tea and plates of lardy cake while the boys listened. All leading somehow back to one September day a long time ago, and an accident down a pit. Words a man will forget when he grows, but which the boy inside never does:

'Only when I see his body will I know he is gone . . .'

'My da is a postman, yours is a thief . . .'

'Now that's how to deal with loss – walk right across a country in a straight line . . .'

Or a challenge set and never completed: 'Make me a feather

from wood that behaves in the air like a real feather – only then are you a real carpenter.'

And more. Some will make plans to go and see the beggar Ianto Jenkins tomorrow, to tell him how things are now. And others will not, believing the beggar may know how things are, anyway.

At Ebenezer Chapel

IANTO PASSCHENDAELE JENKINS WALKED slowly down to the chapel porch last night and went straight to his bench. He did nothing for a while, just watched the late cinema queue, and no one asked him any questions. He did not see the boy Laddy Merridew hanging back in the doorway of the Savings Bank waiting to see if he was all right, relaxing when he saw Ianto find a sandwich tucked into his kit bag. Watching and waiting for Ianto to start eating, but he did not. The beggar sat there, the still-wrapped sandwich forgotten in his hand, staring at nothing.

Laddy Merridew came up the steps in the end and sat on the stone bench next to the beggar. He did not say much, for there was nothing much to say, but he took the sandwich from Ianto's hand and put it back in the kit bag.

'Mr Jenkins, can I say something?'

'You just did, Maggot.'

'I am sorry about your brother, the real Maggot.'

The beggar just nodded.

'And Mr Edwards says it was not your fault. He is coming down to tell you, tomorrow. Mr Philips said he has records in the library, about inspections and things like that. It was not your fault.'

Ianto Jenkins looked up then, but said nothing.

The last of the cinema queue disappeared into the cinema for the last showing, and some minutes later a few latecomers arrived, 'Missed the opening, mun. No point . . .'

'Oh well.'

The latecomers brightened, went to come up into the porch, 'Old Ianto Jenkins'll give us a story . . .' but the boy stopped them. 'Not just now.'

And much later, when the film was done, and everyone had gone, when Mrs Prinny Ellis had put the padlock on the cinema doors and gone, herself, 'Another day tomorrow . . .' the boy left the beggar sitting in the chapel porch, alone.

Ianto Passchendaele Jenkins looked round at his home. At the walls of the porch, square grey stones piled exactly, glued with mortar made from more stones, ground small. At the beams where pigeons roost. At the slates hanging on their nails. At the great grey doors of the chapel, one wedged ajar. At the bench that served him as bed, as chair, as table, closet, platform and pulpit. At his kit bag pushed beneath the bench, packed and ready to move on out every day for as long as he could remember. At the chipped white china mug holding the dregs of his last coffee, finished before he went up the High Street earlier this evening to find Peter Edwards.

The beggar got to his feet and pulled the chapel door a little wider. It was not exactly musty inside. More old. Ianto Jenkins understood that. But there was something different. A scent.

It was too dim to see exactly, what light there was from the streetlights came in only slowly through the painted windows, their figures and inscriptions fighting in the gloom to be understood. But Ebenezer was no longer empty. There on the flags where the box pews once stood, there was a rowing boat. A boat made of a hundred woods, smooth as skin, varnished. Perfect.

Then, maybe, the shadows were full of echoes. 'Is that you dreaming again, Ianto?' 'Ah, let him dream. The world is full of men who do not.'

And in the echoes, after a little while, the beggar may have heard another voice, small, hesitant, hopeful. 'Shall we play, after, Ianto?'

Ianto Jenkins went to the boat and laid his hand on the gunwale. He looked up. Maybe it was a trick of the light, but he could see no roof, just dust, rising and rising without end.

Tomorrow comes, and there is no breeze at all. There is a frost over the town, mist hangs like smoke in the back yards and a sheet forgotten on a washing line in Bethesda Mansions hangs flat as a leaf in a book. Mrs Eunice Harris, up early with her bladder, looks out of the window and shakes her head when she sees the sheet, 'What is the world coming to?'

It is cold in the kitchen of number eleven Maerdy Street where Half Harris will be dipping his bread into a mug of milk, then dipping his finger as well and holding it to the keyhole to feel how cold the air is. He may lick his finger clean before taking a stub of pencil from a jar and drawing a wavy line for the Taff on the back of an old envelope. Then he creeps back up to his bedroom and pulls a blanket from his bed. In the narrow hallway he tucks the blanket into his pram and he leaves the house, closing the front door quiet as anything. His breath makes brief clouds in the air as he pushes his pram along Maerdy Street and he grins, walks a little faster and snaps them between what teeth he has left in his head.

Up the Brychan, Laddy Merridew's gran has left already for the Public Library, telling Laddy he must pack his suitcase soon as his dad is coming to fetch him the day after tomorrow. 'I can't understand it. A boy's place is with his mam . . .' and Laddy did not say that his mam lied to him and his dad didn't, and that was as good a reason as any. He will go down and tell Ianto Jenkins, when he has had his breakfast, and they may make plans for when he comes to stay next time.

But when Laddy does leave the house, there is the Woodwork Teacher stamping up the road waving a fist, his hair wild, 'Think that's clever, do you?'

'Sorry, Mr Evans?'

'You know what I mean. Stealing my boat . . .'

'No, Mr Evans.'

'Varnish hardly dry. Gone.'

'Gone?'

'You bloody lads . . .'

'I haven't seen it, honestly.'

The Woodwork Teacher runs a hand through his hair, 'I was going to sell the thing too . . . pay for a bit of a holiday . . . You keep an eye out, will you?' and he looks hard at Laddy before retreating.

So it is Half Harris who reaches Ebenezer first, and it is Half Harris who parks his pram and takes the blanket and climbs the steps to where Ianto Passchendaele Jenkins is lying still on his bench in the morning.

He sees the beggar, frost in his eyebrows and his mouth just open. His hands clasping his newspaper coverlet under his chin and his cap on his chest. Half lays the blanket gently over, and turns to go. But there is the flutter beneath his ribs of something not quite right, and he turns back to see what it might be. Something not there that should be – no small breath-clouds from the half-open mouth, and something there that should not be – eyes open a little but dull as the eyes of a fish caught yesterday. And Half Harris sits on the flag-stones by the bench and flaps his hands.

And that is how Laddy Merridew finds them both when he arrives a little later. Half Harris rocking and grunting, and on his bench, Ianto Passchendaele Jenkins the beggar, frost silvering his face and hands.

And when Matty Harris and Tommo Price arrive to open up the Savings Bank, they look across at the chapel porch and see Half Harris with one arm round the boy.

Matty Harris jangles his keys, 'What's the matter?' and it is the boy who answers in a small voice, 'It is Mr Jenkins. Can you help?' and Matty Harris comes over to see, then takes a corner of the blanket and begins to pull it over the beggar's face. But the boy stops him, 'No, please . . .'

Maybe the word spreads as words will, and the others will arrive at the chapel porch. Peter Edwards, his cap in his hand, 'We should have come down last night . . .' and Nathan Bartholomew, 'I'm sorry,' and Judah Jones and James Little, 'It was cold last night, ice on the windows . . .' 'It was indeed,' and Andrew Baker Bowen, 'I'm sorry too, I was going to say thank you this morning . . .' and no one sees Half Harris slipping into the chapel, just to be alone.

And even though Ianto Jenkins has been taken away by Tutt Bevan as is proper, the others plan his departing sitting there on the steps, the boy Laddy Merridew in the porch, listening.

Peter Edwards is first, 'Ought to give him a good send off.'

Factual Philips next, 'Right enough. Mind, funerals are expensive, there's oak, and brass nails, and handles, and hearses, and expenses...' and Matty Harris waves a hand, 'I will contribute. And my wife will. Oh yes.' James Little nods, 'I've got those candlesticks in the shed. Matching pair. Georgian. I can sell those. Too big to put in my bag...' and he reddens.

'The wake, at The Cat?' Nathan Bartholomew says. 'A good spread, I can sort that,' Baker Bowen says. Peter Edwards agrees. And Judah Jones says nothing more.

There is talk of dusting off Tutt Bevan's old horse-drawn hearse, and getting the horses from Mr Wigley up Pant. The boy Laddy Merridew interrupts, 'Then what?' and they don't answer him, too deep in their plans, 'Granite headstone. Have to think about the inscription – "Ianto Jenkins" or "Ianto Jenkins, called Passchendaele"? And a nice plot up there in the Kindly Light cemetery maybe, with the others...?'

'No!' and they turn to see Laddy Merridew standing over them, glasses in his hand. 'No. You can't do that to Mr Jenkins.' He searches in his pockets for a handkerchief, and there isn't one, and he is remembering an old man who handed him something like a handkerchief when he fell by a bus stop only a few weeks ago and that just makes things worse...

Factual Philips coughs, 'Someone fetch his gran? She's up the library,' but Laddy doesn't move and his voice is shaking, 'You can't bury him. You can't put him in a coffin. I won't let you.' He tries again, 'It's dark. He's afraid of the dark. He's afraid of being under the ground and stones falling . . .' and in the silence that follows all anyone hears in their heads is the thud of earth on wood, earth on wood.

Laddy pulls at the great grey door of Ebenezer and disappears into the chapel. But not for long. He is gone only the space of a few heartbeats and he is out again, his voice lifting, excited, 'Come in here. Come and see.'

'What?'

But they do go, and they do see.

They see a chapel empty but for dust, and they see a boat. Each rib of the boat a different wood, each plank for the sides. Mahogany, birch, hornbeam, ash, and all their cousins, their colours deepened under coats of varnish, a boat that glows and glows in what light filters through the chapel's windows. And it is not empty. For asleep in the bottom of the boat, curled on his own blanket, his mouth open, is Half Harris.

At the Top of the Last Hill

THERE IS ALWAYS ANOTHER way, especially after discussion, always things to do.

There was a boat that had to be bought from its maker: 'Leave that to me,' Matty Harris said, and he was off to talk to the Woodwork Teacher about finding his boat in a chapel, and about money. And Tutt Bevan, come back now, was making decisions and taking charge as was proper, calling to Matty as he rounded the corner to the High Street, 'See if he has any of my old offcuts left up there. Tell him I need them back.'

Another tomorrow comes, as they always will. Ianto Passchendaele Jenkins's hair is neat, ready for this day as like as any other and as different. He is lying on his bench for the last time, wearing his khaki jacket and trousers, and the watch with no hands is on his wrist. The rowing boat of a hundred woods, made by a Woodwork Teacher, stolen by lads, found by Half Harris, and bought by a Deputy Bank Manager, his Clerk, a Piano Tuner, a Window Cleaner, an Undertaker, a retired Collector of Gas Meter Coins, a Deputy Librarian, a Chiropodist called 'Baker' and a man who was a Collier, was carried out into the chapel porch earlier. The oars, collected from the boat's maker, have been placed across the ribs at the bottom of the boat, one each side, and in the centre between the oars is Half Harris's blanket, neatly folded and waiting.

There is the sound of an engine idling then stopping, and at a signal from Tutt Bevan the beggar is lifted with gentle hands into the boat, as a dray borrowed from the brewery and driven down from Dowlais by Factual Philips waits as close as it can. And then help is summoned from the growing crowd of townsfolk and the rowing boat and its cargo are carried slowly down the chapel steps and lifted onto the dray. Ropes are thrown over and secured while those who readied Ianto Jenkins for this last journey stand round to watch, and Laddy Merridew is the last to come down and take his place, holding Ianto Jenkins's kit bag.

They move off up the High Street at a walking pace. There is no sound except wheels and feet on the road, damp now, for a drizzle has begun to fall, as Ianto Jenkins begins his last journey through the town, up every street and down the next, never stopping, showing those places that do not shift that the journey is all, the arrival just the stuff of a moment.

They leave the cinema and the Savings Bank behind. Past Tutt Bevan the Undertaker's they go. Past the Public Library, the Town Hall, the bus stop where Laddy Merridew fell, and the Kindly Light statue, head bowed, a tumble of coal round his boots. Past the dressmaker's with its deep doorway, a scatter of cigarette butts on the ground. Past the General Stores, and the ladies putting the sign on the door to 'closed' and joining the procession. Past the turning to Steep Street, where Baker Bowen will be closing his door, ready, and the neighbours as well.

And on up the hill, the lorry sighing past The Cat on the corner of Maerdy Street. There is the still-curtained window of the bedroom above the bar, where Maggie is resting while Nathan Bartholomew, acting publican as well as Piano Tuner now, lugs barrels up the cellar steps, for the other publican is gone, some say, to a fancy piece in Abergavenny, but who knows? And he will leave the barrels and come out to join them with a group of drinkers, and walk beside the old Window Cleaner, Judah Jones, and will help him with his bike. Past Maerdy Street, where Lillian Harris is waiting on the corner to join her two sons. And there they are, Matty and Half, both pushing the pram up the hill behind the dray, and Eunice Harris, Sarah Price and Mrs Bennie Parrish in their best black coats and hats walking in the crowd behind, Eunice Harris still refusing to have anything to do with that pram at all.

Past the turning to Icarus Evans's farm but there is no sign of the Woodwork Teacher, last seen collecting brochures from the travel shop in the High Street – and on to the Brychan, where doors open as the procession passes and the lads come out to watch, then go to fetch their jackets and join in. And Laddy Merridew's gran as well, bringing with her Laddy's old raincoat, several sizes too small but better than nothing.

Right out of town, the procession long now, past a drunk in the last doorway, on and up the road, to the top of the hill, and they do not stop there. On towards the next hill they go, the breeze sharpening, the townsfolk following the beggar's body pulling their collars round their chins. A few with umbrellas. But not a word is said. Even the lads. Not a sound. Leaving what sounds there are for the dray to make: the flat hiss of tyres on the damp road, the low grumble of the engine, a cough from the driver Factual Philips and the creaking of the ropes holding the boat steady.

The procession passes between plantations of dark fir trees. Then it turns off the road as the light is falling, onto a track between the firs, until they come out at the very top of this last hill, before the hills become mountains. A high place, a clearing where the land falls away in all directions. North to the Beacons where the breeze comes from, east to another country, west to more hills, more valleys, and there in front, with the mountain at their backs, they look over the lights of the town and down to the coast where the big cities glow across the low sky to the south.

The dray and its boat creak slowly over the grass. Slowly and slowly the people come, until in a while it seems as though the whole town is gathered. They talk in low voices and stamp their feet in an evening drizzle as light as mist and as chilly. There are the shopkeepers, the ladies from the Stores, the grocers and the butchers, the stationers and the sellers of clothes and shoes and hats. There are the fruiterers and the fishmongers, the confectioners, the chemists and the second-hand bookshop owners. There are the steelmen and the colliers who are colliers no longer. There are the craftsmen and there are the wonderers.

There too is Tutt Bevan the Undertaker supervising the untying of ropes, Factual Philips and Peter Edwards organising the lifting of the boat and its cargo to the grass, the boy Laddy Merridew there with Half Harris, and Matty Harris and Tommo Price standing close, and the others arriving out of the crowd. Nathan Bartholomew helping Judah Jones still with his bike.

It is Tommo Price who speaks first. 'Never liked hearing that Ianto Jenkins and his old stories.'

And Matty Harris nodding. 'Nor me.'

And Peter Edwards, 'Could never stop him, mind.'

And Nathan Bartholomew, 'Not easy to hear . . .'

And James Little, 'It is good to have it said.'

And Factual Philips, 'Right enough.'

And Baker Bowen just nods, Judah Jones as well, and Half Harris grunts. And the boy Laddy Merridew hugs Ianto Jenkins's kit bag and says nothing.

There is a pyre waiting, branches from the plantation firs heaped high by Tommo Price and Peter Edwards and the colliers who are no longer colliers, who came up to help and are standing in the drizzle, pulling their collars up round their ears. The pyre sits there, ready, and close by is the Woodwork Teacher's trailer with its load of offcuts collected by Matty Harris keeping dry under its cover.

After a long while, finally, the boat is lifted up onto the pyre and the pyre settles and shifts. The first burning rags are pushed between the branches, the crowd falls silent and they all stand back in the gathering darkness, not wanting to watch the fire, and unable not to. Not wanting to see the branches catching, smell the resin, and see the glow in the night sky from the city lights in the distance eclipsed by the growing fire.

Night falls completely and the fire is still catching hold for the branches are damp. Tommo Price and the lads from the Brychan fetch the dry wood from the Woodwork Teacher's trailer, to add it all to the fire, help it burn. Armfuls of wood, and the fire eating them, hotter and hotter, and the pine branches crackling and flaring. But the boat has still not caught alight.

And then from the bottom of the trailer, it is not wood the lads are taking but boxes, the Woodwork Teacher's own boxes, collected by mistake from his barn, boxes full of wooden feathers carved ever since he was a boy.

Laddy Merridew shouts, 'Stop! Not those!' but the lads aren't listening, and it is too late. The lads throw the boxes onto the edge of the pyre, where the flames are upright one moment, and wavering the next, but strong for all that. All the boxes save one they dropped on the grass.

And the boy Laddy Merridew lets go of Ianto Jenkins's kit bag, picks up the box while the boys laugh, 'Stinker, there's brave . . .' and he thinks fast. Should he take it back to the Woodwork Teacher and try to explain – 'Mr Evans, I'm sorry, your wooden feathers . . .'? But he remembers how angry Mr Evans was yesterday, shaking his fist, his hair wild as anything. Maybe it's best to leave the explaining to Matty Harris, so Laddy takes that last box and throws it onto the pyre himself.

Then the boat, which until now has sat dark and flickering, its varnished sides glowing, catches. First, a single rib catches, maybe a rib of wood born easier to burn than the rest, or where the varnish is thicker perhaps. But one rib catches. And the gunwale. Until the boy, the men and the whole crowd are watching the boat all burning. Every rib catching and flaring, beautiful and final.

And at the same time, the flames find the boxes. They catch the cardboard lids, lift the corners, curl them back to find what is inside. Box after box catches light. Sparks and bright drifts of drizzle talk to each other above the pyre as the flames and the smoke and points of rain work together in the night. And Peter Edwards keeps an eye on Laddy Merridew, tells him not to stand too close, but Laddy is gazing at the boxes and doesn't hear, just pushes his glasses up his nose . . .

Then the fire finds the dry curls of carved wood, the piles of worked shavings that cascade from the burned boxes, to be seen for just an instant before the flames catch them. The shape of the boat is black against the fire, burning now so fast it is night itself come down, and the air above the pyre is a blizzard of sparks whipped by the breeze.

The sparks fountain against the sky, filling it with more stars than there is room for. Laddy Merridew and Peter Edwards stand together now, watching. And as they watch, the breeze catches a single burning feather. Another and another float upwards, caught up in their burning, then a hundred, a thousand, until the sky is alight with bright curls of flame that rise on the air and disappear into the darkness.

Then something white lands on the boy's raincoat. Ash. He brushes it away and it leaves a streak like smoke on his sleeve. But it is joined by another and another, delicate things, almost nothing, falling out of the dark. And the night is filled with a blizzard of white above the beggar Ianto Passchendaele Jenkins's blazing boat, a blizzard of white feathers rising and tumbling on the up-draught before landing gently and perfectly on the grass.

The Kindly Light Generations

The names of those killed down Kindly Light one September morning, underlined.

Thaddeus Evans, Collier *m* wife

The carpenter *m* The seamstress

The Woodwork Teacher, Thaddeus 'Icarus' Evans

Albert Harris, Foreman *m* 'Black-Skirted Nan'

George Harris, Collier *m* wife who died

Lillian Harris

The Halfwit,
Jimmy 'Half' Harris

Matty Harris, *m* Eunice Harris
The Deputy Bank Manager

Benjamin Lewis, *m* Susannah, friends of the baker **William** *m* wife
Collier   **Bowen**

The teacher   The doctor

Andrew 'Baker' Bowen, *m* Mrs Bowen
The Baker

Philip 'Fancy' Philips *m* wife
(who did not help)

'Little Phil' Philips *m* wife
(the solicitor)

The Librarian, Philip 'Factual' Philips *m* Nancy

Grandfather Brightwell *m* Mrs Brightwell
(who went for a walk)

Gareth Brightwell, Collier   Rosie *m* Mr Bevan

The Undertaker, Simon 'Tutt' Bevan

Mad mother

Eve engaged to **Edward Bartholomew**

son (d)   son (d)   son (d)   **Edward Bartholomew** *m* wife
                                    (the blind piano tuner)

The Piano Tuner,
Nathan Bartholomew

Ivy Jones, widow

|

Geraint Jones, Collier *m* **Meggie Jones** (who fell in love with a window)

|

The Window Cleaner, Judah Jones

Billy Price, Collier *m* Mrs Price (who needed proof)

|

son *m* wife

|

The Bank Clerk, Tommo Price *m* Sarah

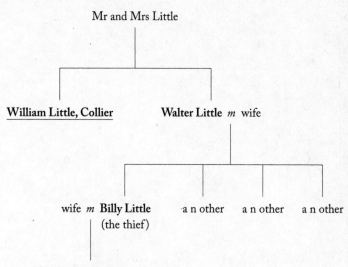

Mr and Mrs Little

William Little, Collier   Walter Little *m* wife

wife *m* **Billy Little**   ·a n other   a n other   a n other
(the thief)

The Gas Meter Emptier, *m* Edith
James Little

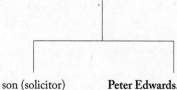

Thomas Edwards, Collier *m* Mrs Edwards

David Edwards *m* wife

son (solicitor)   **Peter Edwards, The Collier** *m* Bella

Other Dramatis Personae

Now

Ianto Passchendaele Jenkins, beggar and storyteller

Ieuan 'Laddy' Merridew

Laddy Merridew's gran, cleaner

Mrs Bennie Parrish, widow

Mrs Prinny Ellis, cinema factotum

Mrs Z. Cadwalladr, Principal Librarian

The colliers who are no longer colliers

Batty Annie, mother of the boy Dai

The publican of The Cat Inn Public House

Maggie, the publican's wife

At the time of the Kindly Light accident

Hannah Jenkins, mother of Ianto Passchendaele Jenkins the beggar

Father of Ianto Jenkins

Ifor Jenkins (the Maggot), younger brother of Ianto

Old Mrs Watkins

The spinster daughters Gwendolyn and Gwynneth Watkins

Mr Ernest Ellis

Mrs Ellis

Author's Note

The Coward's Tale is set in a fictitious town based tenuously on Twynyrodyn, Merthyr Tydfil, in the south Wales valleys. Many places in the novel are (or were) real; this is where both my father and mother were born and brought up, went to school and had their first jobs. However, thanks to the imprecision of childhood memories and the even more imprecise wanderings of a writer's imagination, the topography of the entire area has been changed. Streets have been realigned, renamed, as the story dictated. Buildings have been created or moved to another location, stone by stone, the stones changing colour in transit. I have moved whole mountains.

I would love to have a drink at The Cat on the corner of Maerdy Street and walk down the road to the remains of old Kindly Light pit – but they only exist in these pages.

Acknowledgements

My thanks are due to the following:

Euan Thorneycroft at AM Heath, Helen Garnons-Williams, Erica Jarnes and Holly Macdonald at Bloomsbury's London offices, and Kathy Belden in New York.

Tracy Chevalier and the Bridport Prize; Sam Leith, Louise Doughty and the *Daily Telegraph* 'Novel in a Year' Competition; Miriam Kotzin and Bill Turner of *Per Contra: The International Journal of the Arts, Literature and Ideas*; Andrew G. Marshall, Tania Hershman, Alex Keegan and Niyati Keni; Sue Booth-Forbes of Anam Cara Writers' and Artists' Retreat, Ireland, where *The Coward's Tale* was written; the Arts Council for their support through Grants for the Arts; and Maggie Gee for her insight, guidance and generosity.

My families, both of them, especially my mothers, who might have approved. Last but not least, my husband Chris, whose love and patience sometimes seem limitless.

A NOTE ON THE TYPE

The text of this book is set in Adobe Caslon, named after the English punch-cutter and type founder William Caslon I (1692–1766). Caslon's rather old-fashioned types were modelled on seventeenth-century Dutch designs, but found wide acceptance throughout the English-speaking world for much of the eighteenth century until being replaced by newer types towards the end of the century. Used in 1776 to print the Declaration of Independence, they were revived in the nineteenth century, and have been popular ever since. There are several digital versions, of which Carol Twombly's Adobe Caslon is one.